FEEDING THE TIGER

FEEDING THE TIGER

JC BOURG

ISBN: 0991007611
ISBN 13: 9780991007615
Library of Congress Control Number: 2015913170
Three Greyhounds, Phoenix, AZ

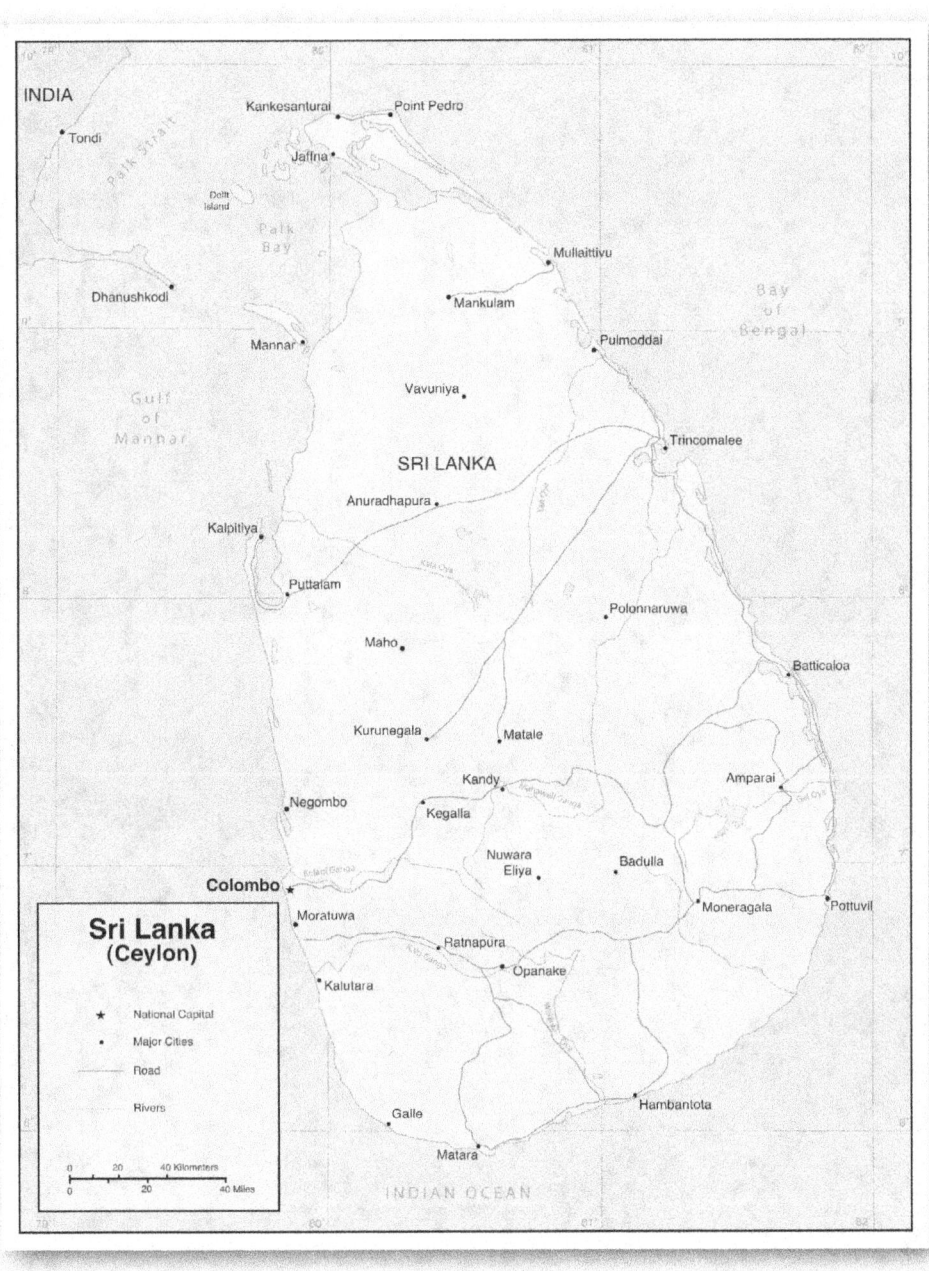

To those who served

AUTHOR'S NOTE

There was a war. The anti-Tamil pogrom and riots in Sri Lanka, during July of 1983 became known as Black July. The tragic event is generally considered the start of the Sri Lanka Civil War, a conflict that lasted for over twenty-five years. Obviously *Feeding the Tiger* is fiction. The cast was created out of my imagination. Any resemblance to any persons living or dead is coincidental.

Death is my business and business is good.

—Unknown

Chapter 1

———⚬❧⚬———

It was November 1983, the year of the pig. An impending storm along the Andaman coast of Thailand defied the end of the rainy season cycle. Lightning sparked. Thunder clapped. Breaking waves crashed. Husky, one-legged Vietnam veteran Raymond Marshall plodded slowly through the soft sand of an isolated Thai beach. Marshall was pushing forty. Graying temples and a Southeast Asian tan suggested sophistication. The excesses of his self-imposed exile had produced a slight paunch. Beneath an easygoing exterior, an explosive temper simmered. His reflex fury existed long before he gave a leg and his youth to an unappreciative country. Searching for traction, his crutch dug deep into grasping sand. The gusty monsoon churned hostile waters. Whitecaps ejected sea spray.

Marshall sucked hard on the salty humid air. Sweat migrated beneath an oversized white T-shirt. A hollow khaki pant leg flapped. Looking up, he squinted at Reno's vacant raised shack. A pitched thatch roof crowned the stilted bungalow. Local rattan furniture occupied the elevated wooden deck. A decorative green glass fishing ball encased in cargo netting swayed. Against a side wall, a loose louvered shutter banged aimlessly. Driftwood and plastic debris littered the ground. A lashing wind whipped through the fronds of surrounding tall palm trees. Swirling sand slapped Marshall's face. "Fuck," he mumbled, lowering his head. Dusk accelerated behind a billowing charcoal canopy. A flash of lightning illuminated the neighboring stilted hovel. Catching a glimpse of the surfboards stored beneath the shanty, he grumbled, "I suppose I should check on the dark surfer's residence as well."

Holding the crutch overhead, he hopped up the grasping incline. His balance teetered. He accelerated. Out of control, he plunged face first into chaffing granules. Plastic waste crackled. Sand shot up his nose. Snorting, he burst out laughing. *There are good days and bad days, and there are one-legged moments that just suck.* He chuckled. Slowly rising, he brushed himself off. Conjuring up saliva, he spat. Snickering, he hobbled forward. Grasping the handrail of his friend's home, he let out a victorious sigh. "Reno better have a couple of cold brews," he mumbled, navigating up worn wooden treads. Leaning against the doorframe, he dug into a front pocket. A house key resisted his searching probe. He paused.

Ominous silhouettes flowed out of Longboard's neighboring residence. The short-statured, thin, cocky shadows approached. The black sky discharged an illuminating bolt. A slick, groomed Asian meandered behind four thugs in training. Wind tousled the scraggly locks of the punks. The apparent leader's lacquered hair defied the gale. His fluttering white dress shirt glowed.

Plopping down in a deck chair, Marshall took a deep breath. *Reno warned me,* he conceded. Focused on the advancing cadre of Chinese gangsters, he grinned. *I'm a badass,* he counseled. *I've faced much longer odds than theses amateurs.* His heart rate accelerated.

The approaching hostiles hesitated at the base of the stairs. Cautiously, they spread out across the face of the raised deck.

"You zipperheads looking for Reno?" Marshall questioned.

Shabby, skinny silhouettes shot curious glances at the shadow sporting a glimmering dress shirt. Stepping forward, a dapper Chinese gangster in a starched linen long-sleeve shirt rubbed his chin. He appeared to be in his late twenties, but guessing the ages of Asians was difficult. His perfectly parted hair sparkled. Squinting at the American, he questioned casually, "What did you say, cripple?"

"Cripple?" Marshall snapped. "You are the one that's obviously deaf. I'll speak louder to compensate for your handicap." Grinning, he rephrased, "I said, 'Are you gooks looking for Reno?'"

"Reno and the surfer owe us money," the thug informed him. "Where are they?"

Marshall snickered. "My friends are out fucking your mothers."

The spokesman flinched. Rage surfaced in his dark eyes. "Kill the gimp," rolled out of a scratchy throat.

"Gimp?" Marshall growled, rising on his one leg. "I'm an Airborne Ranger whose lost track of how many Chinamen I've sent to Buddha. You five would be nothing more than rounding errors."

One of the shadows reached for the small of his back.

Marshall locked his arm and raised a Browning forty-five-caliber pistol. The semiautomatic handgun barked. A crimson plume erupted out of the silhouette's head. The target collapsed. An incoming round shattered the ornamental glass ball. Ignoring the showering shards, Marshall nailed another hostile. The folding shadow wailed. "When I see you at the gates of hell, I'll be standing in the short line," Marshall muttered, exchanging fire.

Chapter 2

———⁂———

It was June 1983. The monsoon rains along the west coast of Thailand had yet to arrive. Dull overcast skies blanketed the shoreline. A stagnant tropical atmosphere embraced this resort community. It was muggy hot. Away from the manicured beaches reserved for tourists, Reno plodded on a narrow path. Foul orders lingered. A pockmarked asphalt road skirted the well-tread trail. The American's throbbing head scanned the broken glass, dog shit, and refuse littering his advance. Sweat infested his forehead, armpits, and lower back. A racing tuk-tuk billowing toxic white smoke idled by. "Jesus," he grunted, fanning his puckered face.

Reno James had recently turned thirty-two. A red rubber band corralled his thick bleach-blond locks into a ponytail. A five o'clock shadow accented a rough tan complexion. Squinting hazel eyes focused on the garbage obstacle course hindering his journey. A tight moist T-shirt proudly displayed the taut physique of a weightlifter. Faded denim jeans and white canvas Bata sneakers completed the ensemble. Not breaking stride, he leaped over a static pond of filth.

Is today Tuesday? he questioned. "Does it matter?" He chuckled, rubbing his damp face. Looking up the inviting stairway of the open-air Jade Tiger Lounge, he grinned. Mischievous laughter distracted his assent. Across the narrow roadway, a pack of local street punks enjoyed a smoke. Instinctively, Reno flexed. The sandaled teenagers, dressed in torn and frayed knit tourist shirts from seasons past, defiantly puffed out shallow chests. An inaudible comment invoked laughter. Among the jet-black-haired Thai delinquents stood a light-complexioned youth with auburn locks. "Half-breed," Reno mumbled. *Departing armies always leave a trail,* he realized. The Roman legions built aqueducts, bridges, roads, and dams across Europe. The American occupying forces populated Southeast Asia with "forgotten children."

A wide reflective grin spread across Reno's face. *I was a forgotten child bouncing in and out of foster homes and trouble,* he recalled. *I was always the new kid at school, dressed in hand-me-downs. Parents didn't want me playing with their kids and definitely not dating their daughters. Teachers despised me. Not all teachers,* he realized. It was a brief scandal at Arrowhead Junior High when Mr. Olivera placed the rebellious Reno James in the advanced math class. *I should have stuck it out,* he regretted. *I owed it to Olivera. At nineteen, I became an expert at hotwiring cars. The San Bernardino County judge was benevolent.* He remembered visualizing the plump gray-haired official in black robes. *He offered me the choice of incarceration or enlistment. I finally found my purpose in the Fourteenth Infantry Regiment. Vietnam was a cruel mistress, the lessons learned expensive. I graduated; many others did not.* He grinned. The excesses of Vietnam were addicting. *I was wealthy by local standards and desired by a hot, insatiable female populous.* A lump rose in his throat. *I have a family now, a family of brothers.*

Looking over at the auburn-haired Thai, Reno flicked his head. The half-breed smiled. "I hope you eventually find your way," Reno mumbled, jogging up the creaking stair treads of the Jade Tiger.

Ceiling fans circulating under a palm frond canopy provided a comforting ambience. From the rafters, black speakers pulsed with a familiar but dated Jimi Hendrix guitar riff. In a white short-sleeve shirt, a skinny Thai bartender behind a bamboo bar scanned a local newspaper. The long ash of his smoldering cigarette defied gravity. In a padded rattan chair reclined the one-legged Airborne Ranger Raymond Marshall. Two twenty-something local beauties flanked the burly unofficial patriarch of the expat community. In a loose-fitting Hawaiian shirt dominated by large white plumeria flowers, Marshall appeared content. His light-brown hair accented with silver sideburns was combed straight back. A grooming gel gave it a wet look. The girls' attire of brightly colored short shorts and tube tops accented the charms of youth. Empty platters of Thai cuisine and beer bottles cluttered the table. Spotting Reno, Marshall perked up shouting, "Afternoon, San Bernardino!"

"Marshall," Reno nodded. "Not wearing your prosthetic today?"

"Nah," Marshall responded. "That plastic peg leg is a pain in the ass. Besides I'd rather lean on Sunnee and Kanya to get around." Grinning, he extended his arms. The girls giggled as they nestled under the embracing wingspan.

Reno sauntered toward the bar. The roused barkeep smiled. The long white ash of his cigarette leaped to the floor. Instinctively, the server retrieved a bottle of Singha beer. After placing the brew on the counter, he searched under the stained surface and pulled out a stack of correspondence.

"Thanks, Aroon," Reno uttered, grabbing the cold amber bottle. Taking a refreshing swig, he closed his eyes, savoring the carbonated refreshment rolling down his parched throat. Grabbing the thick dog-eared pile of blue and brown envelopes, he nodded gratitude and retreated to the sea of empty seating options in the sixties time warp.

"Hey, Reno!" Marshall called across the empty saloon. "I'm having a barbeque Sunday afternoon and would appreciate your attendance. Jackson is heading Stateside. It's either his mother or father. Anyway, one of them is dying. I'm procuring some steaks from one of the resorts to give our brother expat a proper sendoff."

"Count me in," Reno replied, raising a bottle of brew. "I like my meat charred and medium rare."

"Extend an invitation to your mysterious neighbor," Marshall added. "The dark surfer needs to come out of his shell."

"I'll ask." Reno shrugged.

"You need date?" Sunnee questioned. Raising the seductive brows of her symmetric youthful features, she offered, "I'll bring my little sister for you. She clean, very pretty. Make you happy."

"Sure," Reno mumbled, focused on the correspondence. To the heavy organ beat of a Doors tune, he utilized a razor-sharp pocket knife to surgically slice open envelopes. Across the wobbly tabletop, he sorted orders for souvenir small arms. *The ad in* Soldier of Fortune *magazine is netting fish,* he concluded. *My venture to assist fellow veterans in acquiring wartime mementos has expanded to wannabe warriors.* As always, the request for seasoned AK-47s dominated. A few naive consumers sent cash. Reno grinned, stuffing the greenbacks into a denim pant pocket. Shaking his head, he realized he wouldn't cheat a brother-in-arms, and in a word-of-mouth business, he couldn't shortchange any customer. Leaning back, he downed the last swallow of cold beer. Feeling the soothing effects of the brew on an empty stomach, he reached for the ceiling in a comforting stretch.

In front of the watering hole, a polished black Mercedes rolled to a soft termination. Reno sat up. From his perch, he squinted into the vehicle's tinted windows. *Lost tourists?* he wondered.

The driver's side door swung open. Wearing a charcoal suit, white dress shirt, and crimson necktie, a slick confident East Indian emerged. His dark-brown complexion flirted with shades of black. Flexing broad shoulders, he adjusted aviator sun glasses and strutted up the stairway into the Jade Tiger. With thumb and forefinger, he stroked a thick jet-black mustache.

Reno shot a curious squint at Marshall. Marshall shrugged. To greet the overdressed patron, Aroon stood at attention. The new arrival quizzed the Thai bartender in a low, assertive tone.

"What's Gunga Din's problem?" Marshall slurred.

Reno chuckled.

Aroon pointed an identifying finger at Reno. The Indian followed the bar-tender's extended arm and blindly dropped a crinkled wade of colorful local currency on the counter. Shoulders back and head high, he approached Reno. Hovering over the American's cluttered table, he asked, "Are you Mister Reno James, the procurer of small arms?"

"You got that right, chief," Reno replied. "Are you interested in a Vietnam War souvenir?"

"Not at this time," the intruder responded. Extending a polite palm, he shook the American's hand. "Allow me to introduce myself. I am Saravanamuttu Appukutty. I would like to discuss a possible business opportunity. May I join you?"

"Sure," Reno answered, motioning toward an empty chair. Squinting hard at Saravanamuttu Appukutty, he added, "What…what's your name again?"

"Please just call me S.A."

Reno chuckled. "OK, *Ese*. I won't forget that." Seeing his potential customer's puzzled expression, he clarified. "No offense, *hombre*. Where I came from, *ese* is barrio slang for homeboy…a friend."

Ignoring the banter, S.A. sat erect. He reeked of cologne. In an educated, articulate voice, he said, "I am aware that you have a connection to small arms. I however am interested in acquiring light weapons. Would you be able to assist me in this endeavor?"

Reno leaned back, scrutinizing the messenger. Trafficking in piecemeal pistols and assault rifles was forgivable. However, *light weapons* encompassed arms designed for use by several personnel operating as a unit. Softly, he questioned, "Are you in the market for mortars, portable antitank guns, and handheld antiaircraft missile systems?"

S.A. grinned. Beneath his thick black mustache, crooked white teeth sparkled. "And explosives," he answered.

Reno swallowed. "Look," he responded, flashing submissive palms. "I may be able to accommodate your request. However, I am a small-time dealer who operates on consignment. How large of an order are you considering?"

"Cost is not an issue," S.A. arrogantly injected.

"Are we talking about tens of thousands of US dollars or hundreds of thousands of dollars?" Reno probed.

"Mister Reno, I'm more interested in the availability of light weapons than cost. After I'm informed of the extent of your supplier's inventory, we can negotiate price."

"How about the logistics of delivery?" Reno inquired. "Where and when?"

"Not an issue." S.A. sighed. "I will accept ownership anywhere in Thailand."

Attempting to suppress a big smile, Reno nodded. "Let me think about it."

"Thank you for your time," S.A. said, rising from the table. From the breast pocket of his suit coat, he produced a business card. "Once you reach a conclusion, please inform me of your decision."

While the Jade Tiger's few patrons focused on the confidently departing overdressed Indian, Reno, examining the embossed font of the small card, mumbled, "Global Ventures Trading Company…Well, that doesn't tell me shit."

Chapter 3

It was a sweltering Colombo Monday afternoon. Billowing black smoke shrouded the tropical sun perched over the Sri Lankan capital. In the heart of the city populated by over six hundred thousand inhabitants, Chola waited at a crowded inner-city bus stop. He fidgeted in a white button-down shirt, black slacks, and rubber sandals. It was hot, sticky. Most of the public transit commuters were students like he was. At twenty years of age, he stood clutching an accounting textbook and a paperback copy of *Huckleberry Finn*. He was wiry thin with a baby face. His hair was jet black and his skin dark brown. A sprouting mustache anchored his upper lip. A large deep scar flowed down the side of his head; the disfigurement a reminder of a childhood incident involving an out-of-control bicycle and a store's plate-glass window. Before him, the stagnant compilation of diesel-coughing vehicles surged forward. Magnified sunlight reflected off the city's midrise buildings. Horns barked. Looking up at the plumes of black smoke polluting the sky, Chola felt his stomach churn. A foul breeze carried the charred aroma of racial unrest. Spotting his bus bullying its way down the thoroughfare, he took a deep breath. *I'll make it back to Uncle's,* he rationalized. *I know I should have stayed home today, but I couldn't miss the exam.* He grinned. *The test went well.*

A packed faded white-and-red bus rolled in beside the impatient commuters. Surging forward, the boarding throng battled disembarking passengers.

The bus paused, exhaled a cloud of rancid exhaust, and flowed back into the slow stream of rush-hour traffic. Hanging out an open doorway, Chola clung tightly to a rusty chrome handle. A soft breeze tousled his thick hair and caressed his scarred features.

The teardrop-shaped island nation, which Chola and fifteen-million other inhabitants called home, had had many names over a colorful history. Located off the southern tip of India, the isle's deep harbors enticed commerce. Arab traders in the eighth century labeled the landmass *Serendib*. In the early sixteenth century, the colonizing Portuguese knew it as *Ceilao*. For the Dutch and British who followed, it was Ceylon. For the Sinhala people, the majority of the local populous, it had always been Lanka. For Chola, a Tamil, his homeland had no other name but Eelam.

After one hundred and fifty years of colonial rule, Great Britain granted independence to Ceylon in 1948. The British divide-and-rule policy disproportionately favored the Hindu Tamil minority. The Tamils dominated the colonial civil service and the professions of education, law, and medicine. Britannia departed, leaving considerable wealth in rubber, tea, and coconut plantations. She also left behind a simmering caldron of ethnic tension. Over the last several decades, the Buddhist Singhalese majority turned up the heat with discriminatory policies. Adding fuel to the pyre, Tamil militant groups began to surface. On this warm Monday afternoon in July of 1983, as Chola hung out of the back of the rickety overcrowded bus, the simmering racial caldron began to boil.

Chola closed his eyes, wishing he was already home. He visualized the small amah's room he shared with his widowed mother. *The servant's quarters of Rolph van der Wall's walled residence will be safe,* he realized. Uncle Rolph, a privileged white Burgher, had a short temper but was a benevolent man. *Uncle paid for my education and introduced me to the joys of reading,* Chola reflected. Glancing down at the copy of *Huckleberry Finn* tucked under his arm, he grinned. *I will soon be home escaping down the Mississippi River with Jim and Huck. This storm of hate will pass. The past flare-ups always did.*

"All Tamils must pay!" shouted an irate passenger.

Looking up into the bus, Chola spotted the instigator.

A seated businessman angrily clutching a newspaper ranted about the weekend ambush of Sri-Lankan soldiers. "Murdered, all thirteen brave men were murdered by the cowardly Tamil Tigers. Liberation fighters, my ass!" he shouted. "The only good Tamil is a dead Tamil!"

"You got that right," an angry voice responded from deep within the compacted commuters.

The bus's brakes squealed. Balding tires chaffed rough asphalt. Chola jerked back, snorting at the taint of burnt rubber. In all directions, the flowing traffic ground to a halt. A mob brandishing knives, clubs, pipes, and axes and toting cans of petrol wadded into the stream of stalled vehicles. Chola hopped off the bus. Slowly he retreated into the sidewalk audience. The rabid rabble scanned idle vehicles for specific prey. Identifying the enemy was difficult. Although religion and language divided the adversaries, they looked alike. There were slight Tamil tells—like how a woman ties her sari and some religious markings. Out of Chola's red-and-white transport, Singhalese expelled Tamils. Dropping books, briefcases, and groceries terror-stricken men, women, and children ran. Chola took a cautious step back. His heart raced. Gulping hard, he sucked on thin air. Tumbling out of the bus, a Tamil businessman in a light-gray suit spilled onto the hot asphalt. Hugging a bleeding knee and shredded pant leg, he looked confused, disoriented. The advancing horde surrounded him. Stepping out of the hostile mass, a heavy thug in a stained white singlet and blue tartan sarong grinned. The brut, wielding a large bread knife, signaled with beckoning fingers. Wincing in pain, the panting businessman stood. Wobbling on a bleeding knee, he took a deep breath and adjusted his narrow necktie. Sweat rolled down his petrified expression. A quiet pause preceded the goon's thrust of a ten-inch blade into the Tamil's skinny belly. The businessman studied his punctured abdomen. Secreting plasma stained his cotton dress shirt. The rabid pack thirsting for Hindu blood howled.

Chola turned and slowly walked away. *Don't run,* he counseled. In his wake, he could hear the desperate cries of his kinsmen. A high-pitched wail pierced his heart. Sweat leaked out of every pore of his taut skin. His head hung low, he focused on the cracked sidewalk. A side glance caught a police officer enjoying the spectacle with a smoke. *Hide, I need to hide,* he realized. Casually, he turned

down a narrow alley. The growls of the rabble intensified. The deserted alleyway offered no sanctuary. Chola tossed his accounting textbook and *Huckleberry
Finn* paperback on discarded rubble. An hour ago, the texts seemed so important. Out of the pile of concrete at his feet, he pulled out a rusty rod of rebar.
Studying the crude two-foot steel weapon, he took a deep breath. *This may work,*
he thought. Braced against the wall at the alley entrance, he waited. The mob
approached. Exhaling softly, Chola drifted into the passing ruckus. Waving the
rusty bar over his head, he concealed his Hindu heritage.

The torrent of hate flowed randomly through the city. Chola scanned the
passing buildings and storefronts, seeking an escape route. In front of a Tamil
tea boutique, a charred corpse smoldered. The café burned. Hiding behind a
charlatan scowl, Chola fought back surfacing bile.

"This way, brothers!" called out a confident middle-aged ringleader. His
rolled-up starched shirt sleeves revealed a gold wrist watch. Creased cuffed
slacks over black leather shoes distinguished him from the shabby rabble.
Clutching a wad of documentation, he motioned to a line of waiting buses.

Trapped in the herd, Chola boarded the transport. His scarred face blend-
ing in with the faces of the hard men around him.

The ringleader, referring to his crinkled documentation, instructed the
driver. The transport lunged forward. Balanced on polished black leather
shoes, he addressed the passengers. "We need to focus, brothers," he said in
a firm, commanding voice. "For mutilating the corpses of our brave fighting
men, we will drive the Tamils into the sea." Waving wrinkled pages in the air,
he continued, "They can run, but they cannot hide. I have here our objective
for today. We are headed to the factory district of Ratmalana. I will identify
the Tamil-owned textile mills, garment factories, and coconut-oil-processing
plants. Your orders are simple, *kada, adha,* and *gini!*"

Break, haul, and burn.

This is not a spontaneous flare-up of racial tension, Chola realized. *This has nothing to do with the ambush of thirteen soldiers. This is my government declaring war on me
and my people.*

From the bus window, Chola felt relief seeing an abandoned garment
factory. Grasping the rebar rod, he exited the transport and joined the

window-shattering mob. Lifetimes of hard work, sacrifice, and luck burned in the distance. Dark smoke stained the red sky of a setting sun. Entering the vacated facility, marauding looters hastily began hauling off sewing machines. Petrol was splashed on colorful bolts of fabric. In search of plunder, the brigands ignored their skinny scar-faced comrade exiting.

"You, boy, come here!" called out the ringleader.

Chola flinched. Over his shoulder, he spotted the riot captain in a back office doorway.

"Come here, boy," the ringleader repeated, focused on Chola's rusty metal rod.

Sheepishly, Chola approached.

Grabbing the rebar out of the Chola's grasp, the riot captain tested the rod's weight and mumbled, "Perfect."

Framed by the office doorway, Chola observed the groomed thug utilizing the steel pole to pry open a desk drawer. Pulling out a metal cash box, the common thief broke the lock with a well-placed blow. Sitting down in the desk chair, he leaned forward, admiring the spoils.

Stepping into the office, Chola retrieved his metal weapon. Looking down, he observed the transfixed greedy bastard counting currency. Whispered numbers filled the quiet, isolated room. Squeezing the rusty bar, rage replaced Chola's quest to survive. *I walked away from the cries of my brothers,* he thought with regret. Images of the long day fed the growing fury. The iron bar slowly elevated.

Looking up, the startled ringleader questioned, "You still here?" A single blow spilt his skull. Pulsing blood flowed down a shocked expression. The crimson-spouting carcass collapsed to the floor.

I ended a life, Chola realized. *I killed an enemy of my people,* he rationalized. "One," he mumbled, climbing out of the office window.

Chapter 4

—◦◦◦◦—

It was late in the day. A gentle breeze flowed through the courtyard of Rolph van der Wall's residence. Dry leaves tumbled across stone pavers. In clay pots, colorful tropical flowers swayed. A hint of smoke tainted the atmosphere. Under the comforting shade of a mango tree, Rolph reclined on a padded chaise lounge. Although he was sixty-three years old, the overindulgence of a privileged existence penalized his appearance by ten years. Wild gin blossoms infested his fair-skinned face and bulbous nose. A potbelly taxed the buttons of a white cotton dress shirt. A ring of silver hair surrounded his liver-spotted crown. Sipping on a gin and tonic, he wiggled the exposed toes of his bare feet. *This beats sitting in traffic,* he thought. *The racial riots are like a passing storm. No need to venture out in bad weather.*

Glancing up at the soot staining the blue sky, he shook his head. *I'll probably have to stay home tomorrow,* he conceded. Setting down the lime-garnished tall glass, he picked up the daily newspaper, the *Island*. After he had wrestled with the fluttering sheets, the headline slapped him. Bold black font read, "Lieutenant, 12 Soldiers Die in Terrorist Ambush." *So that was the spark this time,* he surmised.

The courtyard bell clanged. Rolph lowered the newsprint. He squinted over the flickering pages. A local family toting luggage stood in front of the compound's rusting wrought-iron gate. The father in a long sleeve dress shirt and navy-blue slacks feverishly yanked on the entrance chime. *Is that Alamar?* Rolph questioned. Craning his neck, he looked into the residence's open doorway. *Is someone going to answer the chime?* he impatiently wondered. The doorframe stood silent. *How about you, Sam?* Rolph questioned, glancing at his idle vehicle. The waxed Baltic-blue Toyota sedan sparkled. Reclining in the driver's seat, the chauffeur snored through an open mouth. Rolph chuckled at the hibernating Sam. "Looks like I'm the designated greeter," he mumbled. "I'm coming!" Rolph declared to the annoying clang. As he slowly rose, his stiff joints groaned. He slipped his naked feet into a pair of slippers. In the comfortable footwear, he shuffled into harsh sunlight. Punishing rays harassed his pinkish complexion. The resonating bell terminated. Stretching dormant muscles, Rolph peered through corroding bars. "What is it, Alamar?" he grumbled.

Gulping air, the distraught neighbor pleaded, "Please...please, Mister van der Wall." He shot a quick glance over his shoulder. "Hide us." Sweat glistened on his dark features. Alamar's wife panted. Three terrified children sucked back tears.

Rolph flinched. "Of course, Alamar," the Burgher responded, unlatching the gate. The desperate family poured into the white man's sanctuary. The creaking metal barrier slammed shut. The Tamil family scuttled past their Caucasian host into the house. In his comfortable slip-on shoes, Rolph followed.

Just inside the doorway of the large parlor, the terrified guests removed their footwear. Attached to the exposed rafters of a high-pitched wood ceiling, two twirling fans circulated moist air. Open windows provided a cross breeze. Framed black-and-white photos of Rolph's ancestors adorned white plaster walls. An ornately carved lacquered bar anchored a corner. Mounted on pedestals behind the counter were two large elephant tusks. In the opposing corner, a sofa and two rattan chairs encircled a color television. Dated magazines peppered a coffee table.

In his bare feet, Rolph strutted across the polished wood floor toward the bar. Floorboards creaked under his heavy advance. Stationed behind the counter, he asked Alamar, "Would you like a cocktail?"

The Tamil responded with a dumbfounded expression.

Rolph shrugged and plopped two glasses on the glossy surface. "I hope you like gin and tonic," he mumbled, pouring the distilled spirit into a stainless-steel measuring jigger. "I don't like drinking alone." Frowning at an empty ice bucket, he called out, "Roshin, we are out of ice."

The petite amah entered the parlor holding a bowl of ice. Submissively, she looked down. A simple smock dress graced a slender frame. A stained apron protected the gown's floral print. Her jet-black hair was pulled back. Modest earrings decorated exposed ears. Stealing a glance at the Tamil family, she froze. Alamar spoke to her softly in their native tongue. Tears welled up in her deep gemstone eyes. Sniffling, she walked over and filled her employer's ice bucket.

"What is it, Roshin?" Rolph politely inquired.

"They are killing Tamils," she whispered. "They are burning them alive." Fighting back tears, her crackling voice added, "Chola is very late...My son has not come home." Concealing her face in her hands, she softly wept.

"Chola went to school today?" Rolph questioned.

Her bobbing head answered.

Rolph's heart sank. "I told him not to go," he reflected. "Chola is such a good kid." He visualized his servant's son as a boy. The lad's quest for knowledge was insatiable. The first book was Dumas's *Three Musketeers*, he affectionately remembered. *I had him call me uncle after that. I wish I was blessed to have a son, an heir like him.* "Don't worry, Roshin," he consoled. "Chola is a smart man. He will find his way home."

After blowing her nose, she took a deep, composing breath. A hopeful smile accompanied a positive nod.

"What is this?" barked Rolph's much younger Sri Lankan wife. Framed by the hallway, she stood defiantly with folded arms. In creased black slacks, high heels, and a designer blouse, the former beauty queen scowled at the Tamil ensemble. A pearl necklace and matching earrings completed the fashionable composition.

Rolph sighed. Utilizing bar tweezers, he dropped cubes of frozen water into tall glasses of measured gin. "Alamar and his family will be our guests for the next couple of days," he declared. Pouring fizzing tonic over the ice cubes, he glanced at Roshin and softly said, "I'm sorry for the late notice, but there will be an additional five for dinner tonight."

"That is out of the question," his fuming spouse informed him. "I don't want any Tamils under my roof." Focused on Roshin, she emphasized, "That means all Tamils." Snorting, she glared at her older white husband. Her ample bosom pulsed.

Rolph bit his lower lip. That was his tell. The gesture was a prelude to the eruption of his famous temper.

Mrs. van der Wall gulped. She took a withdrawing step back. Turning Rolph's, disenchanted possession hastily retreated. The click of escaping stiletto heels faded down the corridor.

Rolph took a calming breath. Lifting a bubbling gin and tonic, he toasted, "Prost." After a victorious gulp, he winked at his housekeeper and instructed, "Roshin, can you show our guests to their rooms?"

She bowed.

"Thank you, sir," Alamar whispered, clutching a cocktail.

"Consider it neighborly hospitality," Rolph responded to the departing family. Grasping the chilled glass, he walked to the open front door. The plumes of smoke scarring the sky had advanced. Sam continued to snooze. Grinning at his napping driver, Rolph took a refreshing sip. *The second marriage was a mistake*, he concluded. Angeline was all form and no substance. In the distance, a rumbling wave of destruction accented with shattered glass resonated. A pipe-wielding youth appeared at the wrought-iron gate. To acknowledge the uninvited thug, Rolph lifted his cocktail. The ruffian hammered the metal barrier with the pipe. Rolph took another taste of chilled gin.

Placing the cocktail on an entry table, he retrieved a cricket bat from an elephant foot umbrella stand. Griping the cane handle, he took a practice swat. *These buggers need to be taught a lesson,* he thought. Sliding into his slippers, he strolled into the courtyard. A cadre of vandals loitered at the barred entry. Shuffling toward the napping chauffeur, Rolph called out, "Wake up, Sam."

Startled, the pudgy driver sat up and grabbed the steering wheel. "We go to Dutch Union Bar now?" he inquired blinking.

"Maybe later," Rolph responded, pointing the cricket bat at the growing threat. "Right now, I need your assistance in repelling borders."

Rubbing a waking eye with a fisted hand, Sam focused. Leaning over, he popped open the glove box. A stub-nose thirty-eight-caliber pistol rested atop crinkled papers. After a satisfying yawn, Sam armed himself.

Burgher and driver walked across the courtyard to greet the invaders, Rolph brandishing a cricket bat, Sam's weapon concealed in the small of his back. In the distance, a fire crackled. Rolph turned to investigate. His wall screened the source. Above the stone structure, he got a glimpse of leaping flames. Billowing smoke polluted the afternoon sky. *The blaze is Alamar's residence,* Rolph surmised. "You bastards," he grumbled at the squad of ten arsonists at his gate. The assailants were young. Some dressed in soiled sarongs, others in patched and frayed shirts and pants. The pipe-wielding vagrant waved his galvanized weapon through the courtyard gate. Tilting his head back, he howled. Sinister laughter indicated appreciation of the performance. Catching a whiff of the intruder's stench, Rolph pinched his pineapple nose. *Who are these vagabonds?* he questioned. *These shanty-town dwellers do not belong in my Colombo, definitely not in my neighborhood. Where are the police? This burning, looting pack of rabid dogs needs to be put down.*

Clutching a five-gallon petrol container, a spokesman hollered over his yelping companions.

"They are looking for Alamar and his family," Sam informed him.

"He's not here," Rolph shouted at the milling mob. "Please vacate the premises."

A wiry youth scaled the barrier. Leaping into the courtyard, the skinny teen teetered backward. His bony ass slammed hard onto the stone pavers. Resting his elbows on bent knees, he chuckled.

The audacity to enter my residence uninvited, Rolph thought. He bit his bottom lip. His face reddened. The veins on his neck pulsed. Grunting, he swatted the invader across the face with the blade of the bat. The hooligan's nose exploded. "How dare you!" Rolph shouted, whacking the collapsing intruder. "This is my house!" accompanied the third blow. In a fetal position, the uninvited guest accepted the beating. Rolph focused on the moaning heap. He grimaced. A shard of pain tormented his aging spine. Hyperventilating, he raised the heavy baton. Sweat rolled down his wrinkled crimson noggin. The bloody splintered cricket bat froze over his head. Snorting, Rolph struggled with the immobile club. "What the...?" he questioned. A tight grip restrained his bat-wielding arm.

"That's enough, sir," Sam said, releasing his employer's wrist.

Gulping air, Rolph concurred. Facing the stunned audience through the bars, he took a deep breath. "I did ask you to disperse," he reminded them, dropping his weapon. Slowly the thugs disbanded. Rolph grinned. *Not bad for an old Burgher,* he concluded. Turning, he discovered Sam targeting the departing spectators with a firearm. Massaging his tender backbone, he instructed, "Sam, can you clean this up? I need to refresh my cocktail."

"Yes, sir," his driver replied.

Chapter 5

———✦———

The setting sun rested on a sparkling royal-blue ocean. The bright-orange sphere slowly descended. Wispy high clouds blushed. A skinny black-gray dog roamed the deserted beach. Small crashing waves pushed colorful plastic-ridden garbage and driftwood up the sandy incline. A large breaking wave startled the mutt. The mongrel scurried into dense surrounding tropical growth. On the rippling water, a lone, patient seated surfer bobbed on his surfboard. An unzipped wetsuit exposed chiseled muscles on a thin frame. The corrosive effects of salt, sun, and wind etched in the leathery creases around the surfer's dark deep-set eyes. He squinted hard into the fading light. The day's last glimmer illuminated a stoic expression accented with sharp cheekbones.

Holding canvas Bata sneakers and a crinkled stack of opened correspondence, Reno strolled along the moist sand at the water's edge. *Did I have six or seven beers?* he tried to recall with a light head and full bladder. The remnants of a rolling wave dowsed his bare feet. *God, that feels good,* he realized. "And so will this," he declared securing his load under a wing and releasing his manhood. Pissing into the ocean, he sighed. To the sound of a steady splashing stream, he focused on the crimson horizon. Catching a glimpse of the undulating surfer, he muttered, "Longboard." *My neighbor is one strange duck,* he reflected, waving at the surfer.

The seated rolling silhouette returned the gesture with a subtle salute.

Two years, Reno recalled zipping up his pants. *For two years, Longboard never spoke, waved, or looked in my direction. It really pissed me off. Marshall warned me to avoid the dark surfer. That was easy advice for Marshall to follow; he didn't share a beach with Longboard. I just assumed the fanatic surfer was a lone wolf. Once a month, a provisioner would arrive at the surfer's stilted shack and deliver food. On several occasions, I saw women, or should I say* young *women, arriving and departing the hut. But day in and day out, all Longboard would do was surf. On bad days, he would just bob in the water. On good days, he would ride waves under the moonlight.*

Strolling in the thick, dirty sand toward his residence, Reno recalled the large waves that pounded the shoreline three years ago.

It was the peak of the rainy season in the fall of 1980. "A new day is born," Reno mumbled, comfortably slouching in a rattan chair on his raised deck. A dark, stormy sky robbed him of dawn's first light. "I live to see another day," he muttered, lifting a cup of joe at the shrouded glow along the horizon. An angry sea churned beneath the stormy sky. Waves crashed with a thunderous roar. A whipping wind seasoned the air with ocean spray. *Never before has my little window on the ocean produced such magnificent surf,* Reno surmised. *Where is the surfer?* he questioned. *My mysterious neighbor should be out there taking advantage of nature's rare gift.* He glanced over at the surfer's stilted hovel. Empty windows stared back. *It's been a couple of days since I caught a glimpse of that arrogant asshole,* he realized. *My neighbor never waves, says hello, or asks me to kiss his ass. The only thing the emotionless specter does is ride waves.* Reno shrugged. Taking a sip of lukewarm coffee, his face puckered. Flicking his wrist, he tossed the balance of the spent coffee over the railing. *Maybe I should check on that aloof prick,* he reasoned. *The surfer is my neighbor after all.*

Standing in the midst of the patches of sad grass and sandy soil that separated the residences, Reno hollered, "Anybody home?" His white T-shirt flapped in the gruff wind. In the distance, rough surf growled. "Shit," he mumbled, strolling over to the tiny hut. Taking a deep breath, he jogged up the worn treads of the stairway leading up to the raised shack. With a fisted knuckle, he rapped on a blistered wooden door. Eerily, it swung open. Cheap rattan furniture housed mismatching stained cushions. A silent reel-to-reel tape deck spun. A full disc slapped a dead reel with a frayed tape tail. There were books everywhere. Teetering columns of paperback and hardback texts rose above a minefield of books littering the hardwood floor. Invading wind woke dormant books. Pages fluttered. Reno snorted. The hovel reeked of shit and vomit. "Hello!" he shouted.

A low groan answered.

Pinching his nose, Reno peered into the back bedroom. On the matted flooring, the surfer, in a fetal position, lay naked in a pool of sweat, vomit, and feces. Reno stepped into the rancid filth. He grabbed a bedsheet off the unmade bed and covered the twitching carcass. Squatting down, he lifted the dead weight onto the bare mattress.

"Water," rolled out of the surfer's gravelly throat, his desperate gaze showing gratitude.

"Sure, sport," Reno replied.

With a plastic bottle of mineral water, Reno attempted to hydrate the sick bastard. "Hopefully you will keep this down," he mumbled, studying the mounted Remington 700 bolt-action sniper's rifle displayed over the bed. It was the M40 variant of the lethal weapon. "Phụng Hoàng" was eloquently carved across the rifle's wood stock. *Is this just another war souvenir?* he wondered. *Or was my neighbor once an assassin in the CIA's Phoenix Program?* "What's your name, sport?" he probed.

"Longboard...I go by Longboard," the surfer muttered, sucking air.

"Please to meet you, Longboard. I'm Reno, the neighbor you ignored for the last couple of years." Failing to evoke a reaction, Reno conceded. "I'll get a mop to clean up this mess and have your soiled linens laundered. Do you think you can handle soup?"

Nodding, Longboard mumbled, "Thanks." Taking a composing gulp, he confessed, "I keep to myself because I have an addiction."

"The heroin beast?" Reno solicited.

A chuckle escaped the trembling patient. "I'm addicted to the gratification of neutralizing life," Longboard clarified. "I surf and read to control the inner demon of my alter ego...Jesse Long."

"You're kinda talking crazy." Reno chuckled. "Now let me go get that mop."

———— ✺ ————

Ascending the creaky stair treads to his stilted residence, Reno glanced over at the surfer's shack. *It's been three years since Longboard survived the bad case of food poising,* he calculated. *Longboard became a good friend and neighbor,* he reflected, *even though I'm his only friend. I have yet to make the acquaintance of Jesse Long.*

On a rough grass matt, Reno wiped his sandy feet. Dropping his sneakers on the covered porch, he entered his humble residence. The furniture consisted of a teakwood couch and chair. The seating option's cushions featured a tropical floral-printed fabric. On the wall over the sofa hung a local artist's oil painting of two elephants frolicking in shallow water. A flat Olympic weightlifting bench sat in the center of the room. Cast-iron weight plates of various denominations littered the floor. Reno tossed the stack of brown and blue envelopes requesting antique weapon souvenirs on a driftwood coffee table. Plopping down on the sofa, he sighed. Reaching under the couch, he retrieved a Romeo and Juliette cigar box. Flipping open the lid exposed a small plastic sandwich bag containing rich dark-green buds of cannabis, a pack of rolling papers, a blue plastic disposable lighter, and several prerolled joints. Flakes of marijuana peppered the bottom of the container. With thumb and forefinger, he delicately selected a half-smoked paper cylinder of weed. A flick of the lighter ignited the drug. A distinctive aroma filled the small room. Inhaling deeply, he sucked the toxic vapors deep into his lungs. After a calculated pause, he exhaled. Enjoying the soothing sensation, he slouched down and took another toke. *Now to the business at hand,* he thought, extinguishing the smoldering joint with a moistened fingertip.

The receiver of a black rotary dial telephone crackled in Reno's ear. *I hope someone's home,* he pondered, listening to a distant pulsing ringtone.

"River City Antiquities," followed an answering click.

"Danny, it's Reno."

"Ah, hello, Mr. Reno James. Danny was expecting your call," Danny replied. "Please proceed."

"OK, Danny, this month's order: twelve Kalashnikovs, four M-16s, and I'll need four Soviet pistols. What type of commie handguns do you have in stock?" Reno asked.

"I still have Markarov pistols," Danny replied.

"Those will work."

"Ammunition?" The Thai chuckled.

"You always ask," Reno replied. "No, the answer still is no."

"Pick up or delivery?"

"I'm going to pick up this month's order," Reno answered. "I may have some other business in Bangkok."

"Danny is your man in Bangkok," Danny quickly replied. "What can Danny do for you?"

"I have a fish on the line," Reno informed him. "I don't know if he is real, but I want to test the waters. I need you to put a fifty-thousand-dollar shopping list of light weapons together for me. That's fifty-thousand US. I'm looking for claymore landmines, antiaircraft guns, mortars, and rocket-propelled grenades."

"No problem," Danny enthusiastically interrupted. "Is your fish going to need export documentation?"

"No, assume this is an FOB order in your pricing. The customer will take the risk and cost of delivery," Reno answered. "Like I said, I'm just testing the waters. If he's real, there may be a bigger or several other transactions. So tell me, Danny, can you deliver?"

"Thailand's modest skimming of the American arms that flowed into Cambodia has filled warehouses. Don't worry, Reno; Danny give you very good bait to reel in this big fish."

Chapter 6

───※───

Cascading rain flowed out of the black night sky. Gusting wind propelled the water across the rough surface of a long, lonely stretch of pockmarked asphalt. Flanking weeds swayed along the narrow roadway. Toads migrated atop the rough surface. The downpour intensified. Falling rain ricocheted off the blacktop. A slit in a man-made mound of sandbags and palm logs emitted a beckoning glow. The escaping light reflected a sparkling sliver across the road. The checkpoint's location was marked by movable metal barricades blocking the deserted highway.

In the depths of the windblown growth, the swirling tropical storm concealed the slithering advance of three militants. Elevated over muddy elbows, AK-47s clawed at dense elephant grass. Progress was slow, wet, cold. Dandak, at twenty-five years of age, was the oldest partisan. A rural peasant farmer, Dandak had never traveled more than ten miles from the mud shack he called home. Long days of toiling in the fields as a child produced callused hands and gnarled feet. A pauper's diet accounted for his lack of teeth. Crawling beside Dandak was Taman, a grocer's son. With a limited education, he had maintained the accounts of the family's fresh-produce stall. Short in stature, he appeared much younger than his sixteen years. Sucking hard on the thick air, he struggled balancing the elevated heavy assault rifle. In front of Taman, the former college student Chola, drenched to the bone, wriggled forward. Parting weeds folded under his sloshing advance.

"Chola," Taman groaned.

Chola paused. He began to shake, and his teeth chattered. A chill had set in. He looked over his shoulder. A low moan flowed out of the dense growth. Reluctantly, he retreated. Utilizing a gun barrel, he parted tall, sharp green blades to investigate. Taman lay on his back, clutching his stomach.

"What is it?" Chola whispered.

Gulping air, the boy muttered, "I'm cut…cut bad."

Chola stretched an investigating hand. In the dark, he found Taman's protected abdomen. "Let me see?" he uttered. Taman's compressing grasp retreated. Warm blood pulsed under Chola's tender touch. In the darkness, a gentle a finger traced a deep gash traversing the length of the young warrior's firm belly.

"I crawled over a broken bottle," Taman informed.

"You'll survive," Chola reassured him.

Dandak poked a curious head through the saturated undergrowth.

"Taman scratched his tummy," Chola said. "Make sure he makes it back. I'll deliver the message."

"By yourself?" Dandak questioned.

Wiping his moist face with the comforting warmth of a blood-soaked palm, Chola plunged back into the thick brush. "It is a simple message," he mumbled.

Chola resumed his crawling advance. The storm subsided. Black clouds appeared overhead. The cloaking growth thinned. Gazing across the glistening ribbon of asphalt, Chola got a blurred image of the government bunker. He grinned. Shadows floating across the lighted narrow gun-port confirmed occupancy. Chola took a deep, sobering breath. Shaking a wet, callused hand, he revived a trigger finger. Fidgeting into a prone firing position, he waited. *Patience,* he thought. Visualizing his mother, he sighed. *I fled Colombo and never said good-bye,* he sadly reflected. *Did she get my letter? How would she react knowing I've killed seven men?* he pondered. Rationalizing that the oppressive regime forced his decision, he proudly accepted the journey he chose.

A burst of laughter resonated from the protective mound. A helmeted silhouette emerged. Still chuckling, the unarmed soldier peered into the floating dark clouds. An ignited cigarette illuminated a young profile. After a satisfying inhale of nicotine vapors, the sentry took a wide stance. Exhaling, he secured the smoldering tobacco between his lips and unzipped his military trousers. Tilting his head back, he sighed and released a steady stream of urine.

Chola's Kalashnikov popped. The occupier, clenching his genitals, collapsed. Toads danced around the crumpled corpse. Shadows scurried behind the bunker's porthole. A husky voice cried out, "Kamal, are you all right? Kamal? Kamal!"

"Eight," Chola whispered, pulling back his weapon's charging bolt. Focused on the bait, he smiled.

The bunker went dark. Gun barrels poked out of the narrow opening. A helmet peered out of the sanctuary. Slowly, in a crouching advance, an occupier approached the carcass. Two quick rebel rounds sent him tumbling backward.

"Nine," Chola muttered.

Chapter 7

—⊗⊗⊗—

Reno, in a white polo shirt, faded denim jeans, and flip-flops, strolled down the meandering path. He reeked of cheap cologne. Longboard, in an untucked Hawaiian shirt and baggy swim trunks, walked beside him. The surfer's bleached locks were greased back and perfectly parted. The fronds of tall palm trees fluttered overhead. The air was clean, the sky blue. A salty sea breeze competed with Reno's sharp, fragrant aroma. Reno stole a glance of his apprehensive neighbor. The surfer kept adjusting his grasp on a sealed bottle of Bacardi rum. *Jackson's farewell sendoff will be Longboard's debut,* he realized.

"Introduce me as Longboard," the surfer mumbled.

"Everyone knows who you are." Reno chuckled. "You're that mysterious local celebrity that bobs in the ocean all day."

"I don't talk about my past," Longboard declared.

"No worries," Reno responded. "The talkers in the veterans' ensemble would rather bloviate, embellish, or just make shit up about their Vietnam tenure. They are not much on probing or listening. The humble heroes remain silent and respect a brother's privacy." Latching onto his neighbor, he added, "It is not a big issue, but a ranger named Joey has some issues. Marshall looks after him."

"Soldier's heart?" Longboard questioned.

Nodding, Reno mumbled, "Shell shock, battle fatigue, post-Vietnam syndrome, whatever you want to call it, Joey is haunted by dark days."

"Thanks for the heads-up," Longboard responded.

"One other warning," Reno announced. "As a virgin audience at the festivities, you will attract the bloviators." Grinning, he added, "If it's any consolation, I've heard every long-winded tale many times."

Squinting, the surfer inquired, "What's your story, Reno?"

Reno paused. A sly smile appeared. "I'm one of those quiet heroes that respect a brother's privacy."

The tropical trail flowed into a wave of rolling laughter. An elevated longhouse resided behind a manicured lawn. From the raised deck, a reel-to-reel tape deck fed a sixties soundtrack into large black speaker boxes. The shadows of surrounding tall palm trees crisscrossed the neatly trimmed turf. A Thai boy tended a folding table draped in linen. An impressive collection of brand liquor bottles anchored an end of the tabletop. A galvanized tub of ice and beer occupied the other. A smoldering oil drum barbecue grill added a festive smoke scent. Standing clusters of thirty- and forty-year-old men chatted and drank. Local girls provided a youthful spice. Other guests sat in an arched arrangement of wooden lawn chairs.

Holding court in the middle of the semicircle seating option, the one-legged host spotted the new arrivals. "Reno!" Marshall called out. "Excuse me," he mumbled to his other guests. Assisted by a crutch, he hobbled across the freshly mowed grass. Balanced on his single limb, he shook Reno's hand. Grinning at the surfer, he repeated the greeting ritual and declared, "It's about time."

Longboard glanced down. Cracking a soft smile, he displayed the liter bottle of white rum and mumbled, "I brought you a gift."

"You do want to become my good friend," Marshall commented, examining the bottle of Bacardi.

"How's Joey today?" Reno inquired.

Pivoting on his leg, Marshall scanned the celebration. At the end of the curved seating arrangement sat Joey. He was thin, clean-shaven, his hair cropped short. Grasping a can of beer with both hands, he rocked softly to the galloping beat of the Cream classic "White Room." "Joey is having a good time," Marshall answered. Leaning into Longboard, he informed him, "Joey and I served in the 173rd Airborne at different times." A gaggle of Thai girls giggled. "Sunee," Marshall shouted at the cluster. "Reno is here."

The female cadre parted. A petite local beauty stepped forward for inspection. Her long dark hair cascaded down her shoulders and back. In black pageboy pants and a sleeveless cotton blouse, she shyly looked down and twisted a sandaled foot in the green grass.

"How old is she?" Reno questioned, examining the innocent belle.

"She'll be nineteen next year," Marshall answered.

Reno chuckled. "Help me with the math. That would make her eighteen?"

"Something like that," Marshall replied, beckoning the girl over. "Daw," he called out. "I'd like you to meet my good friend Reno."

Daw approached. Nuzzling under Reno's arm, she melted into a snuggling embrace.

"Please to meet you, Daw," Reno said, looking down at the party favor clinging to his chest.

"Longboard, let's go drink your rum," Marshall announced, leading the way to the folding table saloon.

"How about a beer, Daw?" Reno proposed to the top of his affectionate escort's head.

"I get cold one for you, Mister Reno," she proudly declared, patting his muscular chest.

Reno admired the Thai filly as she pranced away with his beer order. *That's a tempting bit of trouble,* he thought, focused on her narrow hips. *My six months of bliss with Mali evolved into two years of trying to evict her from the beach house,* he reflected. *Local girlfriends are expensive. Daw will add some seasoning to today's party,* he concluded, *nothing more.* Plunging into the celebration, he caught a whiff of cannabis. Hysterical laughter erupted out of a huddle of sleepy-eyed expats. *Marshall knows how to throw a party,* he concluded, greeting friends with a wave, a nod, or a smile. "Good afternoon, boys," he said, strolling into a conversation between Bear and the departing Jackson.

Jackson was a good old boy from South Texas. He was thin, graying, and fair-skinned; acne scars blanked his perpetually oily complexion. Bear was black. His real name was Cletus Jones. Originally, he hailed from Philadelphia.

The six-foot-four Bear had a barrel chest and a very happy five-foot-tall Thai wife.

Was it Jackson's mother or father who just died? Reno pondered. "Sorry about your loss, Jackson," he offered.

"Thanks, Reno," the Texan responded.

"Hey, San Bernardino," Bear exclaimed, placing a massive paw on Reno's shoulder. "I see you finally convinced the dark surfer to join us."

Jackson and Reno looked over their shoulders. Marshall was working overtime to welcome Longboard into the fold.

"Do you think Marshall is telling the surfer the Odenbach yarn?" Bear questioned.

"Most definitely," Reno answered as Daw's cold, damp hand presented a chilled can of Singha beer.

"I get from bottom of ice tub for you," she proudly informed, latching herself into a snuggling embrace.

"Thanks, sweetheart," Reno mumbled, kissing the top of her head.

"What's the Odenbach story?" Jackson probed. "I haven't heard that one before."

Bear flinched. "How did you miss it? I've heard several versions over the years."

"What?" Jackson playfully snapped. "What did you hear?"

Reno looked over at Marshall. The one-legged host was deep into the Odenbach rant. Reno sighed. "I'll give you the CliffsNotes version," he conceded, wetting his palate with cold carbonation. "Marshall grew up in the suburbs of Denver. In high school, he was a talented nose tackle...all conference or something like that. The quarterback, Ray Odenbach, lived across the street. They were teammates but rivals. They both get drafted by Uncle Sam. Marshall goes to Nam. Odenbach flees to Canada. About four years ago, Marshall returned Stateside to close out his mother's estate. He bumps into Odenbach." Reno tilted his head, draining the can of beer. Daw instinctively confiscated the empty container and departed, seeking a replacement. After wiping moist lips, Reno continued, "Odenbach's illegal Canadian departure was pardoned by Jimmy Carter."

"That was a bullshit move by the peanut farmer," Jackson blurted.

"Fuckin' A," Bear agreed.

"Please save the commentary until the story's conclusion." Reno chuckled, flashing his palms. "Anyway," he continued, "Odenbach is feeling smug about his reprieve. He comments about Marshall's lost limb. Something like…you lost that in Vietnam…good." Bear's nostrils flared, Jackson's oily complexion reddened. "There are several endings to the tale," Reno informed. "The one I like is when the police arrive, Odenbach is pummeled. Marshall is hopping on his one leg; his hands are swollen. His knuckles bruised and bleeding." Reno accepts a fresh beer from Daw and closes. "The cops are vets; they arrest Odenbach."

The trio turns. Marshall, concluding his Odenbach yarn, smacks the air with an open hand and shouts, "I bitch-slapped that deserter."

"That's an alternative ending," Reno commented, taking a sip of brew.

"Don't let Marshall's big heart and pleasant demeanor fool you," Bear commented. "He is one badass that I would never cross." He lowered his gruff voice. "The story you will never hear from Marshall is when he was removed from the battlefield." Bear swallowed. "I was there." Shaking his empty beer can, he politely asked Daw, "Do you mind getting us another round, honey?" She glanced up at her date. Reno winked and sent her on the errand with a playful pat on the tush. Bear spoke softly. "It was a very successful search and destroy. We took a dink camp of company size totally by surprise without a single casualty. The dink body count was high, and the weapon cache we captured…" Bear grinned into the sky and mumbled, "Mortars, AK-47s, explosives…" His expression soured. "A detonated landmine shattered the victory celebration. Marshall lay on the ground snorting like a bull and clutching a bloody stump with both hands. You could see the intense pain in his focused eyes. He never cried out. His gazed softened as he looked at us as if to apologize for spoiling the successful mission."

"Do you think he was in shock?" Jackson questioned.

Bear slowly shook his head, "Nah, I know shock and I know Marshall." Glancing across the lawn at the animated host, he smiled. Refocusing on his audience, he continued, "As a medic hastily applied a tourniquet, Marshall looked at me and asked through gritted teeth, 'Hey, Bear, how about a smoke?'

Can you believe that? There was blood everywhere. A shattered bone stuck out of the mangled mess, and the son-of-a-bitch wants a cigarette. Make no mistake, my white brother was in agony but concentrated on the smoldering tobacco between his lips to camouflage the pain. When the dustoff arrived, he spit out the glowing butt and muttered, 'It's time to go. Can someone hand me my leg?'" Bear looked down and dragged a finger across a sniffle. A reflective grin emerged.

"You OK, Bear?" Reno asked, breaking the silence.

"Yup," Bear responded. "It's funny how those days seem so long ago and then again like the events just happened."

The bubbly Daw skipped into the reflective exchange with a fresh round of cold brews. Pop tabs released carbonation. Bear tilted his big noggin and placed a cup hand behind an ear. "Oh yeah!" he exclaimed as the heavy brass beat of James Brown's "I Feel Good" burst out of the large black speaker boxes. "I feel good," Bear sang out, twisting and turning to the addictive tune, "I knew that I would now." Bear's large feet floated over the dark-green turf. His punctuated screams and shouts complemented the funky classic.

Daw's petite paw accepted Reno's invitation to dance. Swaying beside the euphoric Bear, the Thai nymph's long jet-black hair rippled in the afternoon breeze. Reno, juggling the full can of beer, attempted to mimic his black friend's soulful moves. The white interpretation lacked a certain fluidity. The flock of Thai girls converged on the sod dance floor. Middle-aged men followed. Other partygoers clapped out a steady beat, encouraging the dancers. Bear closed his eyes as the tune's alto sax solo flowed through his body. Reno grinned. *Joey's not the only one having a good time.*

Chapter 8

—⊗⊗⊗—

Bangkok's Rambutti Palace Hotel was located near the Don Mueang International airport. Its clientele consisted mainly of layover flight crews and transit passengers. The hotel bar was quiet for a Friday night. A local band on a small stage phonetically performed the Donny Osmond classic, "Puppy Love." The lead singer's second-language attempt fell short of the original. A heavy American couple cashed out after a quick snort and staggered toward the exit. KLM Royal Dutch pilots and attendants held council in a red vinyl corner booth. The aircrew cackled in their native tongue over a Formica tabletop littered with empty beer bottles and a smoldering ashtray. The air-conditioned room was crisp and cool. The aroma of secondhand smoke hung in the air. A twelve-year-old-looking Thai bartender in a red vest and bow tie stood watch over a long empty counter. Behind him, the liquor selection glowed in soft light. The servers consisted of two Asian beauties in matching sarongs and long-sleeved blouses. Focused on the patrons, the shy girls stood attentively.

Sitting at an isolated small table, Reno used the back of a manila envelope as a scratch pad. Tucking a number-two pencil behind an ear, he pondered the calculations. After a quick shrug, he picked up a glistening glass mug of cold brew. Leaning back in a padded bamboo chair, he squinted hard at the musicians.

"And they call it ruppy luv," the Asian singer passionately sang to a tinny accompaniment.

What is "ruppy luv"? Reno snickered. *I wonder if they know any Led Zeppelin.* Glancing over at the boisterous uniformed Dutch, he focused on a young blond stewardess. *Kinda cute,* he concluded. *A little pudgy, but after a steady diet of petite Thai cuisine, I'd like to sample from the European buffet.* Chuckling, he went back to work. Retrieving the pencil, he scanned a neatly typed laundry list of munitions. Attached to the top of the page, a yellow Post-it priced the light weapons at fifty-thousand dollars. *Danny wants fifty-thousand US for this?* he questioned. Glancing at his scratch pad, he underlined his eighty-five-thousand-dollar quantification of the individual items. *If Danny can produce this firepower for fifty large, he has done me a favor. This is a clearance sale price that I'll mark up to...* He paused to check the numbers. "Seventy-five big ones," he whispered. *S.A. is still getting a bargain at that price,* he concluded. Reading through the list, he mumbled, "M30 mortars, M2 Mortars, M79 grenade launchers, Browning fifty calibers, Claymore mines...This is all American hardware." *A little dated, but made in the USA. The Thais probably siphoned these off en route to the Cambodian civil war in the seventies. In the US and Soviet arms race, you have to dispose of last season's dated weapons to make room for the new, more advanced methods of killing. In my car heisting days,* he recalled, *the new cars were stripped for parts. The older models shipped to Mexico. What one consumer considers obsolete, another cherishes. There is always a market for last year's models.*

Taking a victorious gulp of refreshing beer, Reno squinted at a middle-aged American approaching the bartender. In a Hawaiian shirt and chinos, the new patron strutted with the confident swagger of a warrior. The balding American ordered a whisky with lots of ice. Turning, he scanned the barroom. Focused on Reno, he lifted his glass of chilled bourbon.

Answering the gesture, Reno lifted his shallow beer mug. "To those we left behind," he toasted.

Flexing, Hawaiian Shirt took a proud breath and echoed, "To those we left behind."

The veterans each took a sip to seal the tribute.

"World War Two?" Reno questioned.

Grinning, the middle-aged warrior approached. "World War Two, Indochina, Vietnam, and Laos," he answered, extending a hand. "Tom Roche, originally from New Orleans," he said, giving Reno a firm handshake.

"Reno James from Southern California, San Bernardino to be specific. You care to join me?"

Roche checked his watch. "Sure," he answered, pulling out a chair.

"You served in the Vietnam War?" Reno politely questioned.

Roche chuckled. "Let's just say I was there at the inception of the US involvement in the Vietnam police action. I worked for the Company."

"I was there as the curtain came down on the tragic campaign," Reno volunteered. "I became addicted to the excesses of Southeast Asia and stayed behind. My current residence is a shack on a dirty beach in Phuket. It's still oceanfront property, something I couldn't afford in Southern California."

"If you don't mind my asking," Roche probed, "how do you make ends meet?"

"I traffic in antiques. My specialty is war souvenirs; used Kalashnikovs are my biggest seller."

Roche flinched.

"Are you interested in a battle-scarred AK-47?" Reno offered.

Roche burst out laughing. Holding up an apologetic hand, he clarified, "No offense, Reno." After a trailing snicker, he explained, "The spillage from the supply line feeding the *mujahedeen* in the Afghan civil war is about to flood the global market with AK-47s. I appreciate the solicitation, but I can acquire a virgin assault rifle very cheap."

Squinting, Reno asked, "Spillage? Who is benefiting from this overflow?"

Roche chuckled. "Pakistan is experiencing a windfall. The US, Brits, Saudis, Egyptians, and Chinese are using Pakistan as a conduit to arm those fanatic Muslim freedom fighters. A conservative estimate is the Pakistanis are diverting 50 percent of that military hardware into the black-market." After downing his amber whisky with a single gulp, he checked his watch. With raised brows, he said, "I'd like to have another, but unfortunately, I'm meeting someone in the coffee shop." Standing, he extended his hand. "It's been a pleasure, Reno," he said with a firm shake.

"As well, Tom," Reno responded, standing.

"I hope the oversupplied global weapons market doesn't put a dent in your... antiquities endeavor," Roche offered, winking.

As Roche departed, Reno waved his empty beer mug at a cocktail waitress. The China doll jumped at the request. She returned with a fresh brew and a small bowl of spicy cashews.

"When do you get off work?" Reno asked.

She stood dumbfounded, innocently desiring to fulfill a patron's request she could not comprehend.

"I'm sorry," he said. "I was trying to be funny."

She bowed and returned to her station.

Grabbing a handful of nuts, Reno tossed one high over his head. Leaning back, he caught the cashew with an open mouth. The feat had been perfected in his youth. Crunching on the rewarding treat, he saw the dark-skinned S.A. enter the bar. *Let's see how real this venture is,* he thought as the groomed East Indian approached. "Que pasa, ese?" He snickered.

"I don't understand," responded a frowning S.A. Pulling out a chair, he barked, "Club soda," at the Thai waitress. She jumped. "What do you have for me?" he questioned Reno.

Reno slid the shopping list facedown across table. The scowling Indian picked up the paper and paused. Carbonated water was served. The tentative waitress retreated.

Scanning the laundry list with a sour face, S.A. mumbled, "What's your price?"

"Seventy-five large," Reno whispered.

S.A. lowered the page. "I don't understand?" he inquired, shrugging.

"Seventy-five thousand American dollars," Reno clarified. "Half up front, half on pickup. The goods are in Bangkok."

"Acceptable," the buyer grumbled. "I'm disappointed with quantity not the price. I came here tonight prepared to secure a much larger order."

Reno grinned. "I'll be happy to raise the price to accommodate you."

The Indian's nostrils flared. Through gritted teeth, he asked, "Do you have the resources to fulfill additional requests?"

"I do," Reno boasted, taking a swig of cold beer. Setting the mug down, he added, "If this transaction is successful, it will be the first of many."

Nodding, S.A. leaned way back in his chair and snapped his fingers in the direction of the entrance. A wide brute of a man answered the summons.

His dark skin glistened. Combed-over oily strands of thinning jet-black hair attempted to conceal a balding head. A half-buttoned dress shirt exposed a massive chest and gold necklace. A thick, shabby mustache concealed his upper lip. He leaned into S.A. They conversed in whispers. He nodded before exiting.

"Do you still have my card?" S.A. asked Reno.

Reno nodded.

The henchman quickly returned with a Thai Airlines vinyl carry-on bag. He dropped it beside the table. S.A. rose and said, "Call me at my office to arrange the transfer." Picking up the sparkling club soda garnished with lime, he raised the glass. "To the first of many successful transactions," he uttered. After taking a sip, he and his bodyguard departed.

"What the fuck just happened?" Reno muttered. Plopping the airline carry-on on his lap, he pulled on the zipper. "Holy shit," he quietly declared. Denominated bundles of dog-eared American greenbacks filled the satchel. Taking a calming swig of brew, he grinned, *I should have asked for a lot more.*

Chapter 9

─ ∞∞∞ ─

It was midday. Tropical sunlight bathed a tall stoic palm frond canopy. A sliver of orange-red earth meandered through the symmetric forest of coconut trees. Healthy, thick dark-green growth encroached on the narrow red-clay roadway. The flanking knee-deep grass swayed under a gentle breeze. Bunches of the skull-shaped green fruit hung high overhead. Shriveled brown husks littered the fertile ground. The coughing drone of a sick internal combustion engine pierced the tranquility of the vast plantation. Exhaling puffs of white smoke, a hand tractor attached to a rickety trailer sputtered down the rural roadway. A skinny driver in a stained white sarong steered the shimmering large-looking lawn-mower. Crammed into the jostling trailer, the heads of ten armed men rocked back and forth. The color palette of the rebels' baggy trousers and cotton shirts consisted of beige, brown, gray, and army green. Blood-spatter adorned the sweat-soaked rancid civilian attire. Black rubber sandals protected the soles of soiled feet.

The troop transport jerked violently through a splashing puddle of orange mud. Chola protectively clutched his assault rifle. *A Tiger's weapon is his most cherished possession,* he reflected. "If lost, the weapon would never be replaced," his training master preached. An unarmed *porrali* (warrior fighting injustice) is useless. *Our resources are limited; every bullet must kill an occupier. As a unit leader, it is a lesson I must instill in the Tigers under my command.* Glancing around at his brothers-in-arms, a sense of pride swelled in his throat. *We are the Liberation Tigers of Tamil Eelam, the LTTE,* he thought, choking on emotion. *The government instigated the racial riots that spread from Colombo across the country. Thousands of my people died; hundreds of thousands fled. Our Tamil neighbors on the Indian peninsula schooled us in weapons, explosives, and jungle warfare.* Recalling the intense physical training, he patted his washboard abdomen. The exploring hand grasped the small cyanide vial dangling from a leather tether around his neck. *My commitment to establish a homeland for my people is here in this* kuppa. *I would rather bite into my cyanide necklace than be captured.*

The bobbing heads of the guerilla cadre pivoted to investigate a passing rural farmhouse. The simple one-room mud structure had a pitched weathered tarp for a roof. Furrowed rows of a small garden sprouted edible growth. Scurrying in a small pen, skinny chickens kicked up dust. Standing in the rough wood doorframe, a shirtless peasant in an orange tartan sarong stood protectively over a naked infant. The opened-mouthed farmer nervously twitched. The three- or maybe four-year-old boy enthusiastically waved at the blood-splattered armed men. Smiles spread across the faces of the Tiger unit as they returned the child's greeting.

"I came from a home much like that," commented Dandak as trailing red dust and exhaust engulfed the small structure.

Chola politely nodded at the reminder that his new brothers came from humble roots. *My objective was to one day become a chartered accountant, to disclose financial information. I found enjoyment in reading* Huckleberry Finn, *he reflected. I guess I'll never know what happens to Jim and Huck. Who's to judge that Dandak's rural existence was less rewarding or fulfilling than mine? Dandak's destiny and mine are intertwined. We will drive the occupying government forces from the northern and eastern provinces or die a Tiger's death and become* māvīrar" (great heroes).

Squinting at Dandak, Chola asked, "What happened to your home, *machan* (buddy)?"

"I left to join the cause," Dandak responded with a shrug. Rubbing his chin, he looked into the coconut palm awning. "I have two younger sisters and an older brother. My mother passed from cancer several years back. My father took to drink. *Appa* (dad) loved his arrack. Most of the rewards from our family's labor went to the toddy vendor." Focused on Chola, he added, "During the

July riots, the government shot my brother. The bullet paralyzed him below the waist. The army arrested my uncle. My drunken father identified the tortured remains of his brother five days later. That is when I joined the movement to kill the occupiers." Looking down at the enemies' blood splotches staining his beige shirt, he flashed a tooth-missing grin.

The coconut palms gave way to dense jungle. The roadway faded in and out. Branches scratched and clawed at the passing transport. The blanketing treetops of the rainforest replaced the sunlit blue sky. Insect clamor intensified. Passing birds cried out. The driver raced the motor. The transport stumbled over rocks and logs.

"Slow down, *machan!*" Dandak hollered.

The driver chuckled. His bony arm clutching the throttle flexed. The overworked engine howled. The trailer accelerated. Over his shoulder, the driver shouted, "Relief is near, Dandak. Night comes quickly in the forest."

In the diminishing light, the driver killed the engine. In the middle of the narrow pathway, the shimmering vehicle rolled to a quiet termination. Slowly the stiff and sore passengers disembarked. No one spoke. After a brief, satisfying stretch, they all took a long-anticipated piss. A meal of molding bread and warm water teased empty bellies. After the Spartan meal, the driver reclined next to weapons on the trailer bed and immediately began to snore.

Chola slung an assault rifle over his shoulder. "I'll take first watch," he instructed.

The exhausted rebels under his charge gratefully accepted the order. Laying juke sacks on the moist jungle floor, they bedded down like sardines.

Darkness embraced the jungle. Chilled air flowed down the narrow path. Chola rolled down his shirt sleeves. He paced back and forth to stay warm. *I like first watch,* he surmised. *Sleep will come soon enough.* Glancing in the direction of his snoring companions, he chuckled. *I will be joining you in a couple of hours, my friends.* Critters scurried through the brush. Chola squinted hard into the surrounding black void. *I can't see anything,* he realized. *I've never known a darker night.* A cold wind rustled treetops. All around, the forest groaned under the weight of nocturnal inhabitants. The crackling of a splintering, falling tree preceded a thunderous crash. Chola flinched.

"What is it?" mumbled the awakened driver.

"I don't know," Chola answered, pulling back the charging lever of his AK-47.

A steady crunch of undergrowth accelerated. The ground pulsed. The rebels leaped out of the juke sack bedding. Standing up in the trailer bed, the driver shot a flashlight beam in the direction of the approaching intruder. The ray pierced the heavy darkness. A spot of light illuminated dense growth. The thick brush erupted. The dark eyes of a massive charging beast glistened. Chola discharged a round into the air. The attacking elephant lifted its trunk and responded with a defiant trumpeting blast. Scurrying for cover, the rebels stumbled, slipped, and fell. In a wide stance, Chola stood his ground. His AK-47 spat out a pulsing stream of fire. The large bull staggered forward and collapsed with a thud. Rolling on its side, the dying gray beast emitted shallow breaths and expired.

Looking down at the kill, Chola exhaled. He felt sick. *I killed a noble creature,* he realized. "You should have runaway, my friend," he mumbled to the elephant carcass. "I tried to warn you." Taking a knee, he placed his hand on the victim. "I'm sorry, oh so sorry," he confessed with a heavy heart.

Chapter 10

———⌘———

"Jesus," Reno declared, wiping his sweaty brow with the back of a moist arm. *It must be one hundred and twenty degrees in here.* Standing tall, he flexed broad shoulders. A drenched white T-shirt clung to his muscular frame. Sweltering sunlight poured through the shipping container's open bay doors. Dust particles drifted through the illuminating light. A foul odor lingered in the stale air. Wooden crates resting on pallets blanketed the metal flooring. The narrow spacing between the waist-high boxes allowed uncomfortable access. Brandishing a crow bar, Reno squeezed through the tight maze. *I'm not going to choose an easy one,* he thought. He paused to identify the carcass of a long-dead rat atop a box. Snorting, he utilized the bar to sweep the rodent remains onto the floor. In the depths of the corrugated forty-foot-long metal box, he shoved the flat tongue of the prybar into the nailed lid of a wooden crate. Long nails yielded to the metal bar's leveraging power. Large droplets of perspiration rolled down Reno's face. He gulped down thick, stagnant air. The jimmied lid conceded with a screeching whine. A stale stench escaped. Peering at the contents, Reno sneezed. Straw cushioned the neatly packed munitions. *Probably has not seen the light of day for ten years,* he realized. *But it appears as advertised.* "I'm satisfied," he mumbled, navigating the tight obstacle toward sunlight.

Exiting the oven, he dropped the crowbar on rough concrete. It bounced with a clang. Pulling the soaked cotton shirt over his head, he sighed. A soft breeze cooled his moist torso. Firmly grasping the garment, he wrung it out. A puddle of sweat formed in front of his white sneakers. After shaking the moist cloth, he tossed it over his shoulder. "Time for a beer." He chuckled. On the shady side of the shipping container, he pulled an ice-cold can of Singha form a Styrofoam chest. Titling his head back, he doused the stale dust annoying his senses with carbonated freshness. A few large gulps emptied the can. A flexed grasp crushed the canister. "God, that was good!" he exclaimed. Checking his Casio watch, he determined it was twenty minutes to the exchange.

A glimmering sun hung high overhead. Waves of heat rippled on top of weed-infested asphalt. Neatly stacked white, red, blue, and orange corrugated steel shipping containers baked in the sunlight. A fifteen-foot-high chain-link fence defined the boundaries of the large deserted lot. Swirling razor wire capped the diamond-mesh netting. Beside a large rolling gate, a flat-roofed sentry box housed a skinny Thai in a shabby uniform. The lone guard allowed access and provided security.

Reno grabbed another beer. Placing the chilled can next to his head, he took a deep breath. *This should go smoothly,* he counseled. *The promise of a bigger, better deal is my insurance today. They are not going to kill me over thirty-seven thousand dollars. I wonder what their break point is? One hundred thousand, two hundred thousand,* he pondered. The larger the transaction, the bigger the risk, he realized, popping open the beer. Leaning against the steel box, he took a relaxing sip. A white Toyota, followed by a flatbed truck towing a forklift, stopped at the gate. The Thai Barney Fife exited his post and rolled back the chain-link entrance. The vehicles entered with a crunching advance.

S.A., in a navy-blue business suit, minus a tie, stepped out of the passenger door of the air-conditioned vehicle. His face puckered at the change in atmosphere. The beefy bagman from the Rambutti Hotel exited the driver's door. The bulge in his blue blazer confirmed a holstered weapon. A splayed white shirt collar highlighted a thick gold chain necklace. From the backseat, a skinny East Indian in gray business attire got out. Sporting the mandatory mustache, he methodically surveyed the deserted lot. Beneath his oversized gray jacket, he modestly concealed an Uzi or compatible machine pistol. Two Thai laborers hopped out of the flatbed lorry's cab, a lifetime of hard work and low pay etched into the wrinkles of their disconnected gazes. Methodically, one grabbed the dowel handle of the wood tool box. The duo plodded past their employers and disappeared into the shipping container. The sound of splintering wood resonated from within the sweatbox.

Shirtless in faded denim jeans, Reno took a big gulp of brew and stepped into the sunlight. "Looks like I'm underdressed," he mumbled. "Afternoon, S.A.," he hollered.

The slick S.A. nodded.

"Care for a beer?" Reno offered, displaying his can.

S.A. frowned.

"I'll take that as a no." Reno chuckled.

S.A. flicked his head at his wide accomplice. The brute nodded and flowed past Reno to inspect the merchandise. Reno took a casual sip off his can. A laborer scrambled out of the shipping container and fired up the forklift. Coughing white smoke, the lift truck emitted an annoying beep.

"Satisfied?" Reno questioned the stone-faced S.A.

Frowning at the American, S.A. shouted, "Gerard?"

Wearing a wide smile on a sweaty noggin, the henchmen appeared and answered with a thumbs-up.

S.A. attempted to smile. "Yes, Mister James, we are very satisfied," he answered. "My only disappointment is that it was not a larger order. A much larger order," he emphasized.

Reno nodded. "In this business, I wanted to establish a…relationship…a degree of trust before upping the ante."

"Ante?" the Indian questioned.

"It's a poker term," Reno clarified. "Raising the stakes?" he offered.

S.A. shrugged.

"Let's just say that now that we completed a successful transaction, we can focus on your *larger order*." Grinning, Reno probed, "How much you willing to spend?"

"If you can procure the same quality of munitions and unit pricing as this order, a larger order would be in the two-million-dollar price range," S.A. responded.

Reno's heart leaped into his throat. A sip of beer allowed a sobering pause. *Holy shit,* he thought. "That is a large order," he conceded. "All light weapons or are you seeking small arms as well?"

"We are in need of small arms; however, for assault rifles, we prefer the ruggedness of the AK-47 over the finicky M-16," he clarified.

"I'll prepare a shopping list for your review," the American offered.

"Splitting the purchase price up front and on pickup is acceptable; however, I don't want to deal in cash. Payments will be in the form of wire transfers. I can recommend several discreet Thai financial institutions," the Indian stated as nonnegotiable.

"Fair enough," Reno mumbled, realizing he would have to do some homework.

"Now let's conclude this deal," S.A. said, motioning to the vehicle.

The Uzi-toting associate retrieved a Cathay Pacific flight bag from the vehicle's backseat. Stone-faced, he handed it to the shirtless American. Flicking open the carry-on bag's zipper, Reno confirmed the currency contents.

"Do you want to count it?" S.A. asked.

"Naw," Reno responded, slinging the logoed vinyl satchel over his bare shoulder. "As businessmen, we need to establish a degree of respect for one another."

S.A. appeared puzzled. "Coming here alone and unarmed, Mister James, you appear to be a very trusting person."

Tilting his head back, Reno downed the last of his beer. Scanning the deserted lot, he placed the empty can on the hood of the white Toyota. "Oh, I'm not alone," he declared. Mimicking a handgun with an extended finger and upturned thumb, he added, "I'm also armed." Targeting the beer can with the extended finger, he flicked his thumb. A muffled pop echoed. The beer can flew into the blue sky. S.A. jumped back. Brandishing a compact submachine gun, the gray-suited henchman leaped in front of his boss. The hefty Gerard drew a shoulder-holstered pistol. A laborer dove off the forklift and seeking cover rolled under the truck. With a clink, the Singha canister landed on the hard asphalt. The mythical lion logo ripped open by a large caliber bullet. Celebrating the shot, Reno softly blew on his extend finger.

A wide smile emerged on S.A.'s stone face. He started to laugh. Gerard snickered. Slowly nodding, S.A. confessed, "Forgive me for underestimating you, Mister James." Extending his hand, he declared, "I'm looking forward to a long and prosperous relationship."

"Me too, *ese,*" Reno responded with a firm handshake. "Gentlemen." He chuckled at the armed escorts. Turning, he adjusted the vinyl strap and headed in the direction of the sentry box. Looking into the sunlight, he blinked. *Not a bad day,* he concluded. "My commission is twenty-five thousand dollars," he mumbled. *My expense is a thousand-dollar bullet. The cost of Longboard's single shot was worth it. If I'm going to pull off a two-million-dollar deal, I needed to establish street credit. My cut on a transaction that size would be...*He grinned wide. *Fuck-you money.*

Chapter 11

⸺⸙⸺

The Air Lanka wide-body commercial airliner hummed. The aroma of new carpet and fresh plastic lingered in the chilled atmosphere. Turbulence jostled the scarcely occupied coach cabin. Twenty-seven-year-old Sandra De Witt awoke from a shallow sleep. She swallowed with a dry mouth. To combat the nip in the air, she rolled down the long sleeves of a baggy cotton blouse. Glancing at her watch, she sighed. Three more long hours, she realized. Pulling a small black band from a breast pocket, the Dutch blonde secured her long locks in a ponytail. *It seems we left Amsterdam ages ago.* Twisting her lean, tall athletic frame, she startled the middle-aged Brit seated by the window. Apologetically, she smiled. He nodded. *What a pleasant man,* she concluded. *I usually have to fend off the flirtatious advances of traveling companions. My wedding ring used to be a slight deterrent.* Examining the empty ring finger, she shrugged. The marriage was brief, the divorce quick. Two medical students made a mistake. *I don't know what Gustav is telling people,* she pondered. *What do I care? As far as I'm concerned, I was never married.*

Two petite stewardesses rolled a drink cart down the narrow aisle. The flight-attendants matching turquoise *sarees* exposed firm youthful midriffs. The olive-skinned beauties giggled like schoolgirls. Smiling wide, a timid attendant approached Sandra and whispered, "What can I get you?"

"I'm parched," Sandra declared. "How about a cold beer?"

The stewardess nodded. As she poured the carbonated pilsner in an ice-filled plastic cup, the other attendant mumbled, "Ask her."

Serving the sparkling brew, the stewardess inquired, "Excuse us, missy. But we wondered if you are in the motion pictures."

Sandra grinned. "I'm flattered," she responded. "But I'm not an actress. I practice medicine."

"You are very beautiful," the attendant informed her. "I have never seen eyes so blue."

"Thank you," Sandra mumbled. Sipping on the cold beer, she hoped to defuse the awkward praise.

The Brit in the window seat ordered a scotch. He appeared forty, maybe fifty. The full head of snow-white hair made guessing an age difficult. The black frames of thick lenses gave an educated quality to the creases around his dark-brown eyes.

"Cheers," he offered, raising the amber-filled plastic cup.

"Prost," Sandra responded.

"I'm Owen Napley by the way," he volunteered, extending a hand.

"Sandra De Witt," she replied, gently squeezing his palm. "Please call me Sandy."

He grinned. "My oldest daughter Cassandra goes by Sandy," he informed.

"How many children do you have?" she asked as a reflex.

"Three girls," he delightfully replied. "Two have found husbands and left the nest. My wife is still mourning their departure."

A topic change is required, Sandra concluded. "Is your final destination Colombo?" she politely asked.

"Yes, it is," he responded. "I've been going there for holiday for many years. As a barrister, I need some quite time away from the law and more importantly the family. I wasn't going to let that ruckus with the Tamils disrupt my plans. I've been told the tourists have nothing to worry about."

"I hope your information is correct," Sandra commented. "This is my first time in Ceylon...or should I say Sri Lanka." Pivoting on the fabric seat, she looked at the Brit and asked, "What have you found in the Pearl of the Indian Ocean that beckons you to return?"

Choking on a sip of whisky, he snorted. Composed, he dabbed his nostrils with a paper napkin and muttered, "Excuse me."

Dutch frankness persisted. "Owen, where do you holiday in this tropical paradise?" she playfully probed.

Taking a breath, he answered, "I usually stay at a hotel in the Negombo Beach area but wouldn't recommend it. It is very rustic." Downing his whisky, he checked the time. "If you don't mind, I'm going to try to get a little sleep before we land."

"Sure, Owen," she mumbled. *What a strange man, she thought. Must have a local girlfriend or lots of them.* She chuckled.

Air Lanka Flight 515 passengers slowly descended a grated metal gangway. The tropical air was thick. A setting sun ducked behind a rainforest horizon. At the bottom of the galvanized steel stairway, a terminal bus idled on a moss-stained tarmac. Jet-lagged, Sandy migrated with the disembarking herd. She preferred to stand during the short bus ride. As they entered the terminal, a blast of sobering cold air slapped the new arrivals. Sandy took a deep, refreshing breath. *A hot shower and clean sheets will soon be mine,* she fantasized. Most of the herd headed toward the transit passenger lounge. The long-legged Sandy, the now-aloof Owen, and a dozen travelers followed the marked linoleum corridors to immigration and baggage claim. The airport was quiet. It appeared deserted. *Customs should go quickly,* Sandy hoped. *I really don't want to stand in a long queue.* Helmeted armed troops in army-green fatigues strolled by. Other heavily armed soldiers appeared. *They are not making me feel secure,* she realized. The small passenger contingent flowed into a large high-ceilinged room. Idle passport procession stations lined the far wall. A lone customs official slowly stirred in the only occupied booth. Sandy grinned. *This should go quickly.* The disinterested official blindly stamped her travel document. *Just need to pick up my luggage, find my driver, and the shower and comfortable bed will follow. I need to add a cold beer to the wish list.* She chuckled.

The automatic glass door swung open. Sandy navigated an overloaded baggage cart through the doorway. It was dusk. The moist air was heavy. A large male crowd behind a barricade erupted in solicitation clamor. She froze. In the midst of the enterprising mob, she spotted her name on a placard. "That's me," she declared pointing at the sign.

Surprisingly, the masses parted. A tiny thin local in a frayed dress shirt, black slacks, and rubber sandals victoriously stepped forward. "Welcome to Colombo, Doctor De Witt," he said, taking control of the baggage cart. "I'm Nadji," he informed her, sticking out a bony chest. "I will be your driver in our nation's capital."

"Please to meet you, Nadji," she replied. "But please call me Sandy."

"Very well," he said, pushing the cart. "My car is this way, Doctor Sandy."

She grinned, no need to explain. *I guess I'll go by Doctor Sandy,* she conceded.

Tossing Sandy's large duffel bag in the compact car boot, Nadji grimaced. After several failed attempts to close the trunk, he began to secure the lid with twine.

Standing watch, Sandy spotted Owen tipping a young porter. The barrister studied the attendant with a lustful smirk. His persona turned ugly, his leer predatory. *What is your story?* she wondered. "Hey, Nadji," she questioned. "What does a single old man do in Negombo?"

Crouched down behind the vehicle, Nadji squinted at his passenger. Following her gaze, he saw the polished middle-aged Brit. He sighed. "Foreigners seeking boy lovers holiday there," he sadly replied.

"What?" she exclaimed. "This is tolerated?"

Standing up, Nadji joined her curbside. He shrugged. "Tourism has suffered greatly do to the Tamil unrest. However, there are few vacancies in the Negombo guest houses that cater to tourists seeking young boys. Sri Lankan children are naturally friendly and desperately poor."

Sandy felt ill and suddenly lightheaded. Her stomach turned. Her breath accelerated. The queasiness faded beneath surfacing rage. Scowling at the pedophile, she growled, "You perverted cancer."

Owen shot her a puzzled expression.

Extending her arm, she pointed an indicting finger and mumbled, "Child molester." Standing beside her, Nadji flexed. The doctor and her protective driver watched the identified pedophile scrabbling into the sanctuary of an idling taxi.

"Thank you, Nadji," she whispered.

"Don't worry, Doctor Sandy. Nadji watch over you in Colombo," the tiny man proudly declared.

Sandy slouched down in the warm vinyl backseat. The shrill toot of the compact car's horn announced departure. The vehicle slowly exited the terminal. A rusty security fence surrounded the airport. Behind the barrier, a gathering of young girls sat atop a grass-covered hill. A gentle breeze caressed the girls' bright-orange, blue, red, and purple sarees. All the local girls' jet-black hair was uniformly pulled back into tight buns. An aircraft roared overhead. The female audience gazed skyward. With childlike innocence, they marveled as a British airliner took flight. Some applauded. Others cheered. Sandy smiled at the joyful display. "Who are those girls?" she questioned.

"Those are Juki Girls," Nadji answered.

"Juki?"

"They are garment workers," he clarified. "Juki is a Japanese sewing machine. Most are village girls. They come from all over Sri Lanka to work in the factories around the airport. After a long day, they find the takeoffs and landings entertaining."

Sandy leaned back in the warm seat. *When I was a child, Papa would to take me to the airport,* she recalled. *I haven't thought about that in years,* she realized. *I loved sitting atop his shoulders, watching those metal birds take flight.* She grinned. *Thank you, Papa. I miss you.* A warm breeze flowed through the vehicle's open windows. Conceding to the fog of jet lag, she closed her eyes.

Chapter 12

———∞∞∞———

A colorful Thai long-tail speedboat chugged slowly down the narrow canal. With only two white passengers the boat rode high in the churning water. The wiry local pilot in an oversized singlet sucked on an expiring cigarette. Through sleepy eyes, he steered the water taxi down the familiar route. A small puddle sloshed around his bare feet. Tossing the smoldering butt over the side, he yawned.

Stilted shacks and shabby teak-wood houses lined the banks of the *khlong*. The residences accessed the waterway by back porches, slated platforms, and small piers. A woman, squatting on her haunches, vigorously washed a bright-red blouse in the murky brown water. Inhabitants stared out of open windows. A teenage girl in a floral-printed wraparound poured a pail of water over her soapy hair. The young bather ignored the catcalls from the boys next door. Rounding a bend, the coughing long-tail veered to avoid a small flat-bottomed watercraft piled high with tropical fruit. The paddling produce vendor was someone's grandmother. In a wicker hat that resembled a flared lampshade, the old woman easily navigated by the long-tail.

Reno leaned back on the uncomfortable bench seat. He propped his feet up on an empty backrest. *I need another look.* He delightedly sighed. Carefully he unzipped the vinyl flight bag. Soft light illuminated the bundles of US green-backs. *Most of this is mine,* he happily realized. *Hell, maybe I should cash in a few chips tonight in Bangkok and celebrate the transaction.* He glanced over at Longboard. The retired assassin sat erect. Stoic chiseled features studied the horizon with a dark, disconnected gaze. At his feet, an electric guitar case concealed a sniper rifle. *He is definitely not much of a talker,* Reno thought. *Maybe he'll loosen up after a few celebratory beers.*

The long-tail exited the residential *khlong.* A revving powerful engine accompanied rapid acceleration. A soft refreshing mist flowed over the bow. A whipping wind swirled under the Pepsi logo canopy. The water taxi spilled into the congested Chao Phraya River. Sunlight caressed the surface of the natural watercourse. Crossing ferries bobbed on the drab liquid. River busses packed with commuters crisscrossed the waterway. A massive flat-bottom barge laden with heavy goods struggled against the current. Reno sat up.

Longboard stood up and walked toward the bow. The former assassin peered over the hull. His Hawaiian shirt, dominated by coconut trees, flapped. Before him, temples, high-rise office towers, and Bangkok's luxury hotels flanked the glistening beige transportation artery.

Taking a deep breath, Longboard stepped up onto the boat's bow. Bending his knees and extending his arms, he looked at the driver. "Do you think you can knock me off?"

The pilot grinned widely, accepting the challenge. The colorful long-tail expertly wove through rush-hour traffic, a nimble surfer riding atop the bow.

Standing on an active pier, Reno paid the pilot. "I'm impressed," he commented to the surfer. "Several times, I thought you were going to take a plunge into that liquid filth." Handing Longboard the guitar case, he pointed up the dock. "River City Antiquities is that way."

The shop was small and cluttered. Carved wooden elephants of various sizes dominated one wall. Bins overflowed with colorful silk scarves. Glass cases housed bronze and stone Thai figurines. Two large white women grazed over an embroidered-silk-filled trough. A cute Thai sales clerk attentively watched the rummaging hefty American tourists.

"How much?" a cow in a floppy pink hat mooed.

"Three hundred baht," answered the soft-spoken clerk.

"That's not even worth negotiating," grumbled the wide woman. "Let's get out of here, Agnes."

Reno and Longboard jumped out of the way of the stampeding tourists. "Hello, lil' darling," Reno greeted the salesclerk.

The Thai angel blushed. A cupped hand suppressed a giggle. "Hello, Mister James," she responded.

"Longboard, I'd like you to meet a dear friend of mine," Reno announced. "This is Palm."

The stone-faced surfer nodded.

"Please to meet you, Mister Longboard," Palm replied with a slight bow. "Reno, Danny is expecting you. Let me buzz you in."

"Danny?" Reno questioned. "I only come here to see you, Palm," he flirted.

Her blush resurfaced. Reaching under the cash register, she pressed a button. A buzz resonated. Behind the counter, the large silk print of an elephant swung ajar.

Reno pulled pack the hinged concealed door and entered. Longboard followed. A short drywall corridor led to a sizable back room. The temperature dropped. An air-conditioning unit below the ceiling hummed. Cigarette smoke tainted the cool atmosphere. Ancient Cambodian sculptures lay on the floor. The pillaged Khmer stone carvings of Shiva, Vishnu, and Buddha displayed the chiseled scars that severed them from temple walls. Logo boxes of brand liquor blanketed a wall. Around a lacquered round table, four locals played cards. Beer bottles and two smoldering ashtrays infringed on the glossy playing surface.

A pudgy card player folded his hand. He appeared to be about thirty years old. His large round head was capped with bowl-cut black hair parted down the middle. He looked up, and a wide grin spread across his fat baby face. "Hello, Reno," he said in a soft, effeminate voice. "Do you have a package for Danny?"

"Yes, Danny," Reno replied. *Why does Danny always refer to himself in the third person?* he wondered.

"And who is your friend?" Danny questioned with a tilted head.

"This is Longboard," Reno informed him.

Danny giggled. "Oh my."

The surfer frowned.

Danny clapped his hands. His Thai associates hastily cleared the tabletop and exited. "Please be seated," he offered with an open palm. "Would you care for a Coke or beer perhaps?"

"I'll have a beer," Reno responded, pulling out a hardwood chair.

Longboard shook his head and wandered over to admire the Khmer stonework.

Danny retrieved an amber bottle of Singha from a small fridge. He placed it in front of Reno and took a seat. "Let's see what you've brought Danny," he probed with wide eyes.

Reno placed a bundle of one-hundred-dollar bills on the table. A paper band around the currency quantified the stack at five thousand US dollars. Danny salivated over the money brick. Reno put another four greenback bricks on the varnished tabletop. He then zipped up the carry-on bag, grabbed the cold bottle of brew, and took a hearty swig.

Danny thumbed through the first bundle and grinned. His smile widened with each subsequent fanning. "I like a transaction where everyone is happy," he announced playfully, stacking the bricks into a neat pile. "I assumed the buyer is happy, you are happy, and Danny is very happy."

"The buyer is happy," Reno confirmed. "He would like to place another order...a much larger order."

"What is your buyer seeking to spend?" Danny questioned.

Reno sucked on his beer. Placing the glass bottle the table, he whispered, "One and a half million American dollars."

The pudgy Thai flinched. "That makes Danny nervous...very, very nervous."

"I share your concerns," Reno mumbled. "But do you have the resources to fill my buyer's request?"

"Inventory is not the issue," Danny clarified. "I fear a *kong*...a swindle. First deal goes smoothly, everybody happy. We all make money. Profit makes us comfortable, trusting."

"Half up front and half at pickup should alleviate most of your apprehension," Reno counseled.

"Setting up transaction this size has cost. Danny does not want to be played as fool." Rubbing his chin, he offered, "You give me deposit. I put list together. You disapprove of munitions; I refund deposit. You approve; deposit nonrefundable, applied to purchase price."

Reno glanced at the Cathay Pacific travel bag and asked, "How much is the deposit?"

The Asian grinned. "Two hundred thousand American dollars," he stated, "Nonnegotiable."

Reno grunted. "Now I'm the one getting scammed."

"Reno," Longboard called out from across the room. "You really need to see this."

Reno turned. The surfer stood in front of a shapely female sculpture popping out of large stone blocks.

"That's an Apsara, the female spirit of clouds and water," Danny informed. "The piece is from Angkor Wat."

Taking a sobering breath, Reno got up to investigate. "It is impressive," he mumbled, focused on the stone breast and nipples.

"I know a hard money lender," the surfer whispered. "We can borrow the two-hundred-K deposit."

"We?" Reno questioned.

"I'm willing to share the risk for a slice of the pie," Longboard proposed. "Would you consider taking on a 20 percent partner?"

Reno grinned. "Absolutely," he answered, extending a hand. The two neighbors sealed the venture with a handshake.

"I'm going to need a piece," the surfer announced. "Do you think Danielle over there has any handguns in stock?"

Reno shrugged. "Hey, Danny, do you have any pistols in the shop for sale?"

"Danny has Remington forty-five calibers and a Smith and Wesson nine-millimeter," he replied.

"We'll take the nine-millimeter," Longboard chimed in.

"Two-hundred dollars?" Danny proposed.

Longboard nodded and looking at Reno said, "It's part of our financing cost so should come out of petty cash."

Reno chuckled, pulling out his wallet. "What's the name of your loan shark?"

"Fourteen-k Triad," the surfer answered.

Chapter 13

—⦿⦿⦿—

Chola leaned back against the trunk of a mango tree. Overhead, rotting fruit emitted a sweet stench. Running his fingers through wet hair, he sighed. His tongue delightedly inspected recently brushed teeth. *It feels good to be clean,* he thought. In search of optimal comfort, he shifted an exhausted frame. Observing the partisans still frolicking in the cleansing irrigation tank, he grinned. Other Tigers slept in the cool shade of the abandoned grove. *We made it to the rendezvous point,* he realized, scanning the encampment. Old men and boys dug bunkers and filled sandbags. Focused on the fifty laborers toiling in the hot sun, Chola took a deep, proud breath. *They come from surrounding villages to fortify our position,* he realized.

A sweat-glistening silver-haired volunteer climbed out of a trench. The ditch digger shaking the dirt from a soiled sarong smiled at Chola. Chola bowed his head in gratitude. A warm breeze rolled down the sloping terrain. Dust swirled around the bones of a farmhouse. *A Tamil family once called this home,* Chola reflected. A single wall remained of the mud-and-brick residence. Pots, pans, and shattered dishes mingled among the bricks and splintered wood spilling across the grounds. Shredded and faded rags flapped on a clothesline. *The family must have left in a hurry,* he concluded. *The government shelling comes without warning.*

Chola flinched and instinctively reached for his assault rifle. He smiled. Six women draped in colorful orange, red, and blue sarees strolled down the path of the renegade mango orchard, large misting pots balanced atop their heads. Four uniformed schoolchildren toting sacks accompanied the *ammas*.

"Warm food." Chola sighed. *The prelude to battle is a hot meal,* he realized, swallowing back surfacing saliva. The women spread out under fruit tree canopies to feed freedom fighters.

"Thank you, *amma*," Chola said to the woman setting the large pot beside him.

She was breathing heavily. Sweat rolled down her dark face. Dishing out a steaming bowl of rice gruel, she mustered a smile and said, "I'm the one who should be thanking you."

The little boy beside her stood transfixed on the assault rifle. "Have you killed many soldiers?" he asked.

"Nine," Chola answered.

"Good," the wide-eyed boy replied pulling flat bread from his satchel. "The soldiers killed my *appa*."

Holding the appetizing bowl and bread, the *amma* tilted her head and asked Chola, "Are your hands clean?"

"Yes, *amma*." Chola chuckled, taking the hot meal.

As the widow and her son walked away, the little boy exclaimed, "Mum, did you hear that? He killed nine soldiers."

Chola dipped his fingers into the warm bowl. He paused. *Hot food,* he thought, staring at fingers of enticing rice porridge. Sucking his fingers clean, he mumbled, "So good." He rotated between gobs of gruel and strips of layered flat bread. Swabbing the bowl with the last piece of bread, he swallowed with a very full belly. Closing his eyes, he savored the moment.

"Chola," a whisper nudged.

With one eye, Chola gazed up. Dandak's silhouette hovered beneath the sunlight fluttering through the overhead branches and leaves. "What?" Chola quietly inquired.

"The commander requests the immediate presence of group leaders for a mission briefing," Dandak replied.

Chola rose painfully on stiff joints. Taking a deep breath, he slung an assault rifle over a tender shoulder. Throwing back his shoulders, he realized he could not display a hint of fatigue. At a brisk pace, he marched out of the orchard.

Karu, the other group leader, joined Chola on the trek across the rebel bivouac. The gaunt, battle-hardened Karu was in his thirties. At well over six feet, he was tall for a Tamil. Rage burned deep in the dark eyes of his disconnected gaze. He rarely spoke. His journey to this point in time was a mystery. Nobody knew, and nobody dared to ask.

The group leaders approached a pitched army-green tent baking under a heavy sun. The front and rear flaps of the heavy fabric command post were pulled back. A warm breeze flowed through the canvas structure. A salvaged hardwood dinner table dominated the earthen floor enclosure. Four stones secured a fluttering torn and frayed map to the tabletop. The rebel commander in camouflage fatigues stood hunched over the weathered diagram. An oversized matching cap adorned his pudgy head. Dark sunglasses shielded his eyes. A mandatory thick mustache blanketed his upper lip. Glancing up at the team leaders, he nodded.

"Master," Chola uttered.

The stoic Karu remained silent.

"Brothers," the officer said, rubbing his chin. "The Mullaitivu District is of strategic importance to establishing a sovereign Tamil nation. It is at the crossroads of our northern and eastern provinces. Tamil families have cultivated its rich soil and fished its abundant waters for generations." As he paced back and forth, his volume increased. "The government gave our Tamil brethren forty-eight hours to vacate their homes, fields, and way of life. Leases were terminated. Property rights ignored. Those brave souls who defied the order were executed. The government then turned over houses, shops, schools, and farms to common Sinhalese criminals. *Mullaitivu* is Tamil!" he shouted, pounding the table. "It is time to avenge the blood spilled by our brothers and evict the trespassers." He paused, seeking a response.

Chola concurred with a nod.

Kura stood stone-faced. His breathing accelerated.

"Chola, this is your objective," the commander instructed, pointing to a farming village on the map. "And, Kura, this is your team's responsibility," he announced, identifying a fishing settlement. "Under the cover of darkness, your thirty-men units will be bused to the respective targets. Simultaneously at daybreak, your mission is to terminate the unlawful occupation with extreme prejudice and seize any goods and chattels that would be beneficial to our movement." Stepping back from the war map, he took a deep breath. "I must emphasize the eviction needs to be served on the soldiers, police, and male inhabitants. I repeat *male* civilians." Looking into the faces of his focused audience, he calmly added, "We do not want any women or children casualties."

Chapter 14

—⊗⊗⊗—

It was late. Rolling grilles and security gates protected the storefronts of a narrow Bangkok side street. Foul water meandered down a curbside gutter. A feral cat pawed at a pile of rubbish. A lone open establishment emitted an inviting glow. Its plate-glass window radiated soft interior light. Across the transparent barrier, "Home of Fine Cantonese Cuisine" in bold font endorsed the restaurant. A bulbous red vinyl replica of a paper lantern hung over the door. Chinese calligraphy adorned the round ribbed lampshade. Arched scripted neon identified "The Red Dragon." The "D" in *dragon* flickered.

Reno studied the faulty signage. "You ever notice," he commented, "no matter where you go, there is a Chinese restaurant."

Longboard shrugged.

"I understand it here in Southeast Asia," Reno continued. "But across the US, every podunk town has a gas station, convenience store, and a Chinese restaurant."

The indifferent surfer reached into the small of his back and adjusted the nine-millimeter handgun holstered in his waistband.

"The other thing I find amazing," ranted Reno, "is the Chinese cuisine invasion. A Mexican restaurant closes, and two weeks later, the Asians hang red lanterns on an adobe structure and call it the Golden Place."

"You ready to do this?" Longboard asked.

"Sure," Reno answered, taking a calming breath. Squinting at the surfer, he probed, "You're not much of a talker, are you?"

"Think of me as your silent partner," Longboard mumbled as he entered the Red Dragon.

White-linen-covered tables filled the dining room. A small bar secured the corner. Behind the counter, glass shelves displayed a limited selection of brand liquors. A solitary chopstick-wielding patron shoveled noodles into an open mouth at close range. A Chinese waiter sorted receipts. A cigarette dangled from his lower lip. The remnants of a bow tie hung around an open collar. Grinning wide, a young gangster stepped from behind the bar. He appeared to be in his late twenties and was thin. His pressed black slacks and starched pinstriped shirt displayed fashionable sharp creases. Wearing the good looks of youth, he paused to suck on a fresh cigarette. After an enjoyable exhale, he muttered to Longboard, "Hello, Johnny."

"Evening, Chin," the surfer replied.

"You are here to discuss a financing arrangement?" Chin asked, tilting his head.

"I didn't come for the wonton soup," Longboard answered.

Chin snickered. Flicking a beckoning finger, he mumbled, "This way, gentlemen."

The corridor was wide and long. Rice-paper partitioning walls lined the passage. Chinese lanterns overhead provided filtered light. A large scroll depicting a colorful tiger hung at the end of the hall. In front of the Chinese scroll painting sat a large thug. In a shimmering sharkskin suit and tight knit turtleneck, he stood with a grunt. A crew cut accented his wide, flat head.

"You know the drill, Johnny," Chin informed.

Longboard raised his hands. Reno followed suit. Taking a deep breath, the wide brute squatted. Intruding fat fingers grabbed Reno's ankles. Inquisitive flabby hands slowly worked up the American's legs. A quick squeeze checked his crotch. After a torso pat down, the goon completed the inspection.

"I'll save you the trouble, Oddjob," Longboard said, retrieving the nine-millimeter from the small of his back. With thumb and forefinger, he surrendered the weapon.

Chin grinned and issued a brief command in Cantonese. Somewhat relieved, the thug returned to his post with the confiscated pistol. Chin pulled back a rice-paper partition. "Gentlemen," he announced, extending a welcoming palm into the private dining room.

A fat, middle-aged Chinaman dined at a large round table. A young Thai girl snuggled against his flabby chest. Focused on a sultry platter of sweet-and-sour pork, he utilized chopsticks to stuff a chomping mouth. His jowls glistened with candy-red sauce. The smack of bad manners resonated. His right hand fed his face. His left arm hung protectively over the adorable nymph, her spandex-covered bottom secured in his firm grasp. Looking up, he scowled at the intrusion. In the center of his flaccid cheek, a black mole anchored ten inches of scraggly hair.

Reno pointed to the side of his mouth. "You missed a spot, chief," he informed.

The kingpin flinched in disbelief.

Chin spoke in Cantonese. In the midst of the cackling roller-coaster-pitched rant, the name Jesse Long surfaced.

The mob boss cast his gaze on the surfer.

Longboard flexed. His tan taut facial features sharpened. Staring back at the fat man, the surfer's assassin persona materialized. The mask of death appeared.

The fat man nodded respectfully. In a low, soft voice, he musically rambled in Cantonese.

Chin leaned forward to listen. He nodded. Looking at the Americans, he translated, "Your two-hundred-thousand-dollar loan has been approved. Let's go to my office to discuss terms."

Focused on the obese gangster, Reno scratched at the corner of his mouth. "Right about here, you left a little sauce."

Instinctively, the slob sent out his tongue to investigate. The tasting organ made a sweeping attempt to cleanse the spillage.

Exiting the private dining room, Reno mumbled behind Longboard, "Should I have said something about the hairy mole?"

Chin strutted into a small, windowless back office. The Americans followed. Scooting around a metal desk, Chin spun the dial on a massive cast-iron safe. The vault's thick door creaked open. Neatly stacked bundles of international currency dominated metal shelves. The Hong Kong dollars and Thai baht made colorful contrasts to the drab US greenbacks. Also on display, brown paper parcels wrapped in twine contained heroin or possibly cocaine. Chin grabbed a large stack of American currency. "Ten, twenty, thirty, forty..." he whispered, placing the cash on the metal desktop.

Standing beside his partner in the doorway, Reno observed and counted silently.

"One hundred and ninety," Chin muttered. Turning, he sealed the vault.

"We may need a recount," Reno commented.

Chin smirked. "These are the terms." He placed his hands on the money pile. "The loan is two hundred thousand. The interest is ten thousand a week. I've deducted your first payment from the principal. In thirty days, two hundred and forty thousand is due."

I have a month to conclude the munitions transaction, Reno realized. He looked at Longboard. The silent partner nodded.

Under the flickering signage of The Red Dragon, Reno slung a leather satchel of money over his shoulder. As the two Americans strolled down the dark, lonely street, Reno asked, "Why did the slick gook refer to you as Johnny?"

"Chin refers to all whites as Johnny. He's not the first Southeast Asian to use that unflattering terminology." Stopping, he adjusted the retrieved nine-millimeter in his waistband.

"If you knew we would be frisked, why the pistol?" Reno probed.

Resuming their leisurely pace, Longboard shrugged. "It was a prop. I wanted the triad to think I was still active. They approached me after the war for some contract work. A white assassin is a powerful tool." On the deserted sidewalk, he squinted at Reno. "I hope you realize, the collateral for the loan is my potential future services for the Triad."

Reno nonchalantly dropped his shoulders. "So foreclosure means we work off the 14K triad debt."

"Not *we*, partner, *me*," Longboard informed. A rare grin appeared on the dark surfer's stoic features. "They are just going to kill you."

Reno started to chuckle. The chuckle evolved into a hard laugh. Patting the surfer on the back, he took a calming gasp. "Time is of the essence, partner. And don't worry; I always pay my debts. Now let's go drink to a successful venture."

Chapter 15

─── ∞ ───

Headlights of a rickety diesel bus illuminated a rural dirt road. The lights rocked back and forth. Insects played within the piercing beams. The lamps went dark. Squealing brakes terminated the journey in a painful skid. The tropical horizon glowed in anticipation of the rising sun. Focused assailants on ripped and cracked vinyl bus seats sat quietly. *Yesterday, we frolicked like school-children in an irrigation ditch,* Chola reflected. *Today we are LTTE, the Liberation Tigers of Tamil Eelam. A death sentence,* he realized. *We are here to administer a death sentence for trespassing.* In the stuffy transport, the other executioners panted and snorted. The tension was thick. *Is there any Tamil who has not suffered at the hands of our enemy?* Chola questioned. *All my brethren's heavy hearts beat with a sense of loss...of injustice. We cannot live in peace with these rogue occupiers. Our only objective is establishing an independent Tamil state.*

The troops simultaneously rose. Rubber-sandaled feet shuffled off the transport. Stepping onto the dirt road, Chola slipped into a heavy chest rigging, the assault gear's pouches loaded with AK-47 magazines. Grenades dangled from the harness. Utilizing hand signals, he divided the unit. Chola's squad calmly strolled down the farm road.

The village appeared. The predawn air was cool. A soft wind blew trash across the village square. A skinny dog pranced in front of the police station. The concrete structure emitted soft interior light. Shadows floated behind illuminated drapes. The predators, keeping to the shadows, advanced. Fifteen heavily armed men salivating for blood surrounded the building. Standing at the entrance, Chola's heart beat heavily. His right forefinger pulled the Kalashnikov's fire selector all the way back into semiautomatic mode. The assault rifle clicked. Casually, he swung open the door. A policeman sat at a desk sipping morning tea. Chola squeezed an anxious trigger. A loud blast launched a lead eviction notice. The projectile shattered a teacup and tore into a shocked expression. The officer's head jerked back. Distant gunfire crackled. The assault had begun. The Tiger squad poured into the concrete station. Chola raced down a narrow corridor. On his right, a doorframe exposed two waking men. On separate single unmade beds, they sat upright with open mouths. They showed the armed intruder surrendering palms. Chola plugged one with two quick rounds. Gunfire echoed. The other occupier vigorously shook his capitulating hands. Behind him, pornographic pictures of large-breasted white women adorned the wall. Stone-faced, Chola shot him at close range. Blood splatter sprayed across the glossy naked images.

"Twelve," Chola muttered. Glancing at the blood-speckled pornography, he shook his head. *My enemy has no discipline.*

The squad exited the police station. Terrified residents spilled into the street. Fleeing families disappeared into darkness. Automatic weapons growled. Ravenous Tigers mowed down disoriented civilians. Surrender was not an option. A woman wailed over her fallen husband. Beside her, a confused naked child flinched at escalating gunfire. Chola slapped a fresh magazine into his weapon. He strutted through the carnage. Sunlight sparkled on the horizon. Rancid smoke filled the air. Popping fires consumed shops and residences. Dawn's first light illuminated death's harvest. *Tamil families once called this home,* Chola thought, throwing a grenade through a plate-glass storefront. *It was a peaceful rural community for generations,* he reflected. The explosive detonated. Erupting glass shrouded a female cadaver on the sidewalk. Twinkling shards danced in arriving sunlight.

"Master," Dandak hollered.

Pivoting, Chola spotted his grinning companion in front of corrugated tin storage shed. With a grunt, Dandak shoved open a sliding metal door. Neatly stacked cardboard boxes labeled "Canned fish" filled the tiny warehouse. *Spoils of war,* Chola thought. "Nice find, machan," he complimented. "Start placing the bounty in the street. I'll send for the bus."

Disappointed that his discovery was rewarded with labor, Dandak's shoulders drooped. Reluctantly, he leaned his assault rifle against the rippling metal structure. An armed specter burst out of the shed. The exiting apparition plugged Dandak with three quick rounds. Chola turned. A bare-assed man wielding a revolver lunged into the rough surrounding foliage. White as a sheet, a teetering Dandak wobbled into the dirt road. He stared at Chola. His mouth opened. Before he could speak, he collapsed face first in a cloud of dust.

Chapter 16

———— ⸎ ————

An inviting stairway led down to the Boiler-Room Pub. Chalkboard signage promoted cheap beer prices and a late-night happy hour. The surrounding Bangkok tourist traps had long since closed for the night. Ruckus laughter floated out of the basement saloon. In the windowless enclave, five frat brothers slowly emptied a bottle of Johnny Walker. Slouched in Windsor chairs around a scarred round table, they embellished their evening's sexual exploits. Explosive laughter occasionally punctuated the slurred dialogue. The vacationing students' attire embraced a pastel color pallet. Oblivious to his friends' conversation, an undergrad in a soft pink golf shirt played with an antique Zippo lighter. Feathered hair framed his boyish looks. A sinister smirk surfaced as he ignited and extinguished the tiny flame.

The only other bar patrons sat in the shadows of a quiet corner. Celebrating a successful loan closing, Reno and Longboard sipped on rum-and-Cokes. Reno's cocktail was garnished with two limes. A leather satchel containing one hundred and ninety thousand dollars occupied a vacant chair. Beneath the frat boys' clamor, a tiny chrome-plated Zippo emitted a repetitive click.

Squinting at the college boys, Reno asked, "Did you ever go to college?"

Longboard shook his head.

"In my last days in Nam, I thought about taking advantage of the GI Bill," Reno confessed. "That dream quickly faded."

"How so?" Longboard probed.

"I was frustrated with my homecoming reception. That irritation turned to anger. Now nobody spat on me." Reno snorted. "But it was little things." After a reflective pause, he shared, "I landed at Travis Air Force Base with optimism. I served my country and proudly wore its uniform. I took a shuttle to the San Francisco Airport to catch a commercial flight to LA. At SFI, I was greeted with cold shoulders and cowardly murmurs. I was happy to board the flight. Sitting in a window seat, I watched the plane fill up. It was a full flight. Suddenly, this thin bird in a peasant blouse comes fluttering down the aisle. You know the type—long, straight hair parted down the middle, no makeup. She wasn't that pretty, but given the opportunity, I would have fucked her. At the very least enjoyed flirting for the next couple of hours. Well this anti-war bitch refuses to take her assigned seat next to me."

"What happened?" Longboard asked.

Reno shrugged. "After a little commotion, a stewardess rearranged the seating chart. I flew to LA next to an old Chinese woman who snored through an open mouth."

"So you get snubbed by some skank," Longboard commented. "That shouldn't have derailed your quest for higher education."

"The skank is not the point." Reno frowned. "It wasn't just my haircut or uniform. I didn't fit in. I learned quickly not to put Vietnam vet on a job application. The revelation was that I was not welcome in the village." He motioned toward the pastel boys. "What are they? Nineteen, maybe twenty years old? Enjoying the fruits of their parents' labor? When I was that age, my contemporaries were nineteen-year-old men. In the shit, there was no racism, no class system. Just men bonded together at the edge of the abyss. Now that is a very exclusive club." Taking a deep breath, he declared, "And one I'm proud to be a member of."

"I got to tell you," Scotty McPherson mumbled, igniting a dancing Zippo flame for the umpteenth time. "For fifty bucks, I went around the world with that petite Thai whore." The collegiate audience quieted as their leader spoke. "In the States, I dropped a hundred and fifty on Cindy Cornwall with dinner and a movie and barely got bare tit." Flipping open the lighter, he produced and extinguished the flame with a deft motion.

"What is with that lighter?" Brian, the smallest puppy in the pack, questioned.

Scotty closed his eyes. Rubbing his thumb across the tiny chrome box's inscription, he muttered, "Death is my business, and business is good, 82nd Airborne." Grinning, he looked at his entourage and informed, "The Thai antique dealer told me it came off a dead GI." Admiring his new toy, he mumbled, "That's pretty cool."

"Isn't that a little morbid?" Brain questioned.

"Don't be such a pussy, Brian," Scotty snapped. "The former owner probably used this to light his dope pipe or burn down some peasant village. The poor bastard was probably some backwoods hillbilly who couldn't figure out how to slip through the government draft net. One thing for certain, he was a racist. All the American troops were. The invading force referred to the Vietnamese as gooks and dinks. In a racist fury, they decimated the local population and celebrated success with a high body count."

"Excuse me, cocksucker," Reno politely interrupted.

The young vacationers looked up. Reno, shadowed by Longboard, stood stroking his chin. "I couldn't help overhearing your conversation." Squinting hard at the group's alpha, he questioned. "It sounded like you said you wanted your teeth knocked out."

Scotty glanced around the table at his troops' puzzled expressions. Over his shoulder, he surveyed the empty tavern. Looking up at the insulting intruder, he questioned, "It's just the two of you?"

"Yep," Reno casually declared.

"Buzz off," Scotty scowled, flicking the lighter.

His proud minions snickered.

Reno joined in the levity. "I'll buzz off, sonny." He chuckled. "After you apologize for your slanderous racist rant or..." He motioned for the punk to stand up. "...face the music."

Grinning across the table at a companion, he instructed, "Moose, please show these gentlemen the exit."

In a striped blue-and-white knit golf shirt, a mountain rose amid the giggles of his drinking companions. Moose was well over six feet tall and wide. On broad shoulders, his head and neck appeared as a single unit. Short black wavy hair capped the summit. "I think you should leave now," rumbled out of the depths of a massive gullet.

Closing an eye, Reno looked up at the intimidating giant. "When did you start walking erect?" he playfully questioned. "Was it Tuesday?"

Moose swatted his chair aside with a sweeping paw. The tumbling chair crashed into the hardwood floor. Moose's neck flared. His shoulders inflated. A flared nostril snorted.

Longboard gracefully stepped into the fray. Planting his feet, he flashed open palms and cocked his hip back. In a fluid motion, he pivoted forward, locking an elbow. In a flash, he fired the heel of his hand into Baby Huey's face. The crack of a broken nose resonated off the windowless tavern's walls. With both hands, the pudgy youth grabbed his exploding face. Gushing plasma spilled through clutching fingers. A sweeping kick by the surfer took the boy out at the knees. The mountain came tumbling down. Moose hit the floor hard.

"Stay down, Moose," Longboard quietly recommended.

Heeding the advice, the giant embraced the beer-stained flooring.

"Any other cards you would like to play, boy?" Reno questioned the instigator. "And don't tell me you are going to call your parents. As a bastard, I always resented that defensive strategy."

"No, sir," Scotty squeaked.

"Well," Reno persisted over Moose's low moans.

"I'm sorry," eked out of Scotty's panting mouth as he slid the lighter across the table. The other pastel boys pushed their chairs back.

Reno picked of the dated Zippo. "Three things," he mumbled, examining the souvenir. "One, this maybe a fake and is no more than a cheap Chinese knockoff." Addressing the terrified focused audience, he continued, "Two, the Airborne Ranger left this in Southeast Asia after his tour of duty." Slowly nodding, he concluded, "Three, the original owner's name is etched on *the Wall* in DC with over seventeen hundred sky-soldiers who gave their lives in service to their country." Throwing the lighter to Longboard, he asked, "What do you think?"

Like a cat, the surfer plucked the smoking accessory out of the air. Rubbing his thumb across the small chrome-plated box, he grinned. "It's a fake," he declared, tossing the Zippo to its owner.

Scotty flinched. The lighter careened off his twitching palm. It clinked as it hit the floor.

Tiny Brain stood. He looked like a fifteen-year-old. Swallowing, he offered, "Gentlemen, I apologize for my friend's drunken rant. Please excuse our ignorance."

Reno nodded his acceptance as he and Longboard retreated back to their rum-and-Cokes. "So much for higher education," he mumbled, sitting down. "They don't know shit."

Watching the children assisting Moose off the floor, Longboard commented, "You know there were a lot of bad apples stationed in Nam."

"I know," Reno mumbled, taking a sip off the sweet libation. "For me, it's a family matter. Even if the criticism is warranted, I take it personal." Raising his brows, he clarified, "Now that punk's broad-brush assertion that all those who served were racist was way out of line." Staring into the carbonated caramel-colored cocktail, he reflected, "In Nam, my tenure was handicapped by drug addicts, cowards, disenchanted officers, and just plain psychos." He grinned. "Every family has its black sheep."

"How about you, partner?" Longboard nudged. "Did you break the code of military justice?"

"Oh yeah," Reno exclaimed, pinching his face.

Leaning back in his chair, Longboard muttered, "Example."

Reno smiled. "OK, I'll feed you a soft infraction." After wetting his palate, he confessed, "It was at this isolated firebase near some village we referred to as Suc Muc Dic. The platoon leader never left his bunker. The only thing that mattered to this pansy-ass lieutenant was surviving his six-month combat rotation. He didn't mind sending us boys, as he referred to us, out into the shit. Apparently since we were young without families, we were expendable. His only mission was to run out the clock and return to the *world*. After a particularly bad day I was having, I tossed a smoke grenade into his sanctuary." After grinning wide at the recollection, he concluded, "The bitch suffered minor burns. I don't think he found Jesus after the fumigation. But he realized the Vietcong was not the only threat to his life." Downing the last of the spiked cola, he motioned with the empty glass. "It's your turn."

Sitting erect, Longboard responded, "I'm not presently disposed to discuss any operational infractions. Nor would I be disposed to discuss any such violations if in fact they did exist."

Reno snickered.

Chapter 17

⸻

The Tamil schoolhouse was a simple single-story structure—white plaster walls, red tile roof. Windows and doorways opened to the elements. Interior walls divided the boxcar building into six identical classrooms. It was a beautiful day. An afternoon sun hung high in a cloudless royal-blue sky. A soft breeze kept the heat and humidity leaning toward comfortable. It took a day to convert the small campus into a field hospital run by the Medecins Sans Frontieres. Across the playground, shell-shocked Tamil refugees huddling in family units conversed in whispers. Powdered milk was provided courtesy of the Red Cross. Six bodies covered in white linen shrouds lay on a sidewalk morgue. In a crowded classroom waiting room, grief-stricken mothers held wounded children. In the adjoining space, nurses cleaned and stitched up wounds. A queue of donors snaked out of a classroom blood bank. A medic at the door screened the potential contributors. Only those with cards identifying their blood group could donate. A groaning generator lit the operating room. Three surgeons challenged death on the more complex cases.

Removing jagged pieces of metal fragments from a young Tamil girl's back, Doctor DeWitt sighed. Fatigue from the tedious task surfaced across Sandy's shoulders. She flexed. The discomfort traversed down her spine. Focused, she ignored her body's cries for a reprieve. Another removed particle clinked in the metal receptacle. A nurse blotted the sweat from her forehead. Extracting the last damaging shard, Sandy took a victorious breath. Stepping back, she nodded to the nurse. The very capable assistant began closing the wound. Stretching, Sandy realized the innocent girl was a casualty of the government's retaliation to a Tiger attack on a farming village. "The conflict is escalating," she mumbled beneath her surgical mask. *It's the children,* she reflected with a heavy heart, *their small frames have a hard time surviving shrapnel gashes.* "Be strong, little one," she whispered to her young patient. "Please be strong."

"Sandy," Doctor Ondaatje called out. "Why don't you get some air, and check on our generator's fuel supply?" Between his surgical cap and procedure mask, the local surgeon's dark eyes smiled. Blood splatter decorated his theater blues. The short doctor, Tom Ondaatje, hailed from Colombo. Unlike his Hindu Tamil patients, he was Singhalese, a Buddhist.

"Thank you, Tom," Sandy muttered with a grateful nod.

The Dutch doctor, peeling off her surgical scrubs, stepped out of the classroom. Warm sunlight greeted her. She took a cleansing deep breath. After blinking into the bright light, a suffering audience came into focus. Desperate eyes gazed back. "Does anyone speak English?" she hollered.

"I speak English, doctor," a thin youth declared, stepping forward. His age distinguished him from the mostly women and children refugees. A deep scar ran down the side of his head. "How may I be of assistance?" he inquired.

Sandy flinched. "'You speak very good English," she responded. "What is your name?"

"Chola," he answered.

"Chola, we desperately need petrol to feed our generator," she informed him.

He confirmed the request with a nod and turned to run the errand.

"Don't you need some money?" she questioned.

Glancing over his shoulder, he grinned. "I'll get your fuel, no charge." Looking at the displaced refugees, he added, "Thank you for caring for my brethren."

The setting sun created long shadows across the schoolyard. After making her final rounds, Sandy wandered into the empty blood bank classroom. She opened an antique refrigerator. The dated appliance hummed. An interior light illuminated crimson blood bags. The bottom rack stored a dozen amber bottles of beer. The exhausted Doctor DeWitt retrieved a chilled liter bottle of Lion Lager. The grasp of chilled glass was rewarding. Utilizing the edge of a counter, she popped off the bottle cap. On stiff legs, she strolled outside. Bottle in hand, she rounded the corner to the back of the schoolhouse. Six laborers standing in a waist-deep hole dug up the playground. Beside the deepening pit lay a log pile of palm-tree trunks and a mound of sandbags. "Our bunker," Sandy whispered, leaning against the plaster schoolhouse wall. She slid down into a comfortable sidewalk seat. Taking a large anticipated swig, she closed her eyes. The carbonated brew rolled down her dry throat. Holding the bottle to her forehead she sighed. *I need to shower and get some sleep,* she realized. Her body told her *not now.* She agreed, retrieving a cellophane-wrapped cheroot from a breast pocket. A plastic lighter ignited the tiny cigar. Closing her eyes, she enjoyed the smoldering scent. Visualizing her stogie-smoking papa in his beige trench coat and red scarf, she grinned. *This is my moment,* she thought, puffing on the relaxing tobacco. Another healthy chug of cold beer triggered a satisfying belch.

"Excuse me, Doctor," asked an approaching silhouette. "I hope I'm not intruding."

Squinting up at the shadow, she recognized the scar-faced youth. "Chola?" she questioned.

"Yes, it is," he replied. "I wanted to inquire about a patient I brought in. He was about my age with several gunshot wounds."

She nodded. "I know the case. Your friend lost a lot of blood. Fortunately all the projectiles were removed. He has a fighting chance."

"Can I take him with me tomorrow morning?" Chola inquired.

Sandy snorted. "That is out of the question. If he is moved, he will die."

Squatting down on his haunches, Chola looked into her blue eyes. "If he stays here and is discovered by the army, he will die a slow, painful death."

"He is a Tiger?" she whispered.

Chola nodded.

"And you?" she probed.

Sitting beside her, he mumbled, "Does it matter?"

"Nah," she answered, taking a fresh puff of rolled tobacco. "They don't call us Doctors without Borders for nothing." In a reassuring bedside manner, she added, "I'll look out for your friend and let you know when he can be moved." Frowning, she emphasized, "He won't be traveling tomorrow."

"Thank you, Doctor," he responded, leaning against the wall beside her. Focused on the bunker construction, he asked, "I hate to intrude, but are you American?"

She chuckled. "No, I'm Dutch."

"The Diary of Anne Frank," Chola mumbled.

Squinting, she asked, "You've read *The Diary of a Young Girl*?"

"I did." Chola nodded. "I identified with Anne's story about the persecution of a religious minority. I just chose not to hide in an attic."

In no mood to discuss the justification for armed conflict, she questioned, "Why did you ask if I was American?"

Chola snickered. "I wanted to know if you've read *The Adventures of Huckleberry Finn*. I was halfway through it when the Colombo riots broke out." He shrugged. "I want to know how it ends."

"Next time I'm in Colombo, I'll pick up a paperback version," she offered. "You never know; our paths may cross again." She took a quick toke. "Consider it my appreciation for feeding our generator."

Chapter 18

⸻

Adjacent to the port of Bangkok, the Klong Toei slums groaned. It smelled of rotting fish and fresh garbage. Ghetto cooking fires sent dancing smoke strings into an ominous dark sky. Reno walked briskly through the tight compilation of less fortunate. Naked children gawked at the passing white man. "So much for this shortcut," he mumbled, snorting at the stench. "Next time, I'll take the scenic route."

An old woman standing in a shanty doorway tossed a pail of soapy water across the narrow path. *I should have worn shoes,* he realized, treading cautiously through the moist, slimy puddle in sandals. *At least I had enough sense to pack Longboard's prop,* he chuckled confidently, patting the pistol concealed under his untucked Hawaiian shirt. He broke stride, stepping over a vagrant. Behind him, hastening footsteps advanced. Slowly he turned. A teenage stalker dashed into the shadows. "Shit, this is all I need right now," Reno muttered. *I have a nonrefundable deposit at risk on an arms deal with a buyer who won't return my calls. My life is collateral for a short-term loan with a Chinese Triad. More than likely, my feet will develop a rash from this rancid shortcut.* He sighed. *And to top it off I have...Pausing, he focused on the sound of predators. Two, possibly three hostiles,* he concluded.

Doorways and windows began to shut. A wiry punk brandishing a pipe blocked the American's advance. In a pair of red gym shorts, the nearly naked teen stood defiantly on bony bird legs. A combination of dirt and grease soiled his bare torso. Cheap black sunglasses shielded his gaze. Reno stopped and glanced over his shoulder. Three street children in rags blocked his retreat. The shortest of the trio, barking in Thai, flashed a blade. His comrades snickered. "Just great," Reno sighed. "I get to add the Dead End Kids to my list of troubles."

"Money, Johnny," the pipe-wielding mugger said, rubbing his thumb across his fingertips. "Give us all your money."

"Fuck you," Reno grumbled. "I'm having a real bad day. I'm trying to find Global Ventures Trading Company at the port of Bangkok. Can you point me in the right direction?"

The thug flinched. Composing himself with a scowl, he slapped an open palm with the galvanized pipe. "Money, Johnny, or I break your leg," the teen-ager threatened.

Reno drew his pistol. Extending his arm, he targeted the boy's head. "Is it this way?" he questioned. Glancing behind his back, he continued. "Is this the direction to get out of this shit hole?"

The assailants politely stepped back. Cautiously, they began to retreat.

"Hey!" Reno shouted. "I really need directions."

"At end of street is *khlong*," the pipe wielder informed him. "Turn right and follow the canal to the docks."

"Thanks, boys," the American declared, securing his weapon. "Hey, kids!" he shouted, pulling an orange-red one-hundred baht note out of his billfold. Tossing the currency on the slimy ground, he added, "I appreciate it."

Exiting the shantytown, pedestrian traffic thinned. Large cargo trucks flew down an asphalt roadway. Traversing the litter-strewn shoulder, Reno plodded through the transport's dusty wake. His floral-printed shirt clung to a moist torso. Beads of perspiration rolled down his shiny forehead. Looking into black clouds, he chuckled, "At least it's not raining."

A directional sign for Global Ventures on a chain-link fence provided hope. Skirting along the mesh fencing, he spotted his objective. "Holy shit," he whispered, looking across the blacktop parking lot. A two-story warehouse labeled "Global Ventures Trading Company" sparkled. A massive ship's anchor fringed by modest landscaping provided aesthetics. *This is no PO box front.* He snickered.

Mopping his sweaty brow with a moist hand, he took a deep breath. *Hold firm to the price,* he counseled, *but concluding a quick close is the objective.*

Reno's moist hand pushed open the glass storefront door. A chilled atmosphere greeted him. Closing his eyes, he inhaled the pleasant air. The time out was brief. The dark wood-paneled reception area was small. A petite Thai beauty manned a greeting desk. Behind her, a metal art globe adorned the wall. Two frayed cushioned chairs and a weathered sofa provided soft seating. A steep wooden staircase disappeared into the ceiling.

"May I help you, sir?" inquired the soft-spoken Thai doll.

"Yeah," rolled out of Reno's dry mouth. He swallowed. "I need to see…" He reached into the front pocket of faded denim jeans. Examining a moist, crinkled business card, he repeated, "I need to see…Saravanamuttu Appukutty." Squinting at her, he added, "Or something close to that."

"I'm sorry," she offered. "Who do you want to see?"

Slapping the tattered business card on the lacquered wood counter, he grumbled, "This is whom I need to converse with."

"S.A. is not available today," she replied with a submissive shrug.

"Then who is?" he questioned.

"Please take a seat," she offered, politely smiling. "Let me see who is available."

Reno retreated to the soft seating area. The well-worn sofa engulfed him. *Just great,* he thought, watching the receptionist converse in whispers into her headset. Angst gnawed at his guts. *Is there even a deal to be made?* he questioned. *Do I throw in the towel now? Try to renegotiate the terms of the Triad loan. That won't work,* he concluded. *The Triad wants to foreclose.*

"Can I get you anything to drink?" the receptionist offered from her perch.

"Bacardi and Coke," Reno responded. Flashing a peace sign, he added, "With two limes."

"I…we…I…Can get you a Coke?" she countered.

"That'll work," he nodded. Sliding deeper into the mushy cushions, he watched her exit. Focused on her swaying departure, he grinned. *Before I admit defeat, let's see what the lackey they send down has to say.*

Grasping the feminine Coke bottle, Reno sucked the carbonated sugar water through a plastic straw. With the active plastic tube between his lips, he squinted up the stairway. Heavy descending footsteps pounded wooden treads. S.A.'s bullnecked bodyguard Gerard came into view. His thick, scraggly mustache still needed a trim. Slurping the last few drops of cola from the bottle, Reno looked up at the hovering wide brute.

"Mister James," the lackey muttered, extending a massive paw. "I'm Gerard."

"Very well, Gerard," Reno said, rising from the couch's smothering embrace. Giving the oily dark hand a firm shake, he continued, "What is going on?"

"S.A. is out of the country on urgent business," the henchman informed. "He will contact you when he returns in a couple of weeks." Slightly bowing, Gerard mustered an insincere gold-toothed smile and took an exiting step back.

Time to double down, Reno thought. *If gun running was easy, everyone would be doing it.* "I've attempted to contact your boss," he said to the large departing errand boy. "Due to S.A.'s lack of response—or should I say professionalism—I was forced to find another buyer."

"No," Gerard mumbled.

Leaning into the tree trunk, Reno whispered, "Somalia warlords." Patting the thug on the shoulder, he added, "No hard feelings."

"We had a deal," barked Gerard.

"Then let's do business," Reno responded. "And stop wasting my time."

"S.A. is the only one who can authorize a wire transfer of funds," Gerard confessed.

"Can you arrange a parlay?" Reno inquired.

Gerard stood stone-faced. Beneath the thick black bristles of his facial hair, a sparkling smile evolved.

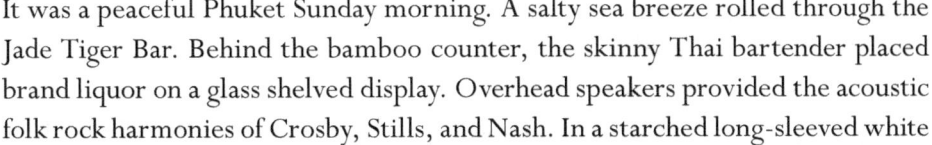

It was a peaceful Phuket Sunday morning. A salty sea breeze rolled through the Jade Tiger Bar. Behind the bamboo counter, the skinny Thai bartender placed brand liquor on a glass shelved display. Overhead speakers provided the acoustic folk rock harmonies of Crosby, Stills, and Nash. In a starched long-sleeved white dress shirt, Reno scanned a glossy travel brochure and sipped on a hot mug of java. A packed army-green duffel bag rested at his feet. Tossing the colorful advertisement aside, he checked his watch. *Where is Longboard?* he wondered.

Assisted by a crutch, the one-legged Marshall sauntered toward the veterans' drinking hole. He easily hopped up the stairway entrance. Securing the padded brace under his arm, he scanned the empty saloon. Spotting Reno, he grinned. "Morning, San Bernardino. What's with the dress shirt? Did somebody die?"

"Hello, Marshall." Reno chuckled. "Nobody died. Longboard and I are flying out of town today on business."

Looking at the bartender setting up shop, Marshall hollered, "Aroon, I need a couple of eggs and a cup of joe." The skinny Thai nodded. "And…" Marshall gazed into the slowly rotating ceiling fan. "A bloody Mary, and make it spicy." Hobbling over, he pulled out the chair across from Reno and inquired, "So where are you two off to?"

"Sri Lanka," Reno answered.

"Where the fuck is that?" Marshall snorted.

Reno placed an index finger on the sleek brochure. The cover depicted stilt fishermen against a colorful sunset. He pushed it across the table. "It was formerly known as Ceylon."

Unfolding the tourist propaganda, Marshall approvingly nodded at the imagery of majestic beaches, ancient cities, and attractive locals. "Isn't there some political unrest in…" Reading from the advertisement, he continued, "The pearl of the Indian Ocean."

"Apparently nobody informed the Sri Lankan Tourism Board about the civil war." Reno snickered.

"Wait a minute," Marshall declared, leaning back. "You are going there to peddle your vintage Kalashnikovs."

"Something like that," Reno muttered. "Can you keep an eye on our beach houses? I'm hoping this will only take a couple of days."

"No problem," Marshall answered.

Leaning forward, Reno said quietly, "If our business takes longer than a week, there may be some hostile creditors looking for us." Tilting his head, he confessed, "I missed an interest payment."

Squinting, Marshall inquired, "How hostile?"

"Extremely," Reno defined. "Don't engage."

A wide grin spread across the disabled veteran's face. "I appreciate the warning, Reno. But don't forget your audience. I will always be a badass Airborne Ranger. I'll water your plants. If a bill collector knocks on your door, he's got a problem."

Chapter 19

———⟡———

The compact Toyota taxi announced another passing move with an annoying toot. Accelerating around a lorry, the cabbie tapped on his horn. Swinging back into the left lane, it beeped the successful maneuver. *Jesus,* Reno thought. *If you honk your horn in the States, it signals you're pissed or all hell is about to rain down. It means something. In Sri Lanka, it seems the cars are communicating to each other in a tooting Morse code.*

Longboard stared out the other passenger window. A colorful populous flowed by. Opened storefronts lined the narrow highway. Distant midrise office buildings grew larger. The taxi decelerated. Traffic thickened. A late-afternoon sun illuminated a polluted haze. The soiled white taxi waded slowly through Colombo rush hour. Strolling cows and horned bulls added to the congestion. Attempting to enter the trickling stream, the aggressive cabbie challenged defiant vehicles.

"Is it always like this?" Reno questioned the driver.

"Oh no," replied the dark-skinned cabbie. "Sometimes the traffic is bad."

Longboard snickered.

In the shadow of a towering hotel, the taxi exited up a sweeping landscaped drive. Manicured tropical growth swayed. Under a protective structural overhang, polished vehicles jostled for position. Businessmen flowed in and out of wide glass doors. The Hilton logo was prominently displayed across a shimmering granite wall.

Reno handed the driver a handful of crisp colorful bills. "Thanks, chief," he commented. "This is close enough; we'll walk up."

The two arms merchants slung army surplus duffel bags over their shoulders and strutted toward the luxury hotel's entrance. Reno stopped. Across the polished stone wall, signage identified the facility's restaurants. The oriental font of the Emperor's Wok popped out. "What did I tell you?" Reno commented. "Wherever you go, there is a Chinese restaurant?"

The surfer insincerely nodded.

A gauntlet of bellboys attempted to relieve the Americans of their canvas luggage. Two doormen timed a synchronized opening of double glass doors. A blast of escaping cold air dowsed the gun runners. The lobby was crisp, clean, and bright. An array of seating options spread across a terraced stone flooring. Boisterous, casually dressed tourists slurped on fruity cocktails. In business attire, locals sipped on whisky or beer and conversed in low tones. Bowtie-wearing waiters scurried about.

Reno dropped his duffel bag at the front desk. An olive-skinned beauty in a navy-blue business suit greeted him with a glowing smile. A gold name tag identified her as Angelina. Beneath accenting brows, her deep dark eyes sparkled. "How may I help you, sir?" she inquired.

"Reno James," he responded in a loud, clear tone. "My partner and I are checking in."

"Yes, sir," she answered. "We've been expecting you." She slid a folded packet across the granite counter and informed him, "These are your room keys for the corner suite. Mister van der Wall has taken care of all your expenses." Handing him an envelope, she added, "You had one message."

"Thanks," Reno mumbled, examining the Colombo Hilton–labeled envelope. "Can you have someone take our bags up?"

"Of course," she said, summoning a bellboy. "Enjoy your stay."

Smiling back into her angelic features, he winked. "You bet we will, Angelina."

Watching a skinny kid in a bellman's uniform struggling with the army-surplus baggage, Reno whispered to Longboard, "Want to get a drink and figure out the next move in our covert venture."

"Who is van der Wall?" the surfer questioned.

Reno shrugged. "I have no idea, but he is picking up the tab." Tearing open the envelope, revealed a small handwritten note: "Tomorrow 2:00 p.m., Poolside Bar. Rolph van der Wall." Handing the message to the surfer, he added, "I guess we'll find out tomorrow. Are you ready for a drink?"

"Let's find the Indian Ocean first. I miss having sand between my toes."

"Hey, Angelina!" Reno shouted. "Which way is the ocean?"

"The Hilton's pool, tennis courts, and the Indian Ocean are across the street, Mister James," she answered, flashing those deep, dark magical eyes.

"Thanks, doll." He winked.

Exiting the hotel, Reno mumbled to his partner, "What do you think of Angelina?"

"The clerk?" Longboard frowned.

"Yeah," Reno mumbled.

"I got to tell you, Sri Lankan women are stunning," the surfer confessed, squinting into the sunlight. "After a steady diet of Vietnamese and Thai cuisine, I may need to sample a local curry dish tonight."

Reno chuckled. "For me, I'm craving a home-cooked meal."

"Something like that," the surfer declared, nodding in the direction of the tennis courts.

On a grass court, a long-legged thoroughbred in a seductive white tennis skirt pranced. Flaxen blond locks flowed out of a white visor. A local in a Hilton-logoed shirt sprinted to return a strategically placed volley. Her subsequent lob did him in. Standing on the baseline, she crouched, awaiting his serve. Sweat glistened on her bare skin. The lime-green ball flew over the net. Her long, lean torso rotated. A powerful two-handed backhand fired back a nonreturnable crosscourt shot. The Hilton tennis pro showed respect by pounding an open palm with his racket. Awestruck, Reno applauded. She reacted to the American's approval with a curious squint.

Longboard placed a hand on his partner's shoulder. "Let's head down to the beach for that drink before she notices you drooling."

In the shade of a thatched roof poolside cabana, Reno sipped on a beer. Longboard departed to the beach. Mostly empty lounge chairs surrounded the large inviting chlorinated pond. A white uniformed attendant served green coconuts decorated with tiny umbrellas to a pod of large, frumpy Europeans. The whine of a blender resonated from the bar. Native beach boys frolicked in the water. A suave mustached local youth applied lotion to a middle-aged tourist. She giggled under his caressing touch. The splashing boys in the pool froze. Bobbing in the water, they all focused at the main bar. Reno turned to investigate.

The tennis thoroughbred sauntered into the lounge. A tennis bag slung over her shoulder. Wiping herself down with a terrycloth towel, she ordered a beer and pointed toward an empty table. Plopping down in webbed chair, she lit a tiny cigar. *That is just sexy,* Reno thought, watching her puff on the maduro cheroot. Politely tilting her head back, she blew a plume of smoke into the rafters. A beach boy slithered out of the pool. Wearing a Speedo and armed with a sparkling gold chain necklace and overflowing confidence, he ambushed the blonde. Hovering over her, he rubbed his dark chest and washboard belly, making small talk. Turning away from the talkative half-naked local, she caught Reno's gaze. Raising her brows, she took a shallow breath. Her rich blue eyes said, "Help me."

Reno winked.

She grinned.

"Hey, Mowgli," Reno said, approaching the aggressive beach boy. "Thanks for keeping my gal company." Looking at the snickering blonde, he pulled out a chair and chuckled. "Honey, I thought we were going to meet in the lobby bar."

"I'm sorry, sweetheart," she improvised. "I lost all track of time."

The dejected gigolo retreated to stalk on older, easier prey.

"Thank you," she whispered. Raising a brow, she questioned, "Mowgli?"

"*The Jungle Book.*" He snickered. "It was a Disney cartoon."

"I got the Kipling reference, Yank," she confirmed.

"And you?" he squinted. "Your slight accent...German?"

"Please," she snapped. "I'm Dutch." After a quick puff on the petite stogie, she placed the smoldering cheroot in a carved coconut ashtray. Extending her hand, she said, "Sandy DeWitt. Thanks again for coming to my rescue."

"Reno James," he replied, giving her petite palm a gentle squeeze. "What brings you to paradise?"

"Paradise?" She snorted. "I'm an aid worker providing humanitarian assistance in the north. I hopped a ride on a Red Cross chopper yesterday for a forty-eight-hour reprieve." Her pleasant facade faded. Taking a sobering breath, she scanned the luxurious hotel's excesses. "It's bad in the north, really bad. An hour's helicopter flight away, an ethnic civil war rages. The only thing the combatants agree on is the sanctity of Ceylon tourism. The beach resorts, heritage sites, elephant orphanage, and booming sex trade are open for business." Gazing at the American, she smiled. "I'm optimistic this cease fire may lead to peace."

Reno leaned back. *Cease fire?* he questioned. *That explains the delayed weapons transaction. Peace would terminate my deal,* he realized. His stomach churned.

"What brings you to Colombo?" she inquired.

"I can assure you it wasn't sex tourism." He chuckled. "I'm investigating a potential business venture. I traffic in antiques."

"Let's drink to the success of your venture," she toasted, touching her bottle to his.

"And to your minivacation," he commented. Taking a large, refreshing swig of lager, he sealed the sentiment. *Small arms from the Cambodian civil war qualify as antiques,* he justified.

Sandy retrieved the smoldering cheroot. A quick flick discharged white ash into the coconut receptacle. A soft puff illuminated the red tip.

"Where did you pick up the habit?" Reno inquired.

Studying the small cigar between her long, delicate fingers produced a reflective grin. "My papa," she delightfully answered. Focused on the string of smoke flowing out of the tiny cigar, she continued, "My mother left us when I was quite young. After her passing, it was always papa and me." She took a long, satisfying toke and exhaled. Gazing into the rising plume, she smiled. "My father was a handsome man. As a tailor, he ran his own haberdashery in Amsterdam. Our flat was located above the shop. We were inseparable." She chuckled. "Except for Thursday nights, that was papa's billiard night."

"So he approves of his little girl's smoking addiction?" Reno teased.

"He only saw me smoke once." Her tone stiffened. "My father was a vain man. When he was diagnosed with terminal cancer, he prematurely surrendered to the fate through euthanasia."

"I'm sorry, Sandy," Reno consoled.

She smiled. Tears welled up in her rich blue eyes. "It was a gorgeous Sunday morning. Colorful boats meandered down the city's canals. After a pancake breakfast, we stopped for a cup of coffee at a sidewalk café. My always punctual father was late for his appointment with death. In the nurturing sunlight, we smoked cigars, my first and his last." She took a quick puff. Blushing, she apologized, "I'm sorry. I don't know why I shared that."

"That was beautiful," Reno responded softly. "No apology necessary."

Leaning back, she took a healthy swig of brew. "Tell me about your American family," she probed.

"Well," Reno answered. "Like you, my mother left me when I was quite young. Only she left me at the doorstep of child protective services and walked away. I never knew my father. I suspect my mother wasn't sure who he was either."

"I'm so sorry, Reno," rolled out of Sandy's shocked expression. "I had no idea."

He chuckled. "Why would you?" With a shrug, he concluded, "When life deals you a bad hand, you play the cards you've been dealt."

"Another round?" questioned an attentive poolside waiter.

The couple exchanged unsure glances. Smiles emerged.

Checking her watch, Sandy toyed, "Do we have time for another drink before dinner?"

Beaming, Reno declared, "Another round."

Chapter 20

───❦───

Dense growth shielded the night sky. Warm, moist stagnant air hung beneath the canopy's embrace. "Heave!" Chola shouted with a parched, raspy voice. Grunts and groans answered. "Heave!" His repetitive command pulsed. Brush crackled in the darkness. Sandaled feet sought traction. Logs under the heavy load's skid rolled forward. The rain forest abruptly ended. The bow of a boat peeked out. Barren white sand stretched out in both directions. Soft waves caressed the deserted shore. Billowing white clouds shrouded the starry sky. Strands of escaping moonlight sparkled on the rippling sea.

Seeing the beach, Chola took a deep breath of salty air. Attempting to conjure up saliva, he swallowed. His brown tartan shirt was soaked with sweat. Staggering forward, his feet sank into soft sand. Around him wobbled the Tiger unit under his command. Like dominos, his exhausted troops fell to their knees. The panting pack of partisans gulped down the warm air.

"We still have a long night before us," Chola informed the huffing, puffing choir. "Let's launch the craft. You can catch your breath on the water." A comforting ocean breeze embraced the hunched-over bundles of exhaustion. No one stirred. Chola straightened his back. Muscle and bone pleaded for a reprieve. Gritting his teeth, he growled, "Do I need to repeat myself?" The fallen rose. Chola grinned. *These are good rural boys,* he concluded. *You never know*

your limitations until you are pushed to the edge, and that chasm is a long way off.
"Heave!" he ordered with a gravelly throat.

The open-hull craft raced across the dark water. Twin two-hundred-and-fifty-horsepower outboard engines growled. The ten-man unit sat against the hull's ribbed frame. Spray shooting over the bow dowsed downcast heads. Salt water tainted with petrol sloshed at their feet. The fifteen-year-old Alak threw up. The young Tiger's returning meal joined the swaying swill.

Chola hugged the barrel of his assault rifle. His teeth chattered. He turned his head. *I cannot show weakness to my men,* he thought, running a moist hand over his face and through saturated hair. A spark of light flickered on the horizon. "*The Adventures of Huckleberry Finn,*" he whispered, focused on the objective. "The King tells the revival meeting that he was once a pirate on the Indian Ocean," Chola mumbled. *It was a beautiful Colombo Sunday,* he recalled. *I was at the beach, lost in the Mark Twain text. I'll never forget reading that passage and gazing across the Indian Ocean. That existence is no more than a pleasant dream. Unlike the grifter in the Mark Twain fantasy, I am a pirate on the Indian Ocean. A privateer,* he clarified. *The capture of merchant shipping in a time of war is justified.*

The racing engine went silent. The shallow boat bobbed on choppy surf. Chola stood in a wobbly stance. Assisted by field glasses, he studied the target and mumbled, "It's a feeder vessel flying a Malaysian flag, possibly three thousand tons. Boarding should be easy."

"I'm sick, Master," mumbled the quivering Alak.

"What?" Chola barked at the boy wearing vomit.

"I can't do this," whispered the petrified Alak. His wide young eyes pleaded for mercy.

Chola scanned the faces of his men. Determination burned in their returning gaze. *This new boy is going to be trouble,* he realized. *Now is not the time for compassion,* he concluded, looking down at the scared puppy. Snorting, Chola whipped back his arm and unleashed a backhand slap across the boy's tender features. "Feeling better now?" he asked, shaking his hand. Whimpering, Alak bobbed his head. "Good," Chola responded. Addressing the troops, he ordered,

"Jagger, I want you to board first, fasten the line, and use your blinding speed to secure the bridge."

Beaming from the compliment, the tall, wiry Jagger flexed his thin frame and answered proudly, "Yes, Master."

"Speed and precision are our allies," Chola preached. Squinting in Alak's direction, he concluded, "No one hesitates."

The twin engines coughed. The watercraft slowly approached the cargo ship. A four-story superstructure overlooked a main deck blanketed by red and blue shipping containers. Floodlights lit up the tower, containers, and ship's perimeter. The speedboat maneuvered alongside its large prey. A smoking sailor on the deck gazed down. With an assault rifle strapped to his back, the lanky, barefoot Jagger wrapped a thick hemp rope around his waist. He leaped out of the boat onto a dangling tire bumper. In seconds, he was on the ship's deck fastening the line. An armed barefoot raiding party followed.

"Secure the bridge," Chola called out, climbing over the gunwale. Racing bare feet pounded the metal deck. Four seamen knelt, their hands in the air. Behind the hostages, Alak pulled back the charging bolt of an assault rifle. The bright light illuminated the scolded boy's swollen red cheek and a trickle of blood mingling with the puke staining his chin. "We are here for your cargo, not your lives," Chola informed them in perfect English. The sailors confirmed the message with nervous twitches. Chola shot a reassuring glance at Alak and instructed, "No one dies."

The young partisan nodded.

Chola sprinted toward the radiant superstructure. Partisans flew up the four-story external stair tower. Chola followed. Callused feet pounded diamond plate treads. Metal grating vibrated. Winded and sucking air, Chola entered the bridge. Three bewildered Malays stared down the barrels of automatic weapons.

"Who's in charge?" Chola inquired.

A skinny, middle-aged man with innocent boyish features stepped forward. A half-buttoned light cotton dress shirt exposed a bare chest. The thin fabric of a breast pocket displayed a red-and-white pack of Marlboros. "I am Tan Boon Eng," he confidently announced, "Captain of the *Saipan Pearl*."

"Did you send out a distress signal?" Chola questioned.

"We tried." Captain Eng shrugged.

"You are trespassing in Eelam waters," Chola announced. "The penalty for this violation is your cargo. Set a course toward Trincomalee," he calmly instructed, "and I need to see your manifest."

The *Saipan Pearl* slowly swung around heading toward shore. At the helm, Captain Eng tapped out a cigarette. After lighting the smoke, he politely flashed the pack of Marlboros to the heavily armed invaders.

"We are LTTE," Chola declared. "We don't drink, smoke, or fornicate."

The easygoing Malay shrugged. With a subtle smirk, he secured the nicotine treats in a breast pocket. After very long and satisfying toke, he blew a plume of smoke over his head.

The hijacked feeder vessel sliced through choppy waters. The air was thick. Sweat glistened off the tense occupants of the tiny bridge. Alak arrived with his prisoners. The Malaysians shot concerned glances at one another. No one spoke.

Chola's flexed finger scanned the ship's manifest. "Furniture, fabrics, mining equipment, farm implements," he mumbled in English. His extended finger paused. He grinned. "Four tons of Indian rice," he whispered triumphantly.

The lights of the east coast port city of Trincomalee twinkled. Way up the dark shoreline, a single beam of light reached across the black water. "That beacon is our destination," Chola instructed. "You're going to need to pick up speed. We are going to beach the *Saipan Pearl*."

The captain's shoulders dropped. Sighing, he revved the engines. The vessel leaped forward. The beckoning beam grew brighter. Silhouetted, tall palm trees swayed across the dark shore. A narrow buffer of white sand appeared. The captain turned his head. His face puckered. The *Saipan Pearl* let out a low grating growl. The ship's pain escalated into a high-pitched screech. Listing heavily port, the feeder vessel sliced its way up the sandy beach. Hostages and hijackers tumbled down the sloping floor. Glass shattered. A cargo container broke free. A massive storage unit rolled off the deck into shallow water. A second and third container followed. The two blue ones sank. The red one bobbed.

The hijackers leaped to their feet. The Malaysian captain and crew lay where they fell. Squatting beside the reclining captain, Chola spoke softly. "You have been cooperative. To show my appreciation, I'm going to release you and your men down the coast. From there, you can trek to Trincomalee." The dumb-struck Malay captain responded with an open mouth. "This option requires an immediate evacuation," Chola clarified.

"What…what about food, water, our personal belongings?" Captain Tan Boon Eng questioned.

"I'm offering you life, nothing more," Chola declared. "My superiors don't always agree with my compassionate sentiment. Time is of the essence."

The captain graciously nodded.

"Jagger!" Chola called out from his crouched repose. "I want you and two brothers to transport the Captain and his crew in the speedboat down the coast and release them."

"Yes, Master," Jagger answered.

Standing up, Chola looked down at the captain and whispered, "Good luck." Staggering on the tilted floor, he leaned into Jagger and instructed, "Drop the Malays off on some secluded beach, make sure they have water, and point them in the right direction."

Sunlight peeked over the horizon. The listing crippled vessel cast a long shadow across the white sand. The successful raiding party lingered at the bow of the beached rusty beast. Chola was the first to slide down the slanting deck into the shallow turquoise water. He miscalculated the depth. Saltwater engulfed his torso as his naked feet searched for the sandy bottom. Water lapped at his chin as his toes found pay dirt. High over his head, he held his precious assault rifle. A wave rolled over his head. The saltwater baptism was refreshing. *A great way to start the day,* he thought, plodding out of the rippling surf. Soft waves lapped at his bare feet. Behind him, his men wadded toward shore.

The tree line came to life as a Tiger Battalion emerged from the jungle. A rebel colonel led the sweeping procession. Soaking wet, Chola trudged up the grasping sand to greet the Tiger commander.

"Well done, machan," the colonel proclaimed.

"Thank you, Master," Chola responded. Triumphantly, he announced, "There is four tons of Indian rice on the captured vessel."

"Excellent!" the colonel exclaimed. Raising his brows, he questioned, "The crew?"

Chola turned to investigate the whine of an outboard engine. The speedboat with the hostages skimmed across the shiny surface. Answering his superior, he said, "There were no causalities. Captain and crew were cooperative. I made the decision to release the captives in neutral territory."

The colonel's nostrils flared. "Do you think that was a wise decision?"

Instinctively, Chola flexed. "Yes, Master, I think it was," he confidently responded to the scowling superior.

The colonel's lecturing persona subsided. Slowly nodding, he confessed, "I'm impressed by your battlefield tact. It is easy to see why the political wing of our movement has requested your services."

"Master?" Chola questioned.

"Chola," the colonel mumbled, "I hate to lose my best group leader. However, our struggle is in need of university-educated patriots with your language skills. You have been assigned to the political division."

Chola glanced over at his soaking-wet companions. Sitting in a circle on the beach, the young pirates laughed and joked over a warm cup of tea. Chola's heart sank.

"Cheer up, machan," the colonel chimed. "You are being groomed for a leadership position in our liberation journey."

"Yes, Master," Chola acknowledged.

"You are to return to the Mullaitivu District," the officer instructed. "There is an American...an arms merchant heading north. He is important to our cause. Your assignment is to shadow him as an ambassador of Tamil Eelam."

Chapter 21

———— ❧ ————

The year was 1970, the year of the dog in the Vietnamese highlands. The sky was gray. A thick, milky-white morning fog blanketed scorched earth. Beneath the concealing vapor, bomb craters in the red clay soil exhaled wisps of smoke. Decapitated palm trees stood watch over shredded foliage. At nineteen years of age, Reno James cautiously advanced in a sweeping line of twenty-four combatants. As the platoon rookie, he was referred to as "the f'in' new guy." It was a web-gear-only operation. Each soldier carried only his weapon, ammo, canteen, and first-aid kit. Reno's jungle boots calculated each step. He glanced down. A horde of large red ants feasted on a gnarled, severed hand. Charred air spiked with the aroma of rotting human remains filled his nostrils. Sweat rolled down his back. He took a deep, composing breath.

Rubin, a chunky Puerto Rican from the Bronx, was the point man. He smiled a lot but was a quiet man. Considered an "old-timer," Rubin was counting the final days to the end of his tour of duty. Even though he would be going home soon, it was his turn on point. The likeable Puerto Rican never shirked his responsibilities. Moving forward in a low crouch, Rubin held up a fisted hand. The squad stopped. A breeze stirred the misty haze. A Vietnamese boy and girl in soiled black pajamas and conical hats materialized. Like ghostly apparitions, the motionless children scrutinized the invaders with deep-set dark eyes, their stoic expressions smudged with battlefield soot. The boy was probably ten; behind him stood his presumed sister. She was more than likely a young teenager. Fog eerily twirled around the stationary children.

"This is a free-fire zone," growled the crusty seasoned Sergeant Bach. "There are no civilians here. Everyone is considered hostile." He raised his M-16, targeting the local specters drifting in and out of the haze.

"No, Sarge," Reno declared. "These are lost children."

Bach lowered his weapon. Thickening fog engulfed the Puerto Rican. He and the children vanished in the dense vapors. An explosive blast erupted within the milky-white haze.

Reno awoke. Covered in sweat, he gasped. Chilled air flowed out of a wall vent. A glowing digital clock clicked over to 3:00 a.m. An ornate ceiling fan stirred a gentle down-draft. The caressing breeze rippled across high-thread-count linen. Focused on the rotating palm-leaf blades, Reno patted his chest. *It's been a while since I revisited the Rubin Flores incident. I made a mistake. Rubin paid for it with his life, and Sergeant Bach had me, the fucking new guy, as his scapegoat. I never questioned the harsh penance in a fee-fire zone again,* he reflected. Focused on the illuminating radiance of the digital clock, he sighed. *I got other problems to worry about now. What have I got myself into?* he wondered. *If there is a Sri Lankan cease fire, peace is on the horizon. The fantasy of fuck-you money is replaced by a two-hundred-and-forty-thousand-dollar Cantonese Triad obligation. I can't run and hide,* he realized. *I did that once. Hell, I've been holed up in Phuket for the last decade.* Shifting on the comfortable bedding, he grinned. *Before conceding defeat, let's see what tomorrow's meeting with van der Wall brings. It's never over till it's over. What am I whining about? Yesterday was a great day. Longboard hired a curry dish for the night. And I got a long overdue taste of white meat.* Closing his eyes, he reflected on the satisfying Sandra Dewitt coupling. Blindly, he reached over in search of the Dutch thoroughbred. The bed was vacant. Propped up by an elbow, he scanned the luxurious suite. Drapes fluttered around the balcony's open sliding glass door. He rose. Putting on a pair of faded denim jeans, he investigated. In the open doorway, warm, moist air embraced his naked torso.

In a terrycloth bathrobe, Sandy leaned against the balcony's railing. City lights twinkled. The dark blanket of the Indian Ocean stretched to the horizon. Random illumination identified ships on the black sheet of glass.

"Good morning, sweetheart," he whispered.

She turned with a soft smile, her blue eyes moist with tears. He hugged her. She melted into the embrace.

"It's the children," she confessed. "They are so innocent, confused. They don't understand what is happening to their world."

"Can anybody really comprehend the horrors of war?" he consoled. Stroking the back of her head, he added, "I've seen it as an active participant. Life sometimes is nothing more than a very bad joke."

"I'm apprehensive about heading back up north this afternoon," she disclosed.

He chuckled. "Anticipation is a double-edged sword. As a kid, I learned that Christmas Eve was always better than Christmas morning. I was so excited the night before, always disappointed the next day. In Nam, I slept better on recon patrols dreaming about R&R, than in a Hue hotel dreading deployment." He kissed the top of her head. "You'll be just fine, Sandy."

She clenched him tight. "Thanks, Reno," she whispered. "Thanks for making my R&R memorable." She sealed the sentiment with a soft kiss.

Longboard can quantify his experience with a local girl monetarily, he concluded. *Unfortunately for me, the emotional cost of my evening with Sandy DeWitt will be far more expensive.*

The Hilton Hotel's chlorinated crystal pond sparkled. Under the protective lee of a poolside umbrella lounged a middle-aged frump dog. In a flowing floral-printed muumuu she sipped on a fluted glass garnished with a fruit salad. Beside her squatted a young half-naked beach boy. Pulling ornate seashells out of a rough cloth sack, the gigolo entertained his mark. The giddy grandmother beamed.

Seated in the empty poolside bar, Reno observed the flirtatious charade. "What did that curry dish cost you last night?" he questioned his partner.

"One hundred bucks with tip." Longboard chuckled. "It was worth every penny." Raising his brows, he added, "I didn't get a receipt, but I'm still going to submit it on my expense report."

Shaking his head, Reno snorted out a laugh.

"That's it?" the surfer questioned. "I anticipated one of your long rants. In fact, you've been very quiet today." Leaning back, he grinned. "You're smitten," he declared. "That Dutch vixen got to you."

"Sandy, Sandy DeWitt," Reno muttered. "She was sharp, witty, and definitely out of my league."

"Do you think you'll ever see her again?"

"I sure hope so," Reno mumbled, checking his watch. Scanning the open-air bar, he declared, "Our host is late."

Out of the sunlight, a tall potbellied senior strutted into the tavern. Scruffy gray chest hair peeked out of a half-buttoned linen shirt. Close-cropped silver bristles encircled a liver-spotted bald head. White slacks completed the milk man ensemble.

"Looks like a Rolph," Longboard commented.

"Gentlemen," the arrival announced, approaching the Americans. Flexing his tall frame, he stood at attention. Bowing slightly, he proudly informed them, "I am Rolph van der Wall."

The Americans rose and introduced themselves with handshakes.

Pulling out a chair, Rolph snapped his fingers in the air and barked, "Arrack," at the bartender. His demanding persona faded, "Have you tried our local coconut whisky?" he politely inquired.

"No," the Americans simultaneously muttered.

Rolph reached for the rafters. His fingers snapped. He shouted, "Make that three arracks, two with ice." Addressing his guests, he confided, "I know how you Yanks are addicted to frozen water." Sitting tall, he continued, "I hope your stay has been enjoyable. I wasn't sure if you were seeking companionship? Let me know your desires, and I can have someone sent up to your room."

"We appreciate your hospitality, Rolph," Reno chimed in. "But who the fuck are you?"

A boisterous belly laugh answered. Rolph continued to snicker as the liquor was served. Grasping a small glass of caramel whisky, he mumbled, "Prost," and took a soft sip.

"Dutch?" Reno questioned.

"My ancestors were some three hundred years ago," Rolph replied. "I'm known here as a Burgher by most, a white cockroach by others."

"Do you know S.A.?" Reno persisted.

"S.A.?" the Burgher questioned.

"Saravan…amuttu Appu…kutty or something close to that?" Reno clarified.

"Oh Saravanamuttu," replied an enlightened Rolph. "Our mutual client uses several aliases. I don't think anyone, in particular Interpol, knows his real name."

"Mutual client?" Longboard questioned, shaking an ice cube in an empty glass.

"I, or should I say, my family is in the boat-building business. Our mutual friend is in the process of acquiring a small fleet. He asked me to welcome you to Colombo and assist with your northern journey."

"What?" Reno snapped.

Rolph lowered his voice. "I'm aware that you have another buyer for your product. Africans, I believe. S.A., as you call him, needs to approve the purchase. I will arrange transportation for that parlay. If all goes well, you'll be back here at poolside in a couple of days." Lifting his whisky glass, he took a calculated sip.

"Will you be accompanying us?" Longboard questioned.

The Burgher snorted. Whisky shot out of flared nostrils. A sweeping forefinger wiped his leaking nose. He chuckled. "Of course not. Didn't you hear? There is a war going on."

Chapter 22

⸺⸺⸺

It was 4:00 a.m. The elevator cab smelled of polished wood. A soft chime signaled the lobby. Automatic stainless-steel doors parted. An industrial cleaning machine hummed. A frail old local, in an oversized Hilton janitor's uniform, held tightly to a floor buffer. The appliance's drone echoed throughout the deserted entrance hall. Reno tossed his army-green duffel bag over a shoulder. Stepping onto polished stone, he yawned. Longboard followed, blinking at the annoying brightly lit lobby. Out of the empty sea of soft seating, the silver-crowned Burgher rose. A blue blazer now adorned Rolph's white milkman attire.

"Gentlemen," Rolph called out, "I trust you've had a good night's sleep."

"Mornin', Rolph," Reno mumbled.

Longboard grunted.

"Your driver and vehicle await," Rolph informed them, sweeping an arm toward the door.

"Were you able to fulfill our request?" Reno asked.

"Ah yes," the Burgher replied, scanning the vacant foyer. Pulling a miniature handgun from a coat pocket, he rechecked the perimeter and handed the pistol to Reno.

Examining the pimp pistol, dwarfed by his palm, Reno questioned, "This is it?"

"Yes," Rolph calmly replied. "In addition, my cook prepared fried chicken for your journey, and there is a small ice chest with beer and Coca-Cola." After smiling at his generosity, he headed toward the exit saying, "This way, Yanks."

Shaking his head, Longboard peered down at the peashooter.

Reno chuckled. "You have to admit, it is kinda funny. We are international arms dealers heading into a war zone with a derringer."

Motioning for the sidearm, Longboard grumbled, "I fail to see the humor."

Reno surrendered the weapon. "OK, you can be in charge of our fire-power...but I get the chicken breast."

The hotel's canopy trapped warm, stagnant predawn air. A tarnished four-door red Toyota awaited them curbside. A crack traversed the windscreen. On the side of the vehicle, black tape spelled out "AP." Behind the wheel, a driver with an open mouth snored.

"AP?" Reno questioned.

"Associated Press," Rolph clarified. "Your driver has made this trip several times. His name is Sam." Flexing into a formal pose, he nodded. "Have a safe journey."

In the front seat, Sam tapped on the horn. Beside him, a vibrating Styrofoam ice chest squealed. The Toyota passed a rural bus bulging with passengers. A thin margin of error separated the AP-labeled vehicle and an oncoming lorry. The car accelerated down a rare straightaway. A rough wood shanty blew by. Wetlands flanked the pothole-infested asphalt strip. Sam yielded to an antique tractor slowly chugging across the road. In a canal, a family splashed water on an elephant.

"This is beautiful country," Reno muttered. Addressing Longboard, he asked, "Are you OK with heading into the war zone?"

"We don't have a choice," the surfer mumbled.

"But do you like it?" Reno probed.

Turning, Longboard faced his partner. A wide grin spread across his taunt tan features. "I love this," he confessed. "I've never been more alive than in combat. Time stopped. Everything you do or don't do affects your survival. An untied shoelace can determine life or death."

Reno nodded. "I appreciate a challenge but prefer working with a net."

Looking forward, the surfer reflected, "There are certain disciplines you are born with. Some are naturally good at math. Others are musically inclined. Particular physiques can be honed to a specific sport. As an assassin, I was a gifted prodigy. When you discover your talent, you realize your purpose. I'd lie in a bed of tall grass. A tick nibbled on the back of my neck. I'd know the parasite would overindulge and fall off. Undetected, motionless, enduring, waiting for an unsuspecting target is my skill. The payoff was exhilarating." Slowly nodding, he concluded, "I miss it."

"Why did you turn down the Triad's employment offer?" Reno wondered.

"Please," Longboard replied. "I'm an assassin not a serial killer."

"How did you end up in Vietnam?" Reno nudged his unusually talkative silent partner.

Tilting his head back, Longboard gazed at the discolored automobile's headliner and mumbled, "My father remarried."

Reno flinched. "How did that punch your ticket to Nam?"

"My father was a real-estate developer in Southern California," Longboard reflected. "When business was good, it was very good, and when the cycle ended, Pop would declare bankruptcy. During a peak in the market, he married my mother, his receptionist. She was his second wife. Technically, his third marriage," he clarified. "Dad had a previous matrimonial contract annulled so it wouldn't be counted in the marriage tally. His previous families drifted into the forgotten past. My mother sealed her relationship with my birth. I attended prep school and spent the summers surfing at our beach house."

"Growing up, I despised your tribe," Reno confessed.

"Within the gated community, we felt the masses' scorn but didn't care." Longboard chuckled. "At seventeen, it looked like a college deferment would exempt me from the draft. It was about that time Dad found wife number three or four, depending on the count. My mother was exiled from the privileged bubble, and I moved into the ranks of less-educated inductees."

"What happened to Mom?" Reno poked.

"With the last flicker of her youth, she snagged a tow-truck driver in Pasadena."

"And Dad?"

Longboard laughed. "The swordsman died of a heart attack while fucking his secretary."

"Augh," Reno uttered.

"At least he died happy." Longboard snickered.

The vehicle decelerated. Portable metal barricades blocked the roadway. Helmeted soldiers in combat fatigues searched a rusting light utility truck. A family of seven stood attentively beside the vehicle. The mother, in a bright-red sari, hovered over two wide-eyed children. An officer in a military cap grilled the father. Sam rolled down the driver's-side window. A toot on the horn and a friendly wave got the attention of the harassing officer. The official scowled at the interruption. Sam grinned and flicked a thumb in the direction of his passengers. Enlightened, the officer nodded and barked out an order. The troops quickly relocated the galvanized metal blockade. The AP Toyota rolled through the checkpoint. Baby-faced soldiers waved at the passing Americans. Reno and Longboard returned the gesture.

"What was that all about?" Reno questioned the driver.

Over his shoulder, Sam mumbled, "White privilege."

Reaching into the front seat, Reno took the Styrofoam lid off the squeaking ice chest. A block of murky ice chilled amber bottles of beer and thick, contoured glass bottles of Coke. An irregular-shaped aluminum foil package rested on top of the clinking glass containers. Grabbing a perspiring bottle of Lion Lager and the tin foil parcel, he retreated to his seat. "Remember, I get the chicken breast," he said.

Snacking on juicy white meat, Reno watched the countryside drift by. The compact car's interior reeked of the fresh aroma of cold fried chicken. Residences slowly appeared. A cadre of women in colorful flowing saris walked alongside the road. Umbrellas shielded the women from the afternoon sun. In a hitched-up red-and-white sarong, a wiry boy peddled a bicycle overloaded with large bunches of bright-yellow and orange king coconuts. Open storefronts replaced the homes skirting the highway. Motorcycles buzzed about.

Pedestrians darted across the thoroughfare. A teacher herded a gaggle of uniformed schoolchildren past an open-air saloon. Reno washed down the moist meat with a swig of brew and commented, "I guarantee you; there is at least one Chinese restaurant in this town."

Sam sucked a chicken drumstick clean. He tossed the remnants into the Styrofoam bin. "This is the last government-controlled city," he informed them. "We have to stop and show papers."

Commercial trucks, busses, and a few cars idled in a long line. It was late in the day. A high sun reflected off the coughing column of hot metal. Sam rudely squeezed past the queuing vehicles. The AP Toyota, hugging the shoulder of the road, rolled to the front of the line. Military presence was heavy. Sam fidgeted with the contents of a tan leather travel satchel. A helmeted young soldier rapped on the driver's window. Sam rolled down the window. Subtly, he passed an expediting fee to the youth. A wide grin accepted the bribe. The Toyota idled forward. Rolling up the window, Sam muttered over his shoulder, "The vehicle has cleared. Leave the pistol."

Exiting the car, Reno and Longboard stretched.

"This way," Sam announced, slinging a travel satchel over his shoulder. The Americans blindly followed.

In a large barren field, rough wood barricades collected hundreds of northern travelers in a zigzagging queue. Foot traffic had ground the dirt base into a fine powder. A warm breeze shoved trash and wisps of soil across the exiting checkpoint. The silent crowd slowly flowed through the maze. Armed troops observed. A young couple quieted a whimpering child.

The Americans followed their driver past the gawking horde. As he caught a whiff of a pungent, spicy human odor, Reno's expression soured. Rubbing the back of his sweaty neck, he mumbled, "Looks like we are going to the head of the class."

"Caucasian privilege." Longboard shrugged.

Under the protection of a tattered white tent canopy, a half dozen officials scrutinized travel papers. Sam approached the first available station. The driver tossed a stack of documentation in front of the administrator. Slowly, the official's wrinkled, expressionless features glanced down. He turned over the cover page. The image of Benjamin Franklin on a crisp US hundred-dollar bill stared up. The administrator methodically collected and pocketed the inducement. Rocking a rubber stamp across an ink pad, he took a deep breath. The seasoned bureaucrat artfully inked, flipped, and stamped the official authorization on all seven copies.

Chapter 23

———

The setting sun flirted with the horizon. A singed aroma hung in thick air. Incoming rounds had taken large bites out of the narrow roadway. Sam downshifted. The AP Toyota entered a trash-strewn roundabout. A ghost town surrounded the junction. Gaping holes adorned cement walls. Bullet wounds riddled idle storefronts. Squeezing past the scorched metal carcass of a bus, Reno shook his head. *We left the Colombo Hilton this morning,* he reflected. *The Southern beach resorts might as well be on another planet.*

Dusk settled in. Dense growth embraced the battle-scarred path. Headlight beams illuminated the foliage tunnel. Slowly rounding a bend, the vehicle coasted to the journey's end. Uniformed rebels in camo-fatigues stood defiantly. A scar-faced youth brandishing an assault rifle stepped forward. Sam switched on the dome light. The driver rustled through his travel satchel. "Get out slowly," the driver instructed. "We have to show travel papers."

Reno sarcastically frowned at Longboard and questioned, "Travel papers?"

As they stepped out of the vehicle, gravel crunched underfoot. The aroma of ripe men floated in the night air. A *poorali* began refueling the vehicle from five-gallon cans.

"Greetings, Sam," the scar-faced spokesman said in English.

"Good evening, Chola," replied the surprised driver. "It's good to see you."

"Can you get this to my *amma*?" Chola asked, offering a sealed letter.

"Consider it done, *thambi*," replied a beaming Sam. "It will make your mum happy." After filing the correspondence in his travel satchel, he retrieved the Americans' papers. "Everything is in order," he declared, handing over the documentation.

"I take it the Americans are in your charge?"

Chola nodded.

Walking past his white passengers, Sam popped open the trunk. "Good luck, gentlemen," he declared, pulling out the canvas baggage.

"Thanks, Sam," Reno responded, tossing a duffel bag over his shoulder. Extending his hand, he emphasized the sentiment with a shake.

"Safe journey," Longboard stated.

After relieving himself, Sam climbed back into the compact car. The vehicle purred to life. Bugs danced in the sweeping headlights' beams. The glow of the Toyota quickly disappeared down the dark, deserted jungle road.

"My name is Chola," the translator informed them.

"Reno James," one American responded with an extended hand.

The gesture surprised the partisan. Timidly, he shook the American's hand. "Please to meet you?"

"Call me Longboard," the surfer announced, forcing a second handshake on Chola.

Chola picked up a kerosene lamp. "Follow me," he instructed, raising the lantern high.

The well-traveled path was wide. The dark jungle crackled. Insects challenged the elevated lantern. "After a long day in that Toyota sardine can, it feels good to stretch my legs," Reno commented. Adjusting the duffel bag strapped across his back, he asked, "How far are we going?"

"Not far," Chola answered.

Firelight flickered in the distance. Conversation flowed out of the surrounding darkness. Beside the trail, rough wood poles supported a palm-frond canopy. In the tiny open-air guard box, a lone sentry snored. A cluttered small table elevated his callused bare feet. Snarly toenails capped the exposed soiled digits. A tiny flame fluttered in a coconut-oil lamp. Insect casualties floated in the oil. A paper spike impaled random pages. A rubber stamp rested atop a sealed ink pad. A pair of black-framed spectacles lay on a weathered official's cap.

"Good evening, machan!" Chola shouted.

Jostled, the guard tumbled onto a planked wood floor. Slowly, the official got up, repositioned the hardwood chair, and sat down. Clearing his throat, he secured the spectacles behind his ears. Methodically, he placed the hat on his head. A tug on the cracked leather visor perfected the fit. Stone-faced, he exposed an upturned palm. Chola tossed the Americans' travel papers on the table. After a quick review, the bureaucrat artfully flipped, stamped, and inked the official authorization on all seven copies.

"I'll be damned." Reno chuckled. *The Singhalese and Tamils live in different worlds,* he surmised. *Their cultures are divided by religion and language. The only thing they share is a passion for the inefficient and inflexible policy of bureaucracy. It's only a matter of time before this haughty bastard learns he can charge for flexibility.*

The official filed two copies on the paper spike. Chola collected the balance of the approved documentation. Holding the lantern overhead, he led the way down the trail. A warm breeze rustled the embracing growth. The dense brush thinned. Out of the shadows, a frontier town emerged. Kerosene lanterns beckoned customers to a tea shop. Sitting on discarded ammunition boxes, armed partisans and civilians enjoyed a hot cup of tea. The patrons paused to inspect the passing white men. A curious gaggle of young boys ran up to the Americans. A one-legged boy on a wooden crutch brought up the rear.

"Brings back images of Nam," Reno mumbled.

"Yep," grunted Longboard.

Behind a large bunch of bright-orange king coconuts, a hunched-over middle-aged woman sat on a three-legged stool. With desperate eyes, she spotted potential customers. She rose. Mustering a soliciting smile, she waved an inviting hand at the produce.

"Why not?" Reno declared, spinning around. A waving finger counted the gawking boys. The calculating digit included Chola and Longboard. "A baker's dozen," he mumbled, flashing flexed hands followed by three fingers.

Beaming, the vendor picked up a machete and hacked away at an orange coconut. Expertly using the tip of the blade, she carved a small hole in the top. She quickly filled the order.

Amid his new young admirers, Reno chugged sweet cool nectar from the bulky sphere. Digging a two-thousand-rupee note from a pant pocket, he attempted to pay.

She retreated back a step and spoke to Chola. "She cannot make change," he translated.

"Keep the change," Reno said, winking.

Bowing graciously, she accepted the currency.

"Gentlemen," Chola insisted, leading the way.

"Where to now?" Reno questioned.

"Dinner," the guide answered.

The Americans followed the young English-speaking rebel to one of the few concrete structures in the shantytown. Chola paused at the base of three steps leading up to a planked wood deck. An open doorframe glowed. Dialogue laced with laughter resonated from within.

"Enjoy your meal," the departing Chola commented.

Reno looked at his partner. Longboard shrugged. Adjusting his luggage strap, Reno plodded up the stairs. Framed by the doorway, he scanned the room. A pigeonholed cabinet secured the back wall. In the sorting slots, coconut-oil lamps quivered. *A former post office,* he concluded. Three servers in white button-down shirts, tartan sarongs, and white gloves stood behind rolltop chafing dishes. Out of the steaming trays escaped the aroma of hot seafood. A round dining table set for five centered the room. Looking up from a formal place setting, S.A. grinned. Beside him, in clean, creased camouflage fatigues, sat two rebel commanders. The Tamils all sported mandatory scruffy mustaches. "The officers club," Reno muttered. *While I was trekking through the shit in Nam, the decision makers in private enclaves sipped daiquiris.*

"Mister James!" S.A. exclaimed. He stood. The officers slowly followed his lead. Chairs scraped the planked flooring. "Who is your companion?" he inquired.

Reno released his duffel bag. Glancing at his partner, he replied, "He goes by Longboard."

The surfer squinted at the dinner party. He flashed the demon persona of an assassin. The Tamils nodded respectfully.

"Please join us," S.A. offered with an inviting, open palm.

The Americans accepted. Taking a seat in a stiff-backed wooden chair, Reno politely inquired, "Are you ready to parlay?"

S.A. waved off the suggestion. "Let's eat first," he responded. "We can discuss our business later, over a cup of tea or coffee if you prefer." Blindly, he snapped his fingers.

White-gloved waiters surrounded the table. Simultaneously, they served stuffed crab, prawns, and rice on white bone china. Like famished lumberjacks, the rebel officers dug in. Lips smacked. Glistening fingers fed open mouths. A more refined S.A. used a knife and fork to slice shrimp into edible portions.

In the limited light, Reno observed the gluttonous commanders. *They are only here for a free meal,* he concluded. An officer held up an empty glass and barked at a server. *Oh how the brass loves to bitch,* Reno reflected. *I guess it doesn't matter the army or the war.* Enticed by the spicy aroma, he closed his eyes and inhaled. *God, that smells good,* he realized. Extracting a chunk of soft, delicate crab meat, he popped it into his salivating mouth. The zesty, tender meat rolled across his tongue. Swallowing, he glanced at Longboard. The surfer took a satisfying bite out of a dangled prawn. "This is really good," Reno whispered.

Longboard nodded, taking another ravenous bite.

Looking over the tropical flower centerpiece, Reno questioned the host, "No alcohol?"

"Tigers don't drink, smoke, or fornicate," S.A. informed them. "We are focused to the cause of independence."

"Good for you!" Reno exclaimed. Shoveling in another salivating mouthful of gourmet cuisine, he chuckled. *While you prohibit specific vices, the ruling class doesn't mind eating like kings.*

Waiters removed the fine china and shellfish debris. They filled the dinner guests' cups with black tea. A carafe of warm milk, a bowl of sugar, and a plate of bite-sized fruit were placed on the stained linen tablecloth. The rebel officers snapped up the lion's share of the fruit tray. Blowing on a misting cup, S.A. asked, "Would you gentlemen prefer coffee?"

"No, this is fine," Reno answered.

"Thank you for meeting me in my homeland," S.A. said, slowly stirring the hot brew. "Unfortunately, due to the gray area of the law in which I operate, I was forced to flee Thailand." Tapping a spoon on the porcelain cup, he grinned. "I was wondering...if you have another buyer, as you threatened, why would you travel all this way to seek me out?" Sipping on the tea, he leered at his guests.

That's it, Reno concluded. *You want to flush out my bluff.* "I didn't say I had another buyer," he clarified. "I said I had other buyers, African warlords. My preference is to do a bulk sale with you, a client I know and trust."

S.A. nodded. "Would you consider me purchasing an option on the munitions?"

Reno's guts contracted. *The cease-fire,* he concluded. *No war, no sale—means a Chinese Triad all over my ass. It's time to go all in,* he realized. "I wouldn't consider an option," he grumbled. "Either put up or shut up," he added. "Do we have a deal?"

S.A. took a deep breath. Exhaling, he sighed.

Reno focused on the Tamil's mustache. *What's it going to be?* he wondered.

S.A.'s lips parted.

A rumbling blast of man-made thunder shook the dining room. Tumbling dishes shattered. Dust rained down from the rafters. The waiters and diners fell to the floor. The ground trembled. Crouched down, Reno wrapped his arms around his head. The firestorm faded. He smiled. *So much for the hindrance of a cease-fire,* he concluded.

Chapter 24

⸙

The earthen floor pulsed. Sand trickled out of the palm log ceiling. A nervous gasp resonated in the crowded dark hole. Outside the reinforced bunker roamed stalking artillery. Wedged in the tight compilation of doctors, medics, and nurses, Sandy hugged her knees. She took short, calming breaths. A heavy flak jacket impeded her gasps. Images of her patients riding the storm out tugged on her heavy heart. A rippling blast caused her to flex. Accelerated breaths escaped her open mouth. *I am a doctor,* she rationalized. *I need to stay strong. Beneath the cloak of my title and education, I can endure.* Picturing Reno on the balcony of the Colombo Hilton, she whispered, "Life is sometimes nothing more than a bad joke." *And tonight we sit like herrings in a barrel.* She chuckled.

Beside her, Doctor Ondaatje nervously rocked. He started to weep.

"Doctor," she whispered, "we'll be fine. The storm will pass."

Sniffling, he replied, "Sandra, it's not the shelling." Taking a composing breath, he clarified, "I was thinking of my daughters."

In the darkness, she found his arm. Giving it a gentle squeeze, she reasoned, "Your family is in Colombo; they are safe, Tom."

"A man carried his little girl to the clinic this morning," he informed her. "She looked just like my youngest. The desperate father handed me his child with a glimmer of hope." Patting Sandra's tender grasp, he continued, "I knew she was dead. I don't know why, but I accepted the lifeless innocent bundle.

I checked for breathing and a heartbeat. I suppose I didn't want the father to feel his hospital journey was in vain. God only knows how long or how far he had trekked." His soft voice crackled. "He thanked me with a soft smile and tear-filled eyes. Cradling his daughter's body, he left."

"One," Sandra mumbled. "One life," she clarified. "If we just save one life, our mission is a success."

"Our mission," he grumbled. "I'm Singhalese, a Buddhist, a civil servant. The government is paying my salary, funding my mission." He paused. In the distance, incoming rounds exploded. "Listen, Sandra, to the sound of my hostile government. My mission is a ruse. It's good propaganda. Send in doctors to tend to the displaced and then apologize for bombing the shit out of them."

Out of the darkness, the tall, lanky British aid worker Dane chimed in, "Do you think this strike was intentional?"

"Let's just say I'm suspicious," Doctor Ondaatje replied. "A hospital on the front lines is established. The government provides the staff with flak jackets, helmets, and a reinforced bunker. Tamil casualties are drawn in for care. And then..." he paused. Man-made thunder answered.

"The Tiger tactics are just as devious," Dane commented. "We've all seen the suspicious activity at the farmhouse down the road. I suspect the Tigers use it as a safe haven. From there, they spy on the government troop movements." Clearing a dry throat, he concluded, "The government uses us as bait, the Tigers as human shields."

"Well, the government's assault has just trumped the Tiger's strategy," Sandy answered.

Chapter 25

———❦———

Awell-defined path snaked through the dense forest. Random rays of sunlight penetrated the thick overhead growth. A stream of seasonal rainwater cascaded across the narrow trail. In rubber sandals, Chola did not break stride. His callused feet plodded through the shallow brook. Water splashed. Reno paused at the water's edge. Glancing down at his sweltering combat boots, he wished he could dip his barking dogs in cool water. Behind Reno, the surfer accelerated. Longboard easily leaped over the wet obstacle.

"Looks like I'm bringing up the rear," Reno mumbled, strutting through the water. "Hey, Longboard!" he called out.

The surfer slowed down.

"Do you think this ruse will work?" he questioned.

"I don't see why not. If we encounter government troops, we are lost tourists and the kid is a tout." The surfer assured him, "The unarmed Chola looks the part of a friendly con man and speaks very good English."

"I wouldn't mind running into the government forces," Reno confessed. "We could bribe a ride back to Colombo."

"How much do we have left in petty cash?" Longboard questioned.

"Who is this *we* you are always referring to?" Reno grumbled, shaking his head. Puffing out his chest, he disclosed, "I have about a hundred bucks in my decoy wallet and two grand in a money belt."

"When this kid gets us to civilization," Longboard said, motioning up the trail at their guide, "we should throw him a nice tip."

"We?" Reno questioned. "What you meant to say was: *Reno, you should tip the kid with your money.*"

"That'll work." Longboard chuckled.

The partisan and Americans trekked in silence. The sun rose high overhead. The air thickened. Chola set a fast pace. The gap between the hikers widened. Reno's back stiffened. He readjusted the duffel bag strap. Passing through a cloud of gnats, he snorted. Sweat rolled down his face. Realizing he was about to become a wealthy man, he grinned. S.A.'s handshake affirmed the weapons transaction. It had been a successful business trip. *We hitch a ride back to Colombo,* he envisioned, *fly back to the home office, and make the exchange. Once the funds hit my account, my first order of Bangkok business is liquidating that obnoxious Triad debt.*

"What do you think?" questioned Longboard.

Reno focused. His partner stood hydrating from a plastic bottle of mineral water. Chola squatted on the moist ground. The trail turned to soupy mud before fading into a murky lagoon. Dense encroaching foliage skirted the water's edge. Hot afternoon sunlight reflected off the glossy surface. Insects of all sizes fluttered above the foul brown liquid. Immersed across the stagnant pond rested the skeletal remains of a detonated wood bridge.

"Looks like we are getting wet," Reno answered, hoisting an army-green duffel bag over his head. "It doesn't look too deep."

From his crouched position, Chola held out a blocking arm. His free hand pointed into the waterlogged intruding growth. "Crocodile," he cautioned.

"Did you say *crocodile?*" Reno questioned, squinting into the bright water.

"There along that tree limb," Chola clarified.

"I can't see shit," Reno declared, blinking. Glancing at the surfer, he asked, "Do you see it?"

Longboard nodded. From the small of his back, he retrieved a sweat-glistening pimp pistol. Tossing a canvas bag over a shoulder, he stepped into the sloshing mud. "Try not to splash," he whispered. Focused on the four-foot reptile, he waded into the wet stench. Water lapped at his chest. He held the pistol high. Mosquitoes nibbled at his chiseled face. Reno followed the surfer into the pond. In bare feet, Chola joined the Americans. Perched atop the bridge debris, a long-legged, long-necked white bird observed the trio's crossing. In a fluid motion, the four-foot croc slid into his liquid hunting ground. Longboard froze. A swishing tail propelled the streamlined predator. Rugged eyes and flared nostrils advanced. The surfer extended his arm.

"Are you going to shoot?" Reno questioned.

"Patience," Longboard whispered. At point-blank range, the pistol popped. The long-legged heron took flight. Oozing blood, the crocodile's head sank. A crimson slick stained the murky surface. "You can splash now," Longboard declared, accelerating to the shoreline. Behind the trio's sloshing exit, the soft underbelly of a reptile carcass bobbed.

Reno tossed his duffel bag on high ground. On hands and knees, he crawled over the steep, muddy embankment. Covered in filth, he stood. Turning, he offered a soiled hand to the exiting Chola. After pulling the guide out of the pond, he assisted his silent partner. In the shade of a large tree, they sat on the reestablished trail. Shaking his hands, Reno sent mud splatter flying. "Nothing like a dip in a septic tank to enhance our back-road experience," he grumbled.

Longboard snickered.

Grinning, Chola offered, "There may be a rainwater tank we can wash up in before making camp."

"Camp?" Reno questioned.

Chola used the palm of his hand to measure the sun and horizon. "We won't make it to the refugee hospital by nightfall," he informed them.

A rogue cloud passed in front of a quarter moon. Stars sparked. A tiny campfire crackled. A soft glow glimmered across the encircling jungle. A peacock scream interrupted the whispering forest. In damp, mud-encrusted clothes, two American arms merchants and their rebel guide dined on packets of Maliban biscuits. Reno washed down the dry cookie with warm mineral water.

"I'll stand watch tonight," Chola offered.

The surfer and Reno glanced at each other and grinned. Reno spoke. "We appreciate that, kid. But we'll take our turn. This is not our first rodeo."

"Rodeo?" Chola questioned. "A cowboy competition?"

Reno laughed. "Excuse my slang. Longboard and I have spent more than a few long nights in the shit...I mean jungle."

"I have a hard time comprehending American slang," Chola volunteered. Tossing a handful of twigs on the dwindling fire, he added, "Some of your expressions make no sense."

"I wouldn't worry about that," Reno replied. "Most of the original references are forgotten over time." Leaning back from the popping fire, he continued. "Not my first rodeo is a clever way of saying I have experience."

"I was reading *The Adventures of Huckleberry Finn* when the riots in Colombo started," Chola interjected. "I enjoyed the vernacular English style."

"Vernacular?" Reno questioned.

"The Mark Twain classic was written in the dialect of the day," Longboard chimed in.

"You've read Huckleberry Finn?" the young partisan exclaimed.

"I did in high school," the surfer replied. "It was a good book."

"Do you remember how it ends?" Chola probed.

Spitting into the fire, the former assassin teased, "I reck'n."

Supported by his duffel bag, Reno slumped down. After the day's long trek, fatigued muscles groaned. An empty stomach grumbled. Gazing over playful flames, he grinned. The dark surfer narrated his recollection of the fictional tale of people and places along the Mississippi River. The Tamil Tiger hung on every word. *There is nothing like a well-told yarn to help us escape reality,* Reno thought. Closing his eyes, he drifted into the comfort of deep slumber.

Chapter 26

———∽∾∾∽———

Dark clouds drifted above. The aroma of inevitable rain floated in heavy air. Searching for comfort, Reno adjusted the canvas strap taxing his tender shoulder. On stiff legs, he limped forward. In front of him, Longboard and Chola ambled on the narrow path. The surfer and partisan discussed classic literature. This morning's topic for the fireside book club was the Melville novella *Billy Budd*.

I read that in Nam, Reno realized. *It was the thinnest paperback in a bin of tattered reading material offered at a remote firebase. I discovered like Billy Budd, I was a foundling not an orphan. An orphan's parents are dead. A foundling is an abandoned child. I liked discovering the nuance of my outcast label,* he recalled. "God save the captain!" he hollered into the novella discussion.

Over his shoulder, Longboard squinted at the eavesdropping intrusion. "The line is '*God bless Captain Vere,*'" he corrected.

"I was paraphrasing," Reno grumbled to the back of his apparently well-read partner's head. Shrugging off his lack of literary knowledge, he rubbed a sensitive cheek. A fresh mosquito bite awoke. *Don't scratch it,* he counseled. *Fuck it,* responded clawing fingernails. Vigorously, he tore into the taunting blemish. After igniting the itch-and-scratch cycle, he accelerated his pace. The surrounding tangled thicket of green thinned. A coconut palm grove swayed under a warm breeze. The jungle path intersected with an inland road. Fresh tire tracks signified the hope of transport. "How much further, Huck?" Reno called out to Chola.

The partisan chuckled. Before he could respond, the distant staccato whine of a small engine distracted the trio. A cloud of approaching dust accompanied the high-pitched crackle. Longboard grasped the weapon holstered in his waistband. Reno dropped his duffel bag. Chola stood defiantly. An antique motorcycle billowing white smoke led the charging dust. A local in a cinched-up sarong sat astride the rusty motorbike. A shirtless boy in shorts clung to the man's back. Chola held up a halting palm. The motorcycle skidded to an abrupt termination. Swirling dust engulfed the gathering. Straddling the vibrating machine, the apprehensive rider nodded at Chola. The young, wide-eyed boy focused on the white men.

"That's a BSA 250," Longboard exclaimed, stowing the pistol. Winking at the father, he squatted down to examine the dated machine. Bailing wire secured a muffler. Corrugated tin replaced the original mud flaps. Thick grease stained the stuttering single-cylinder engine. Stepping back, Longboard admired the vehicle. "Looks like a 1960 or '61 model," he shouted over the idling engine. "Ask him if he is interested in selling it," he hollered at Chola.

The partisan translated. The nervous rider silenced the machine. Father and son climbed off the tattered twin seat. Longboard hopped aboard. A kick start brought the engine to life. Revving the motor, he took a short, ten-yard spin. He returned with a wide grin. "What's his price?" the surfer inquired.

"I explained the urgency of your Tamil business," Chola responded. "He is willing to donate the motorbike to the cause."

Reno whipped off his money belt. Unzipping the concealed compartment, he pulled out five crisp folded one-hundred-dollar bills. Fanning the American greenbacks, he smiled at the beaming father. "Tell our friend..." He paused to rephrase. "Tell *machan* this is to show our appreciation for his sacrifice."

Chola translated. The seller accepted the gratuity with a twitching hand. He stared at the windfall, and an enthusiastic gasp escaped his open mouth.

The journey resumed with the partisan sandwiched between the Americans on the vintage motorcycle. Canvas luggage lay strapped across the handlebars. This was not Longboard's first motocross rodeo. The agile surfer expertly steered the whining machine down the twisting, turning rural road. Flanking palm trees flew by. A cooling headwind whipped his bleached locks. A rocky wash dissected the trail. Standing on the bike's pegs, he navigated through the jostling stone-ridden obstacle course.

Straddling the rough seat, Reno grunted. "Can you try not to hit every hole in this basin? Huck and I were planning on having children one day."

Chola laughed.

Revving the small engine, Longboard climbed out of the gully. A charred odor lingered. Headless palm trees inhabited a blackened landscape. Coughing white smoke, the touring motorbike sputtered past the burned remains of a farmhouse. Atop the charcoal wood, a flock of greynecked crows perched. The scooter popped. The birds took flight. Fluttering black wingspans disappeared into the gray sky. Soot blanketed an adjacent irrigation tank. A bloated corpse floated in the dark, soupy liquid. The motorcycle accelerated.

A drop of rain struck the surfer's forehead. Large droplets began to stain the scorched earth. The burnt stench intensified. A glowing vein of lightning lit up the gloomy sky. A blast of thunder growled. As the rumbling crash faded, the heavens released a torrential downpour.

Reno tilted his head back. He closed his eyes and opened his mouth. His parched tongue caught random drops of moisture. *A hot shower and a cold beer,* he imagined. *Another coupling with Sandy needs to be added to the wish list,* he concluded. A jolting bounce interrupted the fantasy. The green landscape had returned. A blue flapping tarp in the dense brush grabbed his attention. Wiping his soaked face with a moist palm, he got a blurred visual of the displaced. Under a frail plastic liberty-blue lean-to, a Tamil family gawked at the crowded motorcycle's passing. A small naked boy waved. Chola returned the greeting. Less conspicuous tents appeared across the hillside. Hastily constructed shelters of mangled corrugated tin and salvaged wood rounded out the refugee hamlet.

"Who are these people?" Reno questioned.

Leaning back, Chola answered, "These are my people. They were driven out of their homes, farms, and businesses by the government. I fight for our right to exist." He patted the American's grasping hand. "Thanks to your weapons contribution, we will be victorious."

Contribution, Reno pondered. *I know nothing of your cause. Profit is my motivation, earning a wad of fuck-you money, the objective.* A high body count was the objective in the Vietnam conflict. Victory was not represented by American flags displayed on a map of Europe or island hopping in the Pacific. Death was the goal. "I envy you," he muttered. "You are committed to a noble cause."

"Longboard said you are both soldiers. What did you fight for?"

Reno grinned. "I fought for what every trench soldier has always fought for," he answered, "the brother beside me in the trench."

The cycle decelerated. The grade steepened. Murky water cascaded down the muddy path. In search of traction, the back tire whipped up muck. Pebbles ricocheted off the homemade mud flap. Longboard raised his hands and planted his feet. "We are not going to make it up this hill," he conceded.

Reno hopped off the back. He grabbed his tender crotch with a massaging hand. "I don't mind walking," he announced. "My balls will appreciate the reprieve."

Chola dismounted the idling overburdened workhorse. He shook his drenched head and gazed up at the falling rain.

Longboard waddled the rutted cycle forward. He wiped his wet face. Focused forward, he visualized the ascent. Vigorously, he shook his hands. After flexing his fingers, he grasped the handlebar. He blinked at the distracting rain, and a wicked grin appeared. "I'll meet you at the summit," he mumbled. The cycle lunged forward. Muddy backwash sprayed Chola and Reno.

Reno examined the speckled mud decorating his drenched clothes. "I think he did that on purpose." He chuckled.

Chola smiled and took a step.

The American grabbed the departing partisan. "You don't want to miss the show," Reno informed him, pointing at the departing motorbike.

Slipping and sliding, the vintage bike accelerated. Puddles exploded. At full throttle, Longboard attacked the hill. Easily flying up the mount, the surfer caught big air before sailing over the crest.

Patting the Tiger on the back, Reno and his tenderized groin limped forward. "Let's hope the motorbike survived the landing."

Chola's bony bare feet clawed up the slick incline. Drifting off the pace, Reno's mud-caked boots gingerly shuffled uphill. The agile partisan disappeared over the summit. *I'm trekking like a Chinese concubine.* The American snickered. Leaning into the driving rain, he accelerated. His mud-fat boots failed. The muck kissed him hard. Face-planted in the mire, he laughed. *This is going to be one of those days,* he concluded. Standing up, he tilted his head back and stretched out his arms. The cleansing shower assaulted his muddy features. After shaking his drenched long blond locks, he continued the climb. Sucking hard on moist air, he strutted onto the hilltop. Breathing heavily, he scanned the horizon. In the valley basin, a strip of black asphalt meandered. The vehicles utilizing the highway appeared as specs. *A hot shower, warm food, and a cold beer are getting closer.* He grinned.

Under the protective canopy of a large tree, Chola and Longboard sat beside the motorbike. Approaching, Reno asked, "How's the bike?"

The surfer looked at the motorcycle and nodded. "This is a fine machine," he declared. "Birmingham Small Arms built a hell of a bike."

"Birmingham Small Arms?" Reno squinted.

"What did you think BSA stands for?" the surfer answered. Winking, he added, "They were arms dealers like us."

"I saw the highway," Reno informed him. "My balls are excited about a smooth ride."

"We are low on fuel." The surfer shrugged.

Reno snorted. "It's going to be one of those days."

Chapter 27

—⚬⚬⚬—

It was dusk. A dark sky threatened. A monsoon wind blew in from a rough sea. Large waves pounded the driftwood, and plastic debris blanketed the shore. The dapper Chinese gangster Chin, in a starched cotton dress shirt, stood on the raised porch of Longboard's dark residence. He reeked of cologne. His perfectly parted hair sparkled. Four street punks in jeans and cheap sandals stood watch. Everybody was packing. In addition to sidearms, the intruding cadre had a five-gallon can of gasoline. Wisps of salty air, fragrant toilette water, and petrol fumes swirled around the deck. Nobody was home.

A doorknob resisted Chin's grip. Stepping back, he twitched his shiny noggin at the secured barrier. An enthusiastic young outlaw threw his bony shoulder at the wood door. The entrance burst open. The skinny battering ram flew into the surfer's sanctuary. Out of control, he landed hard on a planked floor littered with books. Twilight flowed through the doorframe. Cheap rattan furniture appeared. A reel-to-reel tape deck sat idle. Hardback and paperback texts exceeded the occupancy limit of bookshelves.

Chin snorted at the seated subordinate rubbing a tender arm. *The surfer, that smart-ass Reno, and two hundred thousand dollars have disappeared under my watch,* he realized. *Maybe there is a clue about their whereabouts,* he hoped, stepping onto the literature-covered floor. A misstep on a hardback text caused him to stumble.

"Fuck," he growled, kicking the book across the room. *There are no clues here,* he concluded, examining the dimly lit hovel. *Burning it down may flush out those defaulting Johnnys,* he rationalized.

A lackey poked his head through the fractured doorframe. "Sir?" he nudged.

"What?" Chin snapped.

"A one-legged Johnny hopped up the stairs next door," he informed him.

A sadistic grin spread across Chin's youthful good looks. "Let's go see what the cripple can tell us." Checking his weapon, he confidently strutted onto the deck. Squinting in the fading light, he identified the large seated silhouette on the adjacent porch.

The nefarious cadre plodded across pathetic patches of grass rooted in sandy soil. *There is an advantage in numbers,* Chin thought, following behind his men. *Taking the cripple hostage will definitely induce the surfer to show his face.*

"You zipperheads looking for Reno?" the porch shadow questioned.

The intruders stopped dead in their tracks. Confused teens looked at Chin, seeking guidance.

It wasn't what he said but the defiant tone, Chin realized. He swallowed and fired back, "What did you say, cripple?"

The seated American barked out insults.

"Who is this arrogant *bak gwei* (white ghost)?" Chin muttered for the benefit of his troops. "Does he not comprehend his predicament?" Frowning, he hollered back, "Reno and the surfer owe us money. Where are those leeches?"

The snickering American answered, "My friends are out fucking your mothers."

The insult slapped Chin hard. He clenched his fist. His nostrils flared. "Kill the gimp," burst out of his rage.

"Gimp?" the American growled, rising on his one leg. Flexing, he identified himself as an Airborne Ranger and spat about the Chinese he had terminated.

Gunfire sparked. *My god, he's armed,* Chin realized. Beside him, a head exploded. Blood splatter doused his face and pressed linen shirt. Another shot rang out. Another henchman fell. Bullets buzzed in the dark. A decorative glass ball on the porch shattered. Pistols flashed. A street punk cried out. Chin stepped behind a human shield and returned fire. The one-legged silhouette toppled. Chin wiped his plasma-sprayed features with a backhand. A corpse missing the top of his head lay at his feet. On the ground, a shadow writhed in agony. Beside the squirming silhouette, a gut-shot teen whimpered.

I got to fix this, Chin realized. *I shouldn't have killed the American. No matter how obnoxious he was. I came to send a message but not this severe.* Chin scowled at the groaning boy clutching a bloody belly. "Shut him up," he mumbled to the healthy teen providing comfort. *Let me think. The authorities can be manipulated.* "What's your name?" he asked the young hoodlum playing medic.

"Tommy," the youth replied.

"Tommy, fetch the tape deck from the surfer's shack."

The squatting youth squinted up at the request. His hands were covered in blood. "Sir, we need to get these men to a doctor."

"Yes, of course, in due time," Chin responded compassionately. "Now get me that fucking tape deck!"

Tommy took off in a sprint. Chin jogged up into Reno's porch. His patent-leather shoe poked at the American carcass. Squatting down, he turned over the body. A satisfied grin resided across the dead cripple's face. "Who are you?" Chin mumbled. "Airborne Ranger." He chuckled. *Vietnamese peasants defeated you,* Chin surmised. *You were nothing more than a broken soldier who drank, smoked dope, and fornicated with whores to pass the time.* Chin retrieved his handkerchief. Shaking open the hanky, he picked up the American's weapon with a blanketed hand. Descending the shaky stairway, he strutted toward his fallen troops.

Toting the large tape deck on a skinny shoulder, Tommy raced across the sandy lawn.

Looking down, Chin examined his wounded men. There was too much blood to make a visual prognosis. Huffing and puffing, Tommy stood attentively.

"Tommy, do you know these boys?" Chin questioned.

"Decha is my brother," Tommy answered, pointing to the moaning, squirming shadow. "Seni is a friend," he added, identifying the gut-shot victim.

"Give the tape deck to Seni," Chin coaxed.

Tommy looked confused. Cautiously, he placed the heavy reel-to-reel on his whimpering friend's lap.

Chin lifted the American's gun. Tommy gasped. A shot rang out. A bullet to the head silenced Seni's whining. *Two youths for one cripple seems fair,* Chin reasoned. "Now let's get your brother to a doctor," he said.

Chapter 28

⸺⚬⚬⚬⸺

Morning rays peeked over the windowsill. Reno blinked at the intruding sunlight. He rolled onto his back. The army cot groaned. Lightheaded, he attempted to drift back toward the comfort of sleep. The warm, creeping illumination persisted. Opening his eyes, he conceded. Staring at the cracked plaster ceiling, he yawned as a gecko scurried across the rough surface. With his head implanted in a balmy pillow, he kicked off the clammy bedding. Sweat glistened on his naked torso. Slowly, he sat up on the collapsible bed and planted his bare feet on the dusty hard floor. The room was bright. The aroma of mosquito repelling incense lingered in the humid air. In the center of the stained concrete floor lay the spiral ash of an expired mosquito coil. Against the wall sat Chola and Longboard's vacated army cots. *They let me sleep in,* he realized. Muffled conversations flowed through the open doorframe. *We hitch a ride to Colombo today, enjoy the layover before the next flight out of this sweat box, and then finalize the arms deal,* he calculated. Standing, he stretched. *First item on my agenda is taking a piss.* He chuckled. After wrapping a sarong around his naked waist, he slid his large bare feet into a small pair of rubber sandals. In the uncomfortable footwear, he shuffled out the door. Grabbing his crotch, he yawned. The Scots called going sans underwear in a kilt *regimental;* in Nam, *going commando* described that practice. *Regardless of the terminology,* Reno thought, *my boys feel uncomfortable dangling under a skirt.*

The Tiger safe house buzzed. Wobbling on sore joints, Reno meandered into the front room. A rotating rusty industrial ceiling fan emitted a pulsing squeal. A Hindu family shrine in the corner perfumed the air with the fragrance of fresh flowers, fruit, and incense. Above the shrine's smoldering joss sticks hung the ornate, colorful picture of a potbellied, elephant-headed deity. Three uniformed schoolboys sitting on a frayed throw rug cleaned an assortment of vintage small arms. The industrious children greeted the American with beaming grins.

"Good mornin', boys," Reno exclaimed. "Do you know where I can get a hot cup of joe?"

The children responded with tilted heads and questioning squints.

"Coffee," Reno clarified, miming a sip from an imaginary cup.

"Tea?" inquired the tallest of the three.

The American laughed. "Sure." He snickered. "Considering I'm in the midst of a civil war, I'll settle for coffee's homely sister."

"Milk?" the boy offered.

"No." Reno yawned. "I'll take it black."

After placing the order, Reno continued on the water closet quest. Exiting the residence, he gazed into the blue sky. *It's going to be a beautiful day,* he concluded. Healthy green grass skirted a well-tread path. Plodding along the walkway, he snorted at a foul stench. An angled tin roof capped a concrete outhouse. Holding his breath, he entered the sweltering stone box. Stained red tiles surrounded a porcelain squat toilet. Lifting his skirt, he took an overdue urination.

"Tea," the lanky boy announced.

Glancing over his shoulder, Reno dropped his skirt. The tall, lanky boy stood attentive with a misting cup. "Thanks, String Bean," Reno said, taking the ceramic saucer of liquid caffeine. The shy boy nodded before racing back down the meandering path. *Children of war,* Reno reflected. *String Bean should be playing soccer, cricket, or some other British physical activity that I don't understand.* Tugging on the slipping sarong, he took a sip of Ceylon tea. *Coffee's homely sister isn't that bad,* he realized, plodding down the muggy trail. Rounding the corner of the single-story residence, he felt a soft breeze and blanketing shade greet him. The wind rustled through the top of a large tree. Motorcycle parts littered a gravel driveway. Chola stood attentively over the squatting surfer. Longboard's grease-covered hands probed the bowels of the vintage BSA motorcycle. Two gray-haired Tamils in hard wooden chairs observed the American mechanic. The stench of petrol filled the air.

"What are you doing?" Reno questioned.

Longboard shot an annoyed glance at the intrusion. "Nice of you to join us," he muttered, pointing at a screwdriver. Chola obliged the request and retrieved the tool. Wrestling with a tight screw, he answered, "I'm tuning up the company vehicle."

"The plan was to hire a car," Reno responded. "An air-conditioned car."

"This won't take long," the surfer informed him. "I promised Chola a ride to the hospital to check on a friend. Then you and I can hit the open road. The fresh air will do us good."

Chapter 29

———✦———

A blistering sun illuminated the rich blue sky. Punishing rays reflected off the heavy traffic flowing in both directions on a narrow pockmarked asphalt roadway. A government army convoy rolled north. Massive mud tires of dark-green troop transports kicked up dust. Tractor trailers hauling heavy artillery shook the fragile blacktop. Military jeeps accented the war motorcade. Moving in the opposite direction of the juggernaut, a sluggish procession of refugees plodded south. The displaced fled on foot, crammed into compact cars, and standing shoulder to shoulder in the open cargo beds of trucks. Overburdened lorries hauled the salvaged remains of uprooted homes. A vintage BSA motorcycle saddled with three riders leaped out of the migrating caravan. Teasing oncoming military traffic, the recently tuned motorbike purred.

Longboard raced the single-cylinder engine. A strong headwind blasted the surfer, Chola, and Reno. The parade of the less fortunate became a blur, the intercepting front grill of a barreling troop transport a reality. *Time to pullover,* Reno thought. *Now,* he emphasized. Chola closed his eyes. A horn blasted. The surfer grinned. The army truck growled. Blowing a kiss, Longboard merged back into the lazy lane. To the aroma of burnt rubber, the bike's locking tires squealed.

"Cutting it close, partner!" Reno yelled as the motorcycle sputtered forward.

"Always have!" Longboard shouted over his shoulder. "The sweetest meat is closest to the bone."

"The next crossroad leads to the hospital," Chola informed him. "Turn right."

The motorbike crept past a tricycle tractor pulling a cartful of misplaced souls. The single driver sat high on a bouncing metal seat. In the trailer, his human cargo stood in silence with disconnected, emotionless expressions. *The faces of war,* Reno thought. Whether yellow or brown, the mien of fleeing civilians is consistent. *It's in their eyes,* he concluded. *Their gaze reflects the loss of loved ones, a way of life, and an uncertain future.*

Spitting out white smoke, the motorbike exited the sad south-bound parade. Tall trees flanked the rural dirt roadway. Sunlight flickered in the green canopy. Reno leaned back, relishing the comforting shade. Chola tapped the surfer's shoulder and pointed at a curved driveway. Atop the inclined private road, a chain-link fence surrounded a single-story schoolhouse. A red terracotta tiled roof capped the yellow concrete structure. Splintered wood peeked out of a terminated classroom. Roof tiles and chunks of concrete sprouting rebar littered the campus. On the skirting sidewalk, the injured sat and reclined, awaiting care. Caucasian aid workers in pale-blue helmets and flak jackets walked among the wounded. The motorcycle stuttered past two locals digging a trench. Beside the growing mound of earth, three shrouded corpses awaited interment.

Longboard silenced the company vehicle. The motorbike coasted to a quiet termination. Curious squints investigated the arrival.

Reno hopped off. Planting his hands on the small of his back, he stretched. Scanning the carnage, he sighed. "Gives you pause," he said. "Makes me question our business plan. There's got to be a better way to make a living than feeding the fire of war."

"What are you saying?" Chola questioned. "Your services are giving my people a chance to fight for their survival. Yours is a noble profession."

Patting the Tiger on the back, Reno mumbled, "I appreciate that, Huck. Now let's go see how your friend is doing." Taking the lead, he added, "Let me handle this, Chola. Being white has its advantages."

"I'll stay with the bike," the surfer volunteered.

The American approached a huddle of blue-helmeted UN volunteers. "Excuse me, padres," he announced. The thin, effeminate aid worker in front of him turned. Reno grinned and blurted out. "Hello, sweetheart."

A stunned Sandy beamed. Her delight quickly faded. She grabbed his upper arm. Securing the grip, she scolded, "Mister James, I prefer you address me as Doctor DeWitt."

"What?" he questioned. Looking into her pleading blue eyes, he understood. "No disrespect intended, Doctor," he conceded. *She needs the protective shroud of the title,* he realized. *Sandy doesn't make life-and-death decisions. Doctor DeWitt does.*

"Good afternoon, Doctor," Chola injected.

"Chola," Sandy exclaimed. "I knew our paths would cross again. As promised, I have a Mark Twain paperback for you."

"That's very kind of you," the partisan delightfully replied.

"You two know each other?" a puzzled Reno questioned.

"We are old friends," Sandy informed him, winking at the Tiger.

Chola patted Reno on the back. "Let me handle this," he whispered. "Being Tamil has its advantages."

Reno laughed. "Well played, my friend. Well played."

"Sandra," interrupted a tall, lanky Brit. "Let me check on your patients while you catch up with your friends."

"Thank you, Dane," Sandy replied with a slight bow as the helmeted volunteer cadre dispersed.

Reno scanned the sultry Sandy. A chestnut-blond ponytail flowed out of her protective headgear. The helmet's chin strap added emphasis to her symmetric features. The sleeveless flak jacket exposed taut, defined arms. *The Dutch beauty is cut,* Reno realized. *Hell she would look good in anything.*

After craning her neck behind her, she whispered, "Be careful, Chola. The government troops have been rounding up young Tamil males for questioning. They consider every able-bodied youth LTTE."

Responding to the warning, Chola nodded his gratitude. "How is Danak recovering?" he asked.

"Danak?" She squinted. Raising enlightened brows, she answered, "Your gunshot friend was released prematurely a couple of days ago. We feared he would be scooped up in the government net."

"Thank you, Doctor," the partisan replied.

"Danak is young, strong," she interjected. "If he made it to a Tiger sanctuary, he will recover."

Chola smiled softly. Placing a hand on the American's shoulder, he said, "I guess this is good-bye, my friend."

Reno patted the young warrior's grasp. "Do you need a lift back to the..." He paused and shot a quick side glance at Sandy and whispered, "The safe house."

"No, thank you, Mister James," answered the confident Tiger. "I have my own resources."

"Let me get your book," said a departing Sandy.

The arms dealer and the partisan strolled back toward Longboard and the company vehicle. "My people are counting on you," Chola muttered.

"The munitions will soon be in transit," Reno assured him.

With crossed arms, Longboard leaned against the planted motorcycle. "How's your friend?" he inquired.

"He was released a couple of days ago," Chola answered.

The three men turned. Sandy, with book in hand, approached. Her large blue helmet bobbed. Sunlight sparked off the glossy paperback. Extending her arm, she presented the gift. "Enjoy," she declared, smiling.

Studying the prize, Chola grinned. Glancing at the surfer, he teased, "I'm about to find out how accurate your summation was."

Longboard examined the book's cover. He spat. Wiping moist lips with the back of his hand, he said with an exaggerated drawl, "I reck'n."

"Chola's abandoning us," Reno informed.

The fireside book club embraced. "Good luck, amigo," Longboard mumbled.

Chola patted the surfer's back.

In the shade of rustling treetops, a Dutch doctor, an arms dealer, and a former assassin waved farewell. Chola nodded. In his rubber sandals, baggy trousers, and plaid shirt, he ambled down the dirt driveway. His lowered gaze focused on the Mark Twain classic.

"He's a good kid," Reno mumbled.

Chapter 30

———— ⚬⚬⚬ ————

Reno grabbed a chilled amber bottle. Inhaling, he prolonged the anticipation. Tilting his head back, he placed the cool glass opening on dry lips. Carbonated refreshment flowed over his tongue and down a parched gullet. "Ah!" He sighed, wiping his satisfied mouth. Admiring the Lion Beer label featuring the regal beast, he whispered, "I missed ya." Looking across the planked wood tabletop at his partner, he commented, "After five days with the teetotaling Tigers, a cold beer was long overdue."

The tavern was quiet. Nothing drives away customers faster than a civil war. Corrugated tin walls elevated a foot off the ground defined the saloon's perimeter. A soft breeze flowed through the gap and across the earthen floor. A skinny rooster with a shredded black-feathered plume roamed beneath empty tables. In search of an insect meal, the frail bird confidently strutted. Behind a heavy board, resting on rusting oil drums, stood Nagesh, the proprietor. The pudgy local reeked of a fetid aroma fueled by a spicy diet. His dark skin glistened. His oily hair sparkled. Today, he could not suppress his crooked-toothed grin. Today, his humble establishment was graced with white patrons.

In a chipped and splintering Windsor chair, Longboard leaned back. He raised a bar glass. Murky colorless liquor swirled in the cheap tumbler. He took a cautious sip. "Whoa," he exclaimed, shooting a glance at the beaming Nagesh.

A cupped hand shielded the bartender's snickering reaction.

"Can I get a Coke to dilute this paint thinner?" the surfer inquired.

"Coca-Cola!" Nagesh shouted, slamming a bulbous bottle of caramel-colored sugar water on the counter.

Longboard nodded.

"What do you think about hitting the road in the morning?" Reno offered.

Longboard shrugged. "An expensive meter is ticking on our Triad loan," he reminded. "And you want to spend another day in this shithole in the hope that you'll catch a glimpse of that long-legged Dutch dish."

"Sandy is a doctor," Reno corrected.

Displaying jazz hands, Longboard announced, "Reno's girlfriend is a doctor."

Reno chuckled. "An extra day is not going to kill us."

The arms dealers slowly comprehended the true meaning of the cavalier comment. They both burst out laughing.

"What's so funny?" questioned the seductive helmeted silhouette framed by the doorway.

"Sandy," Reno blurted, jumping out of his chair.

Longboard, utilizing the chair's armrest, pried himself up. Bowing slightly, he mumbled, "Doctor DeWitt."

Sandy strutted to their table. She released the chin strap and plopped the blue metal bonnet in an empty chair. The sweat across her forehead twinkled. Matted bird's-nest hair clung to her moist scalp. "What are you antiquities dealers drinking?" she questioned, confiscating Longboard's moonshine tumbler. After an investigative sniff, she downed the potent toddy in a single gulp. "Nagesh!" she hollered at the poised bartender, "Another round."

Reno held the back of an open chair for her. She accepted the invitation and sat down. The gentlemen politely followed. "Someone's in a festive mood," Reno probed.

Sandy shook her head and confessed, "I've been pulling shrapnel out of women and children for the last ten hours. My shift has ended. The tide of casualties has finally receded." She paused as the attentive Nagesh served the next round, a complimentary bowl of cashews, and an ashtray. "Thank you," she muttered to the departing waiter. Holding a jigger of firewater, she concluded, "This moment is mine, and I plan to get good and drunk."

"I'll drink to that," Reno toasted.

Sandy pulled a cheroot from a breast pocket. Holding the scraggly cigar between delicate fingers, she solicited a light.

"If you plan on indulging in the local hooch," Longboard teased, "I wouldn't smoke."

The hovering Nagesh ignited the maduro stogie. Exhaling a relaxing plume, she replied, "Detonating this homebrew is the least of my concerns." Taking a long, satisfying drag, she gazed at her drinking companions through dissipating smoke and questioned, "Just what type of antiques do you Yanks traffic in?"

Reno, grinning at his partner, replied, "Dated weapons from the Cambodian conflict."

"It's funny," she commented. "That revelation never surfaced during our Colombo liaison."

"Nor did the fact that you were a medical doctor," Reno retorted.

Flicking white ash, she replied, "Fair enough, Mister James." Reaching for his idle hand, she conceded, "I'm glad we reconnected."

Longboard pushed back from the table. As he rose to exit, a helmeted aid worker burst through the open doorway. Winded, the tall, lanky Brit scanned the empty saloon and called out, "Sandra!"

"What is it, Dane?" she responded with concern.

Sucking air, he approached and answered, "It's your friend." Panting, the Brit plopped down in an empty chair, adding, "George informed me that the government net snared your friend."

"Who's George, and who is my friend?" she prodded, squinting.

"George is one of our grave diggers," he answered. "Your friend...the one you gave the book to."

"Chola," Longboard mumbled.

The Brit nodded as Reno handed him a cold beer. Dane took a healthy swig.

"What does this mean?" inquired Reno.

"There is an internment camp at the junction," Sandy sadly informed him. "Tales of rape and torture resonate from the barbwire compound, but very few survivors."

"Rape?" Longboard questioned.

"The guards wear the gold wedding necklaces of Tamil women—the *thalis* around their necks as trophies," Dane answered. "Broken shamed women seek suicide as an escape."

"Can't the relief agency do anything?" Reno questioned.

Dane and Sandra exchanged glances. "Our protests get filed in triplicate," Sandra conceded.

Reno looked at Longboard. The surfer understood. "Do you want to rescue Huck?" Reno questioned.

"Abso-fucking-lutely." The former assassin grinned.

"What do you think you Yanks can do?" questioned the Brit.

"Have some faith, Limey," Reno stated. "Armed with white privilege and a thousand American greenbacks, we'll negotiate freedom."

Chapter 31

———⁂———

A candy-red three-wheeler sputtered down the rural road. Its sunbaked black vinyl canopy fluttered. A rusty exhaust pipe spewed white smoke. Billowing dust stalked the tiny taxi, the settling particles tarnishing the flanking dense foliage. The apprehensive driver took deep, calming breaths. On the narrow passenger bench, Reno fidgeted. A tight white T-shirt emphasized his muscular torso. The baggy leggings of army surplus pants were tucked smartly into his combat boots. Preparing for the parlay, the American sorted currency. *It's not so much the cards,* he realized. *It's how you play them. This should cover the admission fee,* he concluded, securing two powder-blue rupee notes in a front pants pocket. For the opening offer, he selected five crisp one-hundred-dollar greenbacks.

The dirt road terminated at a barbwire-encrusted compound. Sharp spiked coils of metal twine capped a twelve-foot-high mesh fence. A single guard tower on wooden stilts vigilantly peered over the surrounding jungle. The nervous cabby silenced the tuk-tuk and slammed on the brakes.

Hopping out of the mototaxi, Reno squinted at the driver. "You wait for me?" he inquired.

The frowning driver defiantly shook his head.

Displaying a twenty-dollar bill, the American repeated, "Will you wait for me?"

The driver conceded, reaching for the inducement. Reno tore the bill in half. Handing a severed potion to the driver, he consoled, "This should not take long."

The sun hung high. The air was thick. Reno took a deep breath, patting the pimp pistol concealed in the leg pocket of his army fatigues. Reflecting on Longboard's commentary, he mumbled, "We need more firepower." Scanning the surrounding hillsides, he grinned. My partner's got my back, he realized. Flexing his shoulders, he strutted toward the main gate. A Tamil woman holding a baby clung to the razor-wire barricade. She stared with tear-swollen eyes into the compound. In the shade of a large tree, other distraught women and children huddled. *Poor souls,* Reno thought, *no doubt the mothers and wives of the incarcerated.* Squinting up into the sunlight bathing the guard tower, Reno detected his arrival being announced. A helmeted soldier in camo-fatigues exited a sentry box. The scowling youth brandishing an assault rifle glared at the approaching American.

"Good afternoon, chief," Reno said, flashing two thousand rupees. He poked the powder-blue bank notes through the wire gate. The surprised guard hastily pocketed the graft. "I need to speak to an officer," Reno informed.

"What for?" questioned the sentry.

"Thank God you speak English!" Reno exclaimed. Flashing a hundred-dollar bill, he winked. "I need a favor."

Displaying a flexed hand, the guard said, "Wait."

Reno watched the sentry return to his post. A warm breeze rippled across the grounds. There were two rows of barracks constructed out of blistered wood. Pitched white canvas tents fluttered in the wind. Uniformed troops mingled around neatly parked military trucks and a lone jeep.

A brute of an officer sporting a thick black straggly beard stepped out of the shanty barracks. Starched creases accented his army-green fatigues. Glossy black boots reflected sunlight. A military cap crowned the top of his fat head. Decorated shoulder epaulets advertised his rank. In a cupped palm, he held a ceramic bowl. Utilizing scooping fingers, he dug sticky rice out of the dish to feed his face. Escaping rice adorned his beard. The sentry intercepted the perturbed commandant. The guard pointed at the American. Reno waved. The officer handed the interrupted meal to his subordinate. He took a deep breath and sauntered to the gate. The sentry followed.

Looks like I'll be negotiating with Bluto, Reno surmised. "Good afternoon, sir!" he called out.

The thug scowled at the American through the thorn wire. His unbuttoned uniform exposed bristly chest hair and four gold Tamil wedding medallion necklaces. "What you want?" he growled.

Reno fanned out five crisp one-hundred-dollar bills. "I'm looking for my guide," Reno informed. "I fear he may be mistakenly detained. I'm willing to compensate you for any inconvenience."

Over his shoulder, the officer grunted. The sentry hastily opened the barrier. Reno entered the compound. The commandant's greasy paw immediately confiscated the inducing currency.

Stepping into the cage, Reno's skinned crawled. Feeling lightheaded, he rubbed the back of his neck. *I've felt this irritation before,* he reflected, visualizing the dead bodies of a Vietnamese farming community. Scanning the barren, dusty internment compound, he did not see any corpses, but he knew death walked the grounds.

"What is your guide's name?" questioned the commandant.

Reno shrugged. Using an extended finger, he traced an imaginary scar down the side of his face and said, "My friend has a distinctive disfigurement."

The officer and sentry exchanged smirks. "This way," the commandant said with a sweeping hand.

Reno accepted the invitation. He followed the burly officer and sentry past the barracks. Curious soldiers peered out of open windows. It was eerily quiet. Powder dust erupted with each step. A whimper resonated from one of the canvas tents. Reno strained to decipher the low female moan. It escalated to a woman pleading in Tamil. No translation was necessary. Grunts and groans of a rapist drowned out the victim's appeals for mercy. The strutting officer grinned while stroking a gold *thalis* dangling from his neck.

Behind the barracks, hundreds of detainees in a concertina wire pen stood in silence. In front of the wire corral were five occupied barbwire beds. Poles elevated the faced-down victims half a foot from the ground. The dry earth below the lashed bodies absorbed trickling blood. Reno recognized the back of Chola's tartan shirt. His stomach churned.

Bluto tapped the side of his head with a greasy finger and snickered. "Long scar, did you say?" He plopped a big black boot on Chola's back. The partisan emitted a shallow groan. Grabbing a handful of the boy's hair, the officer lifted up a pitted bloody face. "Is this your friend?" he politely inquired.

Reno slowly nodded.

"I'm tenderizing this Tamil for questioning," the commandant informed him. Motioning to the caged men, he offered, "Perhaps you would rather purchase a healthy specimen." Glancing in the direction of the rape tent, he added, "Possibly a woman?"

"You've made your point," Reno replied through gritted teeth.

"I think five hundred American is a little light for releasing a Tiger."

Reno tossed the officer his decoy wallet.

The commandant, thumbing through colorful local bank notes and two one-hundred-dollar bills, commented, "I'm wondering why I just don't keep your money and send you on your way?"

"Because I'm not leaving without the boy," Reno answered. "You'll have to kill me. And explaining the death of a white American cockroach requires paperwork." He shrugged. "Save yourself the writer's cramp."

The commandant chuckled. Pulling the US currency out of the billfold, he tossed it back. "I left you with cab fare. Is that acceptable?"

"Acceptable," Reno echoed, securing his wallet.

"Well then, get this filthy carcass out of here before I change my mind."

Reno stood defiantly. "Nah," he replied. "For seven hundred dollars, I expect assistance with my purchase to the front gate."

The commandant barked an order, and his subordinate unlashed Chola. The bloody partisan dangled between Reno and the sentry. Chola's bare feet dragged across the compound; his chest pulsed with shallow breaths. At the gate, Reno accepted the burden. The barrier clicked shut behind them. "Don't worry, Huck," Reno whispered. "I got you."

The tuk-tuk stuttered to life and raced to pick up its designated fare. Reno gently placed the boy in the baby cab. The American's hands and white T-shirt were speckled with blood. He gazed back into the compound. The commandant stood behind the sharp wire gate delightedly recounting the greenbacks. Reno scanned the surrounding hills. He tapped the center of his forehead and mumbled, "Keep the change, motherfucker."

The crack of a single shot rang out. Seven hundred US dollars floated to the dusty ground. The commandant teetered on wobbly legs. A crimson dot stained his forehead. Most of his brain and shattered bone fragments erupted out of the back of his skull.

Spitting white smoke, the candy-red tuk-tuk exited down the rural roadway. A second shot rang out. "What are you doing, Longboard?" Reno mumbled. One shot sounds an alarm, a second draws fire. Craning his neck, he looked up at the concealing hillside. Tracer rounds showered the dense foliage. The strafing-ignited projectiles were a prelude. Concentrated firepower followed. Mortar rounds pounded the rain forest. Splintered timber and earth erupted. The ground trembled. In the sputtering tuk-tuk, Reno lamented, "Longboard's not going to make it." Smoke and dust floated above the targeted scorched landscape. Reno's heart sank. *Why did I signal for Bluto's termination?* he questioned. I should have just walked away. The disconnected costly acquisition groaned. Clotted and dry blood stained the partisan's shredded features. "Don't die on me, Huck," Reno mumbled.

Chapter 32

In the corner of Nagesh's Tavern, a slouching Reno nursed a glass of the local white whisky. The American was the only patron. The other occupants consisted of the pudgy curry-scented Nagesh and a skinny roaming rooster. Hostile sunlight poured through the open doorframe. Fine dust danced in beams of light penetrating the corrugated tin roof. Reno elevated his bar glass into a piercing ray of sunshine. The murky liquor sparkled. *Nothing like liquid poison to dilute reality,* he thought. "To those we left behind?" he questioned. Shaking his head, he muttered, "Not yet." *The surfer is going to make it.* Staring at the illuminated doorframe, he visualized the agile Longboard. Miming a toast, he mumbled, "To friends, neighbors, and partners." A large gulp of potent hooch validated the sentiment.

A tall, shapely silhouette strutted through the blinding lighted entrance. Reno grinned. "Over here, Sandy." He playfully waved in the vacant saloon. "Nagesh, another round," he called out.

"I'll have a Coke," Sandy interjected, nodding at the barkeep.

Reno rose as the long-legged Dutch doctor sat down. "Not drinking?" he inquired.

"No," she answered, shaking her head. "And you need to pace yourself," she advised.

"Make that two Cokes," Reno ordered. Looking into her focused deep-blue eyes, he whispered, "What now?"

"The Tigers took out a helicopter yesterday," she answered. The attentive Nagesh placed two elegant curved bottles of Coke on the rough wood surface. White paper straws bobbed out of the containers' lipped openings. "The government is turning up the heat," she continued. "They ordered the closure of the hospital. All aid workers are required to leave."

"Shit," Reno mumbled. "Your presence has kept the Sri Lankan army in check. After what I saw in the internment camp yesterday, I'd hate to think what that unleashed dog would do without international witnesses." After extracting the paper straw, he took a refreshing swig of sweet carbonation. "Ah!" he sighed, placing the cold bottle on his temple. "So how is our literary friend doing?"

"Chola lost a lot of blood and required more stitches than a ragdoll," she answered. "But our bookish Tiger will survive to fight another day." Lifting the thick glass bottle of cola, she placed her supple lips on the straw. Seductively, she siphoned the fizzing brown liquid through the hollow paper tube. Taking a composing breath, she said, "I'm afraid there is no news on your missing partner."

"I know," he muttered.

"Perhaps he is with a rebel unit?" she offered. "The current rumor is that the Tigers ambushed the internment camp and assassinated the commander." Sucking on the straw, she raised an inquiring brow.

"Ambush!" He chuckled. "I was there, Sandy. No more than two shots rang out."

Focused, she leaned forward. Her impatiently folded arms solicited more information.

He obliged in a low growl. "I negotiated with that fat fucking commander. Intoxicated by his power over the weak, he strutted like a gamecock. I signaled my partner...my friend to terminate the bully. I enjoyed watching Longboard blow out the back of that piece of shit's skull." Breathing heavily, he leaned back. Catching his breath, he confessed in a softer tone. "I made a mistake...I took it personal."

Reaching out and touching his hand, she consoled him. "Making it personal is not a gaffe. It's what separates us from the bureaucrats who view life and death as a statistic." A wicked grin spread across her angelic face. "I would have liked to have seen that fat fucking commandant's farewell."

He gave her tender touching hand a passionate squeeze. "Thanks, sweetheart," he whispered.

"Do you need a lift to Colombo?" she offered.

He exhaled. "I don't know what to do about my missing partner."

"My impression of your partner…Longboard," she confessed, "is that the dark, mysterious surfer seemed very capable of dealing with life's obstacles."

Reno reluctantly concurred.

Chapter 33

———⚮———

A feather of smoke danced at the barrel end of a bolt-action rifle. "Twenty-three," Longboard whispered. He licked his lips, savoring the familiar taste of a kill. The barbwire compound below buzzed. A fat cadaver, sporting a burgundy halo, lay faceup in the dust. Discarded American currency fluttered around the corpse. *The gun sights are dead on,* he realized. *Drop the weapon and reconnect with my partner,* he pondered, spotting the exiting candy-red tuk-tuk. *It's a shame. I'm so close to an assassin's milestone. Do I risk detection to bag number twenty-five?* "Fuck it," he mumbled, rolling into a comfortable firing position. A soldier pulling up his trousers flew out of the rape tent. Longboard's rifle popped. The rapist's head exploded like a ripe melon. "Twenty-four," Longboard mumbled. Fifty-caliber tracer rounds sprayed the hillside. The illuminated projectiles shredded concealing growth. Severed chunks of terrain rained down. *Number twenty-five is too expensive,* Longboard concluded, hugging the sniper's nest. The roar was deafening. Splintered timber fell from the sky. The earth shook. In search of air, Longboard sucked on moist soil. *It's time to exit,* he realized, slithering through the erupting landscape.

Beneath the bellowing artificial storm, a vintage motorcycle purred. A BSA 250cc motorbike catching big air shot out of the lingering hilltop smoke. With a sniper rifle slung across his back, Longboard stood tall on the cycle's foot pegs, gulping down fresh air. Adrenaline shot through his veins. Halfway down the hill, blanketed in knee-deep ferns, he stuck the landing. After fishtailing in the green growth, the agile surfer regained control. Spitting up foliage, the cycle mowed a clean swath down the steep grade. Catching a glimpse of an approaching dirt road, he grinned. Exiting the jungle, he skidded to an abrupt termination. The rear tire hurled a storm of dust and pebbles. Looking back up at the decapitated hilltop, the surfer victoriously revved the single-cylinder engine. Between his legs, the motorcycle shimmied. *It's time to ditch the weapon,* he thought, wrestling with the strap. Over the whining motorcycle, the distant hum of a helicopter escalated. A gunship buzzed overhead. "Shit," Longboard mumbled, tracking the passing chopper. *Did it spot me?* he wondered.

A sweeping turn by the whirlybird confirmed his fears. Gunning the cycle's throttle, he mumbled, "If this is going to be my final ride, let's make it memorable." Hugging the gas tank, he flew down the hillside trail. A dusty wake beckoned the hovering predator. The gunship unleashed side-mounted machine guns. Incoming stalking rounds sparked off the dirt roadway. *I need cover,* Longboard concluded, exiting with a hard right turn. Blindly, the cycle plunged into rough growth. Branches slapped at the surfer. Thick brush clawed at cycle and rider. A low splintered limb ripped pants and flesh. A covey of star-tled birds took flight. Longboard paused. Sweat rolled down his face as he freed the captured twigs, vines, and foliage. The gash across his thigh warranted a quick glance, nothing more. The gunship hovering above the green ceiling began spraying bullets into the briar patch. Clippings and lead rained down. "Trying to flush me out, bitch," Longboard grumbled. The cycle rambled for-ward. The confining growth thinned. Riding high, the surfer cruised down a narrow game trail. Menacing projectiles advanced. The cycle accelerated. The cover receded.

At the edge of the tree line, Longboard took a deep breath. Before him, a series of rice paddies descended. Little dikes framed terraced sheets of liquid murky-brown glass. At the base of the flooded field staircase, a palm grove swayed. Above, a bright sun illuminated a royal-blue sky. Behind the whipping rotary blades of a probing gunship closed in. *If I scurry out of the brush, I'll be spotted by the hound,* he realized. *Hell, I don't have a choice,* he concluded, sputter-ing over to the top tread of the agricultural stairway. Visualizing the descent, he calculated sticking two landings before seeking sanctuary in the concealing coconut orchard. Bringing the vintage bike to a fever pitch, he popped the clutch. At full throttle, he raced down the skinny dike, skirting the top stair tread. Taking a deep breath, he flew over the edge. Airborne, he focused on the landing embankment. Moist clothing flapped. Cool air caressed. Flexing, he braced for impact. The cycle hit the narrow berm hard. A detached chrome muffler shot into the shallow water. Without a regulated exhaust, the antiquated bike wailed. *One jump down,* he concluded. Sunlight sparkled on the smooth surface that fringed the narrow raised dike. Flying down the narrow moist surface, the howling cycle accelerated. The runway terminated. The motorbike took flight. Incoming fire churned the paddy fields below. *That annoying bitch has found me,* he realized. He leaned back. The cycle's rear tire touched down. Skipping down the narrow berm, Longboard struggled to maintain balance.

"Come on, honey; don't let me down now," he mumbled. The gunship flew by. Pumping the brakes, Longboard regained control. The moist landing surface began to crumble. In search of traction, the cycle's rear wheel spat out chunks of earth. The helicopter made a sweeping U-turn. The cycle's rear tire bit. "Good girl," Longboard whispered. The security of the swaying palm grove lay before him. The stalking predator spit bullets behind him. Bike and rider shot into the symmetric forest. Longboard glanced over his shoulder. A fallen coconut palm terminated the escape. The impact ejected Longboard and launched the mangled remains of a classic motorcycle. A tumbling compilation of twisted metal bounced along the moist jungle floor. A trail of metal debris marked the short journey.

The rotors of the government helicopter cut through the humid air above the coconut plantation. The pilot hovered over the smoldering remains of a motorcycle. He grinned as the carcass of the dead bike burst into flames. "What?" He flinched. A projectile pierced the chopper's windscreen. The small hole in the windshield sent cracked tentacles across the glass. The invading bullet bit off the pilot's shoulder. Stunned, he grabbed the pulsing wound. The gunship teetered. Rotor blades dipped into the jungle canopy, severing palm fronds. The forest reached up and grasping the punishing blades, pulled the chopper out of the sky. Spinning out of control, the gunship plunged into the jungle. It broke apart on impact. Flames danced within the dying bird. Detonated munitions popped. A massive explosion sent a tumbling ball of fire into the summer sky.

A wisp of smoke lingered at the barrel end of a bolt-action rifle. Limping out from behind a coconut tree, Longboard mumbled, "Twenty-five." Grimacing, he took a cautious step toward the crash site. Feeling the heat gave him pause. Leaning on the sniper rifle, he determined there were no survivors. "Twenty-five and change," he corrected.

Chapter 34

———— ✦ ————

Dark clouds threatened. A gentle breeze distributed the aroma of an impending storm. Ten sleek modern trucks laden with dry food and tents lined the curve drive of the schoolhouse hospital. It was moving day for Doctor DeWitt and the six other international aid workers. The supplies were a parting gift for the destitute refugees. Local Tamil UN staff hastily unloaded the precious cargo. A burly Aussie, Paul Horn, in a pale-blue flak jacket anxiously paced beside the idle convoy. "Let's pick up the pace, lads," he counseled. Horn, a retired Australian army officer, was the UN security escort. This was his show, and time was of the essence. The stocky middle-aged veteran strutted with confidence. A wide neck secured his big head to broad shoulders. A small patch of close-cropped blond bristles stood defiantly behind a receding hairline. His fair skin was singed red by the tropical sun. The walkie-talkie in his clammy grasp crackled. With a sour expression, he fidgeted with the volume.

"Excuse me, chief," Reno called out.

Looking up from the handheld device, the Aussie squinted. "You're a Yank," he exclaimed.

"Last time I checked." Reno chuckled, extending his hand. "Reno James."

"Paul Horn." The Aussie reciprocated with a vise-grip handshake. "What can I do for you, Yank?"

"I'm looking for a missing friend," Reno replied.

Holding up a silencing palm, Horn blurted, "White?"

Reno nodded.

The Aussie shook his head. "The only thing I saw on our journey was desperate refugees and brown bodies."

Reno's shoulders dropped. "Thanks," he mumbled. After swallowing disappointment, he asked, "When are you departing?"

"Our bailout cannot come soon enough," Horn replied. "Those government buggers got me on a tight schedule. They estimate how long it will take to travel, unload, and return and shave a couple of hours off for their amusement. After all that, we were detained at a checkpoint this morning. Government troops probed every nook and cranny of the transports in search of weapons. A whacker looking for a howitzer shined a light up my clacker."

Reno laughed. "Did they find anything up your ass?"

"Fuck you, Yank." Horn snickered. The Aussie tilted his big crimson noggin. Squinting with a closed eye, he questioned, "Vietnam?"

Nodding, Reno answered, "I did my time in hell." Grinning, he added, "I pegged you as one of those badass Aussies that trekked through dense brush searching for Vietcong."

Puffing out his chest, Horn proudly declared, "First Battalion Royal Australian Regiment."

"Respect," Reno muttered.

"Is your missing mate a brother?" Horn inquired.

"He is a brother," Reno confirmed.

"I'll put the word out to the other convoys," Horn offered.

"Thanks, mate," Reno mumbled.

The Aussie looked past the American. A sly grin spread across his glistening face. "Who is the bonza sheila?" he asked, flicking his large head.

Reno followed Horn's gaze. The stoic Sandy in a Kevlar vest and blue helmet stood conversing with Doctor Ondaatje. The protective gear did little to conceal her seductive charm. "Bonza sheila?" Reno questioned. "She prefers the moniker Doctor DeWitt."

"Does she cook for you?" Horn probed.

"Something like that." Reno snickered.

"Respect," the Aussie declared.

To combat surfacing emotions, Sandy coughed. Looking down at the short, fragile Doctor Tom Ondaatje, she offered a soft smile. He looked like a boy playing army in his large helmet and protective vest. *What an amazing human specimen,* she thought. On the edge of tears, she uttered, "I wish I had a fraction of your courage."

He smiled. "That is kind of you to say, Sandra. But the decision to remain was not difficult. This is my country. My government cannot comprehend the obvious. We are one people sharing an island. Hindus and Buddhists have lived in harmony for centuries. I don't view my patients as Tamil but fellow citizens of a great nation."

A tear broke free and rolled down her soft cheek. "It's been an honor working with you, Doctor," she acknowledged.

"As well, Doctor," he replied. "On behalf of the citizens of my country, I want to thank you for the generous donation of your time and expertise."

In protective armor, the physicians hugged. The bulletproof fabric did not impede the conveyance of affection and respect. Breaking the embrace, Sandy adjusted her uncomfortable helmet. Ondaatje dug into a pants pocket. Pulling out a crinkled, soft blue envelope, he examined the sealed correspondence with a reflective grin. "This is for my wife," he quietly informed her. "I want to avoid the government censors." Taking a deep breath, he submissively asked, "Do you mind delivering it for me?"

Sandy extracted the letter from his grasp. "Consider it done," she answered.

Chapter 35

———— ✦ ————

On his belly, Longboard slithered forward. Crusty mud concealed his light complexion. He grimaced. A painful shard tormented a cracked rib. Slowly, he parted the engulfing elephant grass. A modest mud hut with a pitched thatch roof baked under a high sun. A woman in an orange-red sari wept on the dusty ground in front of the residence. A shirtless embracing peasant farmer attempted to provide support. Two half-naked boys stood beside their sobbing mother. The children focused on the two soldiers lounging in an open-air army-green jeep. The intruders casually brandishing assault rifles enjoyed cold beers. From within the mud shack, a girl screamed out. The plea sent the mother into a lamenting wail. The rapists waiting on deck laughed. *Looks like the troops seeking a little R & R decided to fuck the farmer's daughter,* Longboard surmised. *I won't be able to stop the crime,* he realized. But grinning, he concluded, *I will administer justice.*

Longboard took shallow breaths. Inhaling was painful. His queasy stomach grumbled. *The coconut water quenched my thirst,* he reflected. *The coconut meat filled my belly. Now I get to suffer through the expensive coconut bowel-cleansing side effect. Discomfort is what makes the kill so satisfying,* he thought. *I've endured much worse than diarrhea for a single shot. Patience is a virtue.* He scanned the shooting gallery. Empty amber bottles encircled the military vehicle. The mother's lament was reduced to a whimper. The girl's pleas terminated during the second forced coupling. The rapist shift change confirmed three hostiles. *I have five rounds left to feed my assassin's addiction before heading south,* Longboard realized. *After fornicating, my drunken prey will be relaxed, easy terminations.*

A rapist appeared in the hut's open doorway. Taking a proud breath, he buckled his trousers and shouted an off-color comment. His companions sitting in the jeep burst out laughing. As he strutted into the sunlight, the top of his sweaty head erupted. A bloody chunk of scalp flew into the summer sky. To an echoing blast, he collapsed. The target sitting behind the steering wheel received a penetrating projectile through the back of his skull. Slumping forward, the carcass set off the vehicle's horn. The third hostile, scrambling out of the jeep, fell flat on his face in the dirt. He lay motionless. The jeep's horn howled. Panting and sucking in powdery dust, the survivor raised his head. The peasant farmer, wielding a machete, stood over him. Burning with rage, the father, demonstrating a hacking skill perfected in the fields, decapitated his daughter's rapist with a single blow.

Longboard slowly rose. Standing in the waist-deep grass, he raised a surrendering outstretched hand to the farmer. Holding the bloodstained heavy knife, the farmer mimicked the open palm gesture. The vehicle's annoying horn wailed. *All clear,* Longboard thought, slinging his weapon over his shoulder. As he shuffled out of the concealing growth, dormant muscles groaned. Dragging a painful leg, he wobbled toward the curious farmer. The missing mother was apparently comforting her violated child. Two boys standing in front of the hovel stared at him like a ghastly specter. Longboard rubbed the caked earth on his cheek. *I must look like an extra in* Night of the Living Dead. He chuckled. His sensitive digestive tract contracted. Puckering his face, he realized he did not want to soil himself. The discomfort passed. *Thank God,* he thought. *It would taint my image as a cool, calculating assassin if I shit my pants.*

Approaching the farmer standing over the headless corpse, Longboard kicked the severed head. His cracked rib protested. He winced. The tumbling, leaking noggin disappeared beneath the vehicle. Grabbing the collar of the deceased behind the steering wheel, Longboard pulled the lifeless body back and silenced the obnoxious vehicle. "Tough day," the surfer mumbled to the traumatized farmer.

The peasant answered with a blank, disconnected gaze. Looking into the open-air jeep, Longboard grinned. In a plastic ice chest, a liter bottle of brew floated in chilled water. Dipping his callused hands into the cool liquid, he sighed. Cupped hands splashed his soiled face. The refreshment rolled down his sweat-soaked chest. Grabbing the last beer, he expertly pooped off the cap on the side of the jeep. Escaping carbonation appeared at the amber-lipped glass opening. He pointed the container of cold lager at the farmer. The transfixed peasant did not react to the offer. Longboard shrugged and poured the bubbling luxury down his throat. Tossing the empty bottle in the back of the jeep, he let out a satisfying belch. Pointing at the body on the ground, Longboard stated, "Let's clean this up so I can be on my way."

The farmer shook his head. He answered in his native tongue in a tone that denoted a question.

The wounded surfer attempted to pick up the decapitated corpse. The enlightened farmer took over the task. Tossing the carcass in the back of the jeep, he called out to his boys. The kids assisted in cleaning up the crime scene by picking up beer bottles. Their father did the heavy lifting, securing the intruders' remains in the back of the jeep.

Longboard extracted the colorful local currency from the dead men's bill-folds. "Not much of a take," he mumbled. "Here, friend, you take it," he said, offering the spoils to the peasant. The farmer accepted. Rubbing his hands together, Longboard asked, "Where can I wash up?"

The farmer understood. He instructed his sons. The eldest boy, the eight-year-old, ran into the shack. The farmer mumbled an apology and after a grateful bow went to check on his daughter. The five-year-old tyke reached up and latched onto the American's fingers. Gently tugging, the toddler led Longboard behind the shack. A faded red cast-iron well pump stood guard over a concrete washbasin. The young guide released his grasp and began cranking on the pump's handle. Siphoned water pulsed out of the rusty spigot. Longboard carefully removed his shirt. He tossed the blood-, mud-, and sweat-stained garment into the concrete basin. Insect bites, cuts, and scratches infested his lean, muscular torso. A deep-purple bruise on his side identified a cracked rib. The eight-year-old ran up carrying a bar of lye soap and a frayed white towel.

"Thanks," Longboard mumbled, accepting the homemade soap. He stuck his head under the pulsing faucet. The well water was cool, refreshing. Lathering up, he felt rejuvenated. *Is it the beer on an empty stomach?* he questioned. *The satisfaction of justified kills?* he pondered. *Or a long overdue cleansing? It really doesn't matter,* he concluded. *I'm feeling pretty good.* He dried off quickly with the coarse towel. Ringing out his shirt, he nodded gratitude at the boys. Slipping into the damp garment, he sighed.

The farmer, holding a steaming wooden bowl, rounded the corner of the shack. Extending his hand, he offered the meal. Longboard grinned. With a cupped hand, he scooped out sticky rice. Two handfuls emptied the dish.

Wiping his lips with a backhand, Longboard mumbled, "Thanks."

Father and sons trailed the limping assassin as he headed toward the jeep. Climbing behind the steering wheel, Longboard offered a casual salute and muttered, "Adios, amigos." The engine growled to life. Popping the clutch, the surfer launched the vehicle loaded with dead men. The farmer hollered. Longboard hit the brakes and glanced in the rearview mirror. A severed head lay in the dirt. "Can't forget that." He sniggered.

The sun drifted toward the horizon. Long shadows appeared. As he cruised down the rural road, a dusty wake trailed the army-green jeep. Longboard's unbuttoned moist shirt flapped in the wind. The breeze caressed his moist scalp. Leaning back, he steered with one hand at twelve o'clock. *Sure beats walking,* he thought. *I'll put some distance between the evidence and the farm before ditching the vehicle,* he concluded. A severed cranium rolled back and forth across the passenger floorboard. Lifeless eyes stared up at the relaxed surfer. Glancing down, Longboard scowled, "What the fuck you looking at?"

Chapter 36

⸺ ✦ ⸺

The vehicle's air conditioner crackled. The cool air struggled to comfort the tense occupants. In the passenger seat, Reno stared out of the growing insect graveyard occupying the windshield. *I left a brother behind,* he reflected. *Why did I signal Bluto's termination?* he regretted. An image of Longboard surfing tugged on his heavy heart.

The narrow asphalt road was freakishly quiet. The burnt-out shell of a lorry floated by. An emaciated cow grazed in a field scarred with man-made craters. The Aussie behind the wheel downshifted. The white United Nations four-wheel-drive vehicle entered a roundabout of a deserted junction. A moss-covered fountain of stagnant filth occupied the circular intersection's island. Atop the inoperable water feature, the flag of the Tamil rebels fluttered. The frayed crimson cloth depicted a tiger leaping through a circle of bullets with crossed bayonets. The trailing convoy stirred the defiant banner and the rubbish infesting the flanking abandoned structures.

Checking his watch, the Aussie flexed his foot. The vehicle accelerated. Leaning back, he mumbled, "Are you armed?"

Reno glanced at the likeable Paul Horn. In the backseat, Sandy and three other international aid workers, reflecting on the dependent populous they left behind, did not hear the probing inquiry.

"Yes, I am," Reno whispered.

"What are you packing, mate?" Horn questioned.

Slumping forward, Reno retrieved the pimp pistol from a pant-leg pocket. He flashed the tiny sidearm.

Glancing down, Horn snickered. "Let me see that."

Reno obliged. The Aussie tested the weapon's weight with an open palm, rolled down the driver's side window, and casually tossed the gun out.

"Why did you do that?" Reno snapped.

"Easy, Yank," Horn responded. "No weapons allowed. Besides, if we are attacked, that cap gun would be useless."

"Ambushed?" Reno squinted. "The trucks are empty. We are traveling under an international humanitarian banner." Shaking his head, he questioned, "Who would benefit from an assault on a UN caravan."

"Both sides, mate," Horn answered. "What did you Americans call it in Vietnam?" Looking up, he blurted, "Winning hearts and minds." After answering his own question, he continued, "That pacification strategy was a tough sell on the locals. Considering you Yanks defined success with a large body count." Focused on the open road, he explained, "Now in this Sri Lankan conflict, vilifying your enemy to the international community attracts financial support. It doesn't matter who annihilates a UN convoy. We will be dead. However, the government and Tigers will be pointing indicting fingers at each other over our corpses. Believe me; the warring parties would relish a major diplomatic incident to shine a global light on their respective passionate causes."

Reno scanned the bleak countryside. Sunlight reflected off ponds scattered throughout green marshy fields. He looked up. Billowing clouds graced the blue sky.

"Relax, Reno," Horn counseled. "We are just about out of the kill zone."

"You will let me know when we are no longer a target?" Reno lightly questioned.

"Once we hit traffic, we can take a comforting breath," Horn answered. "Nothing defuses a cover-up like eyewitnesses."

Reno gazed forward. A long, lonely stretch of deserted highway disappeared into the horizon.

Stepping out of the UN-marked vehicle, gravel crunching, Reno squinted at the setting sun. An orange glow hovered over the tropical horizon. It had been a long day. Arching his back woke napping muscles, and he gazed down the long line of idle transports. Truck drivers hopped down out of their respective cabs. Armed troops began inspecting the convoy. Utilizing a mirror attached to a pole, a soldier examined a truck's undercarriage. Reno took a deep breath of warm, moist air. He offered assistance in opening the jeep's passenger door. Sandy emerged. Placing her hands in the small of her back, the tall drink of water stretched. She offered Reno a soft smile. He winked. They migrated to the back of the jeep. A cadre of groggy international aid workers huddled around the Aussie security officer.

"Passports and luggage," Horn announced, popping open the four-wheel-drive vehicle's hatchback. "Don't speak unless questioned," he lectured, pulling out baggage. "Answer all questions direct. Do not elaborate." Retrieving a military duffel bag, he looked at Reno. "No wisecracks, Yank. These officials enjoy flexing authority."

Reno exaggerated an innocent expression. He shot a who-are-you-talking-to glance over his shoulder. Dane, the lanky Brit, snickered. Sandy playfully slapped Reno's chest with a backhand.

"This may go quickly or could last hours," the Aussie continued. "Brace yourselves for a humbling experience. But remember after the belittling ordeal is over, we're heading to the closest boozer to toss back amber fluid."

Reno slung his duffel bag over his shoulder. His right hand clutched a dark-blue American passport. After adjusting the canvas strap, he picked up Sandy's tattered rucksack. "Allow me, Doctor DeWitt," he said.

She responded with an appreciative bow.

On stiff legs, the international aid workers and American arms dealer plodded past the metal barricade blocking the road. A sandbag bunker briefly shielded the exiting sun. The barrel of a fifty-caliber machine gun poked out of a slit in the tall mound of heavy canvas sacks. Soldiers eyed the white parade with disdain. The Aussie accelerated taking the lead. A gravel path led to a moss-stained white plaster single-story building. A pitched red tile roof capped the inspection station. A helmeted guard sat in a metal folding chair beside the open doorframe entrance, an assault rifle on display across his lap. The Caucasian cadre flowed past the sentry into a large open room. Three industrial ceiling fans hung down from crossbeams. Two of the fans slowly twirled. One sat idle. A small gray bird flew through the rafters searching for an exit. A long wooden table spanned the length of the facility. Behind the counter, a dozen dark-brown uniformed government inspectors stood in a cluster. They acknowledged the arrivals by spreading out. A stocky female officer in an ill-fitting brown skirt scowled at the stoic Dutch beauty. Puckering her pudgy face, the official flicked a beckoning finger in Sandy's direction. As Doctor Dewitt's surrogate porter, Reno plopped Sandy's luggage on the counter in front of the uniformed sour broad. The frump dog dismissed the American with a waving backhand. Reno shrugged and slid down the counter. A short, skinny inspector in an oversized military costume patted the table top. Reno placed his duffel bag in front of the small man.

The humid room was quiet. One of the working ceiling fans occasionally squealed. On one side of the long table fatigued travelers stood patiently. Across from them, government bureaucrats rummaged through dirty laundry. Reno's tiny inspector pulled out a tube of Crest toothpaste from the American's toiletry kit. Smirking at Reno, he removed the cap and squeezed the tube. A stream of minty-fresh gel landed atop the pile of the American's clothing. The culprit paused for a reaction. Reno stood disengaged. *Trying to get a rise out of me, sweetheart,* he thought. *It's going to take a lot more than decorating my wardrobe with toothpaste.* Down the line, the inspectors chuckled as the female official held up a pair of Sandy's silk panties. She delighted her colleagues with a lingerie exhibit that included lacy bras and nightwear. Reno struggled not to laugh. *These lackeys are nothing more than spoiled children,* he realized, scanning the room. The Aussie stood proud as an official patted him down. The lanky Brit did not flinch as a government official exposed roll after roll of thirty-five-millimeter film. The destroyed ribbons of the thin plastic strips and yellow Kodak canisters cascaded onto the floor. *These humanitarians faced death to heal the less fortunate,* Reno reflected. *Tolerating bureaucrats elevated by the power of their station is an easy task.* Sandy squatted down to retrieve her undergarments off the floor. *What an amazing woman,* Reno thought. *Brains, beauty, and compassion all packaged in a sexy athletic angel.* His heart sank as he realized she was definitely out of his league.

Chapter 37

—◦◦◦◦◦—

A tropical downpour drenched a cluster of approximately thirty fleeing civilians. To avoid government scrutiny, they chose a rural route. The southern migration's only defense was a herding tactic. They fled as a group. Mothers carried children. Fathers were burdened with bags of clothes, pots and pans, and diminishing rations. No one spoke. Downcast eyes navigated the narrow muddy path skirted by rough foliage. A silhouette shrouded in an olive-green oilskin tarp trailed the procession. The stalking, limping shadow kept its distance. The rough-draping sailcloth deflected the falling rain and concealed Longboard's Caucasian ancestry.

"This scenic route is a bitch," Longboard grumbled, plodding forward in mud-caked boots. *What's worse?* he pondered. *Walking in the rain chilled to the bone or having mosquitoes suck your blood in a sauna?* Glancing up at switchbacks snaking up before him, he grinned. *My last obstacle,* he surmised, *a city that recognizes white privilege resides in the valley over the ridge.* The incline steepened. His breathing accelerated. He closed in on the pack of escaping refugees. Rounding the corner of the last switchback, he got a glimpse of the destitute families standing in the rain at the hilltop. The storm intensified. Sheets of water fell from the black sky. *Something is wrong,* Longboard realized, pausing to adjust his shielding rain tarp. His moist hand confirmed a pistol and sheathed combat knife confiscated off his last kills.

Behind him, the jungle stirred. An ominous shadow exited. A gun barrel jabbed him in the back. Longboard stumbled forward. A local barked out a high-pitched command, emphasized by another threatening poke. *Five-foot-five hostile,* Longboard calculated from the angle of the command and gun prod. Obliging, Longboard briskly trekked to the peak. The gunman's light tread kept pace. *No more than one hundred fifty pounds,* Longboard added to the summation of his captor.

A corrugated tin lean-to beside the narrow path capped the summit. A campfire smoldered beneath its protective lee. Bedrolls and a wood box overflowing with fleeced watches and jewelry occupied the shelter's earthen floor. Two brigands brandishing assault rifles corralled the refugees into a toll line. The trailing bandit shoved Longboard into the back of the queue. A toll-collector plucked a young flower out of the lineup. Wrapping his arm around the innocent girl, he escorted her toward the shelter to extract an expensive fee.

Longboard, elevating his gaze, calculated the kill sequence. The punk behind him slapped the back of the surfer's cloaked head. Longboard licked his lips in anticipation. *You have no idea death is hiding among the flock,* he thought, stealthily unsheathing the combat knife. Savoring the comforting power of the weapon, he tightened his grasp. In a fluid motion, he turned. Expertly, he plunged the blade under the punk's second rib and into his heart. A torrent of blood erupted. A gasp escaped the open mouth of a shocked expression. Jerking the knife, Longboard severed the youth's spinal cord. Death arrived instantly. *It's quick but messy,* Longboard reflected, feeling the warm plasma draining down his arm. He released the impaled cadaver. The lifeless bundle collapsed and folded over in the mud. Longboard flung off his oilskin cape. Catching a gust of wind, the shroud took flight. Drawing his pistol, he extended his arm and discharged two quick rounds. A toll-taker jerked as the projectiles tore into his torso. The gunfire sparked a civilian stampede. Ignoring the fleeing sheep, the assassin followed his extended arm to the toll booth. A disorientated rapist rolled off his prey. A terrified young brown flower hastily covered her bare flat chest. Longboard fired. Holding a leaking belly, the brigand wailed like a girl. Looking up, the wounded thug's eyes pleaded for mercy. Wearing the mask of death, Longboard silenced the whining rapist bitch with a head shot. Stepping into the toll booth, Longboard shook his drenched head. It smelled of smoke. The downpour produced a tinny sound. Drops from a roof leak hissed in the smoldering fire. The rape victim began to weep. Longboard squatted down and tugged on a blanket beneath the dead pedophile. Conceding, the cadaver rolled out of the shelter and into engulfing sludge. After shaking the rough cloth, the surfer draped the cover over the girl's naked torso. Looking up with teary eyes, she graced the assassin with an appreciative smile. Longboard winked. The herd of refugees converged around the small shelter. The defiled child leaped into the embrace of her family. The balance of the shocked crowd's curious expressions sought answers.

"What?" Longboard innocently questioned.

A Tamil teen pointed at the fruit crate sparkling with booty and raised thick, bushy eyebrows.

Longboard chuckled. "Sure," he mumbled nodding. "Knock yourself out."

No translation was necessary. A flurry of hands grabbed at watches, gold necklaces, and rings. The box toppled. Jewelry spilled out of the shelter into soupy muck. The pack quickly confiscated the spoils. After a brief admiration of the plunder, the herd continued on their southern migration. In the back of the fold, the young flower looked back.

Longboard waved at the departing parade flowing downhill. The rain softened. At the basin of the valley, a city appeared under the stormy sky. Spotting field glasses dangling from a rough wood support, Longboard grabbed the binoculars.

Let's calculate my exit, he thought, scanning the vista. A congested asphalt roadway intersected with the town. On the highway, a UN convoy queued up for inspection. *I need to avoid that checkpoint,* he realized. Surveying the dense forest west of town, he grinned. *I can off-road it to avoid the authorities. Four maybe five hours at best,* he determined.

Hanging up the field glasses, he flexed. Fatigued muscles groaned. An empty belly growled. Smiling at the dead man's face down in the mire, he mumbled, "Did you leave me anything to eat?" After pausing for a reply, he added, "Cat got your tongue?" Retrieving the fruit box, he sat beside the dying fire and tested the heat of a black kettle's lid. Tossing the warm cover aside revealed misting curry rice. "I'll help myself," he muttered. Feeding his face with a scooping hand, he chuckled. "With a full belly and a little luck, I should make happy hour at the local pub."

Chapter 38

—⊶⊷—

It was dusk. The tavern was crowded. Dark-brown men with oily jet-black hair indulged in the evening drinking ritual. The dress code consisted of sarongs and cheap sandals. Behind a counter lined with standing patrons, the barkeep, sporting a scruffy mustache and a dead milky eye, served local hooch. A shirtless barefoot boy in shorts stood on the countertop cluttered with beer bottles and Mason jar cocktail glasses. Raising his heels, the skinny kid reached up to light a dangling kerosene lantern. An eerie swaying glow illuminated the drinking rabble.

The stocky Aussie Paul Horn appeared in the doorway. He mumbled over his shoulder at his trailing companions, "This looks like the pub to get rotten." Curious squints investigated his arrival. The chattering bar crowd faded to silence. "Can a bloke get a coldie in this boozer?" Horn hollered at the gawking horde.

The half-naked boy nimbly jumped off the counter. Standing on the hardwood floor, he stuck out his bony chest and exclaimed, "Yes, sir!" Scanning the watering hole, the boy's eyes lit up. He rushed over to a passed-out patron occupying a long picnic table. An investigating nudge did not stir the snoring drunk. The skinny kid took a deep breath and wrapped his arms around the drunkard's torso. Exhaling a mighty grunt, the youth pulled the dead weight onto the floor. Straddling the mumbling carcass, the boy presented the seating option with a big smile and inviting arm. "Your table, sir," he declared.

Horn strutted into the silent tavern. The lanky Brit Dane followed. Sandy's entrance invoked "Ahs" from the dark male audience. Bringing up the rear, Reno placed a protective hand on her shoulder. *An Aussie, Limey, and Hollander,* the American thought. *Well, we know who the drinkers in the international aid community are. The other escaping humanitarians chose a hot shower over a cold beer,* he reflected. *Who's to argue with another man's priorities? Besides, after the third beer, who cares about a bath?*

"Four beers," Horn ordered, swirling a pointed finger at the tabletop. The international social drinkers club scooted into the attached table benches. Soft murmurs resonated from a focused barroom audience. An alpha male staggered over from the bar. He was wide for a local. A potbelly hung over a loosely wrapped sarong. A mangy beard encased sagging jowls. Proudly, he displayed a scuffed motorcycle helmet at the end of a swaying arm. In a teetering stance, he hovered beside the seated white woman. Tilting his floating head, he examined the Dutch beauty from top to bottom. Sandy looked down, rubbing the back of her neck. Horn, Dane, and Reno stood up.

"Nick off," growled the Aussie. The comment's tone surprised the curious drunk. He took a step back and waved with a big, friendly smile. The wide grin exposed a betel nut addiction. Years of chewing areca nuts and tobacco wrapped in a lime-coated betel leaf had transformed his teeth and gums into a reddish-black cesspool.

"I take it your employer does not have a dental plan," Reno playfully said, returning the wave.

The drunk apologetically bowed. Triumphantly sucking in his gut, he drifted back into the festivities.

The chivalrous escorts returned to their seats. The enterprising kid plopped four frosty liters of local lager on the table and a wooden bowl of cashew nuts. Horn picked up his chilled bottle. Raising it high, he toasted, "Cheers."

Lifting his brew, a serious Reno chimed in, "To those we left behind."

"To Doctor Ondaatje," Sandy announced, touching his glass.

"Doctor Tom Ondaatje," Dane echoed.

Reno took a satisfying swig of cold beer. An airborne cashew skimmed across the tabletop. "Some drunk is tossing nuts." He chuckled. *Can't these people hold their liquor?* he wondered. A flying kernel struck him in the back. He defiantly flexed. *Just ignore it,* he counseled. A salty projectile hit Sandy in the back of her head. "Motherfucker," Reno grumbled. "What's your problem?" he growled, turning to investigate.

There he was, sitting in the shadows in a wood chair leaning against the back wall, his mud-caked boots elevated on a table. Soiled, tattered clothes hung loosely over a battered frame. Smirking, he flicked another bar nut.

Reno lit up. His heavy heart vanished under an accelerating beat. Surfacing emotion erupted into a wide grin. "You motherfucker!" he shouted.

"It's good seeing you as well, partner," Longboard mumbled.

Horn squinted at Sandy and flicked his head. "Reno has found his lost brother," she answered, placing an understanding hand on Reno's shoulder.

Reno patted her comforting touch. "Excuse me," he muttered, sliding out of the restraining bench. With bottle in hand, he swaggered over to the dark surfer slouching in the shadows. "Don't get up," he teased.

Longboard chuckled, dropping his elevated feet to the floor. Exiting the comfortable repose, he winced.

"You all right?" Reno probed, pulling up a chair.

Longboard shrugged. "A little worse for wear," he mumbled. "The company vehicle is toast," he added.

Leaning forward, Reno quietly inquired, "I saw the sniper's nest...hell, the entire hillside erupt. How did you escape?"

"The taste of a kill summoned my inner demon," Longboard responded. "My dark side has a strong self-preservation instinct. It has navigated me through much tougher obstacles."

"You're kinda talking crazy," Reno commented.

Longboard laughed. "I'm not crazy, Reno. I'm just very good at what I do."

"I'll give you that, partner," Reno commented, leaning back and taking a healthy swig of cold brew. Wiping his lips with a backhand, he added softly, "You terminated the camp commandant at what? A thousand yards?"

The assassin proudly grinned. He took a sip of the local white lighting. Sitting erect, he responded, "I'm not presently disposed to discuss that operation. Nor would I be disposed to discuss any such operation if in fact it did exist."

Chapter 39

⸎

Chola folded his pillow. He propped himself up in the army cot. The collapsible bed creaked under the shifting weight. Through open windows invading sunlight illuminated the rebel infirmary. Wounded Tigers packed the large room. Casualties occupied hospital beds, cots, and the hard concrete floor. A steady drone of pain and suffering resonated off the cracked plaster walls. The pungent aroma of antiseptic competed with the rancid stench of festering wounds and ripe bedpans.

Chola had gotten used to the soundtrack. It wasn't that long ago he sang in the choir. Carefully he reached under the shallow bed. *No need to pop the stitches holding my shredded flesh together,* he thought. His blind hand found the book. Slowly he retrieved the tattered paperback. Victoriously he held the blood-stained copy of *The Adventures of Huckleberry Finn* against his chest. *Should I read it again?* he pondered. It was a good escape from reality.

An orderly rushed into the ward. He whispered to his fellow attendants. The quiet conversation sparked a sense of urgency. Following his nose, a skinny kid in a large lab coat sprayed disinfectant. His colleagues hastily removed overdue bedpans. A wailing casualty was removed. Curiously scanning the commotion, Chola found the answer in the doorway. A rebel commander and trailing subordinates in crisp, clean camo fatigues strutted into the infirmary.

The leaping tiger symbol of the LTTE adorned the officer's multi-green-shaded kepi. The pudgy leader sported a thick mustache. Passing damaged troops, he respectfully bowed. One of the subordinate officers pointed an identifying finger at Chola. The commander high-stepped through the obstacles of bodies on the floor. Chola, attempting to sit up, grimaced and retreated to a horizontal repose.

The senior officer appeared at the foot of Chola's bed. "Relax, machan," he whispered. "You need to heal." A hovering subordinate handed the commander a crinkled page. Scanning the wrinkled document, the commander summarized, "The doctor says you will be able to return to active duty soon."

"Yes, Master," Chola replied.

"Get me a chair," the officer growled over his shoulder.

The lackey jumped and relayed the request to an orderly. The officer's impatient scowl observed the retrieval and unfolding of a collapsible metal chair.

The gray metal creaked as the commander sat down. He leaned forward, resting his elbows on his knees. "Chola, wars are fought on many fronts," he quietly informed. "We can defeat the enemy on the battlefield only if our supply lines continue to flow. There is no shortage of brave Tigers to take up arms. What we lack is financial support. Most of our funding comes from the Tamil diaspora." Pausing to gauge his audience's comprehension, he asked, "Do you understand?"

A focused scar-faced Chola nodded. "The war has scattered our citizens across the globe. The displaced Tamils donate to the movement. One day, they will return to their homeland, Tamil Eelam."

Raising his thick eyebrows, the delighted rebel leader quizzed, "And how do we encourage our dispersed brothers to continue feeding the cause?"

Grinning, Chola uttered, "Information."

"Excellent, machan...excellent," the commander mumbled. He leaned back, and his volume increased. "The western-leaning government's propaganda has vilified us to the international community. Our victories are called massacres. Our freedom fighters are labeled terrorists. Documented and photographed accounts of our enemy's barbarous atrocities never see the light of day."

He grinned. "An opportunity has arisen to reach out to the international press. I want you to deliver our message."

"Me?" Chola swallowed.

Slowly nodding, the commander replied, "Yes, you, my educated Tiger. Your fluency in English makes you the perfect spokesman to articulate the justification of our movement."

Chapter 40

The sun was just a dot sparkling in the cloudless blue sky. Through the dark-green protective lenses of aviator shades, Reno glanced at the simmering ball. Hot rays baked his oiled flesh. Drifting toward sleep, he closed his eyes. A booming splash and spray of cool water nudged him back to consciousness. Sitting upright in the chaise lounge, he removed water-spotted spectacles. A pudgy bleach-white kid seeking attention frolicked in the hotel's pool. "French?" Reno questioned the fat brat's repetitive cry for recognition. *Chubby is going to burn in this topical heat,* he concluded. *Serves him right,* he chuckled, cleaning his sunglasses with the soft billowing white pool towel.

The Colombo Hilton's pool was a chlorinated oasis in the congested city. Neatly trimmed palm trees swayed under a salty breeze. The cough of traffic and chorus of car horns echoed off the surrounding midrise buildings. Attentive servers scurried around the concrete pool decking. Tourists hydrated themselves with fruit drinks spiked with distilled spirits.

"Can I get you another beer, sir?" questioned the silhouette blocking Reno's sunlight.

"Sure," Reno conceded. "How about you, Doctor DeWitt?" he teased. "Are you ready for another liquor-laced fruit salad?"

The reclining white-bikini-clad Dutch beauty mumbled, "No, thank you, Mister James."

The waiter bowed and rushed off to place the order. Reno took a satisfying breath. The aroma of coconut butter filled his nostrils. Concealed by dark lenses, he took a lustful journey down his poolside companion's exposed taut flesh. Her oiled skin sparkled. Beads of sweat resided across the sleek surface. The skimpy swimsuit strategically shrouded her charms. Sandy's firm muscular belly pulsed. *I need to pursue her,* he concluded. *Who knows where this relationship will go? If I don't make the effort now,* he realized, *I will always regret it.*

An eclipsing shadow spilled across her athletic frame. Reno, anticipating a cold beer, looked up to investigate. The dapper Burgher Rolph van der Wall hovered at the foot of Sandy's chaise lounge. Sporting a lecherous smirk, he admired the sunbathing doctor. "Good afternoon, Mister James," rolled out of the side of his mouth. Still focused on Sandy's exposed curves, he added, "Forgive my intrusion."

"Afternoon, Rolph," Reno said, rising.

Sandy stirred. Propped up on her elbows, she scrutinized the intruder.

"Sandy, this is Rolph. He is a...business associate," Reno enlightened her.

"Rolph," Sandy responded, sitting up and relocating her sunglasses on the top of her head.

"Business associate," Rolph mumbled with an accepting nod. "And what might your affiliation be with Mister James? If I may be so bold."

Reno flinched. *Why the fuck would you ask that?* he pondered.

Sandy chuckled. "Hij is mijn vriend."

Rolph grinned wide. Patting Reno's oily bare back, he said, "I'm envious."

"I'm in the dark here," Reno announced.

"It's all good, Yank," Rolph declared. "I'm your business associate, and you are this stunning creature's boyfriend."

Reno caught his breath. He fired an affectionate wink at Doctor DeWitt. She reciprocated.

"Mister James, if you don't mind, I have a brief bit of business we need to discuss," Rolph said, extending a soliciting arm in the direction of the shaded poolside bar. Enjoying a parting glance of the sultry Sandy, he bowed, "Jonge dame" (young miss).

"Tot ziens" (see you later), Sandy replied, reclining back into a sun-basking repose.

Strutting toward the comforting shade of the red-tiled poolside cantina, Rolph repeated, "It's all good, Yank." Reaching into his pleated linen pants pocket, he retrieved a crinkled sheet of onion paper. The open-air bar was empty. A blender whined in the distance. Pulling out a rattan chair from a quiet table, Rolph sat down and tossed the wrinkled wad of paper next to a carved-coconut ashtray. The blade wash from an overhead fan teased the fluttering document. Reno sat down and instinctively grabbed the crumpled paper.

"It's the confirmation of your wire transfer," Rolph whispered. Snapping fingers high over his head, he barked, "Two gin and tonics...with lots of ice."

Reno unraveled the document. Below his Thai bank account number, "US $2,000,000" leaped off the page. He swallowed with a dry mouth. The haunting inequality images of thrift-shop clothes, hand-me-downs, barren Christmases, and foster homes seemed trivial. Flexing a finger, he dragged it across the seven-figure numeral. *A million-three and the deposit goes to Danny,* he calculated. *Two-hundred large pays off the Triad loan. The vig on the loan is forty,* he reflected. *That was forty thousand last week,* he realized. *The Triad should be satisfied with fifty,* he reasoned. *The partnership take would then be four hundred and fifty big ones,* he figured. *Longboard earned his 20 percent,* Reno reckoned. The surfer should be delighted with ninety thousand dollars. A satisfied grin grew into a wide smile. "Three-hundred and sixty," he mumbled, realizing he had fuck-you money.

"Congratulations, Mister James," Rolph toasted, holding up a fizzing tall glass of sparkling gin.

Reno's hand had a slight twitch as he touched glass. He downed the cool lime-accented cocktail with several gulps.

Leaning forward, Rolph whispered, "There is a sense of urgency with this transaction. Our mutual client decided to pay for the goods in full to expedite delivery." After wetting his soft-spoken palate with a gentle sip, he added, "The Tamils have demonstrated extraordinary faith in you, Reno. Do not disappoint them."

Enjoying the soothing effects of gin, Reno leaned back. "You made my day, Rolph," he declared, rattling cubes of ice in an empty bar glass. "The shipping containers have been collecting dust awaiting payment. I'll book myself on the next flight out of this tropical paradise and arrange the transfer of goods."

"Excellent," the Burgher mumbled.

"If you will excuse me," Reno announced, pushing back from the table. "I have to make some travel arrangements."

Rolph glanced in the direction of the sun-bathing Dutch *dame*. "Would that be travel plans for two?" he poked.

Reno followed the Burgher's gaze. Both men watched as the long, lean, glistening Sandy rose. Oblivious to a gawking poolside audience, she strutted to the sparkling water's edge. After taking a seductive breath, she plunged into the inviting chlorinated pond.

"I sure hope I can convince Sandy to join me," Reno answered. Squinting at the Burgher, he asked, "Any advice?"

Rolph beamed. He offered, grinning, "She is Dutch. They like cheese."

Reno laughed as he rose. Extending his hand, he declared, "It's been a pleasure Rolph." Shaking hands, he added, "Let's see how well I can incorporate dairy products into the invitation."

Reno jogged into the sunlight. Dropping his sunglasses on Sandy's vacated chaise lounge, he accelerated and dove into the hotel pool. Cool water jolted his senses. Before him, the blurred image of Sandy's long legs. *I'm a rich man,* he realized, propelling toward his objective. He surfaced right in front of her. She wrapped her arms around his neck. Sucking air, he asked, "How do you say 'boyfriend' in Dutch again?"

"*Vriend,*" Sandy whispered into his ear.

"I like the sound of that," he conceded. Swallowing, he took a composing breath. "Sandy, I have to leave on the next flight out." She pulled back. He grinned. "Come with me?" he asked. "I'd like to spoil you with a holiday."

"Where...where would we go?"

"I have one maybe two days of business in Thailand," he informed her. "After that, you can pick the destination."

"Can I think about it?" she asked.

Reno, nodding in defeat, mumbled, "I understand. It was a lot to ask."

"Oh, I'm going," she blurted. "I just need some time to think about the perfect holiday locale."

As the fat French kid splashed in the pool's shallow end, Reno planted a passionate kiss on his Dutch girlfriend's sultry lips.

Chapter 41

⸻❦⸻

Reno strutted through the hotel lobby in moist swim trunks, his rubber sandals squeaking on the polished stone. His long, damp blond locks flowed across broad shoulders. Playfully, he swung Sandy's grasping hand. The air was cool. Cocktail chatter resonated from occupied soft seating arrangements. Sandy's simple white cotton bikini cover-up attracted attention. The short transparent tunic top exposed her long legs. Straw platform sandals accented toned calves.

"Let me check on departing flights," Reno said, changing course to the concierge desk.

Sandy paused. "I need to take a shower," she announced, giving him a peck on the cheek.

"All right," he conceded. "But I just want to throw this out as you ponder our vacation objective." She raised a brow. Leaning forward, he whispered in her ear, "Australia."

Sandy laughed. "I'll take it under advisement," she responded, departing toward the bank of elevators.

"Oh, I can get used to this," Reno mumbled, admiring her seductive gait. Glancing at his watch, he realized Longboard's massage should be concluding. *My partner will be happy with his ninety-thousand-dollar payday,* he reflected, strolling to the concierge station. Hovering in front of the polished dark wood desk, he flashed his room key.

"How can I assist you, Mister James?" inquired the local olive-skinned beauty manning the post.

Reno flinched. *She knows my name?* Focused on the gold name tag attached to the breast pocket of her navy-blue blazer, he declared, "Angelina...I'm flattered you remember me."

Glancing down, she suppressed a childlike grin common among island inhabitants. "Please be seated," she offered, motioning to a cushioned chair.

"I'm still wet from a plunge in your pool," he said, declining the offer. "Angelina, I need your assistance with transportation."

She anxiously picked up a ballpoint pen.

"I require three tickets on the next available flight to Bangkok."

Scribbling down the request, she glanced up and asked, "Do you have a seating preference?"

Reno paused. *What the hell?* he thought. *I'm a wealthy man.* "First class if available," he playfully responded.

"Very good, Mister James," she replied, making the notation. "I'll send a list of options up to your room."

"Thanks, sweetheart," he offered. The comment evoked another innocent blush. Heading toward the lift, he paused. *I don't want Sandy to think I'm a slob,* he thought. On the dark wood paneling behind the hotel's front desk, a series of clocks denoted the time of day at major cities around the world. It was approaching 5:30 p.m. in Bangkok, ergo it was happy hour at the Jade Tiger in Phuket. Reno envisioned Marshall holding court at the local watering hole. *Maybe I can get one of Marshall's girl's relatives to clean up my beach house,* he thought. *I'll have them stock my fridge with beer, wine, and...cheese.* He chuckled. *Nothing shows European sophistication like fine wine and compressed ripened curds of milk.* Making an about-face, he returned to the obliging Angelina. She was on the phone. Acknowledging his presence, she politely held up a pausing finger.

"Change in travel plans, Misters James," she asked, hanging up the phone.

"No," he responded, shaking his head. "I need to make an international call. And prefer not to do it from my room."

"Do you know the country code and number?" she inquired.

He nodded.

"You can use one of the house telephones," she offered, motioning to a row of partitioned stations along the wall. "However, the charges will be billed to your account."

"That's fine," he acknowledged, departing.

Woven palm leave panels provided privacy for a beige touch-tone phone; a glass bud vase and a single orchid added ambience. Reno punched in the familiar digits. Static crackled.

"Jade Tiger Lounge," interrupted the hiss.

"Aroon, it's San Bernardino," Reno playfully announced.

"Reno, where have you been?" questioned the Thai bartender.

"All over." Reno chuckled. "But I'm heading home. Is Marshall there?"

"You don't know?" Aroon declared.

"Don't know what?" Reno questioned.

"Marshall is dead."

Reno froze. His breathing accelerated. Closing his eyes, he visualized his happy-go-lucky one-legged buddy. Taking a deep breath, he asked, "What… what happened?"

"His body was found at your place. The police concluded Marshall stumbled upon a burglary."

"Fuck," Reno growled. "Fucking Fourteen-K Triad." *I warned Marshall not to mess with those dinks,* he reflected. Rage competed with sadness. He was panting like a dog, and his stomach churned. "Fuck, fuck, fuck," he mumbled, pounding his forehead with the tan receiver. The handle emitted muffled dialogue. "What?" flowed out of Reno's gasping mouth.

"I said, Sunee is having an honoring ceremony for Marshall on Tuesday."

Ignoring the funeral update, Reno questioned, "Are you buying the burglary story?" Static answered. "Hello? Hello?" he snapped.

"I don't know, Reno," the barkeep sheepishly replied. "I don't want any trouble…and neither do the authorities."

Reno abruptly hung up the phone and muttered, "It was the chinks." Picturing the fat kingpin and his hairy mole, he mumbled, "You think your vig is steep." He pounded out another familiar number. A distant chime pulsed in his ear. "Pick up, pick up," he impatiently chanted.

"River City Antiquities," answered Danny.

"Danny, it's Reno."

"Oh the missing Mister Reno James finally surfaces," Danny toyed. "Your absence has been making Danny and his partners very nervous."

"I've got your fucking money, Danny," Reno snapped. "I will be in Bangkok tomorrow to finalize payment and transfer. That is not why I'm calling."

"You make Danny very happy man. What else can Danny do for you?"

Reno snorted. "I need to place a small order. I need half a dozen assault rifles and sidearms and a dozen hand grenades."

"Make and model?" the conduit questioned.

"It doesn't matter. I just don't want any crap," Reno declared. "I'll need five magazines of ammo per small arm."

"This is the first time you request ammunition with a small order." Danny giggled. "Do you need export documentation?"

"No," Reno softly said. "This order is for me." Hanging up the phone, he focused on the single orchid decorating the phone station. Recalling Marshall welcoming Longboard into the fold, he grinned. *The one-legged ranger had a temper,* he reflected. *Marshall really was a badass. However, if you were a brother-in-arms, you were always welcome at his campfire. Hell, he basically adopted Joey and all his wartime issues. I've got to get home to avenge my brother,* he realized. Turning, he spotted Longboard in a casual button-down Hawaiian shirt and faded denim jeans strolling in his direction. A relaxed grin dominated the surfer's chiseled features.

Approaching the stoic Reno, Longboard inquired, "What is it?"

"The Triad murdered Marshall," Reno whispered.

The surfer's worry-free expression faded. The mask of death appeared and muttered, "No prisoners."

"Absolutely," Reno concurred.

Plush corridor carpeting cushioned Reno's heavy tread. Strategic floral arrangements accented the long hallway. *I need to focus on the mission,* he realized. *Will*

Sandy understand? Would anybody who wasn't baptized in combat? How do I explain the necessity of avenging my brother? There is no debate, he concluded. *I'll state the facts, grab my belongings, and head to the airport.* Taking a deep breath, he inserted the room key. The hotel room's lock clicked. Sunlight flowed through a large open window. The Indian Ocean sparkled in the distance. The posh suite was crisp and clean. An active shower resonated through an open bathroom door. Beneath the cleansing cascade, Sandy hummed a simple tune. *Ah fuck,* Reno thought. *This is not going to be easy.*

"Is that you, Mister James?" Sandy called out. The running water terminated. "Don't forget I have a letter to deliver before our departure."

"I have bad news," Reno declared.

"If it's about Australia," she joked, "I'm very flexible." She exited the bathroom in a courtesy terrycloth robe. With her head hung low, she vigorously dried blond locks with a billowing white towel. Glancing at the American's hard expression, she paused. Dropping the towel, she stood erect. "What is the matter?"

He stood speechless, studying the tall, slender wet-haired beauty. Her deep-blue eyes tightened. "I was just notified that a close friend of mine in Thailand was killed doing me a favor...a fellow vet...a brother." His voice cracked. Stating the fact confirmed reality. Marshall was dead.

She stepped forward. They embraced.

Squeezing her tight, he smelled clean, moist hair. "I'm sorry," he mumbled. "Marshall's termination requires my focused attention. I...I have to leave."

Locked in his arms, she whispered, "Does this mean good-bye?"

"I hope not," he answered, kissing the top of her head.

Snuggling deeper into the embrace, she muttered, "Me too." Flexing, she pushed back. Her tone stiffened. "As a physician, I know the importance of staying in character. The shroud of the title alone has helped me deal with life and death. I don't know what you have to do...and I don't care. I just don't want to be the distraction that jeopardizes your task. Good luck, Mister James. Drop me a line after you fulfill your responsibilities. Today is not the day for good-bye."

Chapter 42

———◈◈◈———

Night receded. A gray sky slowly appeared over the Bangkok shipyards. Bright lights illuminated massive cranes loading and unloading colorful shipping containers. A chorus of grinding, coughing machines converted power into motion. Falling metal rang out. A late-night shower had doused the docks and surrounding roadways. The air was moist. The scent of rain lingered. Behind steel grate and rolltop security doors, businesses slept. A welcoming light poured out of the open storefront of the Wheelhouse Pub. The beckoning rays spilled across a glistening asphalt frontage road. Inside the brightly lit cantina, four exhausted Thai dockworkers shared a breakfast pitcher of beer. Scarred yellow hard hats cluttered their round blistered red table. In matching black rubber work-boots and tired dark-blue jumpsuits, they slouched in wooden chairs. They sat quietly. Sucking on cigarettes, they celebrated the end of a graveyard shift.

The Wheelhouse's proprietor was a skinny silver-haired Thai. With an arched spine, he lugged a sloshing red plastic pail of used dishwater past the solemn laborers. On the damp sidewalk, he dropped the heavy bucket and sighed. Taking a motivating breath, he lifted and tossed the soapy solution far into the deserted street. A wave of frothy liquid slammed into pitted blacktop. Wiping a moist hand on a soiled bib apron, he pointed at the empty beer mug occupying a sidewalk seating option. The lone white patron nodded. The old barkeep picked up the plastic pail. Weary bones groaned as he slowly shuffled to retrieve another morning beer.

I probably should have got a coffee, Reno reflected. Swiping his somnolent expression with a clutching palm, he leaned back. Ripe clothes clung to his clammy body. *A hot shower and cool sheets would be nice,* he fantasized. "Business before pleasure," he mumbled, accepting a foamy mug of cold brew. In the distance, a freighter navigating down the Chao Phraya River blasted a low, defiant horn. The warning echoed down the murky-brown waterway. *I feel your pain,* Reno thought, haunted by Marshall's untimely exit. *I took his generosity for granted. All the misfits in our expat community did.* Focused on the rising bubbles in the golden-yellow pilsner, he reflected on better days.

It was Christmas Eve 1976. Sporting scraggly hair and a George Harrison beard, Reno meandered down the congested Thawiwong Road in Phuket. Sweating in a long-sleeved white cotton dress shirt and bellbottomed denim jeans, he stopped in front of a beer stall. A sweaty, rancid Thai in a ratty Santa hat sold him a cold can of beer. Sucking down the cool carbonation, he resumed his aimless trek. The tropical sun descended. Holiday lights strung across the traffic-burdened boulevard came to life. Red, green, blue, and white bulbs twinkled. Outdoor cafés were packed. Food stalls released pungent odors. Laughter flowed out of bars, promoting young Asian flesh. Bing Crosby's rendition of "White Christmas" resonated from a seafood restaurant.

Wiping his damp forehead, Reno stopped in the stream. Pedestrians flowed by. *Where is the Southeast Asia magic?* he wondered. *Does it exist in the Kingdom of Thailand? My Stateside welcome was less than hospitable,* he reflected. Slowly turning, he snickered at a plywood snowman nailed to a palm tree and mumbled, "My god, the Buddhists impaled Frosty." Maybe it was Christmas. The holiday was not kind to foster children. *The fat man in the red suit never hopped down my chimney.* He grinned. *Best Christmas was a lukewarm turkey dinner in Nam with my brothers.*

"Hey, soldier!" a gruff voice hollered.

Reno scanned the crowd. Asian and tourist faces drifted by.

"Over here, Yank," the deep voice beckoned. Sitting at a sidewalk table, a burly American in a white Stetson waved Reno over. Empty beer bottles occupied the tabletop. A painted Thai beauty snuggled next to the cowboy.

"What is it?" Reno questioned as he approached.

The cowboy attempted to rise. Retreating to his seat, he chuckled. "Forgive me for not getting up. I forgot. I only have one leg."

Reno acknowledged the black humor with an uncomfortable grin. "What can I do for you, Tex?" he probed.

"Tex," the cowboy barked. "I'm from Colorado." Extending a hand, he added, "Raymond Marshall, 173rd Airborne."

"Reno James, Fourteenth Infantry Regiment."

"Merry Christmas, brother," Marshall accented, tightening a firm grip. "Let's drink to the birth of the Christ child," he offered, shooing away the working girl with a greenback gratuity.

Accepting the invitation, Reno slid into the whore's seat. The frail folding chair wobbled. Standing up, he repositioned the chair on the rough concrete sidewalk. Satisfied, he sat down. Sitting idle, he felt his sweat accelerate. "Whoa," he exclaimed, unfastening two shirt buttons.

Craning his neck, Marshall hollered over his shoulder, "Bobby, two beers and two tequilas."

"You don't appear to be a tourist?" Reno questioned.

Marshall snickered. "Home is where you hang your hat." Flexing an index finger, he lifted the brim of the Stetson. "For the last five years, home has been a Thai longhouse." A busy Asian waiter plopped two amber bottles of Singha and two shot glasses of golden tequila on the cluttered tabletop. The table rattled. An empty glass dead soldier fell and rolled off the edge. With catlike reflexes, Marshall caught the escaping bottle just before impact. "Still got it," he mumbled, placing the bottle back in formation. Picking up a tequila jigger, he solemnly muttered, "To those we left behind."

Reno nodded, touching his glass to Marshall's. The harsh spirit stung. His nostrils flared. A swig of cold beer doused his burning throat.

Studying the empty shot glass, Marshall echoed, "To those we left behind." Looking skyward, he smiled softly. His reflective expression faded, and squinting, he inquired, "The Fourteenth Regiment are the Golden Dragons?"

Reno nodded. "My regiment has deep roots in American history. The Golden Dragon nickname and symbol dates back to the Boxer Rebellion at the turn of the century. The Fourteenth's motto, '*Right-of-the-line*,' comes from the Civil War."

After taking a healthy swig, Marshall's face puckered. "Just what is *Right-of-the-line* supposed to mean?"

Reno chuckled. "The story goes that during some famous Civil War battle, a commander asked the general where he should put the Fourteenth Infantry Regiment. The general replied, 'Where they belong, right-of-the-line.' The general's comment was a military historical reference. Apparently, when the Italians conquered Europe with shields and swords, their right side or sword hand was vulnerable. The Roman Legion's best troops held the position on the right."

"The 173rd Airborne's legacy does not date back that far," Marshall informed him. "Probably because the Roman Empire did not have any fucking planes to parachute out of."

Reno laughed. "OK, Sky Soldier, maybe you can enlighten me on why the 173rd was nicknamed the *Herd* in Nam."

Marshall slowly nodded. "That moniker evolved from an event with true military historical significance." Leaning back, he proudly puffed out his chest and asked, "Do you remember the western TV series *Rawhide*?"

"Now that was a good show," Reno replied, raising a longneck bottle. "Although I must admit, I enjoyed the theme song more than the thirty black-and-white minutes of cowboys chasing cows."

"Precisely," Marshall exclaimed, reclaiming the spotlight. "The theme song was motivating. A colonel would play that catchy tune over the PA during all battle formations. The scurrying paratroopers kicked up a lot of dust and were nicknamed the Herd."

"I'll be damned," Reno commented, emptying the bottle.

Marshall tilted his wide-brimmed hat back and hollered, "Another round." After placing the loud order, he asked, "You do have time for another toot?"

Leaning back, Reno stretched out his legs and confessed, "I have nowhere to go."

"Are you passing through as a tourist?" Marshall prodded.

"More of a wanderer," Reno responded, feeling the distilled agave warming his belly. "After my discharge, I spent some time in San Bernardino, California. That's where I originally hailed from. It seemed dull, slow. The adrenaline rush of Nam changed my perspective of reality." He paused as the second round arrived. Clutching the cold amber bottle, he shrugged. "I bought a one-way ticket to Thailand looking for..." Shaking his head, he sighed.

Marshall burst out laughing. "If I got a nickel every time I heard a Vietnam vet sing the blues, I'd have a shitload of nickels." He shifted. The flimsily chair groaned. "Tell me, San Bernardino," he questioned, "do you have any plans for Christmas?"

Reno exchanged his grip on the cold bottle for the jigger of tequila. After tossing back the warm shot, he wiped moist lips with a backhand and answered, "You're looking at it."

"It's your lucky day, amigo," Marshall declared. "Every year, my Mexican brother in Arizona sends me a couple dozen of his mamacita's tamales to celebrate Jesus's birthday. Not to downplay turkey, ham, or Christmas goose, but nothing completes the holiday festivities like corn-husk-wrapped pork tamales." Raising his brows, he nudged, "Are you in?"

Secreting saliva lubricated Reno's mouth. He swallowed. "Fuckin' A," he declared.

Marshall grinned. Leaning forward, he disclosed, "I have a live-in Thai girlfriend. I'd appreciate if you don't mention the arm candy I was drinking with."

"Sure, buddy," Reno acknowledged. "I understand."

The air horn of a distant ferryboat blasted its presence. Reno looked up from his beer. *That was my best Christmas,* he concluded. The reality of Marshall's departure churned his gut. *The funeral's going to be tough,* he realized. It began to drizzle. Under the protective lee of a green awning, Reno took a big, cold swig of brew to dilute his grief.

The Bangkok shipyards awoke. Roll-down security doors receded. A cyclist peddled down the slick roadway. A motor scooter sputtered by. A rambling old woman pushed an aging blue canopied food cart. Three Tamils strutted down the wet sidewalk. The drizzle leaned toward rain. S.A.'s barrel-chested bodyguard, Gerard, led the procession. Two young lackeys tried to keep pace. The trio sported fresh blue Global Venture—logoed windbreakers. The moist light jackets flapped in a soft breeze. Reno leaned back. The Tamils approached.

Absent his harsh persona, Gerard grinned. "Good to see you again, Reno," he said, seeking shelter under the protective canopy. His young companions stood attentively in the light rain.

"We all good?" Reno asked the hovering gentle giant.

Gerard squinted. "I don't understand."

No slang, Reno realized. *My customers speak the queen's English.* "Are you satisfied with the merchandise?" he rephrased.

Nodding his comprehension, Gerard declared, "I am…all good." Behind the enlightened smuggler, his companions whispered like schoolchildren.

"What are they snickering about?" Reno asked, pointing at the murmuring dialogue with a beer mug.

Gerard glanced over his shoulder. The youths resumed an attentive posture. Nodding slowly, Gerard turned. "They heard about your rescue of a Tiger from the internment camp."

"The commandant's head exploded like a ripe melon," Reno toasted.

Gerard beamed. "Our relationship has evolved from negotiating factions to friends." Extending his hand, he sealed the sentiment with a firm handshake. "Cheerio, Mister Reno," he added, departing with a playful two-finger salute. His companions waved good-bye.

"Adios, amigos," Reno muttered to the exiting terrorists.

Rounding the street corner, the trio disappeared. Reno focused on the narrow alleyway across the street. The rain intensified. In a hooded dark-green poncho, Longboard emerged from the shadows. The downpour careened off his waterproof garment. The surfer secured a pistol in the small of his back and jogged across the street. Misplaced steps detonated puddles. Under the protection of the Wheelhouse's awning, he flipped back his hood. Water pounded the overhead canopy. After running moist fingers through wet hair, he took a dry seat beside his partner.

"Coffee," Longboard shouted into the pub. The frail proprietor nodded. Frowning at Reno, Longboard barked, "If you're going to sit there and drink beer while I have to wade in wet garbage to shadow you, we need to renegotiate our split." The hunchbacked owner handed Longboard a hot mug of Java. The surfer clutched the warm cup with cold, damp hands. Leaning forward, he inhaled the smoldering aroma.

Reno chuckled. Raising an almost empty beer mug, he said, "Upper management does have its perks."

Chapter 43

Sandy took a sip of strong black coffee. It was late morning. The hotel's restaurant was nearly deserted. Most of the tourists had already gorged themselves on the elaborate breakfast buffet before departing on sightseeing excursions. An island of chafing dishes occupied the center of the open-air facility. Stainless-steel bins of crisp bacon, sausage, and ham emitted a tempting pork aroma. A hint of curry lingered from the local selections offered. A chef in a white double-breasted jacket and stovepipe hat manned an omelet station. Sandy took a bite of toast blanketed with cheese. *I should have just settled for coffee,* she realized, setting the slice of charred bread on an empty platter. *My appetite departed with my American lover,* she concluded, conjuring up an image of Reno. *I wasn't going to derail his mission, but we should have negotiated a contingency plan to reconnect.* "Can I smoke here?" she mumbled, picking up a small cigar. With the cheroot balanced between delicate fingers, she scanned the upscale establishment. Spotting two local businessmen reading newspapers at a corner table, she took pause. *I saw them poolside yesterday,* she reflected. *I thought it odd that they would spend the afternoon under an umbrella and not loosen their ties. Were they at the lobby bar last night? Am I being monitored? Reno coached me to be careful.*

A waiter appeared and flicked a lighter. "Thank you," she responded, accepting the flame. Leaning back, she took a calming toke. *Tobacco and coffee,* she thought, *not a bad way to start a brokenhearted day. I'll make my delivery, try to get some tennis in, and then decide the location for the next chapter in my life.* After a few quick puffs, she rose, extinguished the dark tobacco, took one last gulp of java, and departed.

Sandy's tennis shoes squeaked as she strutted across the lobby's polished stone. A quick glance over her shoulder did not detect stalkers. *I shouldn't be so paranoid,* she counseled. An attentive bellman in a pillbox hat opened the main door. Warm, humid air invaded. The doorman in a double-breasted purple coat and glossy patent leather military cap approached.

"Taxi please," Sandy instructed.

The commissionaire blew into a silver pea whistle. The lead vehicle in a long line of yellow taxies broke ranks. The grumbling Toyota screeched to an abrupt termination curbside.

"Where to, miss?" inquired the polite doorman.

Presenting the powder-blue envelope addressed to Doctor Ondaatje's wife, she asked, "Is this far?"

"No," the doorman replied. "Your destination is located in Colombo 10. That is the adjoining district." Bending over, he instructed the cabbie in Singhalese. Standing at attention, he handed her a Hilton-logoed business card displaying the swirling and curlicue Singhalese alphabet. "When you need to return, show this to any taxi driver."

"Thank you," she replied, exchanging a folded rupee note for the return directions.

As she climbed into the vinyl backseat, warm plastic squealed. It smelled like an ashtray. The cab lunged forward and skidded behind a tourist bus spewing diesel fumes. Searching for fresh air, Sandy gazed out the open passenger window. Observing her business-attired shadows quizzing the doorman, her heart sank. *They are stalking me,* she realized. *Reno was right. I need to be careful.*

The taxi followed the toxic coughing tour bus out of the buffed hotel grounds. As she exited the Hilton sanctuary, Colombo appeared as a congested urban hive inhabited by the haves and have-nots. Traffic purred and coughed. Horns tooted, howled, and wailed. Half-naked bony men sat cross-legged on the sidewalk hawking tropical produce. Behind the skinny vendors flowed women in colorful saris, businessmen, and uniformed schoolchildren. Sandy's cabdriver preferred rapid acceleration and braking to navigating through the maze. It was muggy, dusty, and smelled like ripe garbage. Trash infested the gutters. Idling beside a cow grazing on a patch of grass in the median, Sandy cranked up the rear window. As the backseat temperature approached unbearable, the taxi's brakes screamed. Sandy jerked forward. The cabbie turned and blindly slapped the meter off. A crooked yellow-toothed smile announced the destination.

After paying the fare, Sandy exited the sweat box. A warm breeze welcomed her on the shaded sidewalk. Passersby slowed to gawk at a white woman. Ignoring the stares, Sandy referenced the addressed envelope to the midrise apartment building before her. *This is it,* she thought, smiling at the sleeping security guard in a webbed patio chair. *I can't blame him.* She snickered. *This sweltering heat induces the urge to nap.*

"Excuse me, Doctor DeWitt," snapped a firm, invading voice.

Sandy jumped. Turning, she stood before the two stalking businessmen, each sporting dark-green sunglasses and mustaches. The wide one in a tan suit shadowed the short, frail spokesman dressed in a wrinkled pinstripe ensemble. "Who are you?" she gasped, catching a breath.

"Our apologies, Doctor," Shorty offered, smirking. "We did not mean to startle you." Taking a step back, he gazed up at the residential complex. "We see you are here to visit Doctor Ondaatje's family. It is unfortunate that the physician chose to disobey the evacuation edict and remain in harm's way."

"I asked who you are," Sandy growled.

Chuckling, he answered, "We are here to ensure that no disinformation disseminates from the conflict in the north." Raising a brow, he asked, "What is the nature of your visit?"

Sandy smiled. *Now the monkey comes out of the sleeve.* "Doctor Ondaatje spoke lovingly of his wife and daughters. I felt compelled to meet them before departing your wonderful country." Flashing the powder-blue envelope, she added, "And to deliver this letter."

"May I see that?" he inquired, extending a confiscating hand. Reluctantly, she placed the correspondence in the anxious palm. Snatching the letter, he secured it in an inside coat pocket and informed her. "After inspection, we will deliver the good doctor's mail." Flicking beckoning fingers, he continued, "Your handbag please."

"I have nothing to hide," Sandy declared, surrendering her purse.

The spokesman's wide accomplice intercepted the exchange. His massive paw rummaged through her personal effects. After a disappointing shrug, he returned the leather tote bag.

Slinging the purse over a shoulder, she asked, "Am I free to go now?"

Slowly nodding, Shorty interjected, "Keep your conversation with the doctor's wife light. We wouldn't want any false rumors resonating from the Ondaatje residence."

Casually walking toward the building's double glass doors, Sandy' felt her heart pounding. She could feel the glare of the stalking security men. Standing on a frayed red welcome mat, she looked down at the snoozing gatekeeper. *Wake up,* she thought. *Please don't delay my entry.* "Excuse me," rolled out of her dry throat.

The doorman snorted and peered up with an open eye.

"I'm here to see Tamara Ondaatje," Sandy announced.

The slouching sentinel scratched his head. Smacking his lips, he reached under his metal seat and retrieved a clipboard. Disconnected sleepy eyes scanned the top fastened page. A wide yawn accompanied his perusal of subsequent sheets.

Sandy bit her lip. *I'm being shadowed by the Gestapo,* she thought. *On the other side of the glass barrier is sanctuary,* she realized, glancing at the double entrance doors. *But before I can escape my stalkers, I have to tolerate this waking tortoise.*

The doorman slowly rose and after placing a cap on his head allowed access. Sandy nodded as she passed the guardian into the security of the building foyer. The air-conditioned white-tiled room was small. Between two elevator doors, a clay pot housed a dying palm plant. Sandy strolled into an open cab and pressed the sixth-floor button. Looking up, she could see the security agents observing her from the sidewalk. With a soft, grating groan, the lift's stainless-steel doors slid shut. A victorious smile appeared on the Dutch doctor. *Thank you, Mister Reno James, for teaching me the advantages of a decoy to throw off predators,* she reflected. Squatting down, she pulled up a pant leg. A Hilton Hotel envelope containing Doctor Ondaatje's correspondence poked out of her white gym sock. The elevator chimed as she retrieved the correspondence she had promised to deliver.

Sandy rapped gently on apartment six-twelve's door. Immediately, it swung open. In an exquisite orange sari trimmed in gold lace, Tamara Ondaatje, flanked by her daughters, greeted her guest with a shy smile. Tamara's pudgy round face inflated the features of a former beauty. The local gown exposed her soft midriff. The thin girls wore matching school uniforms consisting of a white collared smock dress and blue necktie. The preteen stood gawking, and her younger sister suppressed an infectious giggle with a cupped hand.

"Welcome to our home, Doctor DeWitt," Tamara muttered softly, looking down. "I am Doctor Ondaatje's wife, Tamara, and these are our daughters, Hashini and Chandrika."

"Please call me Sandy," the Dutch doctor replied, shaking the nervous hostess's sweaty palm and shooting a friendly wink at the girls. "And this is for you," she added, handing the smuggled letter to its intended recipient. "Please excuse the envelope exchange; I wanted to avoid the government censors."

Tamara gingerly accepted the correspondence as if it were marked fragile. "Please come in," she muttered, focused on the letter. Sandy followed the retreating family into the antiseptic-smelling flat. The walls were bleach white. Dark grout defined polished white-tile flooring. A cassette tape deck on an end table emitted soft jazz. On the far wall, a lacquered wood chest supported a portable color television. A teakwood sofa setting surrounded a glass coffee table. The low table was set with a silver-lined porcelain teapot, cups, and a platter of British biscuits. Beside the kettle, a half-full bottle of Johnny Walker Black Label stood proud.

"I've prepared some tea for our visit," Tamara announced, placing the letter on the coffee table. "If you would prefer a spirit, I can offer you some fine scotch."

"Ceylon tea is a real treat for me, thank you," Sandy responded, taking a seat on the cushioned sofa.

Young Chandrika plopped down beside her and looked up with pure innocent curiosity. Sandy recalled the faces of her young patients, scarred, mutilated, and terminated by war. Her heart sank. Swallowing, she refocused, "Your daughters are even more beautiful than Tom described."

"He cherished his girls," Tamara offered, serving tea.

"And you as well, Tamara," Sandy reassured the fragile Mrs. Ondaatje.

The hostess smiled. "I was never sure he did," she confessed. "Ours was not a *love marriage*."

"I don't understand," Sandy probed, accepting a misting cup.

"Our families arranged our union," Tamara informed her, taking a seat. "My husband was dedicated to his profession, to his family, and to his daughters." Behind welling tears, she confided, "When he defied the order to return home, I feared it was because he never grew to love me."

"Read his letter, Tamara," Sandy counseled. "I can assure you, one of the finest men I ever met loves you very much."

"Thank you Doc…Sandy," Tamara replied, picking up the envelope.

Sandy sipped tea. The young girls snacked on cookies. Mrs. Ondaatje read. *Theirs was an arranged marriage,* Sandy realized. *In life's journey, I would hate to be paired with the person assigned to the seat beside me. My first marriage was a "love marriage,"* she reflected, *more of a very big mistake.* Stealing a glance at the focused, beaming Mrs. Ondaatje, Sandy felt warmth as tears of reassuring passion rolled down the Sri Lankan beauty's soft cheeks. Picturing Reno, Sandy wondered if he was the one. Grinning, she realized Reno James did very well in his initial interview as a companion. *Only one way to find out,* she surmised. *Looks like the beaches of southern Thailand will be the stage for the next act in my life.*

Tamara religiously folded her husband's letter. Placing it over her heart, she looked at her guest and mouthed, "Thank you."

Chapter 44

⁂

It was a gloomy day. The sea was calm. Soft waves rolled in. Three beached long-tail boats awaited the bereaved. Like a lost herd, the funeral crowd migrated down the powdery sand. Sunee, in a short black dress, led the procession. Her grieving attire accented every curve of a youthful frame. Holding the powder residue remains of Army Ranger Raymond Marshall in a wrapped white cloth, she struggle in high heels. Stumbling behind Sunnee in a tight off-shoulder black gown, Kanya held a framed photo of the deceased master sergeant.

Reno slowed his advance. Granules seeped into his penny loafers. He rolled up the long sleeves of a white dress shirt and loosened his tie knot to combat the heat. Spotting Bear, he gave an acknowledging nod to the large black man. In a charcoal suit and thin black tie, Bear comforted his petite, modestly dressed Thai wife. Beads of sweat flowed off the Bear's big black noggin. Squinting at a thin Mexican in a tan wide-lapel suit, Reno assumed the Hispanic man must have served with Marshall. Other unfamiliar faces popped out of the somber expatriate gathering. A lanky Jethro-looking hillbilly sporting a scraggly goatee and wearing an uncomfortably warm tweed jacket patted the Mexican's back. The Hispanic lit up, displaying sparkling gold incisors. *Definitely brothers,* Reno realized.

In jet-black high-water slacks and exposed white socks, a disoriented, sniffling Joey bullied his way into a watercraft. The traumatized Joey sat twitching as he gazed into open water.

"It looks like Joey is having a bad day," Longboard whispered.

Reno nodded and mumbled, "We all are." Glancing at the surfer in a happy floral shirt, he said, "Marshall took care of Kanya and Sunnee with a life insurance policy. Unfortunately, Joey is on his own."

"He can stay with me," Longboard casually committed.

Reno's face puckered.

The surfer grinned. "I control my inner demon. Maybe I can assist Joey with his."

As he climbed into a wooden boat, Reno's dress shoe sunk into moist sand. *I should have worn sneakers,* he thought. Diesel engines coughed to life. Shore attendants launched the three long boats. A sea breeze soothed the sweltering passengers.

"The locals call the tossing of ashes in open water *loi angkarn,*" Longboard informed him quietly. "They believe the sea will wash away Marshall's sins and ensure a smooth journey to heaven."

I like that, Reno thought, as the grieving armada bobbed in a tight circle. In the boat across from Reno, Sunnee carefully dropped the white cloth containing Marshall's ashes over the side. The bundle drifted across the deep blue surface and then slowly sank. Sunnee and Kanay wailed while others scattered flowers on the water. From the back of each boat, the pilots fired rockets into the darkening sky. Glancing up at the fireworks erupting across the gray clouds, Reno grinned. My bighearted brother is dancing in the afterlife. *And if he didn't make it to heaven for his past sins,* Reno chuckled, *he is fucking the devil's daughter.* Leaning into the surfer, he muttered, "Now let's drink in commemoration of an Airborne Ranger."

Longboard nodded.

Looking forward, Reno mumbled, "Tomorrow, we seek vengeance."

The sleek sampans sliced through the rolling deep blue sea. Under a gloomy sky, no one spoke. The short voyage terminated in soft sand. Shore attendants offered feeble disembarking assistance. Somber passengers plodded up the grasping granular incline. Huffing and puffing, Bear broke the silence. "I don't know about anyone else, but I feel like I'm toting the Sahara in my wingtips."

Polite rippling laughter responded. Muffled conversations emerged. The beach faded into encroaching grass. Marshall's usually festive longhouse stood quietly. Lifeless dark windows graced the facade. Across the trimmed lawn, empty folding white resin chairs surrounded round linen-draped tables. Under a protective canopy, a Thai bartender in a red vest and black bowtie offered libations. Standing behind a bamboo bar, he focused on the advancing well-dressed horde and took a deep breath.

Bear plopped down at the first seating option. His massive frame dwarfed the tiny chair. Tola, his petite Thai wife, stood attentively at his side. Pulling off a size-thirteen scuffed black wingtip, he poured out a handful of the beach. "Reno," he called out, shaking the shoe. "Have a seat. We need to talk."

Reno and Longboard accepted the invitation and pulled out glossy white wood folding chairs. Empting his other shoe, Bear looked at his wife. "Flower," he muttered. "Get us a bottle?" Glancing at Reno and the surfer, he questioned, "Rum?" They nodded approval. Leaning back, he closed his eyes and puckered his lips. She gave him a quick peck and departed. "Don't forget the glasses, ice, and Cokes," he called out.

"Thank you, Mrs. Jones," Reno offered.

Bent over, tying his shoes, Bear growled, "Who killed Marshall?"

"Later, Bear," Reno sternly answered. "First, I want to drink to the memory of the brother I lost."

Bear slowly nodded. "You're right," he mumbled. Raising a brow, he probed, "But you do know who killed him."

"We do," Longboard answered.

"Then later it is," Bear conceded. Scanning the crowd, he grinned. Out of the side of his mouth, he said, "There is someone you boys need to meet." Bear stood and hollered over polite chatter, "Hey, Bandito!"

A thin Mexican in a tan three-piece leisure suit standing in the drink queue turned to investigate. Beneath a thick black mustache, a wide smile emerged. Golden teeth sparkled. Vacating his place in line, he strutted to respond. "Hey, Bear!" he shouted. "Did you ever figure out who your father was?"

Bear let out a barrel laugh. "No," he answered. "But I whittled it down to a short list. If your sister is still looking for a prom date, I'll share the prospects with her." The two men embraced. "I never thought I'd see you again, Ochoa," Bear confessed as they parted.

Ochoa frowned. "Really, amigo? Did you really think I'd miss Marshall's farewell?"

Reno and Longboard rose.

The Hispanic stuck out his hand and announced, "Oscar Ochoa, only brothers can call me Bandito."

"Please to meet you, Bandito," Reno responded with a firm grip. "It's Reno James; however, the moniker San Bernardino occasionally surfaces."

"I go by Longboard," the surfer said, completing the introduction ritual.

The tiny Mrs. Jones arrived, juggling a bucket of ice, plastic cups, logoed red cans of Coke, and a liter bottle of dark rum. Somewhat relieved, she carefully unloaded the burden on the barren side of the table. "Thanks, Flower," Bear mumbled as she set up shop and poured four healthy rum-and-Cokes. After serving the men, she bowed and departed. "She is a good wife," Bear mumbled as he raised his plastic cup and toasted, "To my brother, Master Sergeant Raymond Marshall."

"To Marshall," the table audience echoed.

Ochoa looked down into the fizzing dark caramel concoction. "I was only in country for about a month," he mumbled. "The platoon was sweeping a ridge line. The point element consisted of Marshall, me, and two other unlucky *putas*. We walked into a classic U-shaped ambush." Ochoa paused to wet his palate. A focused audience obliged. He continued, "A strafing machine gun cut the point element in half. I dove for cover on coarse rock shale. I clawed at the hard surface. I needed to get lower. Communist bullets buzzed all around. Shredded growth rained down. Incoming fire sparked off the surrounding rocks. Then it happened. My face exploded. Everything went black. A shot to the head blinded me. Shattered teeth rolled down my throat. I lay there thinking about the Catholic faith I was born into but ignored. Could I slide into heaven on a technicality? I wondered." His voice crackled. He took a deep, composing breath. A soft golden smile emerged as he continued, "Out of the darkness, I felt massive hands latching onto my chest rigging. Marshall barked over the battlefield clamor, 'Hey, Bandito, you ready to get the fuck out of here?' I told him I was blind. He told me that was a good thing because exiting is going to be one ugly bitch." Ochoa quickly tweaked a sniffling noise. "I've never told that story to anyone," he confessed with a catch in his throat.

"I provided covering fire," Bear interjected. "How the two of you never got hit amazed all of us." Glancing at Reno and the surfer, he clarified. "Oscar never got shot in the face. Rock shrapnel had sprayed his Mayan good looks."

Grinning wide, Ochoa displayed gold front teeth. "I lost two incisors that day."

A ruckus at the canopy bar distracted the conversation. The skinny Thai bartender sat on the ground. He looked bewildered. Swinging his arms defiantly, Joey with beer in hand stomped away. Bear's petite wife assisted the confused barkeep to his feet. Squints and puzzled expressions tracked the departing Joey.

"Joey's short fuse is lit," Bear mumbled. "Hey, Joey!" he shouted. "Come join us."

Joey acknowledged the invitation with a scowl. He popped open his beer. A fountain of spraying carbonation erupted. Gulping down the rapidly escaping white foam, he walked around the table. Hovering over Reno, he sucked back tears. He snorted, and his fair completion turned soft red. Sniffling, he shouted in a high-pitched crackle, "Marshall is dead because of you."

"We are all grieving," Reno softly replied. A half-full beer can hit the ground. Joey's torso pivoted. *Here it comes,* Reno realized, nothing like telegraphing a punch. Reno rolled with the blow. The grazing fist stung. Rubbing a tender cheek, he watched Joey running toward the beach.

"You OK?" Bear asked, placing a comforting paw on Reno's crouching back.

"I saw it coming," Reno answered, taking a deep breath.

Longboard pushed back from the table. "I'll check on Joey," he volunteered.

"Do you know something about Marshall's murder?" Ochoa questioned.

Reno nodded.

Ochoa's pleasant demeanor faded. Focused on Bear, he demanded, "Do we have a strategy?"

Seeking a response, Bear squinted at Reno.

"Look," Ochoa barked, breaking the silence. "I didn't max out my credit card for a trip to Thailand to watch the sprinkling of flower petals on the ocean."

"Marshall's assassins are extremely powerful," Reno cautioned.

Bear snickered and mumbled, "Born in the north to die in the south." Clearing his throat, he spoke in a low growl. "Vietnamese regulars would tattoo that prediction on their arms. Bandito and I fulfilled many of those prophecies."

Reno bowed his head in respect. Checking his watch, he muttered, "The war council will meet at twenty-three hundred hours in the Jade Tiger Lounge." Glancing around at the buzzing bereaved, he concluded. "Until then, I'm going to celebrate and drink to the memory of my friend and brother."

Chapter 45

Pounding rain cascaded off the thatched roof of the Jade Tiger Lounge. It was a dark night, the downpour deafening. Slouched down in a rattan chair beside the brightly lit bamboo bar, the barkeep Aroon snored through an open mouth. The illuminating light faded across a sea of vacated tables and chairs. In the darkest corner, five veterans of the United States' undeclared Vietnam War held council. Cletus "Bear" Jones chomped on the moist end of a smoldering dark cigar. Martin "Stretch" Bickhum, a tall gangly hick from some Southern backwater sharecropper's shack, sucked on an unfiltered cigarette, his bony fingers stained with a nicotine addiction. Between puffs, he stroked a scraggly billy-goat beard. Oscar "Bandito" Ochoa politely waved at the growing cloud of secondhand smoke. Longboard sat stoic, focused on Reno.

After wetting his dry throat with a swig of cold brew, Reno glanced around at the ensemble. "Gentlemen," he opened.

"Before we get started," the hillbilly interrupted, pushing back from the table. "I got to take a piss."

Reno shook his head as Martin lethargically headed toward the facility. "What's his story?" Reno whispered.

Bear and Ochoa, reflecting on an inside joke, grinned. "Don't let his Jed Clampett persona fool you," Bear answered. "Stretch is one of the best jungle fighters I ever saw. The country boy was right at home in the dense wilderness.

You would think he had x-ray vision the way he spotted dink spider holes," Bear chuckled. "Growing up in an urban jungle, I was lost in that sea of green growth. The cracker looked out for us inner-city soul-brothers."

Stretch emerged from the facilities. Enjoying an unshielded wide yawn, he zipped up his fly. Taking his seat, he let out a comforting sigh.

"Can we begin now?" Reno emphasized.

"Yep," Martin declared.

"My retaliation plan is simple but infested with risk," Reno stated. "The adversary is formidable."

"Who killed Marshall?" Bear barked.

"A Chinese Triad," Longboard answered.

"What's a triad?" The hillbilly questioned.

"It's like a street gang," Ochoa chimed in. Glancing around, he added, "Maybe closer to the Mafia."

Bear snickered. "I'm from South Philly. I know about street gangs and organized crime. They are tough motherfuckers, no doubt. Hell, as a kid, I remember this bag lady for the mob. This scrawny gray-haired old mama collected the receipts for the numbers racket. Every junky and street punk knew she was toting thousands in cash." Looking through the hovering smoke-filled haze, he grinned. "Nobody touched her out of fear, fear of retaliation." Leaning back, he took a reflecting toke. "I thought I knew some real badasses growing up in Philly. Then I went to Nam. The toughest street gang to march across the planet wears army green."

"We are no longer in a war zone, Bear," Reno counseled. "More than likely, we will have to face the Thai criminal justice system. And the death penalty is alive and kicking in the Kingdom of Thailand."

"Shit," Martin snorted. "After Nam, I returned to the world. My first week back at the local Piggly Wiggly some hippie bitch called me a baby killer." Snickering, he added, "One thing for sure, baby killers don't give a shit about the police."

"So what's the plan, amigo?" Ochoa asked.

"Just a simple search and destroy," Reno tossed out. "We eliminate all hostiles present, burn down their hooch, and immediately withdrawal. There will be no dustoffs, reinforcements, or supporting artillery. I'm optimistically calculating that a brazen day raid may dissuade the Triad from retaliating." He shrugged. "And if they do, I'm prepared to go to war." Grinning, he concluded, "A blatant assault may have the same effect on the authorities. Christ, the local police, fearing the Triad, swept Marshall's murder under the rug. Maybe they'll show us the same courtesy."

Slowly bobbing heads accepted the mission.

Longboard broke the silence. "I respect your bold assault strategy, partner. However, I ply my trade in the shadows."

"Understood," Reno mumbled.

Bear pointed his big noggin at the open-air bar's entrance. Pivoting heads investigated. Joey stood soaking wet. Water dripped off his drenched silhouette. At his feet, a puddle grew on the hardwood floor. In a flash, he rushed the table, slammed down a deck of cards, turned, and flew out of the saloon into the dark wet night. Bear opened the frayed box. It was not a full deck. He fanned the cards facedown on the tabletop. Each card was logoed with the red, white, and blue wing and sword insignia of the 173rd Airborne. Martin, Ochoa, and Bear religiously admired the emblem.

With a dealer's expertise, Bear rolled the cards over. Every card was an ace of spades. "The death card," Bear mumbled. "Nobody touched the bag lady in South Philly because of the stiff mob penalty. Everybody knew who would be collecting the penance." Holding up a single card, he added, "The Triad will know who did this."

"One other thing, gentlemen," Reno stated. "Do you remember the battlefield etiquette that your kill's weapon became yours? And anything else the dink might be carrying?" Reflective nods answered. "Well, nothing eliminates debt like killing your creditor. A successful raid ensures me of a two-hundred-and-fifty-thousand-dollar windfall, which I will share equally."

"What does that mean?" Martin pondered.

"Fifty thousand dollars, amigo," Ochoa answered. "I'm doing this for Marshall," he clarified. "Not money."

"I understand." Reno nodded. "But the money will ease your angst just a little."

Chapter 46

———— ✺ ————

Two Brahma oxen fastened to a heavy wooden yoke plodded methodically up a dusty road. Behind the beast of burden, a rickety wooden cart creaked uphill. The trailer was empty. The only passenger was a hollow-eyed old man with thin silver hair and a scruffy gray beard. Clothed in rags, his emaciated dark-skinned torso rocked to the rhythm of the jostling assent. A swatting switch motivated the castrated bulls. It was hot. Flies buzzed. The humped cattle ground to a standstill. Trailing dust engulfed the timber vehicle. The weary driver raised a downcast gaze. Two Tamil guerrillas in camo fatigues, carrying assault rifles and bandoliers of ammunition, blocked the roadway.

A Tamil Tiger approached the driver. A deep scar ran down the side of his face. Fresh cuts and scrapes crisscrossed his youthful features. A scraggly moustache decorated his upper lip. "Where are you going, *thaathhaa* (grandfather)?" Chola politely inquired.

"Away," the old man muttered. "Wherever the dumb beasts take me."

"Don't flee, Grandfather," Chola counseled. "Victory will soon be ours. We will push the invading government forces into the sea."

"You push, the soldiers retaliate, the innocent die," the old man muttered. His ghastly gaze scanned the young zealot. "A helicopter arrived with the sun. Bullets rained down. Hundreds of soldiers arrived by truck. The uniformed animals smashed, looted, and killed. Survivors fled into the jungle. The village of my father's father was set ablaze. The invaders were gone by noon."

"When was this tragedy?" Chola asked.

The old man shrugged. Shaking his head, he thwacked a fly-infested ox's backside. A cloud of flies erupted. The cart rolled forward.

"Safe journey, *thaathhaa*," Chola mumbled. The old man's tale was all too familiar. The government's strategy was to eliminate all the Tamil villages surrounding the port city of Trincomalee. The harbor and its commercial enterprises were the prize. Economics was a powerful motivator. Chola flicked his head and continued down the dusty trail. His companion followed.

The dirt road snaked downhill toward the wounded remains of a farming village. Weeds infested uncultivated paddy fields. A burnt hut graced the hillside. Unwanted growth swayed under a warm, foul wind. A rancid stench slapped the Tigers.

"What is it?" snorted the round baby-faced Gajaadhar.

"Dog," Chola informed, pointing to a bloated carcass on the side of the road. The light-brown short-haired mutt had a white fur collar and stocking feet. A bullet hole between large pointed ears was the apparent cause of death.

The partisans accelerated. Upwind, death's aroma dissipated. *A farmer's beloved pet,* Chola reflected, visualizing a happy, tail-wagging canine.

"I have two dogs," Gajaadhar mumbled.

"What are their names?" Chola asked.

The fresh-faced terrorist grinned. "Lord and Lady," he exclaimed. Reflecting, he mumbled, "They are good dogs."

Mud and brick houses displaying battle wounds appeared. Bullet holes adorned walls. Broken glass lined hollow window frames. Charred walls supported a collapsed roof. A burnt aroma lingered. The uninhabitable structures appeared deserted. A frail dark boy wearing short pants dragged a bulging gunnysack out of a doorframe. Soot covered most of his naked glistening torso. Spotting the heavily armed Tigers, he froze. Gaunt features faded. A smile blossomed. Abandoning the loot, he approached the freedom fighters.

"*Thambi* (little brother), are there any soldiers about?" Chola inquired.

"No, *iya* (sir)," the skinny boy replied, flexing. "But two white men arrived in an automobile. They are talking to adults at the library."

Glancing at Gajaadhar, Chola mumbled, "This is the place." Addressing the boy, he commanded, "Take us to the library."

"Yes, sir," the beaming boy responded.

Beside Chola, the boy proudly strutted down what remained of Main Street. Destitute inhabitants materialized. Nods conveyed respect. The Tigers politely acknowledged traumatized admirers. A soft wind teased a large pile of ash in the roadway. The polluted breeze engulfed the Tigers and their young guide. Chola snorted. Gajaadhar sneezed.

The skinny kid pointed at the extinguished pyre and informed them, "The soldiers burned all the library books."

Chola approached the heaping pile of ash. *My adversary has no soul,* he realized. *The government will not stop until the Tamil cultural heritage is reduced to a powdery residue.*

"It's only books," Gajaadhar offered.

"No, machan," Chola mumbled. "Men live and die, but a people's journey through time survives in literature. The government is attempting to erase the footprints of our race with fire." Chola glanced up from the cremated remains. Parked in front of the gutted public library sat a mud-splattered Range Rover. Mingling locals peered into the open doorway and broken windows of the simple white plaster structure. "Thanks, little brother," Chola muttered to his scrawny young guide.

The Tigers approached the library. The small crowd parted and bowed. An angled wooden door hung from a single hinge. Chola entered through the shattered doorframe. Gajaadhar stood watch. The bookshelves were empty. Index cards blanketed the floor. Whispers resonated. Chola quietly walked around a toppled cabinet. Four men sat around a table. A peasant farmer spoke softly. A casually dressed local translator relayed the dialogue. A balding middle-aged white man took notes. Scribbling, he remained focused. Beads of sweet clung to his smooth scalp. In a khaki photo vest, another white man with long, scraggly black hair fidgeted with one of the many cameras tethered around his neck. A full beard complemented his scruffy appearance. Puffing on a cigarette, the photographer appeared bored.

"Good afternoon, gentlemen," Chola announced in perfect English.

The startled session flinched. The translator and farmer smiled at the *poorali* (freedom fighter). The white men jumped up.

"I...I am John Kohn, reporter for the *New York Times*, and this is photojournalist Alec Russing."

"Are you a Jew?" Chola asked.

Examining the assault rifle, Kohn swallowed. He shot a questioning glance at the longhaired Russing. "Yes...yes, I'm Jewish," he replied. "Why is that relevant?"

"Because a Jew would have a passionate comprehension of the realities of ethnic cleansing," Chola replied.

"Whoa," Kohn gasped. "Who are you?" Taking a sobering breath, he added, "If I may inquire?"

"I am a Liberation Tiger of Tamil Eelam," Chola proudly declared. "Our objective is to create Tamil Eelam, a homeland for Tamils in the northern and eastern provinces. I've sought you out to relay our struggle to the world beyond our shores. The Colombo press characterizes us as Marxists and religious extremists." He held out his AK-47. "My weapon is Soviet made, and the Tigers are a secular movement; beyond that, there are no other similarities to Communism. Socialism is not the objective. The portrayal of a religious conflict between Tamil Hindus and Singhalese Buddhists is also false. Buddhism is not under attack. The culture of the Tamil people is systematically being destroyed by the Sri Lankan government. I picked up arms to defend a long and valuable heritage." Chola's voice crackled. He took a composing breath.

Kohn looked up from his note pad with an open mouth. Focused eyes pondered a response.

"Are you familiar with the book burnings in Nazi Germany?" Chola asked.

"Of course," Kohn blurted.

"Are you aware of the burning of the Jaffna Library two years ago?" Chola inquired.

Slowly nodding, Kohn answered, "I'm aware of the criminal act; regrettably the incident did not receive much press coverage in the West."

"The Sri Lankan government destroyed one of the largest libraries in Asia. The Jaffna Public Library contained irreplaceable palm-leaf manuscripts, original texts, and historical documents of the Tamil culture." Chola gazed around the empty bookshelves. "This barren room is evidence to the regime's tactic of erasing my heritage." He smiled at the peasant farmer. "I don't know what *anna* (elder brother) is telling you. But I'm familiar with my people's tales of woe. I've been tortured by the authorities, witnessed the rape of Tamil women, seen the innocent incarcerated...executed." With a contemptuous smirk, he concluded, "And I'm the one labeled a terrorist."

"Please...please sit down," Kohn offered, motioning to the chair occupied by the translator. He flicked his head. The local quickly obliged. "I have so many questions."

Reluctantly, Chola sat down.

Beaming with an anxious pen, Kohn asked, "Tell me about you...name, age, education?"

Chola massaged his scruffy moustache and confessed, "I have family in Colombo." He took a deep, reflective breath. "To protect them, I need to respond in generalities." Squinting at the cameraman, he said, "No pictures." Grinning, he offered, "You can call me Huck. I'm twenty-one years of age. I attended university as a business student."

"I must confess...Huck," Kohn responded. "I'm impressed by your linguistic skills and knowledge." The reporter swallowed. "Would you like to comment about the deaths of Singhalese civilians and execution of captured soldiers by the LTTE?"

Chola flexed. His scarred features hardened. "The cycle of violence exists in every conflict. I am a product of my oppressor. The choice I was given as a Tamil youth was flee my homeland, face incarceration and torture, or fight for secession from the Singhalese regime. I chose the latter. On the atrocity ledger, the LTTE tally is miniscule compared to our adversary's."

"*Machan!*" Gajaadhar shouted into the structure. "I've spotted vehicle dust on the hillside."

Chola grabbed his weapon and leaped out of the chair. "Thank you for your time, gentlemen," he declared in a hasty exit.

"Good luck, Huck," Kohn offered.

Chola paused. Looking over his shoulder, he grinned. "Don't worry; this is not my first rodeo."

Chapter 47

⸻ ✺✺✺ ⸻

It was late afternoon. Urban exhale tainted the clear day. The sun hung high behind the polluted veil. Bangkok pulsed with congested sidewalks. Savvy pedestrians shielded their lungs with surgical masks. Others tolerated the aroma of diesel exhaust. Traffic slowly meandered down overflowing streets. Grumbling vehicles conversed in a chorus of blasting horns. A dated white Mercedes sedan exited the main drag. Like a stalking predator, the metal beast navigated through a maze of side streets. Entering a trash-strewn alley, the driver killed the engine. Balding tire treads coasted to a sloshing termination over murky slime. Three-story moss-stained brick walls lined the narrow passage.

Focused on the sliver of smoggy sky illuminating the alley's exit, five passengers sat quietly. The pause was brief. Four car doors simultaneously swung open. Combat boots exited onto the slick surface. Five veterans in army fatigues walked to the back of the vehicle. The car's boot popped open. A large black man, a gangly country hick, a gold-toothed Hispanic, a stoic surfer, and Reno gazed down. An impressive array of small arms lay across the trunk bed. It was a web-gear-only search-and-destroy mission. The aging warriors slipped into camo-green chest riggings. Pistols were loaded, checked, and holstered. Hand grenades hooked to harnesses. Ammunition pouches filled with backup magazines. The metal click of virgin AK-47's resonated off the moist brick enclosure. Longboard reached in and retrieved his Remington bolt-action sniper's rifle. Reconnected with the dependable tool of his trade, he closed his eyes. A soft grin appeared.

Martin reached into the pant leg pocket of his baggy fatigues and pulled out a face-paint stick. Utilizing two fingers, he streaked his hatchet-face a deep green. Bear shot him a questioning squint.

"I like going into battle wearing war paint," Martin mumbled. "Not all of us were blessed at birth with a night-fighter's complexion."

Bear chuckled as his back teeth secured a fat maduro cigar. A tarnished Zippo lighter ignited the tobacco log. Tilting his head back, he released an O-shaped ring of smoke. With a satisfied grin, he tracked the dissipating circular band.

"We all saddled up?" Reno questioned.

Confident, reassuring nods answered.

"I'll take point and walk through the front door," he declared. "Longboard will cover me from the shadows or whatever dark enclave he's comfortable killing from."

The surfer snorted a chuckle.

"Hopefully the late-lunch crowd will exit before the fireworks." Addressing the Airborne Rangers, he continued, "You sky soldiers enter through the rear kitchen door." With a slight shrug, he recommended, "Allow the cooks and dishwashers a minute or two to evacuate before spraying the premises."

Bear blew another confident smoke ring. Ochoa fidgeted with his Kalashnikov's fire selector, setting and resetting it between semiautomatic and full automatic. The goblin-faced Martin stroked his billy-goat beard with green, oily fingers.

Reno turned his wrist over. Focused on a cheap Casio digital watch, he said, "This should not take more than ten minutes. Let's synchronize. Set your watch's timer to zero."

The cadre fiddled with time pieces. Bewildered, Martin stuck out his arm; his watch emitted a repetitive beep. "Can someone do mine?"

"Si, señor," volunteered Ochoa, silencing the annoying toot.

"This is the rendezvous point," Reno declared. "If our retreat is blocked, we'll commandeer another vehicle." Looking around at the squad, he took a deep breath. "I would not fault anyone for walking away now."

Bear snickered and took a relaxing puff. Ochoa's finger set his weapon's fire position on full automatic. Longboard slung his scoped weapon over a shoulder.

Martin swallowed. "This is not Vietnam." Spitting out of the side of his mouth, he added, "This is personal."

"Let's do this," Reno announced. Simultaneously, they hit a tiny button on their watches. The countdown began. The mission was a go.

Proudly brandishing overwhelming firepower, the adopted brothers of Army Ranger Raymond Marshall exited the alley. Produce and dry-goods shops lined the thoroughfare. Vendor wares flowing out of open storefronts spilled onto the sidewalk. Consumers examined fruits and vegetables. Merchants solicited customers. Street hawkers served up cheap cuisine. Pedestrians migrated down the obstacle-strewn sidewalk. Overhead, electric cords, cables, and lines wove a confusing web. A hodgepodge of sleeping neon signs awaited dusk. At the end of the block resided the unsuspecting Red Dragon Restaurant, "Home of Fine Cantonese Cuisine."

In the center of the asphalt roadway, the five veterans walked abreast. The setting sun was at their back. Long shadows marked their advance. Bear randomly puffed on his stogie. Martin fondled his beard. Ochoa flashed a gold tooth to spit. The surrounding buzz of commerce abruptly terminated. A baffled civilian audience took a comprehending pause. Panic ensued. Foot traffic accelerated. Merchants hastily collected sidewalk inventory. Roll-down security grates slammed shut.

A young Royal Thai police officer in a light-brown uniform strolled out of a barbershop. Fresh-cut black hair sparkled. Oblivious to the commotion, he admired his reflection in the barber's plate-glass window. Taking his time, he placed a military cap on his newly trimmed look. Adjusting the patent leather visor, he froze. The image of five heavily armed American soldiers drifted across the barbershop window. Slowly, the officer of the law turned. An open mouth gulped down polluted air. The passing cadre of death squinted in his direction. Hyperventilating, the cop glanced down at his holstered sidearm. His knees turned to jelly. Lightheaded, he took a seat on the sidewalk.

"Rough puff," Reno mumbled at the policeman. "Why don't you sit this one out?" Enjoying the intoxicating sense of power, Reno took a proud breath. *Today you will be avenged,* he reflected, picturing the bighearted Marshall. The fact that the safety net of war didn't exist made this more significant. After serving up a healthy dose of vengeance, he would gladly face the consequences. Now was not the time to hesitate. The plan was in motion.

The squad split. Reno casually walked into the Red Dragon. The air was cool. The scent of fried fish lingered. A local businessman in a cheap suit dined alone. A young couple swooned at each other over empty dishes. A waiter assisted a busboy in clearing a cluttered large round table. "Time to leave," Reno announced, displaying an AK-47 across a relaxed arm. The businessman accepted the invitation for a free meal and flew out the door. The young Romeo displayed chivalry. Standing in front of his date, he shielded her as they exited. The employees stood dumbfounded. Reno pulled back his weapon's charging bolt. The servers dropped an overflowing tray of dinnerware. Plates, platters, and serving bowls shattered on the checkered linoleum floor. Crunching glass accompanied the waiter's and busboy's exodus competition.

The slick gangster Chin stormed into the room. "What's going on?" he barked, brandishing a perturbed scowl. He flinched. A smirk appeared, "Hello, Johnny," he uttered, drifting toward the bamboo bar. "You here to pay your debt," he playfully questioned.

"Nah," Reno answered, shaking his head. "I'm here to collect."

After migrating behind the bamboo counter, Chin carefully placed his hands on the lacquered surface. Brand liquor on glass shelves occupied the wall behind him. Tilting his head, he stated, "I don't understand?"

"Yes, you do," Reno insisted.

With an enlightened grin, Chin conceded, "Oh yes, the cripple." Shaking his head, he mumbled, "The one-legged gimp had a very disrespectful tongue." Exposing his palms, he offered, "I lost two men that evening...very unfortunate. Let's call the loss of comrades even?" Chin raised his brows and slowly lowered his right hand.

A sniper always trumps a concealed weapon, Reno thought.

The restaurant's plate-glass window popped. Chin's chest exploded. Open-mouthed and wide-eyed, the dapper mobster went sailing into the liquor display. He hit the wall hard. Shards of glass rained down. The antiseptic aroma of fine spirits engulfed the dining room. Lying in a pond of alcohol and broken bottles, Chin gulped for life. Blood flowed out of his gasping mouth. The fabric of his white starched shirt surrendered to a growing crimson stain. Focused on his right hand, he attempted to grasp an idle handgun. Looking up at the hovering gun barrel of an assault rifle, he growled, "You're a dead man."

"Yeah," Reno responded. "And you are the picture of perfect health." Squeezing the trigger, he launched a single round. The projectile entered a little left of center on Chin's shiny forehead.

Chapter 48

—∞∞∞—

Skirting along the side of the restaurant, the sky soldiers heard the crack of Reno's assault rifle. A single window perched above overflowing trash cans occupied the red brick wall. Flies buzzed over moist refuse. Foul stagnant air stank. "Secure the flank, Bandito," Bear instructed over his shoulder. Ochoa stopped. In a wide stance, he focused on the dark windowpane. Panicking shadows darted within.

Bear and Martin accelerated around the corner. The Red Dragon's back door swung open. In hairnets and soiled bib aprons, the Asian kitchen staff poured into the alleyway. A pudgy middle-aged Thai woman fell hard onto grease-stained asphalt. She scrambled to her feet. Blood flowed out of scraped kneecaps. A fleeing teenage coworker shoved her forward. Displaying the survival instinct of flushed birds the employees took flight. The thump of escaping sandaled feet dissipated into the shadows of surrounding alleyways.

The Airborne Rangers peered into the abandoned kitchen. The lid of a large kettle battling escaping steam clinked. A deep fryer sizzled. A vacant stove burner emitted a low blue flame. The room reeked of pungent Asian condiments. Taking a cautious step through the doorway, Bear snorted. An arm bar halted his advance. He squinted at the hick. Martin held up a single digit. Looking down, he adjusted his assault rifle to semiautomatic. Framed by the entrance, the hillbilly whistled an obscure bird call. A snappy Triad soldier's coiffed head slowly rose up above a counter cluttered with plucked ducks. Martin discharged a single round. A bullet smacked the curious gangster's forehead. As the collapsing corpse hit the floor, Martin entered the galley.

"Uncanny," Bear mumbled as he followed the sharp-sighted redneck. Pulling a playing card from an unlatched breast pocket, he dealt an ace of spades into the burgundy puddle migrating across the tile floor.

Through the porthole of a swinging door, Martin spotted Reno. Reno acknowledged the sighting with a wink.

"Where's Ochoa?" Reno asked Martin as he entered the dining room.

"Securing an exit," Bear answered, bringing up the rear.

The three invaders gazed down a long, wide corridor. Tasseled red lanterns ran down the ceiling. Rosewood lattice inlaid with rice paper adorned the walls. Armed silhouettes scrambled behind the translucent screens. The faint click of small arms preparing for battle resonated.

"Kitchen staff?" Reno mumbled.

"They hightailed in search of high cotton," Martin answered.

"The lunch crowd?" Bear inquired.

"Evacuated," Reno answered.

Simultaneously, they pulled back charging bolts. "The Red Dragon is a free-fire zone," Reno declared. "Anything that breathes is considered hostile."

Veterans schooled in the American warfare strategy of superior firepower unleashed assault rifles. Spitting out spent cartridges, three AK-47's wailed. Shell casings showered the checkerboard flooring. A deluge of copper-plated bullets sprayed the ornate hallway. Plaster rained down. Splintered wood erupted. Sparks flashed. The volley lasted twenty seconds. Empty Kalashnikovs went silent. The synchronized trio detached drained banana box magazines and reloaded. A dangling red lantern crashed. A misting gun smoke floated over the battlefield.

A paper partition burst open. A pistol-wielding wide thug stumbled into the hallway. Powdery dust clung to his sweat-soaked crew cut. Blood splatter decorated his shiny sharkskin suit coat. Off balance, the charging bull fired a small caliber round skyward. A concentrated barrage of tremendous firepower tore into his muscular torso. On wobbly legs, he teetered. A dangling, lifeless arm released the handgun. A shocked, confused expression briefly analyzed the

American assailants. Death arrived. His eyes disengaged. Falling backward, he hit the debris-littered floor with a thud. The Americans reloaded.

Focused on the alleyway window, Ochoa's heart raced. In the bowels of the Red Dragon, a salvo of assault rifles reverberated. The blackened windowpane rattled. The brick wall pulsed. Sweaty palms held his weapon. *Rosa,* he thought, visualizing his wife. The image predated their four children. He always saw her as thin. She was a beauty once, he reflected. *She still is,* he conceded. *Her soft smile is timeless. I have a good life in Arizona. A successful tile and grout business, good neighbors, and four boys,* he quantified. *Will I lose it today? Will my sons grow up fatherless?* A grin emerged. *If it wasn't for the gringo I would not have a life.* The voice of Marshall dragging him off the battlefield came to him. *"It's just like crossing the border,' Marshall joked in the swarm of Communist bullets. I was blind, a burden. Marshall should have saved himself, but didn't. There are moments in time that define you,* Ochoa realized. *I owe a debt to Marshall that I can never repay.*

A chair crashed through the window. Broken glass spilled into the alleyway. Ochoa targeted the dark opening. A gunman in a flashy white suit and burgundy turtleneck hopped onto the windowsill.

"You terminated my guardian angel," Ochoa mumbled. Scowling, he barked, "Hijo de puta!"

The perching prey, discovering the irate, snarling gold-toothed Hispanic froze. Surprise, confusion, anxiety, fear, and panic flashed in the condemned man's wide-eyed, open-mouthed expression.

"Adios pendejo," Ochoa growled, spraying the crouching thug with a short burst. The handful of heavy penetrating cartridges propelled the remains of the Triad soldier back into the structure. Terrified chatter followed the crash of the rejected escapee. Ochoa unhooked a hand grenade from his web gear. Embracing the red brick wall, he pulled the pin. "Fire in the hole!" he hollered, tossing the deadly pomegranate into the open window. A blast shook the building. The window vomited chunks of plaster, wood chips, loose paper, and sparkling glass. A soiled smoke rolled out of the window frame. Catching a soft breeze, the plume swirled skyward.

"Flank secured," Bandito muttered.

A billowing brown cloud rolled down what remained of the corridor. Reno snorted at the engulfing dust. Blinking eyes combated the irritating mist.

"Jesus," Martin declared. "I can't see shit."

"That was Bandito," Bear said. "Didn't you hear the warning?"

"Let's finish this," Reno announced, waving a hand at the dissipating blanket of filth.

The trio advanced. High-stepping, they cleared the wide carcass. Bear dropped death's business card. Heavy combat boots cracked, littering wood fragments. Glass crunched. Martin pulled back the remnants of a lattice rice-paper partition. Bullet holes adorned grass cloth walls. A meticulous Chinese painting of flowers and birds swayed on a single peg. A large round table draped in red cloth lay on its side. Toppled and fragmented chairs, fractured serving dishes, and wasted food spilled across the floor. Among the private dining room carnage, four well-dressed Asian gangsters reclined in various poses of death. Lifeless disconnected eyes relayed everlasting expressions of shock, fear, and defiance. Expired hands still clutched unutilized pistols.

Martin grinned at the angled table. The camo-face-painted hick sprayed the crimson tablecloth with a quick burst. Chunks of wood flew off the hard surface. The red shroud floated to the floor. An armed henchman leaped out from behind the barrier. The Southern boy's second volley terminated the hostile. The deafening blast faded. A child's whimper rolled out of a cowering dust-covered bundle of black spandex in the corner. Martin cast a high-pitched whistle at the trembling, curled-up human ball. A petite Thai girl's head emerged. Tear-swollen black gemstone eyes submissively scanned the American's boots. Plaster residue tainted the teenager's tousled long black hair a silvery-gray. Panting like a scared puppy, she made eye contact.

Sucking on his cigar, Bear questioned, "Free-fire zone?"

"Nah," Reno answered. "Vamoose, papoose," he offered, flicking a thumb toward the debris-strewn exit.

The terrified party favor, in a short, snug fitting dress, sprang to her feet. She was all legs. In stiletto heels, the nimble gazelle leaped through the carnage. The rapid click of her sharp footwear accelerated as it faded.

Bear casually pulled a chunk of playing cards from a breast pocket. A flick of the wrist launched the Airborne Ranger calling cards. The death cards fluttered as they slowly descended across the dining room morgue.

The eagle-eyed hillbilly took point. Bear and Reno covered his advance. A wood door blown off its hinges lay in the corridor. Martin glanced through the splintered doorway. An empty window frame marked Ochoa's post. "Hold your fire, Bandito," Martin hollered.

"Si, Señor Stretch," Ochoa acknowledged from the alley.

Martin scanned the Spartan room. Blood splatter and steel fragments decorated white plaster walls. A humming air-conditioning vent battled humidity flowing through the open window. Wooden legs of an overturned table pointed up at a ceiling fan dangling from a frayed cord. White bone mah-jongg tiles lay across the seat of the room's only upright wooden chair. A stack of perforated and damaged cardboard boxes of brand liquor leaked. A booze pond peppered with colorful engraved domino-like game pieces blanketed the linoleum floor. In the glistening alcohol and plasma cocktail puddle, the limbs of a facedown hoodlum in a T-shirt and denim jeans twitched. The twisted grotesque carcass of a street punk lay beside the convulsing casualty. Sprawled out in front of the window lay a snappily dressed thug in a bullet-riddled white suit.

On the wet floor in the corner slouched another dead man. The blast had removed his face. Martin's nose snorted at a shit-house stench. *Faceless must have soiled himself,* he concluded. "All clear," he relayed to his backup. "I need to pop a round," he announced plugging the sloshing saturated casualty in the back of the head. "Hang tight, Bandito," he shouted into the alley. "The show's just about over."

"Gracias," Ochoa responded.

Martin retreated, joining his companions. Reno tested a locked door. Over his shoulder, Bear puffed on a shrinking stogie.

"This is the prize, boys," Reno announced. "The windowless office where I finalized the loan with the devil."

Bear glanced at Martin. "We are not common thieves," Bear declared. "We are here to administer justice."

The southern camo-faced billy-goat nodded.

Reno chuckled. "I'm not referring to the chinks' vault. I suspect the fat fucking kingpin of the Triad is cowering behind a desk."

Bear flashed pearly whites. A smoldering cigar accented the smile. Leaning back, he lifted and recoiled a size-thirteen glossy black combat boot battering ram. A walloped bolted lock surrendered. The barrier swung open through a fractured frame. A pistol popped.

"Son of a bitch!" Reno exclaimed as a small-caliber projectile burrowed into his shoulder.

Bear blindly sprayed the tiny room. Ricocheting bullets sparked off the brick enclosure. A seated chunky gangster and standing thin whore caught the rebounding rounds. Collapsing behind a large metal desk, the girl squealed. The pudgy mob boss slumped back in a swiveling desk chair. Snorting like a pig, he focused on the weapon he had dropped. Behind him an open vault displayed a small fortune in US and colorful foreign currency. Bundles of heroin and cocaine enhanced the steel box's value.

Martin took a knee, zipped open a medical kit, and spilled out the contents. Rummaging through the pile, he retrieved a gauze-dressing package. As he rose, he tore open the packet. "Let's take a look," he asked, ripping open Reno's shirt. "No exit wound," he mumbled, shaking his head. "Apparently missed the subclavian artery and collarbone." He grinned, sliding the bandage over the leaking bullet hole.

Reno took deep, composing breaths. Lightheaded and weak-kneed, he leaned back into the wall. *I got to suck it up,* he counseled. Martin relieved him of his assault rifle. "Thanks," he instinctively mumbled.

Guiding Reno's hand over the wound, Martin instructed, "Keep applying pressure."

Reno nodded. Plasma flowed through his compressing fingers. Lifting his head, he glared through the shattered doorframe at the expiring crime lord. "Did you order Marshall's demise?" he muttered. "It doesn't matter." The Triad killed his friend, and the fat fuck with the hairy mole was in command.

The slouching obese Chinaman made eye contact with Reno. Mumbling in Cantonese, he started to laugh. A trickle of blood rolled out of the corner of his mouth.

Reno stuck his tongue out of the side of his mouth. "Right about there, chief," he informed him. "You left a little sauce."

Bear picked up the mob boss's pimp pistol. Pointing at the gangster's greasy comb-over, he turned his head. The gun popped. The Chinaman's body jumped. The desk chair rolled back. The slumping corpse flowed out of chair onto the floor. Exiting the tiny room, Bear dealt an ace of spades over his shoulder. Ignoring the spoils of war, he declared, "Mission accomplished. Let's get out of here."

"Wait!" Martin exclaimed. Rushing into the office, he grabbed the dead man's soft red pack of Krong Thip Ninety cigarettes. Flicking his wrist, he released a single cigarette from the nearly empty packet of local smokes. Utilizing a complimentary box of Red Dragon matches, he ignited his nicotine addiction.

In a provisioner store across the street from the Red Dragon, Longboard reclined comfortably in a sniper's nest fashioned out of rice gunnysacks. The general store was deserted. Large wicker baskets of apples, oranges, and tropical fruits crowded the floor. Wooden bins displayed a plethora of fresh vegetables. The plastic-lined baskets of various red and green Thai chilies produced a dominant sharp aroma. The ceiling creaked. Probably the grocer and his family riding out the storm in their residence, Longboard concluded. Through a telescopic sight, he scanned the restaurant. After shooting Chin in the chest, the only other potential target was a long-legged hooker who scurried out the front door in spiked heels. *I sure was not going to terminate that nasty kitten.* He snickered. Within the Red Dragon, automatic weapon fire flashed. *It takes courage to engage the enemy at close range,* he surmised. *Exchanging fire with an adversary justifies their termination as survival instinct. It's an excuse not afforded a sniper. To patiently wait for that one shot that will terminate life takes skill. To live with it is an assassin's true talent. A calloused heart is a prerequisite.*

A street gang brandishing machetes, bats, and pistols charged down the center of the street. *The Triad's local muscle,* Longboard concluded. *The dink cavalry has arrived.* Utilizing a scope, he scanned the raucous horde. *Now who is the officer?* he wondered. Every pack has an alpha dog. His gun barked. A stocky singlet-wearing thug collapsed. The advancing throng rolled over the dead man. A straggler retrieved the casualty's cheap revolver. "Wasn't him," Longboard mumbled. A short, cocky kid encouraged the mob from the rear. *Looks like officer material,* Longboard thought, blowing off the top of the punk's head. The rabble stalled. Two gang members examined the scalped corpse. Others began to peel off. The dink cavalry dispersed. "The snake's head," Longboard muttered. To expedite the retreat, he fired a shot over fleeing heads.

Reno, Bear, and Martin exited the restaurant. Bear sucked on a red-tipped cigar. A lazy cigarette dangled from Martin's lower lip. Reno stood tall. Just above the breast pocket of his crimson-stained fatigues, he held a compressing bloody hand. Under the arched scripted neon identifying *The Red Dragon,* they paused. Ochoa rounded the corner to reconnect with the team. Across the street, Longboard emerged from the depths of a vacant grocer's. Chomping on a bright-red apple, he crossed the street. Sirens wailed in the distance. Reno dropped his hand, unhooked an incendiary grenade from his web gear, and pulled the pin. Casually, he lobbed the Willie Pete into the restaurant. Martin took a satisfying toke and flicked his cigarette. Longboard pitched the core of a very sweet apple into the gutter. The five-man juggernaut proudly strutted down the street littered with two bodies. The grenade exploded. A cloud of white phosphorus ignited the 14K Triad's hooch. The Home of Fine Cantonese Cuisine burst into flames. A wave of hot air rolled down the boulevard. Fire crackled. Panicked neighbors scrambled to protect businesses. The Americans didn't look back. They didn't have to.

Chapter 49

———— ∞ ————

Sunlight poured through an open window. A salty sea breeze complemented the distant grumbling surf. Reno blinked at the warm light. His head throbbed. He kicked off uncomfortably moist sheets. An agonizing bolt shot through his tender shoulder. "Augh," he groaned. Starring up at the woven palm ceiling of his beach hut, he swallowed. *Water*, he thought. *I need cool, refreshing aqua to hydrate my dust-bowl mouth.* Carefully, he sat up, resting bare feet on the grass mat flooring. His light head hung low. In search of liquid, he rummaged through the cadre of beer bottles infesting a nightstand. "Bingo," he muttered, discovering a half-full container. Blindly, he took a big swig. The warm beer was flat, bitter. His face puckered. A parched tongue and dry throat welcomed the sour lubricant. He dropped the bottle. It clinked on impact and jingled as it rolled down the uneven floor. A wide yawn started Reno's lazy healing day.

In boxer shorts, he shuffled across the scruffy bedroom. Pausing, he picked up the arm sling draped over a chair. After poking his head through the knotted cotton cloth, he flirted with pain and gingerly slid his arm into to the support. Once secure, he prodded the damaged shoulder's dressing. He winced. "That was not a good idea," he mumbled. Woozy, he gingerly calculated each step and pierced the beaded curtain that shrouded his kitchenette. The small cooking area consisted of a tiled lime-green counter, a hot plate, a minifridge, and a single sink overflowing with dirty dishes. A flick of a switch sent electrical power to the tabletop stove. Testing the sloshing contents of an idle teakettle confirmed two, possibly three, cups. From the dirty-dish graveyard, he retrieved a fairly clean mug. Placing a Vietnamese small tin brewing chamber over the coffee mug, he grinned. *The Vietnamese know coffee, and they know how to expel foreign occupiers.* A heaping teaspoon of rich dark chocolate coffee grounds filled the perforated hat-shaped disk. Inhaling, he enjoyed the seductive sent.

A soft whistle escaped the teakettle. *Close enough,* he surmised, pouring hot water into the single-serving brewer. Looking into the dark steaming java, he pondered, *What will today bring? Incarceration? A Triad vendetta? A return letter from Sandy?* "Yeah, like a letter from Sandy is in the deck," he mumbled. Shaking his head, he exited through the beaded door. The payback for Marshall was expensive—the total cost yet to be determined. Taking a cautious sip, he realized avenging his brother was worth it. He swung open his squeaky front door. A blast of sunlight greeted him. "Oh shit," he mumbled. *I missed another sunrise.* Blinking, he shuffled onto his raised porch.

Collapsing in a rattan deck chair, he sighed. "Mission accomplished." Warm rays soothed his naked torso. Relaxed, he ignored the trash peppering the white sand and gazed into the sparkling blue ocean. Sunlight winked across the rippling surface. Waves rhythmically swelled before breaking across the shoreline. Two surfers bobbed in the inviting waters. Longboard sat tall on his board. His apprentice Joey lay flat on his belly. A rolling wave lifted the duo. Longboard offered a casual salute. Spotting Reno, Joey cautiously sat up. Rocking back and forth, he enthusiastically waved. Reno lifted his coffee mug in response. *Joey is having a good day,* Reno concluded.

Longboard shouted.

"What?" Reno quietly questioned.

The surfer hollered again. Something about the *Bangkok Post*, Reno deciphered. Glancing around the deck, he spotted a folded newspaper secured under an oyster shell ashtray. Grabbing the journal, Reno held it up. The surfer's head nodded. *Bangkok Post* in bold gothic font titled the daily. It was a week old. The headline "International Gangs Settle Score" took Reno's breath away. He took a calming gulp of hot coffee and read.

At dusk yesterday an unknown number of hitmen barged into the Red Dragon Restaurant on the outskirts of Bangkok's Chinatown. The Cantonese Restaurant was an apparent front for Macau's 14K Triad. In a storm of gunfire, the assailants left sixteen Triad members dead, including high-ranking kingpin Wong Lau. The mob boss was executed gang-land style with a bullet to the head. The crime scene suggests a turf war motive. The suspects list is long, as crime syndicates from Hong Kong, Singapore, and Taiwan seek to expand business in Thailand.

Reno leaned back and took a deep, comforting breath. Visualizing the jelly-kneed police officer taking a seat before the raid, he grinned. Five GI's became an unknown number of hitmen for convenience. *The authorities appreciated us harvesting bad fruit,* he surmised. *Looks like I can cross off the Thai Justice System from my contingent liability list. Not a bad way to start the day, a cup of coffee and good news.* Clumsily juggling the broadsheet with one hand, he folded it over, scanning the wrinkled contents of page 2.

Bold font declared, "American Reporters Arrested in Sri Lanka." Reno read, Colombo—*New York Times* reporter John Kohn and photojournalist Alec Russing arrested in the port city of Trincomalee in eastern Sri Lanka. A government official said Mr. Kohn and his cameraman entered the country as tourists. They did not process the appropriate journalistic documentation to travel into the conflicted eastern provinces. The reporters are being brought to Colombo to face charges.

Meanwhile the unofficial cease-fire between the security forces and the Tamil terrorists remained peaceful for a second day. Formerly known as Ceylon, Sri Lanka is an island nation off the southern tip of India.

Lowering the newspaper, Reno sighed. *Sri Lanka is such a beautiful country, rich in resources and geographically located to compete on the world stage as an economic power. Just like Vietnam,* he realized. *The cancer of war feasted on Vietnam for thirty years. How long will Sri Lanka endure the disease?* he wondered. *Did I prolong the conflict with my profitable transaction or give the rebels a fighting chance toward independence? There is no answer. Only time will determine the victors to write their version of the events.*

As he gazed out at the sparkling vista, surfacing emotion produced a wide smile on the American. A sleek, long-legged silhouette meandered across the firm sand at the water's edge. White foam lapped at her bare feet. In a sundress holding a pair of sandals, the Dutch thoroughbred paused to take a puff off a tiny cigar. A soft breeze teased the light fabric of her gown. Exhaling, Sandy shot a mischievous grin in Reno's direction. With a smoldering cheroot secured between her fingers, she casually waved at her American lover.

"This is a special day," Reno mumbled. "It's not every day a doctor makes a house call."

Chapter 50

———✺———

It was well past midnight. Bangkok's famous red-light district, Patpong, pulsed to a lecherous beat. Colorful fluorescent tubes of scripted light beckoned. The Kings Table, Hot Stuff, and the inviting Lucky Pussy glowed in the night sky. The go-go bars flanked a bustling night market. Brightly lit stalls hawked designer knock-offs, wood carvings, and silk ties. A large Western sightseeing herd meandered through the tourist tat maze. Touts, pickpockets, and Thai grifters preyed upon the ogling vacationers. It was hot and muggy, the clamor of bargaining commerce deafening. Potbellied Fred Melton from Harrisburg, Pennsylvania, shuffled amid the flock. A wide grin dominated his pudgy face. A sweat-soaked Philadelphia Eagles jersey clung to his flabby frame. Like a giddy schoolboy, the middle-aged Mister Melton peered into the open doorway of The Candy Box. Under an array of multicolored crisscrossing light beams, young Thai girls sheathed in scanty lingerie pranced. Fred's loins stirred.

"Fred!" barked the trailing Mrs. Margaret Melton.

"Yes, dear," Fred instinctively grumbled. Turning, he spotted his wide wife in her favorite blue muumuu, waddling down the sidewalk.

"Slow down," she growled. "My feet are killing me." Beneath a floppy sun hat, a scowl dominated her blemished, sunburned features.

"Yes, dear," he acknowledged, resuming their single-file stroll.

The Meltons drifted down the crowded sidewalk. Ahead, an obstruction diverted the trickling stream. Fred craned his neck. Under the flashing neon sign, Hot Stuff, a pair of bikini-clad female gatekeepers invited patrons into the dark enclave. A dated disco tune escaped the open doorway. In high heels, the thin nymphs with long jet-black hair rocked softly to a seductive beat. Sweat sparkled off their taut bare flesh. Fred accelerated a collision course. Margaret snorted. A swaying Thai angel cast a luring smile at the American. He took the bait.

"You buy me drink?" purred the long-legged nymphet.

Fred nodded. She hugged his arm with gentle, caressing fingers. Sucking in his gut, he flexed. A fragrant aroma engulfed his senses.

"Fred!" hollered his irate spouse.

Floating in the intoxicating scent of youth, Fred glanced over his shoulder. Beaming, he softly said, "This looks like a good place for a cold beer, Margaret." Drooling over the young Thai hostess, he ignored his wife's guttural growl. The seductive usherette tugged on his arm. Playfully, he resisted as she reeled him into the cool cabaret.

The room was dark, the air chilled. A mirrored sphere slowly rotated below a jet-black ceiling. Reflected drops of light cascaded down the walls and across empty seating options. The thumping beat of a popular tune pulsed. A focused bartender stood behind a soft red-glowing counter. On an elevated stage, a pack of local talent swayed. Exposed flesh glistened. Out of the darkness, patrons slowly appeared. A cadre of Japanese businessmen giggled at a barmaid's solicitation. Young girls seeking middle-aged prey circulated in the labyrinth of tiny tables and chairs.

The usherette led Fred to a quiet corner. Behind a small round table, he took a seat. She flowed onto his lap. Latching onto his sweaty neck, she cooed in his ear, "You buy me drink now?"

Fred inhaled her erotic aroma. "Yes," somehow rolled off his tongue.

"You son of a bitch!" hollered Mrs. Melton.

Fred looked up. His eyes adjusted. With fisted hands planted on wide hips, Margaret Melton in her floppy hat and favorite blue muumuu sizzled. Fred swallowed. His new friend snuggled closer. *What have I got to lose?* he pondered. *It's not every day I can have a drink with a young girl. The last time I did, I was twenty.* "Tomorrow, Margaret," he offered. "Tomorrow I will take you jewelry shopping. But tonight…tonight I'm going to enjoy a cold expensive beer with this angel."

Mrs. Melton's lips puckered. Her harsh demeanor softened. Conceding to the terms, she plopped down in a petite wooden chair and focused on the male-oriented entertainment. Draft beers and a champagne cocktail arrived. Margaret eyed the bubbling mug of pilsner with disdain. Fred took a healthy swig of cold brew. The Thai vixen downed the bubbling broad-bowled stemmed glass of 7-Up in one swallow.

"You buy me another drink?" inquired the doe-eyed temptress.

Fred's impression of a bobblehead doll answered. Margaret rolled her eyes. Grunting, she looked away from her salivating husband. Focused on the exit, she squinted.

The open doorway framed an ominous muscular Asian in pressed black slacks and a starched white cotton dress shirt. Uneven bristles of a prison hair-cut capped an egg-shaped head. Through designer sunglasses, he scanned the dark nightclub. Bony fingers elevated a smoldering cigarette to his thin lips. He took a long, satisfying toke. After a relishing pause, flared nostrils expelled secondhand smoke.

Margaret gasped. "Fred," she nudged, "Let's get out of here."

"One more round," her giddy husband said.

"That man scares me," Margaret pleaded, flicking her floppy hat toward the entrance.

Fred glanced over his shoulder.

With a sense of entitlement, the confident Asian strutted into the cabaret. A roaming beam of light reflected off a thick gold Rolex watch. The bartender flinched. The prancing stage ponies froze. Standing in front of the bar, the new arrival examined the terrified merchandise on stage through dark lenses. Sucking on a cigarette, he ignored the bartender's polite inquiry. At the end of the serving counter, thick purple velvet curtains parted. Escaping crimson light illuminated a concealed corridor. Adjusting a necktie, a local in a wrinkled black suit flew through the drapes and greeted the mystery man with a deep, respectful bow.

"Who is that?" Fred questioned the seductive bundle on his lap.

The young girl's breathe accelerated. "Jimmy…Jimmy Three-Fingers Li," flowed out of her pulsating flat chest. Tightening her embrace, she implored, "Don't leave."

Fred carefully extracted the clinging barmaid. Margaret toppled a chair as she rose. Her wide hips blazed a path toward the exit. Dropping a wad of colorful local currency on the tiny cocktail table, Fred followed his fleeing spouse.

"I like the one on the left," Jimmy Li mumbled.

Following the gangster's lecherous gaze, the nervous manager grinned. "Excellent choice, Mister Li. Her name is Cherry. Would you like to sample her charms now?"

Jimmy held up a disfigured three-fingered hand. "Later," he mumbled. "Hopefully my interview will be brief."

"This way, Mister Li," the manager offered, sweeping an arm toward the velvet curtains.

Red lighting cast an eerie glow down the long corridor. Doorways flanked the hallway. Grunts, groans, and active bedsprings resonated behind closed doors. Open doorframes exposed small vacant bedding chambers. Jimmy paused. In an open room, four whimpering girls huddled together on an unmade bed. The scared children held tightly onto one another.

"Why aren't they working?" Jimmy snapped.

"Village girls." The manager apologetically shrugged. "These rural peasants come to Bangkok dreaming of becoming maids." He chuckled. Studying the trembling children, he forecast, "This group should be ready to take the stage… next week."

"Good," Jimmy mumbled.

At the end of the hallway, a goon stood guard in front of a hardwood door. He stepped aside as the manager fumbled with a ring of keys. A deadbolt lock clicked. The barrier swung open. A metal frame bed anchored the small room. On a stained, worn-out mattress, a Royal Thai police officer in a light-brown uniform sat with his head hung low. As Jimmy Three-Fingers Li entered, the policeman elevated his gaze and swallowed.

"Leave us," Jimmy instructed over his shoulder. The door slammed shut. After tapping out a cigarette from a pack of Marlboros, Jimmy secured the filtered tip between dry lips. Patting pant pockets, he searched for a lighter. Successfully, he retrieved the gold smoking accessory. Taking his time, he ignited the tobacco canister. A satisfying puff completed the ritual. Through dissipating smoke, he flashed the red-and-white pack at the officer.

The policeman nodded. A twitching hand retrieved the gift. Apprehensively, he leaned forward, accepting the small flame dancing out of the sparkling lighter. After a few quick erratic puffs, he leaned back.

Jimmy smiled. Flicking the lighter with his disfigured hand extinguished the tiny flame. After securing the gold-plated accessory, he elevated his designer sunglasses. With the spectacles perched atop his head, he pulled a single playing card out of his shirt's breast pocket. Twisting his wrist, he examined the bloodstained ace of spades logoed with a white bird wing and red sword under the title "Airborne." Holding up the stiff paper, he politely inquired, "Did you see who dealt the death card at my cousin's restaurant?"

Taking a quick puff, the weak-kneed Royal Thai officer nodded.

Chapter 51

———⟨❈⟩———

At an outdoor café on the shady side of the street, Reno, Sandy, Longboard, and Joey sat around a plastic table. A red-and-white checkerboard vinyl cloth protected the serving surface. Bamboo skewers and beer bottles surrounded what remained of a satay appetizer. The restaurant was empty. It was late afternoon. The lunch crowd had departed, and the dinner rush was hours away. Sandy dipped a petite grilled meat spear into a cup of spicy peanut sauce. Joey tracked the serving as the Dutch beauty lifted the misting meat into her delicate mouth. Closing her eyes, she slowly chewed on the street delicacy.

"Is this your first sampling of the spicy Southeast Asian delicacy?" Reno questioned.

Sandy swallowed. After cleansing her palate with a sip of cold brew, she shot the American a playful frown. "Really, Mister James," she teased. "Do you know so little about my heritage?"

"Dutch East India Company," Longboard interjected.

"Thank you." Sandy nodded to the surfer. "Every Tuesday night, Papa would take me to a *rijsttafel*…a rice-table in Amsterdam, the popular restaurants were an import from the Dutch colonialism of Indonesia."

"What did I tell you, partner?" Reno said to Longboard. "Everywhere you go, there is a Chinese restaurant. Hell, it sounds like noodles, rice, and spring rolls have overrun Holland." Grinning at Sandy, he confessed, "And I was told the way to win you over was with cheese."

Sandy chuckled. Addressing Joey, she commented, "There is no cheese in his bachelor shack. The only thing I could find was a case of beer and three black bananas."

The inclusion produced a smile on the fragile Joey.

"I was planning on stocking up on dairy products," Reno countered. "But then...what happened?...Oh yeah...I got shot!"

Joey burst out laughing. Sandy and Longboard joined in.

"Excuse me," interrupted a tall, white, slightly overweight intruder.

Snickering, Reno looked up at the middle-aged man hovering in front of their table. A thick helmet of gray hair crowned his head. It appeared he had slept in his wrinkled blue blazer and khaki chinos. A Brillo Pad of silver hair peeked out of a low buttoned cotton shirt.

"What can we do for you, chief?" Reno inquired.

"Reno James and Jesse Long, I've been looking for you," he calmly answered. "Let me introduce myself." Lightly patting his exposed chest, he announced. "I'm Arch Stanton with the US Department of Justice."

Reno took a deep breath. His stomach dropped. Jesse Long, a.k.a. Longboard, shot an ominous squint at Stanton. Joey's breathing accelerated. Sandy placed a reassuring hand on Reno's arm.

"My apology for the intrusion," Stanton offered. Motioning to the empty restaurant bar, he continued, "I have an urgent matter to discuss that requires your immediate attention."

Reno rose. Instinctively, he flexed. Longboard followed suit and placed a restraining hand on Joey's shoulder. Bending down, Reno planted a soft kiss on Sandy's head. "Order some prawns for the table, sweetheart," he muttered. "Hopefully this won't take too long."

She returned a nervous smile.

The happy-hour crowd had yet to arrive at the vacant bar. Passing a lone server, Reno ordered three beers and pointed at a round table in the corner. As the trio sat down, Reno growled, "What do you want?"

Stanton grinned as the beers were served. Pushing his chilled bottle into the center of the table, he said, "Indulge me, gentlemen. I have a short story, a journey, if you will. It involves the Tamil insurgent organization, the LTTE, and heroin trafficking."

"You want to lecture us about drugs?" Reno interrupted.

Stanton flashed a palm. "Patience, Mister James, or if you prefer, San Bernardino," he said, with a knowing grin. "Oh yes, there is a file on you." Glancing at Longboard, he added, "Although it is not as thick as Mister Long's impressive dossier."

Reno took a swig of cold beer. Conceding, he shrugged. "Please proceed with your narrative."

Stanton took a shallow breath. "The Tamils of Northern Sri Lanka, in particular the *fisherman* caste, have a long history of smuggling, mostly alcohol and tobacco. An opportunity for a more profitable product arose with the Soviet invasion of Afghanistan. The conflict diverted the traditional flow of Golden Crest opium through India. The Tamil Tigers, in need of funding to acquire weapons, embraced the lucrative heroin trade. Tigers are currently running heroin through Europe and into Eastern Canada, the profits funding their guerilla war. In tracing those illegal proceeds, I discovered a two-million-dollar wire transfer that led me to you."

"That's it," Reno snapped.

"Patience, Reno." Stanton smirked. "The poison that flows out of the Golden Crest of Afghanistan and Pakistan is not my concern. I'm in the kingdom monitoring the white Chinese powder smuggled out of the Golden Triangle of Laos, Burma, and Thailand. During my investigation, an informant relayed a plot being orchestrated by a Jimmy Three-Fingers Li of the Fourteen-K Triad."

Reno and Longboard exchanged puzzled expressions.

"I take it you are not acquainted with Jimmy Li?" Stanton probed.

An intrigued audience shook their heads.

Reaching into his wrinkled blue blazer, Stanton retrieved a folded eight-by-ten glossy. After unfolding the black-and-white mug shot photo of the Macau gangster, he pushed it across the table with a flexed finger.

"All dinks look alike to me," Longboard mumbled.

Tapping the image with an extended finger, Stanton warned, "Remember this one. He is looking for you. Specifically Jimmy Three-Fingers has a network searching for five veterans who burned down his cousin's hooch." Leaning back, he concluded, "If I can find you, he certainly will."

"Why?" a puzzled Reno questioned. "Why the heads-up, Stanton?"

Stanton reached over the photo and grabbed the idle beer. He tossed back a healthy swig. After wiping his lips, he sat erect and proudly saluted, "Golden Dragon, sir!"

Reno returned the salute with a reflex response, "Right-of-the-line."

"You were in the Fourteenth?" Longboard questioned.

Nodding, Stanton added, "I suspect we have mutual friends' names etched on the Wall."

"Thank you, brother," Reno acknowledged.

"I was never here," Stanton declared. "And I never told you that Jimmy Three-Fingers has taken residence on the second floor, suite two-twenty-two, of the Orchid Inn. It is a quasi-brothel/hotel with ample security." After downing his beer, he stood and playfully saluting, added, "Best of luck, brothers."

"Well, that's a relief," Longboard sighed, tracking the exiting Stanton.

"What's a relief?" Reno exclaimed. "We are at the top of a Chinese gangster's hit list."

"Precisely," Longboard commented. "Being arrested by the Feds is concerning. Neutralizing a mobster is like taking out the garbage." He grinned. "I'll handle this on Tuesday."

"Why Tuesday?" Reno wondered.

"Dark of the moon," the assassin answered. "Death travels better on a bleak night."

Reno shook his head. "You're kinda talking crazy again."

Smirking, the surfer leaned back and took a reflective breath. "There were hunter teams and killer teams in the Phoenix Program. The Hunters would locate and identify a target. I would be given the location and a photo of the individual to be neutralized." He pointed at the eight-by-ten glossy of Jimmy Li. "Under the cover of darkness, wearing black pajamas and face paint, I would find and terminate the threat."

"That's your plan?" Reno snapped. "You're going to walk through the lobby of the Orchid Inn in a Halloween costume?"

"I liked to ad-lib in the field," the professional assassin responded. "Whether I shoot Jimmy in the head at a distance or crush his larynx and remove his liver while he sleeps, the threat will be eliminated."

Reno's faced soured. "Why would you cut out his liver?"

"Buddhists cannot enter heaven unless their liver is intact," Longboard informed him. "It is the ultimate fuck you." He picked up the photo. Studying the image, he mumbled, "This should be an easy assignment. This punk looks like an amateur." Glancing at Reno, he added, "Now those ill-equipped and starving Vietcong were true professionals, very tough terminations."

"Do you need backup?" Reno volunteered.

"Nah," Longboard replied. "This mission does not require your bludgeon search-and-destroy skills. It warrants the scalpel talent of a Phoenix Program assassin." Pushing back from the table, he added, "Now let's get back to your girlfriend and Joey before our prawns get cold."

Chapter 52

⚉

Chola gazed out the bus window. Downtown Colombo drifted by. It had been almost a year since he had fled the nation's capital. *I once called this home,* he reflected. *It wasn't the same place.* The scars of the race riots were evident by the burnt remains of Tamil businesses. Pessimistic Tamils fled the city; optimistic Tamils endured the oppression of the Criminal Investigation Department. Unwarranted search and seizures, arrests, torture, and rape were common occurrences for the minority inhabitants. *My risk in the city is minimal,* Chola concluded. *As a translating delegate to the peace conference, my safety was assured. Even though my credentials are bogus, the government would not want to jeopardize the fragile cease-fire by the disappearance of a moderate Tamil representative.* Scanning the other delegates, he visualized a flock of sheep. The militant Tigers pressured the government to the negotiating table and then were barred from the proceedings. *The LTTE does have one clandestine participant at the All Parties Conference.* He grinned. *Me.*

Slouching down on the vinyl bench seat, he sighed, "What a waste of time." Visualizing the plump politician bloviating about restructuring local district governments but maintaining police powers, Chola felt his breath accelerate. The Singhalese government's true intent was genocide. *The Singhalese settlements on Tamil lands have increased. Food supplies into the north have been curtailed. Why hold a peace conference? The Tamils want independence. The Sri Lankan government wants the Tamils to capitulate. What is there to negotiate?*

The bus exited the grind of Colombo traffic. It sputtered up the sweeping entrance of the Galle Face Hotel. Constructed in 1864, the hotel was a magnificent colonial architectural reminder of British Ceylon. Air brakes hissed. The bus driver pulled a lever. The transport's folding door recoiled. A salty sea breeze entered. Anxious delegates rose. Chola held his seat. The flock, anticipating the free buffet, stampeded through the exit. *The government that rations provisions to the Tamil north provides the delegates lavish complimentary meals.* Chola smirked. Casually, he exited the empty transport.

Sunlight sparked off the Indian Ocean. Reflected rays flittered across the four-story Victorian facade. Ravenous delegates running up the entry stairway disappeared into a high-ceilinged open-air lobby. Chola slowly ascended the steps. At the top of the stairs, large carved wooden elephants guarded classic columns. The doorman in a white uniform accented with bullion cord epaulettes pressed his hands together. The hotel's famous employee smiled widely beneath a signature handlebar white mustache and muttered, "Long life."

"Thank you, machan," Chola replied as he passed.

The polished stone floor reflected penetrating sunlight. A frayed red carpet walkway directed hotel guest traffic. Flower arrangements emitted a sweet fragrance. Chola proudly strutted through the tourist sanctuary. At the front desk, a sunburned German complained. A blond snapped a photo of his girlfriend hugging a carved elephant. A strolling white couple held the hands of their young daughter. As they approached Chola on the woven crimson fabric trail, the little girl broke her father's grasp to point at Chola's scarred face. "You shouldn't point," scolded the mum. She offered an apologetic smile to the terrorist. Chola nodded his understanding. Ahead, laughter resonated.

Following the carpet trail, he rounded the corner. A terraced lounge overlooked the glistening Indian Ocean. A long dark-wood bar lined the far wall. Ceiling fans circulated salty air. Clamoring Westerners sitting in ornately carved low wood chairs drank and smoked. Ignoring the privileged whites, who were immune to the cruelty of life, Chola gazed out over the twinkling water. *Such a beautiful vista,* he thought. A flock of birds dipped and rose in a joyous dance. *Tamil Eelam,* he thought, *a prosperous land where my people can live in peace.* A tug on his sleeve terminated the fantasy.

"Hello, Huck," whispered the bald, hook-nosed *New York Times* reporter John Kohn.

Chola's stomach dropped. Searching for plainclothes security police, he scanned the bar crowd.

Kohn placed a calming hand on the Tiger's shoulder. "Don't worry, son," he offered. "I've never revealed a source."

Chola looked past the reporter. "Did you get your story out?" he questioned, maintaining a vigilant watch.

"With some effort," Kohn replied. "After our encounter, the authorities terminated my reconnaissance of the region. I was arrested, interrogated, most of my notes and Russing's camera and film confiscated. Under armed guard, we were exiled to Colombo."

"Are you still being watched?" Chola questioned.

"Oh yeah," Kohn declared, nodding.

Chola flinched.

"Relax," Kohn reassured him. "CID agents are watching the hotel entrance from across the street. Venturing out the front door, I've been intercepted and ushered back to this luxurious holding pen." Looking over his shoulder, he observed, "The lobby bar appears safe. Can I buy you a beer? I would like to resume our interview."

"I don't drink," Chola stated.

Kohn chuckled. "I'm not asking you to break your LTTE vow and indulge. But sitting behind a frothy brew enhances your cover."

Maybe this reporter can clarify the absurdity of the peace conference, Chola pondered, accepting the invitation.

In a quiet corner, shielded by a square-fluted column, Chola stared into a glass mug of carbonated pilsner. Friendly bubbles rose to the surface. *Would I ever drink alcohol?* he questioned himself. He reflected on wading through a freshwater lagoon a few months back, his weapon held high over his head. His mouth was dry; he was parched, lightheaded. Bloated corpses floated in the filthy liquid. Succumbing to the craving, he lowered his head and quenched his thirst. *I drank from the cup of the dead,* he realized. *I could drink a beer,* he surmised, *but not today.*

Kohn pulled a handheld cassette recorder out of a weathered leather satchel. Setting it on the table next to a white logoed ceramic ashtray, he hit record.

"What is that?" Chola frowned.

The reporter grinned. "It is a tape recorder."

"It is so small!" Chola exclaimed. Picking up the purring device, he studied it with childlike innocence. "You Americans are so clever," he declared, carefully setting it back down.

"Actually it's Japanese," Kohn confessed. After clearing his throat, he asked, "How is the cease-fire being perceived by the partisans?"

"It's meaningless," Chola responded. "Total annihilation of the Tamils or complete independence for Tamil Eelam are the only results that will end this conflict. This cease-fire is only a pause to one of those ends."

"Then why did the militant groups agree to a cease-fire?" Kohn probed.

"Politics." Chola snickered. "Our supporters in India wanted to intervene in the conflict diplomatically. I'm assuming my superiors agreed to suspend hostilities at their bequest." Squinting hard at the reporter, he softly inquired, "Tell me. How is our struggle being perceived in your world?"

"My world?" Kohn questioned.

"Beyond these shores," the partisan clarified.

Slowly shaking his head, the reporter declared, "The masses are ignorant, Huck. Very few Americans can identify Vietnam on a map, let alone Sri Lanka. And the Vietnam War consumed fifty-eight thousand American lives." Leaning back, he took a nip off his cold brew. "Every Sri Lankan conflict story I submit leads with 'The island nation off the southern tip of India formerly known as Ceylon.' Then I define the Tamils as an aggrieved minority and the government as dominated by the Sinhalese majority. Hopefully the enlightened reader proceeds through the text I risked my life to produce. I'm not alone," he informed. "Other journalistic voices are reporting the Tamil conflict as a struggle for independence. However, the government press is spinning the militant LTTE as a terrorist menace. It is easy to sway the ignorant masses."

"Is anyone listening?" Chola interjected.

"I know the Singhalese president has taken his antiterrorist agenda on the road. A two-week road show seeking support for his war against the terrorist Tamil tigers included stops in Washington, London, and Beijing." Looking into Chola's focused gaze, Kohn concluded, "If the terrorist label stuck, it would have been an easy sell."

"Please report what you saw in the eastern province," Chola asked. "The truth always finds the hearts of good men."

"Being arrested by the government only enhanced my resolve," Kohn replied, leaning back. Stroking his chin, he muttered, "You are an enigma, Huck. You are educated, articulate, and well-read. What motivates you?"

Chola grinned and mumbled, "*Dharma*."

Kohn's face puckered. "The cosmic order of the universe?"

"There is no single English word for the Hindu concept," Chola explained. "Dharma is much more than the proper functioning of existence. It encompasses one's duty and righteous obligation to prevent chaos in the world."

"Preventing chaos?" Kohn squinted.

Chola slowly nodded. "It is a river's dharma to flow, the sun's to provide nurturing light, the moon's to regulate the tides. When there is no peaceful resolution, it becomes a warrior's dharma to fight."

Speechless, Kohn studied the philosophical partisan. "Who are you?" rolled out of his open mouth.

"I told you before," Chola answered. "I have family in Colombo; to protect them, I need to remain anonymous."

The reporter chuckled. "My apologies, Huck. The question was rhetorical. My point was that you are an articulate enigma."

Chola's scarred features blushed.

Kohn leaned into the youth. "There is a blind spot," he whispered. "The jailers of my resort prison are not watching the beach." Looking down, he confessed, "I've exited the hotel on a few occasions for conjugal liaisons at a local brothel and returned undetected."

"I don't understand," Chola questioned, tilting his head.

"If you want to pay a visit to your mum and dad," Kohn clarified, "I'll show you the unguarded back door."

Chola slouched down. When he visualized his widowed mother, his heart swelled. A smile emerged across his tattered face as he recalled the life he once lived. Focused on the reporter, he muttered, "Show me."

Chapter 53

—⁂—

Clicking over to 3:00 a.m. the digital radio-clock emitted a nudging beep. Between high-thread-count linen, Longboard stirred. He awoke as the assassin Jesse Long. His delicate touch silenced the annoying buzz. Anticipating the challenge, he grinned. The hotel room was crisp and cold. A wall-mounted air-conditioning unit hummed. He rolled out of the comfortable bedding onto the floor. Twenty quick push-ups got his heart pumping. His breathing accelerated. Standing tall, he stretched. In his briefs, he shuffled across the carpet in the dark. Parted balcony drapes emitted the flicker of city lights. Sliding open an arcadia door bathed his naked torso with warm, humid air. Two patio chairs and a round end table furnished the platform. Stepping out, he surveyed the Bangkok skyline before peering down. The terrace below was lit. The drapes of the suite pulled back. Shadows danced within. *The target and his henchman are awake,* he concluded.

Exiting the patio, he closed the drapes. Flicking a light switch illuminated a modern but modest hotel room. After a long, satisfying piss, he prepared for the close-quarters assignment. Methodically, he dressed in black, passing on the adult diaper. *Dawn will dictate my exit,* he surmised. My empty bladder can endure a three-hour time frame. Dressed in what Reno referred to as a Halloween costume, a black-face-painted Jesse unzipped a travel bag containing the tools of his trade. He attached a five-inch suppressor to a modified

Smith and Wesson semiautomatic pistol. The covert weapon was nicknamed the *hush-puppy* in Vietnam. It fit snuggly in a custom-made shoulder holster. Examining a razor-sharp US Air Force survival knife, he reflected on the honed blade's history. The cutting tool had severed spinal cords, pierced hearts, sliced through windpipes, and extracted a Communist liver. After sheathing the experienced blade, he tested the tension of a thin wire garrote. Adding the strangulation device to his armaments, he took a deep breath.

In a trance, navigated by his inner demon, the nimble assassin walked through the flowing drapes. Without hesitation, he straddled the balcony's protective metal railing and rolled over the side. A soft landing placed him on the terrace below. A black-gloved hand slowly loosened the bulb lighting the deck. It gradually dimmed before going dark. Crouched in a ball in the shadows, death peered into suite 222. Two henchmen slouched in front of an active television set. The sleepy-eyed Asian thugs appeared disinterested in the local program. Beneath the drone of the TV box, moans of pleasure resonated behind a closed bedroom door. A muffled high-pitch whine of ecstasy evoked snickers from the sleepy guards.

Now comes the hard part, Jesse realized, waiting for the opportunity. *Sometimes it comes quickly; other times it drifts into hours, even days. It requires a vulture's patience. It took me four hours crawling on my belly with a blade of grass between my teeth to neutralize a VC sympathizer,* he reflected. *Trip wires were the obstacle. If the grass between my teeth bent, I knew I'd found a signal wire. It was tedious, but I accomplished the mission. I hated soiling myself,* he recalled. *In a sniper's bed, I filled my diaper waiting sixteen hours for a single kill shot. This assignment's biggest challenge was complaining to the front desk to be relocated over the target. In a hotel that rents rooms by the hour, it wasn't very difficult.*

A henchmen rose. Jesse flexed. The dapper thug with cigarette in hand strolled toward the balcony. *The show is about to start,* Jesse realized, pulling out the thin wire garrote.

The glass barrier slid open. The unsuspecting smoker strolled to the railing. Leaning over the metal baluster, he lit his cigarette. Behind him, a shadow stirred. In an instant, a thin wire was looped over his head and pulled taut. A lit cigarette floated to the ground below. The city lights blurred, and a life faded.

Jesse eased the well-dressed carcass into a deck chair. Drawing his hush-puppy, he calmly entered the suite and fired. The long barrel launched a muffled round. The bullet ripped into a puzzled expression. The gangster's head jerked back. A blood spout erupted.

Bottled laughter from the television shrouded the assassin's advance. The closed bedroom door emitted grunts and groans of lust. An unlocked doorknob did not resist. A pistol-wielding hand slowly pushed open the barrier. The bedding chamber was bright. Like a dog in heat, a kneeling sweat-glistening Jimmy Three-Fingers pounded away. In front of the pumping gangster, an expensive Thai whore on all fours emitted high-pitched delight. A disfigured hand slapped her petite bottom. To the smacking sound of bare flesh, Jesse drifted into the room, raised his weapon, and squeezed the trigger. The hush-puppy's muffled blast fired a bullet into the back of Jimmy Three-Finger's egg-shaped noggin. A hematic mist graced the back of the naked Thai filly. She froze. The butt of a handgun thumped the back of her downcast head. It was a calculated blow. She fell forward. The teetering corpse toppled on top of her. *No need to crack her skull,* Jesse reasoned. *Hell, she just had a client die in her vagina.* Extracting the dead man from the whore, Jesse rolled the body onto the floor. Lifeless eyes gazed up at the popcorn ceiling. Pulling out a six-penny nail and his business card, Jesse Long licked his lips. His parched mouth tasted the addictive flavor of neutralizing a threat. Utilizing the pistol-butt, he nailed an ace of spades playing card bearing a skull-and-crossbones insignia to the dead man's forehead. *Close kills always warrant my calling card,* he reflected. *No need to break protocol.*

Floating through the posh suite graveyard, Jesse exited through fluttering drapes. With a calculated leap and little effort, he climbed into the overhead balcony. After meticulously packing his tools, he shed the sweat-drenched costume. A quick hot shower followed. In a Hawaiian shirt and faded Levi's, Longboard, toting an overnight bag, departed down a stairwell. *My predawn labor has left me ravenous,* he concluded, exiting the premises. In a side street adjacent to the hotel, he paused to gaze at the morning sunlight taunting the surrounding skyline. Craving flapjacks with a hearty side of bacon, he went in search of a coffee shop.

Chapter 54

―――⸿⸿―――

Dark clouds gathered over Rolf van der Wall's walled compound. Framed by the double-wide doorway of the luxurious residence, Roshin gazed at the compound's wrought-iron gates in anticipation. A simple pressed and clean smock dress adorned her petite frame. Her jet-black hair had been pulled back into a tight bun. The widow's chest pulsed with rapid breaths of excitement. Fifteen years ago, an industrial accident claimed her husband. Influenza took her baby daughter. Chola was all she had left in a life punctuated with sorrow. Behind her, wood flooring creaked with the familiar thump of Rolph's large pounding feet. *Mister van der Wall is a benevolent employer,* she realized. *But today is mine,* she rationalized, standing firm in her vigil. *I will return to my duties after my son's visit.* The drone of an approaching vehicle fanned expectations. She sighed as a delivery truck rumbled past the walled residence.

"We are out of ice, Roshin," Rolph informed her.

Glancing over her shoulder, she gazed at her employer through misting pleading eyes.

Standing behind the glossy bar in the ornately decorated parlor, Rolph smiled softly. Holding up an empty stainless-steel ice bucket, he winked. "I'll take care of this," he volunteered. "You need to stand watch for our prodigal son."

"Thank you, sir," Roshin whispered, returning to her attentive post. *What does "prodigal" mean?* she wondered.

Rolph's glimmering Baltic-blue Toyota sedan rolled up to the barred entrance gate. Sam, the driver, leaped out of the vehicle. A wide grin dominated his pudgy face. With a joyous spring in his step, he unlatched and swung open the barrier. Hopping back into the idling car, he drove into the courtyard.

Peering into vacant passenger windows, Roshin's head jerked back and forth. Sam, looking down over into the backseat, emitted a muffled command. Chola's head popped up.

Roshin gasped. Tears tumbled down her dark cheeks. In a trance, she descended the entry stoop. Chola shot out of the vehicle. In the cobble-stone courtyard, adorned with clay-potted flowers, mother and son embraced. Roshin wept. Chola tenderly stroked his mother's back.

In the doorway, Rolf, holding a gin and tonic, enjoyed the reunion. In the Burgher's throat, an emotional lump clawed. Under his sniffling bulbous nose, he dragged a finger.

Roshin stepped back. Her face melted. With a callused finger, she gently traversed the fresh scars crisscrossing Chola's shredded features. Grabbing her hand, he pressed it against his cheek. Closing his eyes, he relished in the familiar healing touch of his mother.

"You need to go inside," Sam instructed, disrupting the tender moment.

Holding tightly to her son's hand, Roshin strolled through the courtyard. "You've lost weight," she mumbled, holding back tears.

"And it looks like you cut yourself shaving," Rolph declared from the top of the stoop.

Glancing up, Chola grinned. "Hello, Uncle."

"Read any good books lately?" Rolph asked playfully.

Laughing, Chola blurted out, "No."

"Well, come in. There is much to talk about," Rolph said, stepping aside. With a sweeping hand, he welcomed the Tamils into the large high-ceilinged room.

With his mother at his side, Chola paused in the doorway. He scanned the elephant tusks displayed behind the bar, the black-and-white photos of Rolph's Dutch ancestors across the white plaster walls, and the sofa and cushioned chairs surrounding the color television. Rolph motioned for them to take seat. Chola squinted at the Burgher. *I lived in this house for most of my life,* he reflected. *I greeted house guests in this room, served drinks, waxed the wood floors, dusted the furniture, and scrubbed the walls. But not once did I ever sit down.*

"I know you don't drink alcohol," Rolph announced, glancing at his fizzing cocktail. "But would you like some tea?"

Chola was dumbfounded. Uncle was treating him as an equal. The Burgher had always been kind to him and his mother. But there was always a haughty aloofness, a sense of privilege shrouding the white man. *Who am I to judge?* Chola concluded. *Uncle paid for my education and introduced me to the pleasures of literature. The blue-blood may have his quirks, but he is a good man.* "No, thank you, Uncle," Chola responded. "I really can't stay that long."

"Nonsense," Rolph snapped. "Please be seated. I have a proposition for you and your mother."

Exchanging puzzled expressions, Roshin and Chola treaded respectfully on the sacred ground encircling the color television. Cautiously, they perched themselves on the edge of the sofa's floral-printed cushions. Rolph plopped down in his favorite easy chair. The teak frame groaned. Leaning back, he wet his palate with sparkling gin. Crossing his legs, he declared, "I have no heirs. But I always felt a kinship to both of you."

"Uncle?" Chola injected.

"Let me finish," Rolph snapped, flashing an open palm. "The war is making me wealthy, and I don't want my shallow wife to squander the fruits of my good fortune." His face puckered at the reference to his tarnished trophy, Angeline. His overindulgent facial features softened. Taking a proud, magnanimous breath, he continued, "Chola, I watched you grow from a boy into manhood. Today, I'm offering you an alternative path for your life journey. After I was informed of your visit, I've made arrangements for both of you to immigrate to Canada." Basking in his generosity, he downed the last of his gin and tonic.

A giggle squeaked out of an overwhelmed Roshin. To suppress the escaping titter of excitement, she cupped a hand over her mouth.

Chola, patting his mother's back, whispered, "I'm sorry, *Amma.*" Addressing Rolph, he replied, "I always considered you a compassionate man. Your proposition enhances my conclusion. However, would you want your son...your heir to abandon his people because he has the resources to do so? I thank you for the noble and gracious offer, but I must decline."

Slowly nodding his liver-spotted noggin, Rolph mumbled, "Very impressive, *Machan*." Grunting, he sat erect. "I respect your sense of duty but implore you to reconsider. Death will be your traveling companion on the course you've chosen."

"We all die, Uncle," Chola stated. "A life in Canada would be infested with regret." His breath accelerated. "I'm a Liberation Tiger of Tamil Eelam," he proudly declared. "I'm devoted to establishing Eelam, a free and independent homeland for my people. If my life's journey is cut short, I will exit with the satisfaction that my existence had purpose."

Roshin wept. Tears welled in the old Burgher's eyes.

A grin erased Chola's stoic expression. "Today is a day of joy not sorrow," he announced. "I have much to tell you about the people and places I've encountered."

Roshin, sucking back tears, sat attentive. Chola was still her little boy who loved spinning a good yarn. He always enjoyed retelling the adventures of fictional literary characters he discovered. *My son has become a hero in the story of our people's struggle for justice.* Proudly, she listened to her articulate *poorali magan* (warrior son).

Chapter 55

———✦———

Infringing the edge of the mattress, Sandy awoke. It was dark, the salty, warm air heavy. The soothing hum of gentle surf flowed through an open window. Flipping off a clammy sheet, she sighed. On her back with her closed eyes, she cautiously advanced a hand into Reno's side of the bed. It was vacant. *Oh yes,* she thought rolling into cooler territory. *What have I got myself into?* she pondered in the solitude of unimpeded comfort. *A doctor and an arms merchant make strange bedfellows. Definitely cramped sleeping companions in this tiny bed.* She snickered. *Reno does have some fine qualities,* she surmised. *Is it his confidence I find attractive? Or is it the loyalty, the sense of commitment he bestows upon his friends. He is fun to be around. He makes me laugh. Is it the excitement, the sense of danger I feel in his world?* The image of her first husband appeared in the evaluation. Gustav was brilliant, an exceptional medical student, and no doubt he became a fine physician. *The intellectual Gustav was too serious for me,* she recalled. *He had no sense of humor. He was cold and distant to my friends and intimidated by the street kids that loitered in front of our flat. Reno and my first husband are polar opposites,* she realized. "Beter een dag leven als een tijger dan honderd als een schaap," (Better to live one day as a tiger than a hundred as a sheep), she mumbled. *Life is too short not to enjoy a scare ride once in a while. I'll take this one day at a time,* she concluded. *That should not be too difficult, as long as we get a bigger bed.*

The aroma of fresh coffee enticed her out of bed. Taking a deep breath, she rose. A men's white T-shirt shrouded her long, lean frame. On the balls of her feet, she quietly exited the dark bedroom. Filtered light floated through the kitchen's bamboo-beaded curtain doorway. Escaping rays spilled across the grass mat floor. Parting the barrier, she entered the kitchenette. A saluting hand shielded her face from the dangling bright light bulb. A glossy amber cockroach scurried across the lime-green tile countertop. Alerted by the departing pest, she quickly scanned the tiny room. Satisfied, she picked up the tempting blue galvanized pot of java off a warming hotplate. Before the pour, she paused and inspected the cylinder of a ceramic mug. *You can never be too careful in the tropics,* she realized. *We are surrounded by bugs.* Warm cup in hand, she strolled through the open front doorway onto the raised deck.

Fading moonlight slowly retreated across rolling dark water. The horizon glowed. A few defiant stars twinkled. Whitecaps rose and crashed along the shoreline. Dying waves lapped at soft sand.

Slouched in a rattan chair, with his bare feet propped up on the deck's bamboo railing, Reno smiled at her entrance. "Mornin', sweetheart," he muttered. "I see you found the coffee."

The platform creaked under her advance. She gave him a quick peck on the cheek before taking the rattan seat beside him. "We have cockroaches," she informed him.

"I'll order chitchats from the provisioner," he yawned.

"Is that some kind of bug juice?" she questioned.

Reno laughed. "No, I'll buy some little lizards, house geckos, to eat the roaches."

"What? Then we will have a hut full of lizards."

"It's not as bad as bugs," he countered. "Just make sure you check the toaster before heating bread and pray they don't fall into an active ceiling fan."

She chuckled. "If I'm going to have to endure the reptile invasion, we need a bigger bed."

"Yes, dear," he conceded, taking a sip of rich hot brew.

A silhouette of a lone surfer rose on the undulating black water.

"Is that Longboard?" she questioned.

"Sure is," Reno answered. "He was out there when I got up. He must have arrived from Bangkok last night and took to the water." Slowly nodding, he mumbled, "I am happy he's back."

"He surfs in the dark?" she asked.

"Nah," Reno replied. "My partner believes the sea will wash away sin. I think the Catholics call it going to confession. A psychologist defines it as therapy."

"Should we be concerned?" she wondered.

"Longboard will be fine," he replied. "Occasionally he talks kinda crazy about his inner demon. Apparently a part of him is addicted to the acceptable sins of war. I wouldn't worry about my partner. He is a good man. When it comes to his vice, I consider him more of a social drinker than an alcoholic."

Dawn arrived. Wispy clouds blushed. Escalating light painted the ocean a deep blue. Sparking white lace accented breaking waves. "My god," Sandy exclaimed. "What a magic moment."

"A new day is born," Reno mumbled, focused on the sunlight peeking over the horizon. "I live to see another day." She placed her hand on his shoulder. He patted her tender grasp and shared, "In Nam, being assigned to a LP, a listening post, was bad news. You were basically ordered to be a human alarm. Outside the perimeter of a firebase, another unlucky bastard and I would ride out the long night. Our mission was to detect enemy scouts probing the encampment's defenses. If the darkness stirred, we tossed out hand grenades. If the dinks detected our position, we were dead. If they attacked the firebase, we were caught in crossfire. Retreat was not an option. Leaving the post, you became a target for the troops inside the perimeter. The black nights with and without incidents concluded with the arrival of nurturing sunlight. The warm rays a congratulatory smile from a friend for surviving the night." He lifted the coffee mug to the ascending sun. "In moments like this, I reconnect with my dazzling guardian angel."

Sandy took a deep breath. Interlacing her fingers with his, she gently squeezed. He reciprocated. A sea breeze blessed the lovers. Sunlight intensified. Long shadows appeared. Reno grinned, realizing the path for the next leg of his life's journey would be wider and smoother and have a slight downward slope.

Chapter 56

I t was late afternoon, the hottest part of the day. A tarnished yellow tuk-tuk shimmied curbside. White smoke sputtered out of its rusty tailpipe. The baby taxi's only passenger was Cletus "Bear" Jones. Chomping on a fat cigar, the massive black man awkwardly dug into the front pant pocket of his denim shorts. Sorting a crinkled wad of colorful currency, he paid the fare with a powder-blue fifty-baht note. "Now comes the fun part," he grumbled, calculating his extraction. Slowly, he pulled his 13-Ds from beneath the driver's seat. Pivoting, he planted his large sandaled feet on the sidewalk. Bowing, he rolled forward. The wobbling baby cab groaned. A gentle breeze graced his exit. Standing tall in an overwashed white tank top, he flexed. Across the front of his tired singlet, faded font declared, "*I Love Thailand*."

"Thanks, Bear," the sweat-glistening Thai cabbie said with a playful salute.

Bear had no idea who the driver was. But he appreciated that his size and black complexion distinguished him as a local celebrity. "Can't forget this," he muttered, retrieving a thin manila envelope from the motorized rickshaw's torn and patched vinyl backseat. After folding the tan folder containing airline tickets and a travel itinerary, he stuffed it into a back pocket. Taking a satisfying puff off his cigar, he savored the fact that he was heading back to Philly. Thanks to Reno's fifty-thousand-dollar gift, he would be traveling with a fat wallet. An image of a Philadelphia in winter surfaced. Visualizing the comforting warmth of his grandmother's small apartment, he grinned. *Nana-Jones is going to love meeting my petite Thai wife*. He imagined strutting through the old neighborhood in a tailor-made suit with Tola in a fur coat dangling on his arm, and his smile widened. The sharp whine of the departing tuk-tuk terminated the pleasant prediction.

A narrow pedestrian road flanked by local vendors led to the modest four-story apartment complex Bear and Tola called home. On the shady side of the street, idle shopkeepers puffing on cigarettes enjoyed a game of dominos. The players paused to acknowledge their black neighbor. A mama-san swept the walk in front of her humble tavern. Food hawkers prepared for the evening trade. In the shade of a large tree, the satay man stood beside his bicycle. Fastened over the front tire, a grill converted from a one-gallon gasoline can smoldered. Utilizing a palm fan, the chef stoked the coals. Spotting Bear, he placed ten bamboo strips of marinated beef over the hot coals. The sizzling meat emitted a sultry aroma. Bear approached, licking his lips. "I'm such an easy mark," he muttered, dropping a handful of Thai coins in the tin can attached to the handlebars. The satay man nodded his acceptance and handed his customer a simmering meat bouquet.

Bear softly blew on the skewered beef before stuffing the entire seductive arrangement into his ravenous mouth. A slow calculated pull extracted the ten tiny bamboo spears. Grinding molars shredded the spicy delicacy. To compensate for the searing heat, he chomped on the greasy treat with an open mouth.

From the beverage vendor, a nimble boy raced up to his regular black customer with a cold amber bottle of Singha beer. "You late today," the boy declared, offering the bottle.

"Thanks, Shorty," Bear responded, accepting the beer and taking a hearty cleansing swig. "You won't be seeing me for a couple of weeks," he said before taking another healthy gulp.

"You renting your flat to Chinese?" Shorty questioned.

"No." Bear chuckled. "Why would you ask?"

"Two Chinamen were here today asking about you."

"About me?" Bear squinted.

"They were polite, well-dressed, looking for a large black man," the boy responded.

"What did you tell them?" Bear barked.

The boy jumped. "Nothing, Bear." Shorty shrugged. "I say nothing."

"Thanks, Shorty," Bear offered, handing the boy the empty bottle. Visualizing Tola, he headed home. His pace accelerated. Reaching into the lazy collar of his sleeveless top, he retrieved the *kunia* dangling from his neck. The solid piece of steel had a three-inch leaf-shaped blade and ring on the pommel. Bear removed the leather necklace tether. Looping a finger through the ring, he concealed the razor-sharp blade in the palm of his hand. Breaking into a sprint, he ran through his apartment complex's courtyard and flew up the exterior stairway to his second-floor flat. Huffing and puffing, he entered.

Tola sat bound and gagged in a dinette chair facing the door. The room was dim. Closed drapes shrouded the sliding glass balcony door. Flexing her wide watery eyes, she attempted to scream. The rag stuffed into her mouth muffled the warning. The cold steel of a short pistol barrel poked Bear's sweaty temple.

The gunman was a fashionable street punk dressed in a yellow golf shirt. A red bandana decorated his butch cut. Large white-framed sunglasses shielded his eyes. The playful design of the eyewear and his upturned shirt collar enhanced a cavalier demeanor. He was a killer. Focused on the weapon at the end of his elevated extended arm, he blindly shut the door.

From out of the kitchen strolled a twenty-something Chinese gangster sipping a cup of tea. A short-brimmed black fedora crowned his thick shoulder-length black hair. Originating at the corners of his mouth, a slender, straight mustache extended past his jaw. A third scraggly tendril was anchored to his chin. The long sleeves of his jet-black dress shirt were rolled up past his elbows. The splayed collar of the low buttoned shirt exposed an ornate golden dragon pendant necklace. "Excuse us for the intrusion," he offered, blowing softly into the ceramic cup. "But we are looking for a cigar-smoking *hak gwei* (black ghost) who served in the military." Setting the steaming teacup on the dinette table beside Tola, he picked up and flashed a framed picture of Bear in uniform.

"Let her go," Bear requested.

"Tell us who and where we can find the other broken soldiers who disrespected the Red Dragon and I will release the whore," the intruder responded.

Ignoring the gun aimed at the side of his head, Bear smiled at his wife and lipped, "I love you." Scowling at the thug, he offered, "Let her go, and I'll tell you what you want to know."

"Do I look stupid?" questioned the spokesman.

"Yes." Bear nodded. "Yes, you do. You have no idea about the wrath that is about to rain down."

From the small of his back, the gangster produced a butterfly knife. He took delight in flipping and fanning the double-handled blade. The performance ended with him grabbing Tola's hair and yanking her head back. "Would cutting off one of her ears advance my agenda?" he questioned.

Bear's barrel chest pulsed with rage. His breath accelerated. Snorting air through flared nostrils, he conceded in a gruff tone, "I'll talk." Smiling at his traumatized wife, he offered a reassuring wink.

"Good," the spokesman responded, releasing the handful of hair.

For a big man, Bear was fast, very fast. Flexing the hand concealing a ring knife, he took a shallow, composing breath. With uncanny speed, he slapped the spiffy goon beside him on the side of the head. The punk's targeting pistol discharged. A grazing bullet dug a deep trench into Bear's scalp before careening into the ceiling. An overhead light fixture shattered. Driven by a massive black paw, three inches of spiked steel pierced the shooter's skull. The impaled head stuck to Bear's hand. The street punk thrashed like a fish on line. Bear used his free hand to dislodge the shiv. The snared body collapsed. A thick stream of blood spouted out of the gouged cranium. Bear charged the spokesman, his vision impaired by the plasma flowing down his face. A pistol sparked. Catching a bullet in the chest, the former all-city defensive tackle from Philadelphia latched onto the hostile and flew through the sliding glass door. The glass barrier exploded. Wrapped in fluttering drapes, Bear and his prey crashed through the second-floor terrace's wood railing. Rough asphalt terminated the short flight. Bear rolled off the moaning Chinaman who broke his fall. Digging deep, he reached over with his spiked hand. Finding the gangster's pulsing neck, he grinned. "Come into my home," he mumbled. "Threaten my wife?" Flexing his hand, he severed the intruder's jugular. Warm plasma graced his hand.

A victorious smile spread across his bloodstained face. Looking up, he spotted Tola standing on the shattered terrace. His petite Thai wife was screaming for help. Nana-Jones would have loved to meet her, he imagined. Distant footsteps grew louder.

Shorty appeared. The boy ripped off his shirt and attempted to ebb the blood flowing out of Bear's chest. "Shorty," Bear mumbled. "Shorty," he attempted again.

With teary eyes, the boy questioned, "Bear?"

Bear beckoned with an expiring finger for the boy to come closer.

Leaning into the local celebrity, the sniffling boy asked, "What is it, Bear?"

"Reno," Bear muttered, coughing blood. "Get a message to Reno...Reno James...The dinks have breached our perimeter."

ACKNOWLEDGMENTS

I am appreciative of my mother, Mary, sharing her passion for historical fiction. The gift became an addictive educational vice.

Many thanks to Mark Nobile, Jamie Marshall, Catherine Ivy, Diane Bertrand, and Scott LeMarr, all of whom waded through a raw initial draft. Their insight, encouragement, and criticism assisted in molding the final text.

And of course all my love and gratitude to my wife and muse, Sharon; her inspiration is the foundation for all my endeavors.